Bride
of the
Summerfields

Bride of the Summerfields

a novel

Book Two
of the
Manor House Series

Nancy Moser

Overland Park, Kansas

Bride of the Summerfields

ISBN-13: 978-0-9861952-3-5
ISBN-10:0986195235

Published by:
Mustard Seed Press
PO Box 23002
Overland Park, KS 66283

This story is a work of fiction. Any resemblances to actual people, places, or events are purely coincidental.

All Scripture quotations are taken from The Holy Bible, King James Version.

Front cover design by Mustard Seed Press
Figure from John Singer Sargent's painting of
Miss Helen Duinham

Printed and bound in the United States of America
10 9 8 7 6 5 4 3 2 1

Dedication

To my darling husband, Mark
Forty years ago I became your bride.
There's nowhere I'd rather be than by your side.
Here's to the next forty years.

Prologue

Autumn 1881

She wore a wig so no one would recognize her. She wore a simple dress of tan cotton, adopting the appearance of a farmer's wife instead of a titled guest.

Though other villagers smiled and linked their arms sentimentally as they gathered outside the country church, she wore a frown and stood alone. As they gathered in small groups waiting for the ceremony to be over, she hid behind a bush and peered in a back window.

The bride, Lila, looked beautiful standing at the altar in her gown of duchesse satin with a pleated edge to the bustled train. The long veil had a scalloped edge, and there were tiny ivory silk roses sprinkled across her shoulders and hair as if she'd just walked through a floral shower.

That could have been me.

"Do you, Joseph Hayden Kidd, take Lila June Weston as your lawfully wedded wife . . .?"

Joseph should have been mine.

To be once-engaged then lose a man to another was a dagger to her heart. Yet Clarissa's loss was not confined to love. She had been Lady Clarissa Weston, the daughter of the Earl of Summerfield. She had held that title her entire life, until the revelation of a forty-year-old secret allowed Lila's father — a mere shopkeeper in the village — to step forward as the older brother and rightful earl. His rise shoved Clarissa's family down a branch in the family tree, and elevated Lila to her Lady Lila Weston title.

Clarissa had gained Lila as a cousin but had lost Joseph as a fiancée.

She had lost a title, surrendering "Lady" to become a simple "Miss."

And since she'd fled to London, Clarissa had also lost a place in the family.

"I do," she heard Joseph say.

Clarissa shut out Lila's vows and looked at her family as they sat in the second row behind Lila's father and brother.

There was poor Father. That he could stay at Summerfield Manor in his demoted position of second son was not surprising. Status had never meant as much to him as it had Clarissa. To Father, the demotion was a relief from the responsibilities that accompanied the title of earl. Clarissa tried not to think less of him for it.

Then there was Mother. Mother had never embraced the countess designation, nor its responsibilities. The demotion from countess to the rather bland title of Mrs. Weston was no strain on her. Over the years she had grown accustom to leaving the duties of her position to her mother-in-law, the dowager countess.

Speaking of . . . Grandmamma looked as lovely as ever, if not even lovelier than when Clarissa had seen her last. She sat close to her husband of less than a year, the love of her life, Colonel Grady Cummings. After decades of being married and dutiful to the late Earl of Summerfield, she'd finally been reunited with her Grady. Clarissa envied their happy ending.

The last family member Clarissa noticed was George, her little brother. In the months she'd been hidden away in London, he'd ripened from a boy to a young man. He'd not minded a whit that he was no longer the heir to an earldom and that Lila's brother Morgan now held that position. As long as George could breed and train horses, he was happy.

Everyone seemed happy, except Clarissa.

"I now pronounce you man and wife."

Joseph tenderly lifted the veil from Lila's face and touched her cheek with a gentle hand as he kissed her. Then they turned as a couple towards the congregation and beamed as though they were king and queen of the world. Joseph raised Lila's hand to his lips before walking together down the aisle.

Clarissa suffered a swell of anger and pain. Why had she come?

Come or not, she couldn't stay a moment longer.

She turned away from the church before the pain within its walls flooded outside and drowned her. For a brief moment she considered lingering, letting her family see her — or letting them think they might have seen her. Yet knowing how the blessings of life seemed to fall upon everyone *but* her, she couldn't take the chance of one final humiliation. And so she ran to the train station that would hasten her escape back to London, where she could disappear from the sight and mind of her family yet again.

If only she could forget them as they'd surely forgotten her.

Chapter One

Autumn 1882

Clarissa Weston sat at the long makeup table in the dressing room of the Savoy Theatre in London. Seated close by her were the rest of the "rapturous maidens" of the Gilbert & Sullivan production of "Patience."

"Can I borrow some cold cream?" asked the girl to her right.

Reluctantly, Clarissa moved the jar so they could share. The girl was always mooching one thing or the other. Even after a year on the stage in London, Clarissa still wasn't used to sharing anything with anyone, much less with a girl who dropped her 'H's and talked in great detail about every man who partook of her favors.

From what Clarissa could see, she had plenty to offer. The brazen way the girls in the chorus traipsed around in their corsets and bloomers was something she would never condone. Proper ladies like Clarissa wore a dressing gown and showed some semblance of modesty.

Yet the Savoy was a huge step above the burlesque halls she'd played during her first acting jobs in London. Those venues were beyond disgusting in regards to their morals, cleanliness, and content. She'd always dreamed of going on the stage as Clarissa Weston, but with the iffy nature of her first roles, she had quickly changed her name to Clara West.

With the matinee over, the girls removed their makeup and chattered about nothing. Clarissa didn't join in. Not that she wasn't used to small talk. Among the society at Summerfield Manor and during the London social season, she knew how to chat about nothing with the best of them. But chatting with a countess or a duke — or even the Prince of Wales himself — constituted a different sort of nothingness, one that owned a modicum of civility and class.

"Oh, bugger," said a girl with the largest bosoms Clarissa had ever seen. "I gots a run in me hose again."

"No one's gonna see it under yer skirt," another said.

"Wanna bet?"

Uproarious laughter erupted around her. It was quickly interrupted when the stage manager popped his head in the door. "Hello ladies."

"Go away, Mr. Mapes. We ain't decent."

He came in anyway, teasing the girls with a tickle up their back or a whisper in their ear as he passed.

Clarissa adjusted the neckline of her dressing gown before he reached her. If only she'd had time to get fully dressed and away before he showed up.

He sidestepped between the moocher and Clarissa, picking up an earring and letting it dangle. "Well, Miss West? Have you considered my offer?"

She noticed the chattering stop. "Let's talk outside," she said.

"Lead the way."

Suggestive *ooohs* followed them as Clarissa led him to the wings of the stage. He moved close, forcing her to hold him back with a straightened arm. "Not so fast," she said.

"So you don't want the role of Patience?"

"Of course I do. I will not perpetually be in the chorus."

He ran a finger the length of her arm. "You know my conditions, Miss *Weston.*"

She looked around to make sure no one else heard his use of her real name. Her family didn't know where she was and she wanted to keep it that way. Once she became a star, she'd let her true identity be known, but until then . . .

"You've given me a hard choice, Mr. Mapes. It is not a decision easily made."

He stroked her hair behind her ear. "I've always wanted to have myself someone as lofty as the niece of an earl."

Clarissa shuddered. Her father and grandmother had warned her about the immoral nature of the stage, but she'd assumed they exaggerated. She was used to the flirtations and innuendo of high society, but to be assailed with the blatant pushiness of those she'd met in the theatre was a constant struggle and an emotional drain.

"So?" Mapes asked. "What'll it be? The starring role for a little nootsy-tootsy or I tell the world who you really are?"

Her dream of a lead part demanded too large a price, but the denial of that dream would cause her another kind of pain. Not just her pain, but her family's. She couldn't go home until she was a star. Only then would her pride of accomplishment make a homecoming possible.

Suddenly a choice was made for her as a prop man approached. "Mr. Mapes, we need yer help. The ropes on the Act Two backdrop are fraying something awful."

Mapes sighed. "Your decision is deferred," he told Clarissa. "For now."

She gladly accepted the reprieve.

Molly Wallace adjusted her newest creation on the padded hat stand, adjusting the tilt just-so.

"That's another beauty," Madam Lupine said. "I especially like the combination of the lace pleating along the brim and the cascade of rose buds hanging from the back."

"Thank you, Madam. Actually, I have a specific client in mind."

"Miss West?"

"She's become a very steady customer."

The shop owner flipped through her account ledgers on the counter. "She has a balance due. I need payment, Miss Wallace. From her, or from . . ."

Me?

"I'll see what I can do," Molly said. She knew Clarissa was three hats behind on payment. She didn't want to call her on it, because she enjoyed seeing Clarissa. She was Molly's only tie to Summerfield and shared the bond of secrecy, as both girls strived to keep their pasts to themselves. Only Clarissa knew that Molly used to be a lady's maid at Summerfield Manor, and that she'd been in love with its heir.

The bell on the door rang and in walked Clarissa. Molly turned to greet her. "Miss West," she said. "How nice to see you again."

Clarissa's eyes scanned the store as if the beautiful hats were as important to her survival as her next breath. She spotted the new hat and rushed towards it. "Oh, Molly. It's gorgeous."

"I thought you'd like it."

Clarissa removed her own hat—a purchase she'd made just last week, and placed the new one on her head.

Molly adjusted a mirror so Clarissa could admire herself. The hat did look beautiful against her dark hair and ivory skin.

Molly saw a smudge of stage makeup along Clarissa's jawline. She handed her a handkerchief and subtly pointed.

Clarissa turned her face towards the mirror and wiped the makeup away. "I left in a hurry." She looked to see the location of Madam Lupine and the other clerk, then added, "Mr. Mapes is being very persistent."

"Is he still threatening to reveal . . .?"

Clarissa picked up a hand mirror in order to see the back of the hat. "I like the tail of the red rosebuds."

"Thank you." Molly lowered her voice and shared something that had been on her mind. "Do you ever just want it over?"

"As in be who we really are?"

Molly nodded. "I miss my family."

"And I miss mine." Clarissa set the mirror down. "Has your sister sent any interesting news from the manor?"

"I've not had a letter in months. The last one spoke of the usual below-stairs drama—though Dottie *has* been elevated from a tweeny to a housemaid."

"Good for her." Clarissa asked a question closer to her interest. "How is my cousin, Morgan?"

It was so like Clarissa to stick Molly with a verbal pin. Just hearing Morgan's name gave Molly pain. "I'm sure he's working hard, learning how to be the next Earl of Summerfield."

Clarissa nodded once, removing the hat. "I'll take it. Put it on my account."

Ah. The sticky point. "Madam Lupine would like payment."

"Next time, all right?" Clarissa said.

"I'm sorry, but I have to insist. If you don't pay, she might make me pay."

With a sigh Clarissa dug into her reticule and pulled out some coins. "There. I'm paid up. Does that satisfy you?"

"It satisfies my boss. Thank you."

Molly wrapped the hat with tissue and was placing it in a hat box when the postman entered the store and handed a stack of letters to the shop owner.

"There's a letter for you, Molly," Madame Lupine said.

"Thank you, Madam. If I may have a moment?"

"A moment. Your sister has not written in quite a time, no?"

"No, she hasn't."

Today's letter only contained two lines: *Ma suffered apoplexy. Come home now.*

There were many strike-outs in the word "apoplexy" as though Dottie had a hard time with the spelling. Molly turned the page over, wanting the obvious questions answered. Was her mother recovering, or worse?

"Is it bad news?" Clarissa asked.

Molly felt the eyes of the other women. Her head swam with logistics. "My mother suffered a fit of apoplexy and my sister says I need to come home. *Now.* I need to go to her."

Madam Lupine pointed towards the back room where the hats were made. "But what of your work?"

"I'll finish it up for her, Madam," said a worker who stood nearby.

"I'll be back as soon as I can," Molly offered.

Madam suffered a sigh, then said, "Go and see your mamma."

Molly kissed her cheek and gathered her things. Clarissa waited for her at the door. "So you're going home. To Summerfield."

There was an odd pull in Clarissa's voice, which caused Molly to clarify. "It's not my home, it's yours."

"You know what I mean."

"Yes, of course I'm going."

"What will you do if you see Morgan?"

A good question. "Why don't you come with me? I'm sure your family would be thrilled to see you again."

Clarissa's head shook in an adamant no. "Not until I'm a success. Besides, the black sheep is rarely welcomed home. I have lived a forbidden and hidden life. I can't let them know the extent to which I have gone against their wishes."

"They'll forgive you. I know they will."

With another shake of her head, Clarissa pointed towards the door. "Go on now. I hope your mother recovers fully and quickly."

"Say a prayer for her, will you?"

Clarissa hesitated. "I fear God doesn't want to hear from me any more than my family does." She offered a weak smile. "Your mother will do best without my prayers."

Molly didn't have time to argue.

Matilda Cavendish looked in the full-length mirror, admiring her new periwinkle day dress. She swayed side to side, imagining how the six-gored skirt would move when she walked. The insets of a lighter blue would peek out, then tuck away, teasing the viewer, and gaining her the positive attention she longed for.

Yet the ensemble needed something to set it off. She retrieved the cigar box where she kept her jewelry.

"Tilda. What's all this mess?"

Tilda pretended not to be startled by her guardian's sudden appearance, "Just going through the dresses I had made for Summerfield Manor."

Mrs. Smith fingered the pleated ruffle on a green sateen. "You're visiting your godfather, not taking over the place."

Tilda shrugged.

"And where did you get the money for all this?"

She shrugged again.

"You don't make enough money cleaning houses. You didn't spend your inheritance, did you? Because that money is supposed to last you for years."

"That money could keep a pauper in rags for years. I need it now, helping me now."

"Your father—"

Tilda knew what words would stop the discussion. "My father despised me and blamed me for Mama running out on us."

Mrs. Smith shuffled her shoulders. "He cared for you in his own way."

"Mmm." She went back to the nearly empty jewelry box. "If you must know, I got the money for the dresses by selling some of my jewelry."

Mrs. Smith shook her head back and forth. "*Your* jewelry. Don't tell me. I don't want to know."

Her guardian's preference of remaining deaf and blind to most of Tilda's doings had come in handy over the years. Tilda grinned and pulled out a necklace of blue lapis. "Don't you think this will look nice with this dress?"

"Where did you get that one?"

Tilda clasped it around her neck and preened in the mirror. "You said you didn't want to know."

"You don't have to steal from every officer's wife."

"And I don't," Tilda said, as she searched the box for the matching earrings. "For my age, I have a very refined taste. I choose carefully."

"One of these days, you're going to get caught."

She plucked out the earrings and put them on. "Tomorrow I'll be gone from Aldershot forever, living the life I've always dreamed about."

"Fancying yourself with pretty dresses and wearing sparklies around your neck doesn't make you a lady. You're still the daughter of a soldier."

"Ah," Tilda said, raising a finger, "but I am also the goddaughter of Colonel Grady Cummings, who just so happens to be married to the Dowager Countess of Summerfield. As an orphan, it's his duty to care for me."

"You don't know if you are an orphan. Your mother might still be alive."

"She's dead to me, as I am dead to her." She blinked the nagging truth away. "Anyway, it's the colonel's duty to care for me until I am of-age."

"If you ask me, you're sixteen going on thirty."

Tilda whipped around to face her. "And whose fault is that?"

"Your father did the best he could, but from my experience few men have the ability and character to effectively manage the well-being of a child."

"His best was leaving his child to manage for herself, growing up sooner rather than later."

Mrs. Smith nodded, and rubbed a wrinkled hand on Tilda's arm. "I know you've had a hard time of it. And you've done real good for yourself, getting a job doing housework for some of the married officers."

"I am never going to clean up after other people again. I'm going to be rich and have others clean up after me. Just you wait and see. If living this life taught me anything it's that the world is not going to give me anything. It's up to me to figure out what I want and make it happen." She offered a satisfied smiled. "Which is exactly what I've done." *So there.*

"I simply worry that you've set your sights too high. I don't want you to be disappointed. Take it one day at a time and be glad your father's solicitor finally found the colonel, and that he extended you the invitation. You're a very lucky girl and I want you to be on your best behavior. Act appreciative and sweet."

"I know exactly how to act."

And how to get exactly what she wanted.

"So, Miss Farrow," said Captain Briggs. "I hear you're sailing with us to England, off to marry a viscount."

Genevieve's mother answered for her. "Morgan Weston is a viscount who will eventually be the Earl of Summerfield. There's going to be a glorious wedding. I wanted it to be in New York, but the groom's family insists it be at Summerfield."

Another woman at the dining table continued the discussion. "I've heard of American heiresses buying themselves a title, but I've never met one."

Genevieve wanted to slide under the table. The entire situation was humiliating.

A baron came to her defense. "I am not averse to the practice," he said. "You have no idea the expense of running and maintaining an estate with dozens of servants."

"But the arrangement is so . . . pecuniary," the woman said.

Genevieve wasn't sure what *pecuniary* meant, but knew it wasn't good.

"It's the American way," the captain said, with a wink at Genevieve. "What we lack in titles, we offer in ingenuity and hard work."

"Here, here!" A banker from New York raised his glass. "To Miss Farrow's future happiness as a . . ." He looked to the baron for help. "A vis-countess?"

"Yes, but it's pronounced vie-countess."

"Sounds even better."

After the toast, Genevieve took a waiter's offering of cod. If only it was the dessert course so she could run back to her stateroom and hide.

"Actually," Mother said with a flirty shift of her shoulders, "the father of my daughter's fiancé, the current Earl of Summerfield, is also unmarried."

"Why aren't you marrying *him*, Miss Farrow?" another woman asked.

Mother answered for Genevieve a second time. "Because he's much too old for *her*. He's more my age."

She was so utterly transparent.

"But isn't earl a higher rank than viscount? Shouldn't your daughter marry — ?"

"Yes, an earl is of higher rank, but the viscount will be the earl someday."

"You're a widow, aren't you Mrs. Farrow?" the Captain asked.

Mother seemed relieved that someone at the table had finally grasped her meaning. "I am."

"Then perhaps you can charm the earl into a marriage. Two titles for the price of one, eh?"

Genevieve pushed back from the table. "If you'll excuse me. I'm feeling a little under the weather."

There was a flurry of chairs being pushed out as the men rose to their feet. She assured them she would be fine, and hurried out of the dining room as if it were a prison from which to be freed.

She stopped at the railing of the ship and breathed deeply of the sea air. If she could swim back to New York, she'd consider stripping to her underthings and jumping into the Atlantic. She'd rather take her chances with the sea than bear the embarrassment of an arranged marriage to a man she'd never met beyond a year's worth of letters.

If only Papa were still alive. He never would have considered it. He'd always called her his "lovely", even though they both knew Genevieve was as far from lovely as America was to England. Everyone knew if they had eyes. She'd been called 'fair' before but didn't dwell on whether it was due to her pallor or was simply her rating in regard to being pretty. Neither alternative spoke well to her beauty quotient. Yet the way Papa had said *lovely* gave her confidence, for she knew he meant she was lovely inside.

At least she had that. For she *was* an interesting person. She was well-read and even witty at times. She enjoyed a vigorous walk in Central Park as much as dancing every dance at one of New York's society balls. She liked to think of herself as being a woman who commanded a modicum of depth.

"Are you all right, miss?" asked a steward walking by.

"Yes, thank you."

"It's a mite chilly out tonight. Can I fetch you your wrap?"

"No, thank you. I think I'll retire."

Maybe if she hurried, she could pretend to be asleep before her mother came back to the room, and delay her inevitable scolding for tomorrow.

She only had four tomorrows left before they reached England.

A scary thought.

Chapter Two

Genevieve did not look up from her sewing when her mother entered their stateroom.

"Here you are."

"Here I am."

Mother closed the door behind her. "I have been looking all over for you. The baron and his wife invited us to join them for a game of Whist."

"I would guess you can find a fourth elsewhere."

"But I want *you* to join us. It's a baron and a baroness."

"I'd rather sew. The lace on this blouse is coming loose at the cuff and—"

Her mother ripped the blouse away from her and tossed it on a bed. "We have Jane to mend our things."

"Her stitches are too long."

"Then tell her to make them shorter. It's her job." Mother checked her reflection in the mirror, and finding it to her liking, left her reflection behind. "Your job is to hobnob with the rich and titled."

"I see no need for that."

Her eyes grew wide. "No need? You are going to be a viscountess and you see no need for socializing with like-kind?"

"The deal is done, Mother."

"Mamma. I have told you to call me Mam-*ma*, not Mother."

Genevieve withheld a sigh. "I will be a viscountess whether I want to or not. I don't see the need to spend time with titled people just because they're titled."

Mother—Mamma—strode towards Genevieve's chair, glaring down at her. "How dare you negate all my hard work! I secured your future—*our* future. I found you a viscount to marry. I negotiated the prenuptial agreement between you."

"In which you agreed on how much you'd sell me for."

Mamma slapped her cheek. Hard.

Genevieve burst out of her chair, taking cover behind it. Her cheek burned and tears welled in her eyes. "You hit me!"

"Yes, I did. And I'm sorry for it. But you make me so angry. When will you accept that this isn't just about you?" Her mother's voice broke as if she too was close to tears.

The only sound in the room was their breathing. Genevieve waited until the sound lessened. "I know you want the title, but—"

"I want it for you."

"But other than being the mother of a viscountess what do you get out of it?"

There was no hesitation. "Excitement."

It was not a word she had ever heard from her mother's mouth.

Mamma held out her hand and waited until Genevieve came around the chair to take it. Then she drew them towards the settee. Once seated she explained. "As you know, we have not always been wealthy."

"I know. I remember."

"When your father was making his start selling sewing machines, times were tough. We had little extra money. We lived in a horrible apartment with a tiny parlor, and no servants. None at all."

Genevieve's memories held a different focus. "I loved that parlor. We'd sit there at night and read aloud from *Moby Dick* and *The Three Musketeers*."

"You and your father read aloud."

"You could have joined us."

"I didn't want to *read*. I wanted to go to the theatre or musicals. I wanted to enjoy life."

"We were enjoying life."

She stood and faced Genevieve. "You two were enjoying it. I was miserable."

Genevieve didn't know what to say. "I'm . . . I'm sorry. I didn't realize."

"Of course you didn't. You and your father only had eyes for each other's company."

"That's not true. He loved . . ." She couldn't finish the sentence because she wasn't sure there *had* been love between her parents.

Mamma strode to the gilt-framed painting on the wall and eased it a fraction to the left. "When your father decided to go into the manufacturing of a new, improved sewing machine that could be used in factories, when he made his fortune, we finally began to live the life *I* wanted to live." She stared at the painting of a New York street scene above the dresser as though transporting herself there. "I will never forget the first time I met Mrs. Astor. She was *the* Mrs. Astor, the head of all New York society, and she talked to *me*, invited *me* to one of her teas."

Where Genevieve had found Mrs. Astor too high-strung. "That made you happy?"

Mamma smiled. "Immensely. And it was more exciting than anything I had ever done. As was moving into our gorgeous mansion on Fifth Avenue, shopping at Tiffany's and Lord and Taylor, and having my gowns ordered from Worth in Paris."

Genevieve decided now was not the time to mention that *she* had little interest in gowns and diamonds.

Mamma's smile faded. "But then, just as we arrived in New York society your father died and I was forced into mourning. I thought I'd smother under that horrible black crape veil. My very soul seemed to die in the widow's weeds, with no parties whatsoever for eighteen months."

"I wore mourning too."

"You were only thirteen, so you could get by wearing white dresses. But as the widow, the grieving fell upon my shoulders."

Genevieve suffered the familiar ache of her father's absence. That her mother discounted the measure of her pain was offensive. "I grieved as much as you." *If not more.*

"I am not talking about the emotion of it, but the total segregation that widowhood entails. When I heard that some society girls were marrying English lords I saw a way out for both of us. I thank God for my brother, who was able to make the initial contact and finalize the contract." She looked directly at her daughter. "This betrothal saved me and has lifted me out of widowhood into a life that promises happiness, light, and excitement. Is that so hard to understand?"

Genevieve did understand.

But there was a vast difference between understanding the reasons behind the game and being a pawn in that game. While Mamma felt excitement and anticipation, Genevieve felt a complete and utter panic.

Déjà vu.

Molly had heard Madam Lupine use that phrase at the hat shop, explaining that it was a strong feeling of being someplace before.

Strolling up the road to Summerfield Manor gave Molly that feeling. Of course, she *had* been here before. Many *befores.* She'd grown up in the village of Summerfield and had worked at the manor from the time she was twelve until she'd run off to London, fleeing a love that could never be hers.

Being in this place, in this moment, wasn't so much a feeling of déjà vu, as a feeling that only a day had passed since she'd been here last. Certainly it hadn't been over a year.

As she walked through the elaborate gates and continued up the drive, Summerfield Manor looked unchanged. The trees that canopied her approach with their leaves of gold and red were imperceptibly taller, and the stone and brick of the manor itself were as solid now as they'd been when the first earl had built it, hundreds of years ago.

Which was the point. Such homes and estates were created to exude permanence and history, a sense of time marching on, world without end, amen.

The exterior was the same, but inside . . . the changes that had occurred within the walls of the manor were the reason she'd left.

The thought of seeing Morgan again made her stomach dance.

And clench.

How was he faring as the Viscount Weston? It was inevitable she'd see him. She hoped to see him. Ached for it. Yet she also feared the meeting because she'd fled without saying goodbye. Would words of parting have healed their pain? Growing up as a shopkeeper's son, he'd been the perfect match for Molly, a lady's maid. But when a secret revealed he was actually the heir she'd had to run away. A clean break was far more merciful than a lingering farewell.

Enough of Morgan. She had her mother to worry about. Her ponderings ended just in time for her to detour to the servants' entrance.

She spotted the earl's valet, Mr. Robbins, shining a pair of shoes on a bench outside the kitchen.

He rose to greet her. "Miss Wallace. How nice to see you."

"It's nice to see you too, Mr. Robbins."

He yanked at the bottom of his waistcoat. "You're looking well."

"Thank you. I am well, but I've come because—"

"Your mother is *un*well." He held the door for her, letting her inside.

There was a happy reunion with Mrs. McDeer the cook, the housekeeper, Mrs. Camden, and the kitchen maids. Molly was peppered with questions about where she'd been and what she'd been doing. Obviously, Dottie had kept her promise to keep Molly's whereabouts to herself.

"Come now," Mrs. Camden said. "We'll have plenty of time to get a full report from Miss Wallace. I know she's eager to see her mother. Fanny, go find Dottie and bring her here."

"How is Ma?"

"I assure you, she's received the best of care."

That wasn't an answer.

"Have you eaten?" asked Mrs. McDeer.

Molly was famished, but hunger had to wait. "Maybe later."

"Of course."

Mrs. Camden nodded to Nick, the footman. "Take her things to the room next to her mother's."

At that moment Dottie ran into the kitchen, straight into Molly's arms. "I'm ever so glad to see you!"

The others dispersed, giving them a moment alone. Molly took a good look at her little sister. "My, my. You're all grown up."

Dottie smoothed her apron. "You've been gone a long time, Mol."

"I know, but . . ." She glanced at Dottie's ample bosom. "I leave you a child and return to find you fully grown."

"Like I wrote you, I'm a full housemaid now too. I took your advice and worked real hard."

"Good for you." She thought of her brother. "And Lon? How is he?"

"As long as he can be outside he's happy. He's become fast friends with Master George." She took Molly's arm and walked towards the back stair. "Master George is fully grown now too."

"He isn't bothering you, is he? I remember how he liked to tease you."

"He's obsessed with horses, so I rarely see him."

Just as well.

"How is Ma?" Molly asked as they began their ascent.

"Not bad and not good. Better than before. At least she's awake. Dr. Peter says that's promising."

"What happened to Dr. Evers?"

"He's still around. Though at the moment he's off in London. Dr. Peter is his son, back from school. He's a doctor too."

Two doctors in Summerfield. What a wonderful excess.

They climbed the back stairs up three flights to the servants' floor. The smell of lemon oil and age accompanied them and brought back memories. Molly had traversed these steps at least a dozen times a day, every day, for seven years. She did the math in her head . . . over thirty thousand times?

Thirty thousand and one.

They reached the servants' floor that opened to a long corridor with bedrooms on either side. Halfway down the hall was a door that separated the men's rooms from the women's. Once through, they passed the room that used to be Molly's. "Who's taken over my job of lady's maid for Mrs. Weston?"

"Old Miss Albers. After you left, and Miss Clarissa left with her maid, Miss Albers was taking care of the missus and Lady Lila, but after Lady Lila got married and moved over to Crompton Hall, Albers only has Mrs. Weston to attend to, so it doesn't matter as much that she's old." She'd answered the question in a single breath.

Somehow it was comforting to know that no new servants had come into the manor and taken her place.

Dottie pointed to the last door on the left. "You ready?"

The fact her sister thought she needed to be *ready* made her nervous. "Of course."

Dottie opened the door and Molly found her mother in bed, her face ashen, her breathing labored. The right side of her face was pulled downward, as though the muscles had surrendered.

"Ma?" She ran to her bedside. "Ma, it's me, Molly."

Ma opened her eyes and managed a crooked. "Mah!" Her words slurred. "You cah!"

27

Molly carefully took her in her arms. "Of course I came." She noticed Ma only used one arm. The other lay limp in her lap.

Ma pointed to a glass on the bedside table. "Wah."

Molly poured some fresh water, and helped her mother lean forward enough to take a sip. Only a portion of the water made it into her mouth, and the small act exhausted her. Molly looked to Dottie.

Dottie shrugged. "She's better'n she was."

Ma tried to open her eyes. "You. Luh-duh?"

Molly stroked her hand, and by the droop of her eyes could tell Ma needed to sleep. She smoothed her covers. "Yes, I've been in London. But I'm here now. We'll have time to talk later. Right now you need to rest. I'll be sleeping right next door so I'll come check on you often." She spotted a bell on the table and moved it close to Ma's good hand. "Just ring and I'll come running."

Molly and Dottie tiptoed out of the room. "I've been checking on her every few hours, but it's hard to get my work done and look after her. I'm glad you came."

Molly had mixed feelings.

Molly spooned some soup into her mother's mouth, a napkin at the ready.

"There you go," she said. "Mrs. McDeer always made a wonderful squash soup."

Ma swallowed with difficulty. "You eah."

Molly glanced at the tray of food that contained her own lunch. She hadn't been downstairs since she'd arrived, but Mrs. McDeer had been kind enough to send up trays.

With the next spoonful, her mother locked her lips shut. "Duh."

"All right. You can be done for now."

"Ree."

Molly took up the novel *Cranford* she'd been reading aloud to Ma before the meal. But before she could begin, there was a knock on the door. "Come in."

As the door opened, Molly stood. A man with striking red hair entered. "Oh. You have company. I can come back."

Molly's mother became agitated, and it was then that Molly saw his doctor's bag. "You must be Dr. Peter."

"I am." He blinked and she could see his thoughts focus. "And you must be Molly, Miss Wallace."

They exchanged a nod in greeting. "Thank you for taking care of my mother."

"It's been a pleasure. Please know that my father is still apprised of the situation. Although I am technically a doctor, I have much to learn. As Father says, 'All I know is I know nothing.'"

She admired his humility. He moved to the side of the bed and took her mother's wrist between the fingers of one hand, while checking a pocket watch with the other. "Strong, but a bit elevated."

Ma smiled a crooked smile. "Mah-eh."

"Of course. You're excited to see your daughter come home." He felt her forehead. "No fever. Excellent. Can you lift your left arm please?"

Ma's forehead tightened as she concentrated on the task at hand. Her arm remained where it was.

"That's all right," the doctor said. He looked to Molly. "Ask her to try as often as you can."

Molly wanted to speak with him alone. "Shall we step outside?"

"Of course." He nodded at Ma. "We'll be right back, Mrs. Wallace."

They stepped down the hall, out of her mother's earshot. "So, Dr. Peter. What is the . . . the . . .?"

"Prognosis?"

"To be blunt, what is the rest of her life going to be like?"

He glanced away, then back again. "There's no way to know. She could regain use of her left side, but chances are it will never be as strong as it once was."

Molly's mind swam with the repercussions. "But she's a kitchen maid. My sister and brother also work at the manor. She can't leave them. She has no home but this one."

His hazel eyes were kind. "I understand. And I continue to pray she recovers fully."

"Prayers are fine, but isn't there something we can do? I can do?"

He took a deep breath. "It used to be thought that apoplexy was a supernatural phenomenon, a punishment for wrong living."

"I beg your pardon! My mother has led a virtuous life."

"I meant no offense."

Molly's mind visited a memory. "She *was* responsible for my father's death, but she was saving Dottie from his . . ." She'd already said too much, but was too tired not to finish it. "His inappropriate behavior."

Dr. Peter's eyes grew wide with understanding. "I'm sorry. I didn't know."

She was glad her family's sketchy past was no longer village gossip. "I'm simply stating that she is a woman of courage. She does not deserve punishment."

He sighed and looked to the floor. "I apologize for even mentioning it. Sometimes my textbook knowledge interferes with practical application. It was wrong of me to bring up an old theory as to the cause of your mother's affliction."

Dr. Peter seemed sincere, so Molly calmed herself. "So what is the new theory as to the cause?"

"A lack of blood flow to the brain. We used to bleed people in this condition, but found that with low blood pressure it did more harm than good." He caught himself. "Again, I digress. *Nowadays,* we see an advantage to getting the blood flowing through the appendages—the legs and arms—to encourage the body to repair itself."

Molly glanced towards her mother's room. "But she can't even walk."

"Perhaps she can—with your help." He pointed down the hall. "You have space to do it."

"I have no training."

"You are her daughter. It might be worth the effort. I believe in you, Miss Wallace. Believe in yourself."

She'd try.

Tilda plopped down on the seat of the train and faced her chaperones with a scowl.

Mrs. White flipped a hand at her. "Sulk if you'd like. We don't much care."

Mr. White put a calming hand on his wife's knee and offered a smile. "I know it's odd to have us accompany you to Summerfield, but Mrs. Smith would not allow you to travel alone, and she is not up to it."

"Besides," Mrs. White said, "A young girl traveling alone is simply not—"

"Proper," Tilda finished. "Yes, yes, I've heard it all. But I think it's silly to be accompanied like a child, when I've fended for myself all my life."

There was an awkward pause.

"Your father loved you very much," Mr. White said.

His wife shook her head. "No, he didn't."

"Ethel!"

Mrs. White nodded at Tilda. "I sense you're a girl who wants to know what's what, yes?"

Tilda nodded, because it was true. Sort of. But to have Mrs. White be so blunt about it . . . "My father made it very clear that my existence was a burden."

"That's not true," Mr. White said. "Your father was simply overwhelmed with the responsibilities of raising a child alone. And he missed your mother."

"Hmph," Mrs. White said. "Drove her out, more than likely."

"Ethel, enough."

Mrs. White shrugged. "That's neither here nor there. You were present when Mrs. Smith interviewed us and that other couple about being your chaperones. She chose us because Mr. White knew your father better than anyone."

"I knew him for over twenty years," Mr. White said.

Drank with him. Gambled with him. Laughed at his off-color jokes.

Tilda knew Mr. White and her father's other drinking companions, but Mrs. White was new to her. And interesting. Tilda had never met someone who was so direct. Directness had its place, but so did discretion.

As the train gained speed, Tilda asked a question that had been dogging her throughout the days of getting ready to leave. "At the interview with Mrs. Smith, you perked up when I mentioned I was traveling to Summerfield Manor."

"You are very astute, my dear," Mrs. White said.

If "astute" meant observant, yes, she was.

Mr. White quickly busied himself with a piece of lint on his trousers. "I've been there. I've seen it from the outside. Everyone who's been through Summerfield is impressed with the grandeur of the estate."

"You were visiting?"

He glanced at his wife.

"Yes, he was visiting," Mrs. White said. "You mentioned that Colonel Cummings recently married the dowager countess?"

"A year or so ago. They loved each other when they were young, but the dowager's parents made her marry the earl instead of Uncle Grady."

"You call him uncle?"

"Papa knew him in the army and he was always kind to us. We didn't see him much, but when I was young and Papa and he were stationed at the same place he brought me presents." She looked out the window at the green pastures flying by. "I think their marriage is romantic. It's horrible her parents kept them apart all those years ago."

Mrs. White put a finger to her cheek, "Let's see . . . would I want my daughter to marry a military man—who may or may not distinguish himself—or an earl?" She let her finger fall to her lap. "An easy choice."

Tilda noticed that Mr. White's face had turned a blotchy red. Was he embarrassed? Perhaps with good reason. Even at middle-age he was only a coachman-for-hire. Clearly his ambition was sorely lacking and he deserved his wife's complaints. But since he was kind — and Mrs. White was not — Tilda wouldn't shut him out. "Mr. White, you've always been very nice to me when I wanted to ride. You know a lot about horses."

"Hmm," said his wife.

But Mr. White smiled. "Sometimes knowing and understanding horses is easier than knowing and understanding people."

At least certain people.

"Enough about your Uncle Grady," Mrs. White said, as she removed a handkerchief from her reticule. "Please close that window, Mr. White. The dust and smoke are annoying my senses." He did as she asked and she continued. "What does interest me, is the situation at the manor. You mentioned that the heir, Morgan Weston, was once a shopkeeper?"

It had all been news to her too, as per the colonel's recent letters. "A shopkeeper's son, I believe. His father was the shopkeeper, and unknowingly was the eldest son of the dowager."

"If you excuse the question," Mr. White asked. "How could he not know such a thing?"

It was getting warm with the window closed, so Tilda removed her gloves. "Apparently, he was stolen away as a child, and the old earl and the countess thought him dead."

"Astounding," Mrs. White said. "To be brought up lowly, then be elevated to a title."

"I don't think being a shopkeeper is *lowly,*" Mr. White said.

His wife huffed. "Compared to being an earl? Don't be absurd. Some people have ambition."

Tilda had never heard a wife talk to her husband this way. It was rather disconcerting, yet there was something intriguing about the control Mrs. White brandished about. Tilda might be able to learn something from her, although a touch of subtlety wouldn't hurt.

"There's nothing ambitious about becoming an earl," Mr. White said. "Either you are one or you're not."

Mrs. White shrugged. "So then. Morgan's mother . . ." she nodded at her husband, "Fidelia. You knew her, didn't you, dear?"

He coughed, seemingly startled by the question, "A bit."

"To know the Countess of Summerfield . . ." Mrs. White said. "Perhaps she will be glad to see you." She grinned. "Though perhaps not."

Tilda tried to remember Uncle Grady's letters. "I'm afraid that's not possible. She died a while back. I don't think there is a countess right now."

Mrs. White's eyes widened. "She's dead?" She turned towards her husband. "Why didn't you know that? We need to know that! It ruins everything."

"Ruins what *everything*? What are you talking about?" Tilda asked.

Mrs. White looked at her husband and said under her breath. "Your connection to Summerfield is dead with her. This entire trip will be a waste."

"A waste?" Tilda asked. What were they talking about?

Mrs. White blinked as if realizing she'd said too much. Mr. White offered a skittish smile, and his wife a fake one. "Ah me. Tis a silly nothing," she said.

"A silly nothing," he parroted.

The air between them seemed to tingle, as if a tension had been disturbed and needed to settle again.

Tilda sensed that there was nothing silly about anything Mrs. White said or did. Nor anything accidental. Tilda would have to keep an eye on her as she set in place her own plan for Summerfield Manor.

Clarissa rushed into the dressing room and yanked off her bonnet. She quickly replaced her street clothes with her costume, relishing the ease of movement afforded by the flowing garment that had no bustle or tight sleeves. Then she sank into a chair at the makeup table and began putting on her face.

The girl sitting next to her leaned close, "He's fuming."

"Let him." Being late had become Clarissa's defense against the stage manager's offense. If there wasn't enough time for him to get her alone, she could avoid him.

"Miss West!"

"Told ya," the girl said.

She swept a brush of blue over her eyelids. "You bellowed, Mr. Mapes?"

There was a tittering among the girls.

Clarissa felt her spine tingle as he approached. The nearest girl made herself scarce.

He leaned into her ear. "Yer late. Again."

"Sorry."

"No, yer not." He stood erect and called out for all to hear. "Five minutes!"

As soon as he left, Clarissa pressed a hand to her chest, trying to calm her heart.

The girl returned to quickly pat a powder puff to her face. "What's he got against you?" she asked.

Clarissa rose from her chair. "I guess he finds me irresistible."

"At least he's noticed you."

If only he hadn't.

Chapter Three

It felt good to go downstairs.

Since arriving at Summerfield Manor, Molly had spent her time on the servants' floor, either with her mother or in her own room next door. All meals had been brought to them, a fact that was both a blessing and a curse. She'd been hesitant about coming back to Summerfield Manor, yet other than walking through the kitchen to enter the house, she could have been in any house, anywhere.

Molly paused one floor down, on the level where the family bedrooms were located. She had spent many hours in these rooms with her mistress, Mrs. Weston, both here and in London during the social season. It would be nice to see her. They'd enjoyed a close relationship, especially since Mrs. Weston had been so reclusive. Molly had been her only contact with the outside world. Mrs. Weston had been instrumental in getting Molly's family jobs at the manor. Molly would always be beholden to her for that.

She continued her journey to the main floor, where she quietly made her way from the back stair to the library, slowing to listen to see if anyone was inside. Hearing nothing, she entered the room. The smell of old books was comforting and she paused a moment to let it settle around her. She moved to the shelf with the novels by Dickens, Gaskell, Trollope, Dumas, and Austen. She chose her favorite, *Pride and Prejudice.* Ma would like the story of sisters in want of a husband, though the issue was distressingly close to home.

She was just about to leave when she saw someone pass by the doorway, then backtrack to peer in at her.

"Molly?" He looked as if he'd seen a ghost.

Her heart skipped a beat. "Hello, Morgan." She bobbed a curtsy. "Lord Weston."

He shook his head at the form of address, and rushed into the room, stopping short of taking her into his arms. "Are you really here?"

He's pleased to see me? "I . . . I am. Here."

"But why? Where did you come from?"

He truly didn't know the reason? "My mother suffered an attack of apoplexy so I came back to help with her care."

He nodded. "I *had* heard that. How is she?"

"A little better. But I fear it will be a long recovery."

He hesitated. "Will you be staying for a while then?"

Without meaning to, she expressed a thought aloud. "Do you want me to stay?"

He paused to swallow. Then he glanced towards the door before whispering. "Of course I do."

She suffered her own pause. Had he really said that?

"I missed you, Mol. Where were you? You left so suddenly. I kept waiting to hear from you."

She was touched. "I'm sorry for your worry, but I couldn't . . ." *Don't go into that now.* "I got a job in a millinery shop in London. Actually, I'm doing quite well for myself."

"I'm glad for that, but . . ." He took a step away from her, busying himself by spinning a globe on its axis.

"How are you and your family doing at the manor, in your new positions, with your . . . your titles?"

"Papa is happy," he said.

"And you?"

"I'm learning to be happy. Trying to be." His eyes met hers, and she melted into their deep brownness. His voice grew soft. "I'm hoping to be happy."

When they heard voices they both looked towards the door. He moved to leave. "Will I see you soon?"

"I look forward to it."

The room felt empty in his absence.

Molly realized she still held the book in her hands. Remembering the first line of *Pride and Prejudice,* she opened to the page and read it aloud: "'It is a truth universally acknowledged, that a single man in possession of a good fortune must be in want of a wife.'"

She laughed aloud, then gave the world another spin on its axis.

The sea went on forever.

Genevieve sat in a deck chair, looking out over the endless ocean that stretched to the horizon in every direction. And above it, the dome of the sky, dotted with clouds that freely moved from horizon to horizon. Endless skies meeting endless seas.

What did their ship look like from above? For though it was large enough to hold hundreds of passengers, in the scheme of the sky and sea it was a mere dot, and she but a pinprick upon it.

She'd never felt so alone and so inconsequential.

In the scheme of the world did it really matter if she married Morgan Weston? Her family's money might help save the Summerfield estate but her gain of an English title didn't make a whit of difference to anyone.

Except her mother.

Genevieve was doing all of this for her mother's sake. Genevieve was content in New York City. She had good friends and had found a sense of purpose working for a few charities. She could easily marry the son of some master-of-industry and raise a house full of happy children. She didn't have to cross an ocean to achieve that end.

She leaned her head against the high back of the deckchair and closed her eyes. *Oh, God, what am I doing?*

"May I sit here?"

Genevieve opened her eyes to see fellow passengers, Mr. and Mrs. Sigmund, standing nearby. "Of course."

Mr. Sigmund helped his corpulent wife into a deck chair, then bid the ladies adieu to take his morning walk.

Mrs. Sigmund groaned and moaned as she tried to get comfortable, and Genevieve helped her adjust a blanket over her legs as a shield against the autumn air.

"There now," she finally said. "Herbert insists I should walk with him, but I am not keen on unneeded exercise. Besides, he doesn't walk, he strides, which is beyond my ability no matter what opinion I hold towards exertion." She sighed deeply, and looked to Genevieve. "So. My dear girl. How are you faring?"

"Tis a lovely ship. The amenities are plentiful."

"I am not speaking of ship amenities. How are you *faring?*"

Although Mrs. Sigmund had been a stranger just four days earlier, she had a way about her that encouraged confession. "I am torn."

"I can see that."

"You can?"

"You don't seem very . . . engaged. Or is that because you *are* engaged?"

She'd pegged it. "I'm just a bit uncertain, that's all. Tis nothing against my fiancé."

"Although you've never met him."

"I have not had the pleasure."

Mrs. Sigmund slapped a gloved hand on the arm of Genevieve's chair. "No wonder you're wary. Have you at least seen a photograph?"

"I have. I find his looks quite agreeable."

"There's half the battle."

I hardly think so.

"Has he seen a photograph of you?"

"He has. Though it was not a good one. Yet as good as it can be, considering . . ."

With an expulsion of air, Mrs. Sigmund angled her body towards Genevieve. "There will be none of that, young lady. Being a beauty is overrated."

Genevieve could have been offended by the woman's comment, yet somehow, was not.

"Looks fade and those who rely on them falter when there is nothing to fall back upon. The woman who endures is the one with gumption, confidence, and a sense of purpose."

Although Genevieve could accept not being a beauty, her lack of the other traits was bothersome. "I'm afraid I have a deficit regarding all those attributes."

"Pish-posh. I've seen flashes of all three in the way you handle your mother and this ridiculous arrangement she's made. The trick is to set those qualities loose. Give them permission to have free rein. If you do that, then nothing that Summerside—"

"Summerfield."

"Nothing that Summerfield throws at you will overwhelm." She leaned close. "They need you more than you need them. Remember that."

"I will try."

"Not try. You will do it."

She hesitated, then said the words that were required. "I will do it."

"That's the way. Now tell me about the wedding plans."

"Is that him?" Mrs. White asked, as the train slowed to a stop at the Summerfield depot.

Tilda nodded, and waved at Colonel Cummings out the window. She hadn't had contact with him very often in her sixteen years, yet his appearance matched her memories. He was tall without being domineering, and from the ease of his smile seemed to be a man who knew about hard work *and* amusement. The only difference from the last time she'd seen him was more gray in his hair, mustache, and bushy eyebrows.

"That must be the dowager countess," Mrs. White said. "Though she doesn't look like one."

No, she didn't. Tilda had expected the dowager to be wearing some fancy bustled gown made of silk or brocade as suited her station, and was rather disappointed to find her wearing a simple bodice with a plain skirt devoid of bustle or drapery. Yet she didn't want to agree with Mrs. White, or argue with her about what the dowager should or shouldn't look like. All Mrs. White did was argue and disparage people, places, and things. Nothing was to her liking. Tilda was picky, but Mrs. White could have argued the color of a blue sky.

Once the train was fully stopped, Mrs. White popped to her feet. Mr. White lingered in his seat, biting his lip.

Tilda didn't have time for either of them. She pushed ahead of the other passengers and exited the train, running towards Uncle Grady. The last time she'd seen him she had run into his arms. But now that she was a young lady . . .

She ran into his arms.

He held her tightly and they rocked side to side. "Oh my dear, Matilda. How good it is to see you."

Tilda was surprised to feel tears threaten. She held onto him a moment longer, until the threat passed. "I'm glad to be here too," she whispered against his chest.

They let go of each other and the colonel held her hands wide. "My, my. You are quite the beautiful young lady." His smile faded. "I am so sorry to hear about your father's passing. He was a friend and a good man."

"Thank you. He thought a lot of you, too."

"Ahem."

Reminded, Uncle Grady turned towards his companion. "Addie, I would like to introduce you to my goddaughter, Matilda Cavendish. Matilda, this is my wife, Adelaide."

He didn't mention his wife's title, so Tilda wasn't sure if she should bob a curtsy or offer a hug. And she had no idea what the dowager should be called. So she just stood there. "Nice to meet you . . ."

"Oh, come here, child." The dowager pulled her into a lavender-scented embrace. "I too am glad you are here with us. You are not alone anymore."

Tilda was touched by her words. "What should I call you?"

The dowager chuckled. "Right to the point. I like that. How about Aunt Adelaide?"

To call a dowager countess Aunt-anything seemed a bit odd, but since she'd offered . . .

"Tilda?"

It was Mrs. White, standing nearby with her husband. Tilda made the introductions. "Uncle Grady and Aunt Adelaide, this is Mr. and Mrs. White who have been my chaperones on the trip." She nodded to the couple. "This is Colonel Cummings and the Dowager Countess of —"

"Yes, yes," Aunt Adelaide said. "Nice to meet you. And many thanks for bringing Matilda safely to Summerfield."

Mr. White gave the colonel a neat nod. "Nice to meet you, Colonel. Your ladyship." He looked to the ground.

There was an awkward moment, then Uncle motioned them towards a waiting carriage. "Shall we?"

"This is where we live," Aunt Adelaide said.

Tilda tried not to show her shock and disappointment, but Mrs. White had no such restraint.

"This is a cottage."

"The old caretaker's cottage," Uncle said. "We've spruced it up a bit and find it suits us very well."

"But it's so . . . so . . ."

"Perfect?" There was a challenge in Aunt Adelaide's voice.

Mrs. White blushed and looked away. "Of course."

"Come in." Aunt led the way.

The inside of the cottage could be seen in one glance. There was a small kitchen area, a dining table for two, a seating area by the fireplace, and a bedroom beyond. Tilda was appalled. The lodging she'd had back in Aldershot was better than this. What good did it do to be invited to live with a dowager countess if they lived in this . . . hovel? She wanted to live in the manor.

Yet in spite of her feelings, Tilda put on a smile. "This is very cozy."

"I'll say," Mrs. White said under her breath.

Uncle laughed. "Lest you panic, this is *not* where you'll be staying."

"Oh, no," the dowager said. "Grady and I have chosen to live a simplified life, but you, my dear Matilda, will live at the manor."

Tilda smiled with relief.

Aunt Adelaide nodded to the Whites. "And you are welcome to stay a few days to see your charge properly settled."

"We would be happy to, Lady Summerfield," Mrs. White said.

"Come. Let's show you the manor," the colonel said.

Tilda couldn't help but gawk as they walked into Summerfield Manor. Her eyes were immediately drawn to a grand staircase that led to the upper floor, where a battalion of stone uprights formed a balcony marking that floor from the one below. A patterned carpet led the way, held in place by shiny brass rails. The floor was white marble and the ceiling was edged with layer upon layer of carved moldings that extended beyond the edge of the walls to form a checkerboard of coffered squares across the ceiling. An immense chandelier marked the middle.

Uncle Grady leaned close and whispered, "Quite the setup, isn't it?"

"It's beyond anything I imagined," she whispered back.

Aunt Adelaide must have overheard, for she smiled as she put an arm around Tilda's shoulders and led her into a grand parlor. Aunt turned to the butler and said, "Tell the others Miss Cavendish has arrived." When Tilda glanced towards Mr. and Mrs. White, Aunt added, "And her chaperones."

Before they had time to be seated five members of the Weston family entered the room. "Well now," said a forty-something man with wide shoulders and a watch chain snaking out of his vest pocket. "You must be Matilda."

"I am," she said with a little bob. "But it's just Tilda. Tilda Cavendish."

"Welcome to our home, Tilda Cavendish," he said. "I am Jack Weston, and—"

"You're the earl?"

He chuckled. "That, I am." He drew another couple close. "And this is my brother and his wife, Mr. and Mrs. Weston."

"Nice to meet you, Miss Cavendish," Mrs. Weston said. "Was your journey pleasant?"

"Yes, thank you."

The older of the two young men stepped forward. "I am Morgan and this is my cousin, George."

Tilda set them right in her mind: Morgan, the heir and the current Viscount Weston. George was the son of the Weston couple and looked to be about her age.

"Nice to meet both of you," she said.

George winked at her and sprawled in a chair.

"Stand up," his mother whispered to him.

He did so with a grin in Tilda's direction. He was quite the cheeky one and Tilda liked him immediately. She also liked his tousled brown hair. Somehow it made him seem more approachable than if he'd been presented with hair slicked down with pomade.

Aunt Adelaide introduced the Whites, yet Tilda couldn't help but notice—with some satisfaction—that she had been singled out first.

"Have a seat everyone," the earl said.

There were plenty of chairs to choose from, at least two dozen, but Uncle Grady patted a place beside him on a settee, and Tilda sat, glad for his proximity. Aunt Adelaide ordered tea. Feeling famished, Tilda hoped there were biscuits involved.

"Well now, Miss Cavendish," the earl said. "I hope you enjoy your stay here."

"Do you ride?" George asked.

"Some." She understated her abilities.

"Well, there you go then," the earl said. "George spends more time at the stables than in the house."

"Always has," his mother said.

The day was getting better and better.

Mr. Weston turned her attention to the Whites. "I assume you were good friends with Miss Cavendish's father?"

"Yes," Mr. White said.

His wife looked at him, as if expecting him to say more. As did Tilda. Of course what could he say? That he and Tilda's father were drinking chums?

Mrs. Weston put a finger to her mouth. "I find that you look slightly familiar, Mr. White."

Tilda piped up, "He's been here before."

Mrs. Weston's eyebrow rose. "Really?"

Mr. White found sudden interest in the brocade that padded the arm of his chair. "I was at Summerfield decades ago."

Mrs. White quickly added, "We are so happy to bring Tilda to you, to such a lovely home." She gave Tilda a cloying smile. "She is a gem who deserves the very best."

Tilda was surprised by her statements, but she smiled sweetly at the compliments. She did want the Westons to like her.

But why didn't the couple bring up the fact that Mr. White had known the earl's wife?

The tea arrived. And luckily, biscuits.

"Is there anything else I can get you, Miss Cavendish?" A maid named Dottie hung up the dress Tilda had worn for the five-course dinner.

In spite of her desire to act like a "Miss Cavendish" who was used to having a maid, a giggle escaped and Tilda put a hand to her mouth. "Sorry," she said. "This is a bit overwhelming."

"I remember that feeling too, miss," Dottie said. "Though of course, I came here as a tweeny, not as a guest."

"What's a tweeny?"

"A maid that works 'tween upstairs and down. That was over a year ago. I'm an upper housemaid now. And at special times I get to help guests like you."

She was clearly proud of her position. In a flash, Tilda realized it could be advantageous to have a friend on the servant side of things. "After my father died, I worked for officers and their wives. Cleaning their quarters."

"Really?"

Tilda nodded. "I know it's a hard job."

"Ain't it though." But then, Dottie must have thought better of her answer, for she said, "But I feel very privileged and honored to work at the manor."

"You don't have to pretend with me," Tilda said.

"I ain't pretending. I mean it." Dottie pushed Tilda's empty trunk under the four-poster bed. "My ma wouldn't be getting the care she's getting if it weren't for her being a kitchen maid here."

"What's wrong with your ma?"

"She had a fit of some sort and can't talk or walk much. Can't use one of her arms at all."

"I'm so sorry." Her concern was genuine. "Papa was sick three months before he died. Not that your ma is going to die, but . . ."

"It's all right. I appreciate the sympathy. And now that my sister Molly is back from London to help . . ."

"Why was she in London?"

Dottie busied herself with the perfume atomizer on the dressing table. "I can't say."

Can't or won't?

Dottie pulled back the covers of the bed and fluffed the pillows. "If you need anything, just yank on that bell-pull over there and I'll come running."

Getting the story of Molly would have to wait for another day. "Thank you, Dottie."

She went to the door. "Sleep well, miss."

Tilda felt the silence as if it had weight. She'd never, ever been in so large a room by herself. More than that she'd never had it be *her* room.

She climbed into bed and pulled the covers up to her neck. The smell of soap and fresh starch greeted her. It reminded her of the myriad of sheets she'd changed and the dirty diapers she'd washed for the families of officers. But it was all different now. Now she had a maid to serve and clean up after *her*.

Tilda spread her limbs to the far corners of the bed and found room to spare. This was the life. This was *her* life.

But as she curled on her side and drew a pillow to her chest, she made a vow: she was not going to merely be a visitor to Summerfield Manor.

Someday it would be her home.

Chapter Four

"It's so nice to have you join the staff for breakfast, Miss Wallace," the butler said.

"I'm glad to join you, Mr. Dixon," she said. "I've been taking my meals upstairs with my mother, but she was still sleeping, so I thought I would seek out some company."

"How is she doing?" the housekeeper asked.

"A little better, thank you, Mrs. Camden."

"She can't talk, can she?"

"Mr. Stallings," Mr. Dixon said. "That is uncalled for."

The footman looked only partially chastened, which was just like him. Nick liked to push boundaries.

"She is trying very hard," Molly said. "Dr. Peter says soon I can help her walk."

"We do miss her in the kitchen," Mrs. McDeer said. "No one chops and dices like your mother."

Molly accepted the compliment with a smile, but thought of her mother's useless arm.

"Now eat please," Mr. Dixon said. "With three guests there is additional work for all."

"Three guests?" Molly asked.

"Miss Cavendish, Colonel Cummings' goddaughter, and a Mr. and Mrs. White, her chaperones."

"Miss Cavendish is nice," Dottie said. "Did you know she used to have a job cleaning officers' quarters?"

"Cranky," Nick said. "I wish some godfather of mine would lift me up outta hard work."

Mr. Dixon glared at him. "Should I tell Mr. Weston you're too busy to be his valet and let Mr. Robbins add those duties to his own?"

Nick reddened. "Of course not, sir. I was just thinking out loud."

"I suggest you think quietly the next time such thoughts enter your consciousness."

The housemaids Sally and Prissy giggled. Nick winked at them, proving he was unscathed by the reprimand. He hadn't changed much during the time Molly had been gone. He was still the flirt and the fun-seeker, able to turn on charm or diligence as needed.

"Miss Cavendish is going riding with Master George and Mrs. Weston," Dottie said.

"How nice for all of them," Mr. Robbins said.

"Are the guests staying long at the manor?" Molly asked.

"Miss Cavendish is staying indefinitely," the cook said, "but the Whites, only a few days. At least I hope that's all. With the others coming I—"

Mrs. McDeer caught a look from Mrs. Camden and didn't finish her sentence. Instead she changed the subject. "Tell us about hat-making, Miss Wallace. I'm betting in such a city as London, you are kept busy."

Molly began her answer, but in the back of her mind wondered about the new visitors. Yet what did it matter to her?

Tilda walked towards the stables with Mrs. Weston. "I'm sorry I didn't have any riding clothes. I should have thought of that." *Not that I had extra money for them.*

"No worries, my dear. You are the same size as our Clarissa, so all is well."

This was not the first time Tilda had heard Clarissa's name mentioned, yet such conversations were decisively short. "Is your daughter married?"

"No, no." Mrs. Weston slowed her walk. "Actually, I suppose she could be."

"You don't know?"

"We don't. She left for London over a year ago."

Tilda knew it wasn't polite to pry, but she was curious. "You don't visit each other?"

Mrs. Weston stopped walking and moved some pebbles with the toe of her boot. "Clarissa has an independent spirit and left Summerfield with a broken heart." She looked at Tilda. "I don't blame her. She was betrothed to Joseph Kidd, but he was in love with Lila, though at the time she was simply a shopkeeper's daughter. Everything changed after Lila and her family discovered their true legacy and titles. As the daughter of an earl, Lila was able to marry Joseph and Clarissa's claim on him was set aside. Clarissa is not one to take rejection well."

"How painful."

"The pain was enhanced by the change in her status." With an awkward smile Mrs. Weston explained how her immediate family was demoted. "I don't mind not being the countess anymore and my husband was so happy to find his brother again he found peace in his lesser title as the second-born son. But Clarissa enjoyed being Lady Clarissa, and witnessing Lila assuming that designation was a humiliation she could not bear."

"She's not Lady Clarissa anymore?"

"She's simply Miss Weston."

"That doesn't seem very fair."

"Perhaps not. But surely, since your father was in the army you have witnessed the inequities in the pecking order of officers."

She was well aware. "I am sorry for her pain," Tilda said with full sincerity. "And yours."

"I have adjusted, but I grieve Clarissa's double loss of love *and* status." She sighed and they began walking again. "She was staying with acquaintances of the family in London for a time, and last we knew she was traveling with them in Europe."

It was odd they didn't seem to know real details. "Does she send letters?"

"Unfortunately, no." Mrs. Weston shook her head as if dispelling the hurt. "But enough of that. The manor has been missing the spirit and liveliness of a young woman, but now that you are here, let us hope the lack can be rectified."

Tilda was very willing to fill Clarissa's shoes.

And riding habit.

There was a certain untamed quality about young George Weston that seemed to belie his status as one of the family versus one of the staff at the stables. When Tilda first saw him there he wore no coat and had the sleeves of his shirt rolled up as he helped the stable-boys saddle three horses. His hair was even more tousled than the first time she'd met him, as if it hadn't met a comb in quite some time. *She* had spent extra time on her own toilette this morning, wanting to make herself out to be one of *them*.

When Tilda and his mother approached, George looked up from his work and strode to greet them. He gave his mother a peck on the cheek. "Good morning, Mamma. Miss Cavendish."

His mother ran her hands over the front of his hair, trying to smooth it into place. "Really, George. Can't you attempt to make yourself the least bit presentable to our guest?"

He winked at Tilda. "I am what I am. You're both lucky I got dressed."

"Oh you," Mrs. Weston said. "Behave yourself."

"If I must." He unrolled his sleeves.

Tilda felt an odd warmth seeing the mother and son showing true affection and teasing each other. She couldn't remember a time when her father had even touched her, much less shared a light moment.

George moved to the smallest horse. "This is Maid Marian. I thought she'd be a good match for you, Miss Cavendish."

Tilda had to ask. "Because she's high-spirited and loves to run?"

His eyebrows rose. "Well then. Perhaps Little John would be a better fit."

"So you ride, Miss Cavendish?" Mrs. Weston asked.

"Not enough, but I think I can hold my own."

"Then Little John it is. Mamma, would you take Maid Marian today?"

"Of course," she said. "She's an old friend."

"And what is the name of your horse?" Tilda asked.

"Robin Hood, of course."

"Of course?"

"You're not familiar with *The Merry Adventures of Robin Hood*?" he asked.

"I'm afraid not." She'd never read much. Papa wasn't the sort to waste money on books.

"It's a great story about an honorable outlaw who lives in the forest. The book is in the library." He nodded at a stable boy, who brought forward a step so the ladies could mount their horses. He helped his mother first, then held Tilda's hand as she mounted. She wrapped her upper leg around the horn of the sidesaddle and let George adjust her stirrup.

"How's that?" he asked.

"Fine," she said. To receive the attention of such a handsome young gentleman made it more than fine. He donned a jacket and mounted Robin Hood with the ease of someone who'd been around horses their entire life.

Then they were off. They did not take the road, but walked overland, across green meadows, among trees that were resplendent with the colors of autumn. Tilda found herself situated between mother and son.

"I'm sorry about your father," George said. "Were you close?"

"George, don't pry."

"Sorry," he said.

"I don't mind answering," Tilda said. *As long as I can lie.* "We were extremely close. He called me his little princess." *Or "girl", or "brat", or "you worthless nothing."*

Mrs. Weston adjusted the veil of her hat. "We're very happy your father's solicitor found Colonel Cummings and that you could join us here."

"As am I." *More than happy.*

George reached up and plucked an orange maple leaf from a branch. He handed it to her. "For you."

She was embarrassed to feel herself blush. "Thank you." When she glanced at Mrs. Weston, she found the woman smiling. People being kind and generous. People smiling. Sadly, these were rare experiences.

"Is something wrong, my dear?" Mrs. Weston asked.

Tilda shook away the negative thoughts. "Not a thing." She grinned at George. "Are we ever going to gallop?"

He answered with a "Hya!" and off he went with Tilda close behind.

Dottie helped Tilda out of her riding habit. "Did you have a nice ride, miss?"

"Extremely."

Dottie set the jacket and skirt aside, and helped Tilda into a green day dress. "Master George used to steal my feather duster and tickle me with it."

It sounded a bit inappropriate.

Dottie must have seen her apprehension. "He didn't mean nothing by it. I was new at the manor and he was just thirteen and liked to tease."

It was easy to imagine.

Tilda began to button the front of her dress, but Dottie said, "Let me do that."

"I'm not used to having help getting dressed. I *can* do it myself."

"I'm sure you can, miss, but don't you see that me being assigned to help you gets me out of sweeping the carpets?"

Tilda caught her smile. "Well then. Button away."

As soon as Tilda was dressed, Dottie gathered her clothes. "Will there be anything else, miss?"

"Have the Whites left yet?"

"Left?"

"Caught the train back to Aldershot?"

"Oh no, miss. Last I saw they were walking in the garden." She bobbed a curtsy and left the room.

Tilda was not surprised the Whites were milking their visit, and she didn't really begrudge them a few extra days of pampering. They'd be gone soon enough, leaving Tilda with Mrs. Weston and George.

On the window seat she spotted the orange leaf George had given her. She picked it up, spun it between her fingers, remembered today's ride . . .

And imagined tomorrow's.

As soon as they disembarked onto dry land, Mrs. Sigmund kissed Genevieve on both cheeks. "The best of luck to you, my dear."

"Thank you."

They both watched as Genevieve's mother accosted a porter and gave him orders as to their luggage. Mrs. Sigmund took advantage of this last moment of privacy. "Remember everything I told you."

Genevieve nodded. "I will do my best to be a woman of gumption, confidence, and . . . and . . ."

"Purpose. The other two will lead to the latter. Above all, remember you're not alone."

"I'm not?"

Mrs. Sigmund pointed to the sky. "God will help you achieve all three. Just ask Him." She looked up when Genevieve's mother joined them. "So you're staying in an inn for the night?"

"I require a chance to regroup."

"So you can descend upon Summerfield Manor bright eyed and bushy tailed?"

Mamma looked appalled. "Most certainly not."

Mrs. Sigmund gave Genevieve's hand an extra squeeze. "I'll say a prayer everything turns out well and you are deliriously happy in your new life."

Genevieve's eyes misted. "I'd appreciate it."

Watching Mrs. Sigmund walk away on the arm of her husband made Genevieve extremely sad. "I'll miss her."

"Don't be ridiculous. You've only know her a few days."

"But she was full of wisdom and treated me so kindly."

"I have all the wisdom you need. Now come. Let's get to the inn to rest. I won't have either of us meeting the Westons with dark circles under our eyes."

After every performance, the backstage area of the Savoy filled with dozens of people wearing expensive clothes coming back to chat with dozens of actors wearing costumes. Reality met fantasy in a loud, pulsating collision.

Clarissa lingered a few minutes before retreating to the dressing room, watching the accolades and kisses from the friends and family of the players. She'd never had a visitor. Her own fault, the consequence of changing her name and living a secret life.

When she'd first performed at the Jolly Tavern, it had seemed necessary to become Clara West, as she'd been embarrassed by the skimpy costumes. Yet she needn't have worried about being recognized, as that sort of theatre was arranged so people could eat, drink, and smoke during the show. Sometimes the smoke was so thick it was like fog on the Thames. And now that she was in a proper play at the Savoy the pseudonym was not as necessary, though she couldn't bring herself to let it go. But just once she wished to have a visi—

"Clarissa?"

She looked in the direction of the voice. "Joseph?" Her stomach flipped at the sight of the man she was supposed to marry.

The man who shunned her for . . .

"Hello, Lila." Clarissa took their hands and kissed each cheek in turn. "What brings you to the Savoy?" She ignored the larger question of why *she* was there.

Joseph answered for them. "I had business in London and thought Lila might enjoy coming with me. But we never expected to see you . . . acting."

"You were very good," Lila said. "You commanded the stage."

"Yes, well . . ." Clarissa resented the compliment because she knew it to be false. She was still just one of the chorus. "How is your family? And how are mine?"

They were clogging the traffic of a pathway, so Joseph led them to the side.

Lila answered. "Everyone is fine. But your family misses you." She looked to Joseph. "We've all missed you and have wondered after you."

"We haven't heard from you in so long. And obviously you've been very busy."

He'd hesitated just a second before his last word. "I have been traveling."

"That's what your mother told us. You've been traveling throughout Europe with the Duvalls?"

Clarissa felt her mouth twitch. She smiled to calm it, and tried to remember the details of her lie. "I've only recently returned and have been so busy performing that I haven't had time to write letters."

"Should we tell your parents that you're in London again so they could write?"

"They'd be proud of your success."

Clarissa let out an *hmmph.* Then she looked past them — through them — before returning to the present. "You know very well they would not be proud. I promised them I wouldn't go on the stage."

"Which is why you've changed your name to Clara West?" Joseph asked.

She laughed it off. "You've caught me in my ruse. Truth is, I didn't want to be found, nor to cause them shame."

"I'm certain they wouldn't be ashamed," Lila said.

I'm certain they would.

"Actually," Clarissa said, "I'd prefer you not tell them you saw me."

Lila looked to Joseph, unsure.

Ah. So that was it. "They haven't truly been worried about me, have they?" She wasn't certain what answer she wanted to hear.

When there was a hesitation, Clarissa made her own conclusion. "See? Life has gone on for both of us." She let her gaze touch them both, though she let it linger a moment on Joseph's face. "All of us."

So there.

To move past the awkward moment, Clarissa continued. "You found me on purpose or by chance?"

"Absolute chance," Joseph said.

"While watching the play I thought I recognized you in the chorus and then I saw your stage name in the program and wondered if Clara was you."

Clarissa's face clouded. "Chorus. Yes. Perpetually in the chorus." She forced herself to smile. "Actually, I alternate the lead with the actress who plays Patience." What difference did one more lie make?

"That's wonderful," Lila said.

"When is it your turn?" Joseph asked. "Perhaps we can come back and see the play again."

Clarissa looked over their heads, pretending to wave at someone. "Sorry. I really must go. It's so nice to see you both."

She moved towards the dressing room, but Lila stopped her. "Where are you staying? Is Miss Sheets still with you?"

Clarissa fluffed the back of her hair. "Yes, Agnes is still my maid. We live in a lovely flat. I do a lot of entertaining so I've had to hire a cook and butler to handle it all."

Lila looked relieved. "So we can tell the family you're all right?"

Clarissa's jaw tightened. "I think not. Tis my secret. My family should understand since they're keen on secrets."

Clarissa walked away quickly, glad for the crowd that filled in behind her.

The man lunged toward her. "Come on, chickie. Gimee what you got."

Clarissa shoved the drunk away. "Watch it or I'll give you what you deserve."

He winked as he put a bottle to his lips. "That's all I's askin' for."

She wasn't in the mood to deal with him, and hurried past, lifting her skirt to step over a pile of steaming horse-droppings. She turned down an alley so she wouldn't have to walk past a pub, preferring to take her chances with the whores along the way rather than more grabby drunks.

"Evening, Patsy," she said to a girl who was doing business against a brick wall.

"Evening," Patsy said with a small wave. Her customer didn't look in Clarissa's direction.

Which was a blessing. The fewer faces she saw in this cesspool the better.

She reached the door to her flat. It was above a tobacconist, which offered her the added bonus of manly smells that reminded her of home, smells that partially masked the stench of rotting buildings, open sewage, and discarded lives.

There was no light on the narrow inner stairway, but Clarissa knew the way. Second floor. Twenty-two steps from street to sanctuary. Not that it was all-that, but it was all she had. From Summerfield Manor to a one-room flat. How the mighty had fallen.

Upon entering, Agnes fell upon her, a hatbox in hand. "Another hat, Lady Clarissa? When we're behind on the rent?"

She'd forgotten about the hat. "You know I can't help myself."

"So I've seen."

"Don't I deserve something pretty once in a while?"

Agnes stormed over to a ceiling-high pile of hat boxes. "Enough 'a while', I think. We're running out of room for your fancy hats. And where are you going to wear them anyway? You don't go out but to work."

If only I did.

Clarissa removed the simple bonnet she wore to the theatre and back. She didn't dare wear the fancy hats and ignite unwanted curiosity. Besides, left in the dressing room during the show, they would surely be stolen.

"And here," Agnes said, draping a navy skirt over her arm. "I spent all evening darning the frayed edge. You wouldn't believe the foulness your skirts pick up. Back at the manor all I had to deal with was a little dust, but here I—"

"Enough!"

Agnes barely flinched. "Hard night on the stage?"

"Not on it, but afterwards. Help me get undressed."

"What happened afterwards?"

Clarissa let Agnes unbutton the front of her bodice. "Joseph and Lila showed up."

Agnes nearly dropped it. "Mr. Kidd and his wife, Lady Kidd?"

"Thanks for reminding me of their marriage, but yes. Them."

"How did they know where you were?"

"They didn't know until they saw me on stage."

Agnes pointed a finger at her. "I told you that would happen. It was inevitable one of your kind would recognize you. I'm amazed it hasn't happened until now."

"I hate them!" She was surprised by the venom in her words.

Agnes raised an eyebrow. "So you've said."

Clarissa paced up and back at the foot of her bed. "Suddenly, there they are, flaunting their marriage at me."

Agnes stopped Clarissa's pacing and turned her around so she could undo the hooks at the back of her skirt. "And how exactly did they do that?"

She whipped around to face her maid, her skirt falling down over her petticoats in front, but caught up on her bustle in back. "He should have been my husband. What they have should have been mine."

"Then take it back."

Clarissa did a double-take. "What?"

Agnes pushed the skirt all the way to the floor, and Clarissa stepped out of it. "I'm tired of your complaining. If it's not about being in the chorus, it's about not being Lady Clarissa, or Mrs. Kidd."

"Well excuse me, Agnes."

"I've told you to call me Sheets."

"I'll call you what I like."

"You insist I call you Lady Clarissa and my lady, when neither are your due."

"How dare you talk to me like this!"

Agnes merely shrugged. "You ask to be called by a name you like and so do I. As a lady's maid, I've earned the right to be called by my surname."

Clarissa rolled her eyes. "You servants are snottier about your position than those of us who are titled. I thought after all this time, living together in tight spaces, I could call you by your first name." She gave Agnes what she hoped was a disarming smile. "You're more than my maid, you're my friend."

"I'm glad for the consideration, but . . ." She swept an arm to the side to encompass the room. "This isn't what I signed up for. Staying with the Duvalls when we first came to London was wonderful, but—"

"But they moved to Paris."

"Before they left they found us a nice flat. Your father was sending money. We would have been fine and I would be happy if we were still staying there."

This was getting ridiculous. "So your happiness is my concern?"

"This is the third flat we've had this year. Running from landlords is beneath us."

Clarissa knew it was her own fault. "You know I've never been good with money. I've had no reason to be."

"There's one simple rule: don't spend more than you have."

"I try not to. But I overspent at first and couldn't catch up."

"You could write your father and ask for more."

"I can't. He thinks I'm traveling with the Duvall's. He doesn't know I'm still in London. He doesn't know any of it."

"Doesn't know that you've broken your promise and are on the stage? That you're destitute?"

"If only Mapes would give me the lead, I'd be making plenty of money."

"Is he still wanting the same payment for it?"

Clarissa sat at the table and started to remove the pins from her hair. Agnes batted her hands away and took up the job.

"I've lost most of my dignity by living as I do. To lose that last bastion of civility . . . I can't do it."

"The landlord was here earlier. He's giving us a week."

One week to eviction. And where would they move to then? There was no place cheaper. "Maybe you could get a job?" she asked Agnes.

The maid stopped her work. "I can't lower myself to do that. I won't do it. I am a lady's maid and have been my entire life."

"'Pride goeth before the fall,'" Clarissa said under her breath.

"Pride in my profession is all I have left. I am proud to be a lady's maid and the truth is . . ."

"The truth is?"

"I am still a lady's maid but you are no longer a lady."

Clarissa popped out of the chair and faced her. "What did you say?"

Agnes took a step back, her hands waving in front of her face. "Now, now. I apologize. We're both frustrated, that's what it is."

Clarissa raised an eyebrow, waiting. "That's what it is, Lady Clarissa." She returned to the chair and let the remnants of the argument settle on the dusty floor.

Only it wasn't settled. "I am sorry, my lady, but things can't continue as they have."

"You have a better idea?"

"You want Joseph? Go get him. For over a year I have listened to your anger. Maybe it's time to fix it for both our sakes."

"And how am I supposed to do that?"

"If he loves you so much . . ."

There was the crux of the issue. Clarissa wasn't certain Joseph had ever loved her or even if she had loved him. The issue wasn't love but defeat versus victory.

Agnes pulled hair from the brush, pushed it into a hair receiver, and reworded her statement. "You grieve losing his love."

"I am angry for having it stolen from me."

"Then steal it back."

"And how do I do that?"

Agnes finished with the hairpins and began to brush Clarissa's hair. "You're an actress. Woo Mr. Kidd away from his wife. If she's as blah as you always say she is, you should have no trouble seducing him."

"I just told you, I won't stoop so low as to offer *that* to any man."

"I'm not saying you actually do it."

The thought of seducing Joseph rubbed her wrong.

"It doesn't matter to me, my lady," Agnes said. "Either you want him or you don't. Either you want revenge against the one who stole him. Or you don't."

Revenge. It was such a harsh word. Was that what she wanted? "I'm no seductress."

"But you can play the part."

"I have nothing to offer him."

Agnes gave her a look. "You're a beautiful woman. That's usually enough, isn't it?"

"But he's a gentleman. Even when we were engaged he was never forward."

"I'm not saying you should throw him on the floor and have your way with him."

"Agnes!"

She sighed. "This life is rubbing off on me."

Clarissa set her hand on her own shoulder, and Agnes took it. "I know how hard it's been."

They let each other go, and Agnes resumed the brushing. "My point is that it might behoove you — us actually — if you at least talk to Mister Kidd and test the waters."

"Surely you don't want me to be his mistress."

"Every other upper class Joe has at least one woman on the side. Tis a fact that's not talked about in polite society, but it's there just the same. You don't really want to marry him, do you?"

Marrying him would mean winning, but marrying him would also mean she'd have to return home to Summerfield. And *that* she could never do. She'd told too many lies and had broken too many promises.

"I just want Lila to hurt a bit. Her family took everything from mine."

"Your family still lives in the manor, so don't act like they're homeless. And you and I didn't have to leave."

"I couldn't stay. Call it pride or vanity or —"

"Pardon me, my lady, but it was both."

True. "I couldn't be there while Lila and Joseph made their wedding plans. I couldn't live in the same house as her, eat meals with her, and engage in small talk as if she wasn't my enemy."

"They why did you torture yourself by going to their wedding?"

Clarissa remembered hiding outside the church, watching Joseph marry her cousin. She'd died a bit that day.

"Well?" Agnes asked.

"I had to see."

"It did you no good."

Clarissa shrugged. "Will seducing Joseph do me any good?"

"It might make you feel in control of something."

Was control the key? "I don't have control over my career, who I love, or how we live."

"If you'll allow me to be honest . . ."

Clarissa turned around to see her. "Could I stop you?"

Agnes shrugged. "You could be in control of how we live if you quit buying those hats. Or better yet, return them and we'll be able to pay the rent and even eat meat once in a while."

Clarissa remembered the hat she'd just purchased, and went to take it out of the box. She put it on, letting the rosebuds flow over her shoulder. It made her look young and vibrant and enticing. If she wore it while visiting Joseph . . . "This hat will help me achieve my goal."

"Which is?"

"Vengeance is sweet, saith the Lord."

"Actually, the verse is 'Vengeance is *mine*, saith the Lord.'"

Same thing.

Chapter Five

Tilda opened the door of her bedroom to go down for breakfast.

As she left the room, she tripped on a small object. There, on the floor of the hallway, was a book: *The Merry Adventures of Robin Hood.* A note fell from its pages: *Enjoy the adventure. George.*

She returned to her room feeling warm inside. She'd never received a gift from a boy. And then she remembered this was her second gift from him.

She retrieved the maple leaf and carefully placed it between the pages. Summerfield Manor was full of surprises. She couldn't remember being so delighted. She couldn't remember ever starting a new day with anticipation. Is this what true happiness felt like?

Leaving a second time for breakfast, she met the Whites in the hall and they exchanged good mornings. Yet their presence put a damper on her joy, a reminder of her un-delightful, less than happy past. If only they would leave. As they reached the top of the stairs that would take them to the dining room, Tilda pulled Mrs. White aside. "I appreciate you accompanying me here, but I am quite settled in."

"Are you wanting us to go?"

The sooner the better. "I was just wondering as to your plans."

Mrs. White clasped her hands and raised them to the crook beneath her bosom. "Is our presence putting a crimp in your new life?"

Tilda considered being polite, but decided against it. "A little." At the very least, they were a reminder of her *old* life.

"Don't be so stingy," Mrs. White hissed. "Don't we deserve to enjoy a bit of a lark for our trouble?"

A lark doing what? "If that's the case, why didn't you accept Mrs. Weston's invitation to go riding yesterday?" Tilda spoke to the husband. "Since you're a coachman, I thought you'd be interested in seeing the stables."

Mr. White looked to the carpet.

Mrs. White answered for him. "We preferred a walk in the garden."

"Tis a very nice garden," Mr. White said. He scanned the entry hall below. "I will say I enjoy being back in Summerfield and seeing the inside of the manor."

Which begged a question. "When we were first introduced to the family, why didn't you tell the earl you knew his wife?"

He looked to his spouse, as if wanting her to offer the answer.

Which she did. "It's of no concern to anyone."

"But it's a connection. I would think —"

"Well stop thinking, all right? You don't want us to put a crimp in your life? We'd like the same favor. Just leave us to our business."

"What business?"

Before an answer could be given, Mrs. Weston appeared in the hallway. "Good morning, all. Are you ready for breakfast?"

Mrs. Weston finished chewing her steamed tomatoes and turned to the Whites. "Did you find your stay here enjoyable?"

Tilda was quick to notice the use of the words "did you" rather than "do you".

"We are much appreciative," Mr. White said.

"When do you plan to return to Aldershot?" the earl asked.

Ha!

Suddenly, Mrs. White set her fork to her plate with a clatter. "Oh my. Oh dear."

"What is it?" Mrs. Weston asked.

"I have a sudden headache." Mrs. White pushed her chair back from the table, causing the footman to rush to her assistance. "I need to lie down."

"I'm so sorry," said the earl. "Should we send for a doctor?"

"No, no," Mrs. White said, stumbling towards the hallway with her husband's support. "I get these often. They are extremely debilitating but my husband knows what needs to be done."

By the look on Mr. White's face, it seemed clear he had no idea what she was talking about. But he led her away, back to their room. The sound of her moans accompanied them.

"Well now," the earl said. "That was sudden."

"Extremely," Mr. Weston said.

"And well-timed," George said with a grin.

Mrs. Weston flashed him a look, then addressed Tilda. "Does she get these episodes often?"

I assume she gets them as often as they suit her. "I really don't know."

"But I thought they were close family friends," the earl said.

"Though I know Mr. White a little, I didn't know his wife until the train."

"He seems like an agreeable man," Mrs. Weston said.

Yes, *he* does.

Mr. Weston looked at his wife. "With twenty-five bedrooms, we obviously have room for them to stay, even with the arrival of the Farrows."

"I know," Mrs. Weston said. "I was just trying to simplify things."

Someone else was coming? Tilda didn't like the idea that she would lose the Westons' full attention. "Who are the Farrows?" she asked.

Morgan took a sip of tea and set his cup on its saucer. "Genevieve Farrow is to be my wife. She's arriving with her mother. Today, unfortunately."

"Morgan!"

He shrugged at his father's rebuke.

"Uncle Grady told me about your betrothal. She's American?"

"Very," Morgan said.

The others exchanged a glance, as if her citizenship was unsavory.

Mrs. Weston drew in a breath and addressed Tilda. "I hope you didn't think I was implying that *you* aren't welcome here, that my 'simplify' comment included you."

"Of course not," Mr. Weston added. "You are very welcome here, Tilda."

George smiled at her. "Very."

Molly stood over her mother, one arm around the back of her, the other holding her weak hand. "Come now. Up. Dr. Peter said it's time for you to start moving about."

With a groan, Ma rose from a chair. Her weight tested Molly's strength but she got a better grip on her until the two of them seemed fairly stable.

"There now," she said. "That's the way."

Her mother's breathing was labored from the effort of standing, so Molly amended her plan to take much of a walk and nodded towards the window. "Shall we take a look outside?"

"Yeah. 'Ure."

With effort they reached the small window that overlooked the front grounds. Molly's gaze was immediately drawn to Morgan, talking with his father on the gravel drive. "I've talked to him. He says he missed me. He still seems interested." Ma shook her head, and Molly added, "I know you never approved of us. And the situation hasn't changed. It's as impossible now as it was when I ran away. He's still a viscount and I'm still . . . me, but I can't help having feelings for him."

With effort, Ma said, "Gheh-e-we..."

"What?"

"Gheh-e-we..."

"I'm sorry. I don't understand what you're trying to say." There was a knock on the door. "Come in," Molly said.

Dr. Peter entered. "Well look at you, up and about."

"We were just taking in the view," Molly said.

"There's a lot of commotion in the house," he said, helping Molly get her mother back to bed. "Apparently the Farrows are expected at any time."

"The Farrows?"

"Gheh-e-we," Ma said.

"That's right," the doctor said with a smile. "Genevieve." He looked to Molly. "Genevieve Farrow and her mother, come all the way from America." He pulled the covers over his patient and addressed her. "I'm sure you would like to recover so you can help be a part of the wedding preparations."

Ma nodded, but Molly had questions. "Is the earl getting married?"

Dr. Peter looked confused. "Not the earl, his son. The Viscount Weston."

When Molly didn't respond, he said, "Morgan Weston."

Morgan. Her Morgan. Molly felt the sting of tears. "If you'll excuse me, I need to get something in my room."

She didn't wait for his response, but fled her mother's room and entered her own. There, she shut the door and leaned against it. The weight of the news made her legs weak and she slipped down to the floor. She buried her face in her knees as all possibility of Morgan seeped away.

"I can't believe the earl or your fiancé didn't come to the station to get us. To be retrieved by a mere coachman as though we are a shipment that's arrived is embarrassing. Even if he is in fancy livery, it's . . . degrading." Genevieve's mother shuddered as she took a seat in the open carriage.

Genevieve was disappointed too, though she would never let Mamma know as much. "I'm sure there's a reason." She looked back at the village train station. "I do hope Jane is managing the task of pointing out our luggage and accompanying it to the manor in the wagon."

"She'll be fine," Mamma said, nodding to the curious walking by.

Out of necessity Genevieve set her worries aside. The trip from New York City to Summerfield had been a never-ending parade of logistics. Odd how she'd never noticed such details on other trips. But then she'd had Father to see to everything. Not that Mamma wasn't adept at giving orders. Yet there was always an aura of the last-minute when traveling with her mother, always a sense that an emergency was imminent and inevitable.

As the carriage left the station Genevieve took a deep breath, trying to rid her lungs of the smell of coal smoke from the trains. "Inhale, Mamma. The whole countryside is alive with the crisp autumn air."

Her mother put a hand to her chest. "Are you actually daring to act enthusiastic?"

Genevieve hated that she'd lowered her guard. She was far from ready to let her mother off the hook for their situation. Not that Genevieve was without complicity. For she'd agreed to correspond with Morgan. She had even enjoyed his letters—though they tended towards the mundane, often contained misspellings, and were far from romantic. She'd tried to enjoy the give and take of their long-distance courtship, but when a deal was struck and marriage became imminent, she'd suffered second thoughts.

A proposal from some American would have precluded this need to leave everything she knew and held dear to travel to a foreign land. Moving from the city to a country estate in the middle of nowhere, with its strange traditions and expectations, was a test she wasn't certain she could pass. There were a thousand reasons why this wouldn't work and but a few why it would.

"Remember to call Morgan, Lord Weston. Or my lord, or his lordship."

Genevieve sighed. "We're engaged. Back home we'd be calling each other by our first names by now."

"We're in England, my dear. Get used to it."

As if she had a choice?

"We are not to question why the British do what they do, but must embrace the fact that Summerfield Manor is in need of *our* money."

"But *I* am not in need of a title."

"You may not be, but I am." With a glance to the coachman, she lowered her voice. "I didn't scrapple from nothing to high society by ignoring opportunities." She pegged a gloved finger on Genevieve's knee. "This is the opportunity of the century. For them and for us."

If she said so.

As the carriage rounded a bend, the wildflowers and groves changed into neat lines of trees, manicured lawns, and gardens. Soon after they came upon a set of massive gates, with scrollwork adorning three sides, culminating in an intricate S at the top.

"I wonder if that's gold," her mother whispered.

Genevieve barely heard her, as her eyes were drawn to the manor itself. It was beyond any mansion she'd ever seen. It was three stories in height and built of red brick. Tan stone adorned the surplus of windows and marked the horizontal line of each floor. A balustrade of shaped stone crowned the upper roof line in front of a line of dormer windows. It was delightfully unsymmetrical, with a massive square tower at one end, and a one-story wing at the other.

"One, two, three . . ."

"What *are* you doing?" Genevieve asked.

"There are seventeen chimneys — that I can *see*. No wonder it demands a staff of sixty. All those grates to clean."

Mamma smoothed her gloves. "Someday you'll be in charge of the staff."

With that daunting thought Genevieve felt her forehead furrow. As the carriage neared the manor, a parade of people emptied out from the double doors in the center tower. The servants, all dressed in their formal black uniforms, formed a V on either side of the entrance. The family emerged but Genevieve only had eyes for Morgan.

She'd seen a photograph of him, but in person his hair was a deeper black than she expected. And he was tall — which was good, since Genevieve was tall herself, being nearly five-foot-eight.

Mamma gave a guess as to the other players. "That stately, older woman must be the dowager countess and the dashing man with a gray mustache must be Colonel Cummings. I would assume the trio of that other couple standing shoulder to shoulder with the teenage boy are Mr. and Mrs. Weston and George. And the middle-aged man without a corresponding female must be the earl. My, he is handsome. Look at how he holds himself."

Genevieve cringed. Her mother was on the prowl even before they'd been introduced. Hopefully, she wouldn't embarrass them. The carriage came to a stop and the liveried coachman quickly opened its door and dropped the steps for their exit. "Lord, help me," Genevieve said under her breath.

"Smile!" her mother whispered.

"Welcome, welcome," said the earl, stepping forward. "Welcome to Summerfield."

Genevieve let her mother take the lead. "Thank you, Lord Summerfield. We are happy to finally arrive."

"Your passage was calm?" the older woman asked as she came forward. She looked directly at Genevieve.

She bobbed a curtsy. "Yes, Lady Summerfield. The seas cooperated quite nicely."

The dowager countess put her hand around Genevieve's arm. "Let me make the introductions. You have already met my son, Lord Summerfield This is my other son, Frederick, his wife, Ruth, and my grandson George."

They shared greetings.

"And this is my husband, Colonel Grady Cummings."

The older man's smile was genuine as he clicked his heels together and offered a smart bow. "Mrs. Farrow. Miss Farrow." He pulled a young lady to his side—a girl who'd been standing slightly behind him, out of sight. "I would like to introduce you to my goddaughter, Matilda Cavendish."

"Tilda," the girl said.

"Nice to meet you," Genevieve said. She felt a little confused, for she'd not heard about Tilda.

The dowager turned towards Morgan and Genevieve felt her stomach tighten.

"And now, let me present you to my grandson, the Viscount Weston, your fiancé."

Morgan stepped forward and bowed. "Tis a pleasure to finally meet you in person, Miss Farrow." He took her hand and drew it to his lips, then stepped back as if he were embarrassed by the whole process. He had lovely chestnut eyes, and she was relieved to see he was taller than she by a good two inches.

But he barely smiled. Although she was pleased with his looks, she worried what he thought of hers. She'd had Jane spend extra time on grooming this morning, but then they'd been on the train with its open windows and Genevieve knew her mousy blond hair wilted easily. And when she was nervous her cheeks blotched more than blushed. She could feel their heat even now.

"And this is Mr. Dixon and Mrs. Camden, who will see that your every need is met."

A butler stepped forward and nodded, as did a middle-aged woman wearing a black dress with a white tatted collar.

Genevieve said, "Hello," then looked down the row of servants. "Thank you for coming out to greet us."

The servants looked uncomfortable at her notice. Had she already made a misstep?

"Well then," the dowager said. "Let us go inside."

Upon entering, Genevieve's eyes were immediately drawn upward, as the foyer was open to the second floor —

first floor in British terminology, she must try to think as a Briton. A massive staircase swept upstairs to a balconied upper corridor. Row upon row of massive portraits lined the walls, undeniable proof of the history and legacy of the manor and its family.

This will be my home? I don't belong here.

"How charming," Mamma said.

It was too small a word, and Genevieve saw the dowager's eyebrow rise. "Mrs. Camden will see you to your rooms where you can freshen up from your travels."

Mrs. Camden stepped forward. "If you'll follow me."

"We'll see you at five for tea in the drawing room," Mrs. Weston said. "Please let us know if you need anything."

Although Genevieve smiled and thanked her, the idea of *needing* accompanied her upstairs as the housekeeper showed them their rooms.

Plural. As in two. As in not having to share a room with her mother.

That's what she needed.

Her mother was shown her room first. The walls were bathed in a lovely sage green. Then it was Genevieve's turn. In her opinion her room was the better of the two. It took her breath away. There was a carved mahogany four-poster bed with a canopy of ivory silk shirred towards a center button on the underside. The bed cover was a pale blue tufted silk. The drapery at the two windows was a robin's egg blue brocade, pooled in perfect yet haphazard puddles on the thick carpet. There was a dressing table with a matching set of jars and bottles, with pink rosebuds adorning the porcelain and back of the hand mirror. A large wardrobe stretched towards the tall ceilings, where curlicues of gold banded the room, interspersed with sprays of spring flowers and an occasional painted cupid.

She drank in the scent of the four vases of fresh flowers and gave one special attention, drinking in the delicious spicy scent of yellow chrysanthemums.

Mrs. Camden adjusted the lace curtains at the window. "There is a lovely view of the lawn from here."

Genevieve joined her at the window. "It is lovely beyond words."

The housekeeper smiled. "We are very happy for your safe arrival, Miss Farrow. Would you like me to close the window? Is it too breezy?"

"Not at all. I am already quite obsessed with the country air."

Mrs. Camden peered outside, then said softly, "It is a balm to the soul."

"What a delightful way to put it."

The older woman seemed to recover herself, and said, "As soon as your lady's maid arrives with the luggage, I'll send her up to help you change for tea."

So we do have to change for tea.

Genevieve must have looked confused because the housekeeper added, "The family has a brief tea at five in the drawing room, and a gong will sound at seven to announce it is time to dress for dinner—which is at eight."

"Not so different from New York—except for the gong."

Mrs. Camden smiled. "You will get used to it. Until then, I could send someone in to help you get comfortable?"

Genevieve removed her plumed hat, holding onto her hair to prevent the hairpins from pulling too many strands free. "I can manage, thank you."

"Very well then. I had fresh water brought to the basin. Again, welcome to Summerfield Manor, Miss Farrow."

Upon her exit, Genevieve removed her traveling jacket. The flow of air through the lesser fabric of her blouse made her feel as though she'd been released from a tight swaddling. She stretched her arms above her head and relished the pain and pleasure as her muscles awakened.

I feel free.

She started at the thought. Free? She'd virtually been sold for a title. How did that equate with freedom? Was it because she had her own room and was free of her mother? She had her own room back home.

Whatever the cause of her elation, she embraced it, flung her arms wide, and twirled in a full circle.

This is my new home where I will live the rest of my life.

What had caused her distress just hours before, now birthed the possibility of joy. Genevieve giggled at the fickleness of her emotions and her circle turned into a waltz. This wasn't her parents' home. Her marriage would mean she was no longer a child under her mother's thumb. She would be a wife and then a mother.

And a viscountess. And eventually a countess.

She stopped her dance. A wife and mother were within the realm of her upbringing.

But being titled? Being raised up among the peerage of England, owning titles that extended hundreds of years into the past? Would the established gentry accept her, or shun her as an American?

Doubts overwhelmed her. She fell onto the bed, turned on her side, and pulled a pillow to her chest.

"Dottie!" Molly whispered, upon seeing her in the upstairs hallway.

But Dottie didn't answer, as a pretty young woman came towards them. Dottie nodded and said, "Good evening, Miss Thompson."

The woman nodded, then entered a guest bedroom.

Molly and Dottie walked to the stairs. "Who's that?"

"That's Mrs. Farrow's lady's maid." Dottie walked faster towards the stairs, meaning Molly had to hurry after her. She grabbed her arm, stopping her progress.

"Why didn't you tell me Morgan was engaged?"

Dottie avoided her eyes, but her expression crumbled, making her look like a little girl again. "I didn't want you to be hurt."

"Don't you think it hurt to be here for days, see Morgan, talk to him and—"

"You talked to him?"

"Quite a bit. During which he told me he missed me and also gave me the impression that he still had feelings for me."

"Oh dear."

"Yes indeed, 'oh dear.'"

"He shouldn't have done that."

Molly snickered at the understatement.

"I was afraid you wouldn't come if you knew about it."

Would she have come?

"Of course I would have come. Ma needs me."

One lie out of two wasn't bad.

At dinner, Genevieve let the conversation swirl around her. Luckily, Mamma was adept at small-talk. Genevieve often thought Mamma could have a conversation with an empty chair. But during dinner, she was glad for it, because it meant she could sit back and observe more than participate.

The dining room was grand yet oddly homey. Perhaps it was the softness of the wall lanterns combined with the candlelight. And the color palette was a soothing gold—not metallic, but warm. The two footmen and the butler stood at the sideboard and were attentive and regal in their formal dress. They would pass for guests if it weren't for the pesky issue of social class and title. She took special note that the two footmen were of the same height and coloring. She'd heard the British enjoyed a matched set and required them to be tall.

The china was intricate, with flowers painted on a field of cobalt blue, and the crystal goblets that had been exchanged with each course were heavy and glinted in the light. She looked at the remaining sterling flatware and realized they'd already used five pieces. Five to go.

"Lord Summerfield, you are so accomplished," Mamma told the earl. "To have risen from shop owner to earl sounds almost American."

Genevieve cringed. To mention the odd situation aloud, much less to the family . . .

"Perhaps it does," the earl said.

"Perhaps it does not," the dowager said with a snap to her voice. "For there are no earldoms in America and no hereditary titles at all." She looked directly at Mamma. "Your country is barely a hundred years old, while this estate alone has been here for over two hundred and forty years. The United States was a rough wilderness when this manor was built."

"We may be a fairly new country," Mamma said, "but we are leading the world with our manufacturing and industrial advancements."

Genevieve felt herself blush. An estate like Summerfield was not concerned with industry. She felt compelled to come to its defense. "The heritage and history of Summerfield inspires me," she said. "Its legacy must be cherished."

"Here, here!" the dowager said. "Well said, Miss Farrow."

Her mother was not cowed. "When my husband rose from nothing to create one of the largest fortunes in New York City, I was by his side, helping him."

Mrs. Weston cleared her throat. Had Mamma offended by mentioning money?

The dowager lifted an eyebrow in disdain. "I am certain he was quite overcome by your enthusiastic support."

Mamma blinked as if gauging if this was a compliment or otherwise. "I was merely pointing out that a wife can be an enormous asset to a man of ambition and ability." She turned her attention to the earl. "You must grieve the lack of a wife, Lord Summerfield. Personally and in reference to the work to be done on this great estate."

Genevieve longed to take refuge under the table.

But the earl recovered nicely. "I do miss my wife greatly," he said. "But I am blessed to have the help and support of my family." He gave Genevieve's mother a glance. "As you stated by reiterating my rise from shopkeeper to earl, I have much to learn, so the lack of a wife allows me to focus my full attention on that goal."

Touché, Lord Summerfield!

Genevieve spotted a flash of color on her mother's cheeks, and watched as she shuffled her shoulders. "I suppose not everyone can handle relationship and responsibility at the same time."

Mamma!

The earl's jaw tightened. "I accept my limitations." He looked away from Mamma, and smiled at his own mother, who nodded — though her own jaw was tight.

To break the tension, the earl and his brother verbally showcased the attributes of the estate. Then young George — the son of Frederick and Ruth Weston — gave an avid overview of the horses and stables. Morgan added a comment here and there, but it was clear this was his father and uncle's show. He'd barely looked in her direction, a point which had initially concerned her. But as the meal wore on his disinterest gave her the ability to relax. Watching people chew — or being watched — was awkward.

The only person as uncomfortable as Genevieve was the young girl, Tilda, who said little and constantly looked to Mrs. Weston as to which fork to use. She had just arrived a few days earlier, which instantly gave the two young women a bond.

Genevieve smiled at her now, and received a wistful smile in return — and a deep sigh, as if the dinner had taxed her too.

Next to Tilda sat the couple who'd brought her to the estate, Mr. and Mrs. White. Mrs. White tried to be a part of the conversation, but Mr. White seemed intent on his plate and glass.

The couple who provided the most interest were the dowager and her husband. Every time they looked at each other, affection passed between them. Mamma had told her their marriage was barely a year in duration, but that theirs was a great love. Apparently, they'd wished to marry when they were young, but had been parted when the dowager's marriage to the previous earl had been arranged. That their love had endured decades apart and had been renewed . . . theirs was a fairy tale.

Genevieve felt on the wrong side of the fairy tale concerning her own arranged marriage. Although she was leaving behind no one-true-love, she was marrying a stranger. Would they grow to deeply love each other?

"Do you enjoy fishing, Miss Farrow?" the dowager asked, for her ears alone.

"I don't know. I've never tried."

"Well then," the colonel said, "my wife and I will teach you. My Addie has turned into an expert angler and can fillet a fish with the best of them."

"By best of them, he means himself." The dowager extended her hand towards her husband, and he grasped it. "Grady has taught me many, many things."

Her blush ignited Genevieve's.

The dowager laughed softly, leaned towards her, and whispered. "Marriage can be quite delightful, my dear."

Genevieve had never heard anyone even hint at the more intimate side of marriage, much less do so at the dinner table. And the dowager fished? And cleaned fish? That didn't seem very proper.

"What are you talking about, you two?" her mother asked.

The dowager rose. "Ladies? Shall we retire to the drawing room and leave the men to their port?"

As Genevieve followed the ladies out of the room, the dowager offered her a wink.

Which made her smile. And wink back.

The dowager laughed aloud.

Chapter Six

Molly *had* to see Morgan today. As soon as possible.

The news that the most recent guest at the manor was his fiancée had kept her from sleeping and caused her to be short with her mother. If Molly didn't talk to Morgan soon, she would crack in two.

After breakfast in the servants' hall, she accosted Nick who was both first footman *and* Morgan's valet. "Nick? A moment please?"

He grinned and tugged at the bottom of his vest. "For you, dear Molly, anything."

Still a shameless flirt.

She led him down the hall towards the laundry, where the smell of soap and starch met them in the corridor. "If you could tell me . . . what are Lord Weston's plans for today?"

His right eyebrow rose. "Well now. So this is how it is. The lot of us were wondering if you were still sweet on him." He smirked. "Trying to arrange a secret rendezvous?"

She hated the presumption. "That is not how it is, and I'd appreciate if everyone would stop speculating about my life."

"Your life is far more interesting than ours. The biggest news below stairs is that one of the laundry maids is sweet on Mr. Robbins."

Molly was taken aback. "He's the earl's valet. That will never be condoned."

"As you know, love knows no bounds."

She dismissed the downstairs drama and got back to the matter at hand. "I simply need a moment to speak with Lord Weston alone. I know how busy he is now that Miss Farrow has arrived."

Nick studied her face, and she hoped he didn't see her true intent. "From what I've heard, there isn't much on the schedule today. They're letting Miss Farrow and her mother get their bearings."

"Could you give his lordship this note for me? Discreetly."

He turned the folded, sealed paper over in his hands. "I suppose I could do that."

"Thank you."

When she turned to walk away he said, "Keep in minit's going to be hard competing with a rich heiress."

Molly didn't dignify his comment with a response.

Molly checked the time on her watch-brooch. It was time to meet Morgan—if he showed up. "I have to go, Ma. I'll be back soon." Since her mother looked curious, and since she couldn't tell anyone, Molly told her the truth. "I've arranged to see Morgan, to have it out with him for leading me on when he was betrothed."

Ma touched Molly's hand. "Sah-wee."

"I know. I'm sorry too."

Molly kissed her on the cheek, then rushed down the back stairs and out a side door of the manor. As she entered the manicured gardens and spotted Morgan, a gardener approached him with a question. Molly held back, plucking a few flowers as though that was her innocent purpose.

The men's discussion ended and Morgan walked towards her. "Good day, Miss Wallace." He looked right, then left. "You requested a meeting?"

Her nerves got the better of her and she made an excuse. "I thought my mother would like a few flowers for her room."

His brow dipped, but he went along with the conversation. "How is she?"

"She is progressing."

"I'm glad to hear it." He fingered the leaf of a bush. "And how are you? Really."

She couldn't deal with any more small talk. "I am horrible."

"Horrible?"

She leaned towards him and hissed, "How dare you speak of feelings for me when you're engaged!"

His face reddened. "I do have feelings for you."

"But you're engaged!"

He stepped away from her, giving his attention to a spread of asters.

Molly continued. "And now your fiancée is here. In this very house. Don't you think I should have been made aware of Miss Farrow's arrival rather than be surprised?"

"I thought someone else would tell you."

She was shocked by his weakness. "Someone else did tell me, but shouldn't *you* have told me, instead of leading me on?"

When he turned to face her, she saw a man, not a title. "I am sorry, Mol. I was wrong. But when I saw you all those old feelings flooded back."

His admission eased her anger. "I . . . I know."

His hand moved an inch towards her, then withdrew. "It's not like I want to marry her. She's not very witty and her letters were quite bland. I suppose she's attractive enough, though . . ." He grinned at her. "She has none of your fire."

Molly caught herself being flattered. "Stop it!"

His grin faded. "I have to marry her. The estate needs her money."

Since when? "I've never seen any indication that the manor is in need."

"You've been gone a long time. And we hide it well."

"Why doesn't your father marry?"

He shrugged. "He still loves Rose, our old family friend at the mercantile, but their love can never go anywhere. So when this alternative solution came forward, Papa and Uncle Frederick decided a wife for me was a way out of our troubles."

It helped that it was an arranged marriage. Yet, that also made it worse.

"I'm truly sorry, Molly. For this…for everything. If I could turn back the years we'd be married." His head shook in small motions and he looked to the sky as if it held the answer. "I always thought those in the aristocracy had the freedom to do whatever they wanted and that we, as commoners, were the ones stuck with our lot in life." He looked directly at her. "But it's not true. My life now is far more restricted than it was when I was a shopkeeper's son. Most importantly, most tragically, I can't marry the woman I love."

Her entire body longed to fall into his arms and feel his luscious kisses. Oh, to return to the days when she'd been the countess's lady's maid and he was simply her beau from the village.

She took a step towards him, hoping he would meet her halfway. But instead, he took a step back. "I'm sorry for everything. But I . . . I need to go."

With that he walked past her, brushing her sleeve with his own.

Molly felt her energy drain away and fell to her knees, right there on the path. *I should leave now as I left before. Run away and never come back.*

"Miss Wallace?"

It was the voice of the gardener. She tried to rise to her feet and he hurried to help her as the heel of her shoe caught in the hem of her skirt.

"Are you all right?" he asked, picking up the fallen flowers.

"I'm fine," she said. "I just stumbled."

Not having the strength to run away, she turned towards the manor.

Genevieve attempted a Chopin etude on the piano, but fumbled it badly. "If I'd known you were going to require me to play, Mamma, I'd have brought my own music. It's going to take me weeks of practice to master this piece."

"We don't have time for that," her mother said. "You need to be proficient *now*." She rifled through a stack of music. "How about this one? It looks familiar."

Luckily it was, and Genevieve began to play the Mozart sonata. She relaxed as her fingers remembered the notes.

"That's it," Mamma said as she waved her arms like a conductor. "Much better."

Genevieve stopped playing. "I don't see why I have to play the piano to impress him. We're betrothed whether I play well or not."

"Your father always said, 'A deal isn't done until the money's exchanged.'"

"Thank you for reminding me that I'm an object being sold."

"Don't be so sensitive. We're here, Morgan's a fine man, and this house is quite elegant—if not a bit run down."

"Hence, the need for our money."

"And your need a title, so that's that."

"I do not need a title. You need me to have one."

"I would grab one myself if it were possible. If only the earl were willing, I would do the work for both of us." She sighed. "I don't understand why he got so testy when I talked about him needing a partner. He took it wrongly."

Because you approached him wrongly. "He isn't interested, Mamma. You have to accept that."

She shrugged. "For the moment. But the question I ask is whether it's wrong for a mother to be ambitious for her child?" She continued leafing through the music.

"Not wrong, just horribly awkward."

"If exposing ourselves to a wee bit of discomfort will help us achieve our goal, I will do it." She glanced upstairs, as though her thoughts were pulled elsewhere. "Remind me to ask Mrs. Weston to give you your own lady's maid. Jane is quite busy taking care of my needs."

"Jane didn't say a thing to me."

"She wouldn't. But the truth is, as the bride, you need your own maid."

"What if I take Jane and you get a different maid?"

Her mother looked appalled. "I think not." Then she plucked a music book out of the stack. "Here. A book of English country tunes you can play *and* sing."

"I will not sing. Ever."

"All young ladies of breeding sing."

"If they are so well-bred then they are wise enough to know when their singing is best left unheard."

She sighed. "It's true you don't have an ear for it."

"I'm glad you realize that."

"As such the piano playing will have to suffice. Continue, my dear. Make yourself talented."

Clarissa hated that her dress was over a year out of style, but it couldn't be helped. It was one of the ensembles she'd brought with her from Summerfield when she'd first escaped to London, so at least it was of high quality. It may not have screamed fashion, but it screamed wealth. And success.

She didn't know for certain which hotel Joseph and Lila were staying at, and had already checked at two. But then she remembered the Kidds had stayed at the Grosvenor during her last London season. She hoped they were checked in here, because the shoes that matched her outfit were chafing her heel.

As she entered the massive lobby she was instantly catapulted to the level of high living she'd left behind. In this hotel guests spent more on a nightly room or for a meal than she paid for a month of rent.

But enough of that. For the moment she had to rely on her actress abilities. She crossed the lobby as if it were her due and approached the front desk, applying her most charming smile.

"May I help you, miss?"

She began her spiel. "I certainly hope so. I was supposed to meet Mr. and Mrs. Kidd for tea yet I am a bit befuddled regarding the time of our appointment. Would you be so kind as to contact them and let them know I am here, waiting?"

"I believe Mrs. Kidd has gone out, but Mr. Kidd is still here."

All the better. "Oh dear, I must have fully forgotten the day and time. Could you send for Mr. Kidd so I can get it all worked out?"

He eyed her with more than a hint of suspicion. "Whom shall I say is waiting?"

She was about to state her actual title of Miss Weston, but needed him to take her seriously, so resumed the title that used to be hers. "Lady Clarissa Weston, if you please."

It did the trick. "Yes, my lady. Right away. If you'd like to wait over there?" He pointed to a sitting area off the massive lobby.

She strolled towards the grouping of chairs, nodding to other ladies and gentlemen as she passed. She prayed no one would recognize her and was glad the space was unoccupied.

She sat on a settee and waited, her mind adapting to the lovely fact that Joseph would be greeting her alone. Seeing him solo had been her eventual hope, but to have the chance so soon was an added bonus.

"Cousin Clarissa?"

She rose and took his hands, kissing his cheeks. "Joseph, I am so glad to find you in." She sat and patted the place beside her.

"I'm sorry you missed Lila. I have a meeting with my family's solicitor so I sent her off with her maid to do some shopping at Harrods."

She began to rise. "If I am keeping you . . ."

"No, no. I have time. I always have time for you."

Clarissa took courage from his last words. This might be easier than she thought. She angled her body so the fabric of her skirt skimmed his leg. "Seeing you and Lila brought back such pleasant thoughts of home and dear friends. I have missed you all so much."

"We have missed you too. We have been worried about you."

"Are you glad to see me well?" She let her eyes seer into his.

He looked away. "Of course. We have been worried about you," he repeated.

She pulled away an inch, and gave him a pout. "Oh no you haven't. You discarded our engagement as if I never meant one whit to you."

"That's not true, Cousin."

"And calling me 'cousin', when we were nearly married is hurtful."

He cleared his throat. "But we *are* cousins now."

"Only through Lila. Not by blood. We are not related by blood." She regained her position, and took his hand in hers, letting it rest upon her knee. "I miss you, Joseph. I miss what we had together."

He gently pulled his hand away. "Your family has missed *you.*"

"I don't care about my family. I care about you. And I."

His brow furrowed. "Clarissa, I am not sure what you are suggesting, but I must remind you that I am a married man." He stood and turned his back to the lobby, lowering his voice. "I'm sorry if I've given you hope of a renewal of old affections, but I assure you that I—"

She put a hand to her chest and rose, stepping away from him. "How dare you imply that I was offering you . . . I never meant . . ."

His face was a mask of confusion.

"What kind of woman do you think I am?"

His mouth was opened to speak, but instead he gave her a bow. "Forgive me for ever implying such a thing."

She lifted her chin and let him suffer a moment. "You are forgiven." Then she added. "If you will excuse me, I will leave you to your errand. Please greet your wife."

"I . . . of course."

Clarissa swept out of the lobby. It hadn't gone as she'd hoped, but as expected.

Then she got an idea.

A little shopping might be just the ticket.

Entering Harrods was like coming home. Clarissa had spent hundreds of pounds in this establishment over the years; her parents, thousands. She spotted the hat department, but turned away. She must keep on task. And so she moved to the other departments, looking for Lila.

There she was. A clerk stood before Lila, waiting for her decision regarding two lace shawls draped across the counter.

"They are both so beautiful," Lila said, fingering the delicate lace.

"Perhaps Lady Kidd would like both?"

Clarissa walked over, making her presence known. "Of course, she would. Lady Kidd deserves all that and more."

The clerk didn't risk a denial and quickly said, "I'll wrap them up for you." Lila's maid stepped away with the clerk to take care of the transaction.

Clarissa put her hands on Lila's shoulders and kissed her cheeks.

"What a happy coincidence," Lila said.

"Not really," Clarissa said, putting a delicate handkerchief to her nose. "Joseph mentioned you might be here."

"You've seen Joseph?"

Clarissa offered a wicked grin. "Oh, yes. I've seen Joseph." She looked directly at Lila. "I met him at the hotel."

Lila glanced at her maid and the clerk, who were obviously listening. She took Clarissa's arm and strolled towards a display of gloves. "Did you have some business with him?"

Clarissa snickered. "You could say that."

Lila let go of her arm. "I don't appreciate your implication. I know my husband and —"

Clarissa's eyes grew wide and she leaned close, her jaw tight. "Your *husband*. My goodness, you simply can't resist gloating."

Lila angled herself so her back was to the clerk and maid, then put a hand to her chest. "I am not gloating. I am merely stating a fact."

Clarissa let out a *harrumph*. "You want to hear facts? Let us talk facts. You stole my husband, my family, and my future."

She hadn't meant to raise her voice, but two other shoppers looked in their direction, and the clerk hurried off. The maid approached, her face pulled with anger. She touched Clarissa's arm. "Excuse me, miss, but you need to be leaving Lady Kidd alone."

Clarissa swiped her touch away. "Miss? Yes, I am a *miss*, only a *miss*, thanks to your mistress. I was Lady Clarissa Weston and now I'm just *Miss* Weston. She lives at Crompton Hall in luxury, while I eat scraps and live in a rat-infested hole and —"

A constable appeared, with the clerk pointing at them. The jig was up.

"Is there a problem, Lady Kidd?"

Before Lila could even try to explain, Clarissa turned on him. "Yes, there's a problem. This woman stole my identity!"

His bushy eyebrows touched. "Pardon?"

Lila linked an arm with Clarissa, patting it, trying to calm her. "Hush now, Cousin. Let's go outside and get some fresh air."

"She's family, your ladyship?"

"Yes, she is."

He pointed at Clarissa. "Then I suggest you do what your cousin says and go outside quietly. If you can't do that . . ." He gave her a serious look.

Clarissa was breathing heavily, and gauged the small crowd that had gathered. It was like she'd been in her own world and had suddenly awakened to find an unwanted audience. It was time to leave the stage. "I'll go. If I must."

He extended an arm in the direction of the exit. Lila kept hold of her and the maid quickly gathered the parcel and followed.

Word had spread to other departments and people watched as the three women made a path towards the exit with a constable trailing behind. "Smile," Lila whispered.

It was good advice, and Clarissa *did* smile as though nothing were amiss. She even spoke to a few as they passed. "Good afternoon." And "Lovely day, isn't it?"

Once they reached the street, the constable led them to the side, away from the entrance. He spoke to Lila, his voice discreet. "Are you all right now, Lady Kidd?"

Clarissa answered for her. "Of course, we are." Clarissa smoothed the fingers of her glove. "Thank you for your assistance, but all is well, thank you."

His eyebrows rose, and he looked again to Lila, who said, "Yes, thank you, constable. I think we can handle it from here."

He touched the brim of his hat and walked away. Lila looked nervous, as if she had no idea whether Clarissa would begin ranting again, or remain calm. Clarissa enjoyed her anxiety.

"Would you like to go for a cup of tea?" Clarissa asked.

"Tea? After that?" Lila blinked. "I don't think so. I don't know what's got into you, Clarissa. We're family and want what's best for you. But that display — whatever it was — it is not acceptable."

"Best? You want what's best for me? Surely you jest."

Lila sighed, clearly giving up. "It was nice seeing you, but I'd better get back."

Clarissa kept her smile. "You do that. Get back. You really need to watch after your husband, Lila. It would be a shame if you lost him."

She walked away. It had been a bit messy, but all in all, mission accomplished.

Lila called after her, "Remember, Clarissa, in spite of everything you're always welcome at Crompton Hall."

Clarissa rolled her eyes and kept walking.

Clarissa leaned against the makeup table, her head in her hands. She did *not* feel up to going on stage tonight. The memories of the meeting with Joseph and then Lila had dogged her all day. Nothing had turned out as she'd planned. The entire thing played over and over like a bad dream.

What's wrong with me? Why did I stir up trouble?

She jerked when she felt cold fingers upon her neck and cringed when she sat upright and found they belonged to Mr. Mapes.

"Eh there, chickie. What's the problem with you?"

She picked up a tin of pancake makeup. "I have a headache."

He kneaded her shoulders and whispered in her ear. "I know a surefire way of getting rid o' it."

The chatter of the other ladies had diminished. They were listening.

Then suddenly, what was a bad thing became a good thing. Clarissa pushed Mapes' hands away and stood, whipping around to face him. "Get your stinking hands off me! If you don't leave me alone, I'll tell the manager, Mr. Carte."

"That's the way," a chorus girl said.

"You tell 'em, Clara."

Mapes' face flushed, and he swung an arm towards the women. "Watch yerself. Carte's given me the power to hire and fire, and more'n that I can do whatever I sees fit with you tramps." He reached for Clarissa, but she batted his hand away. He smirked. "Getting a little extra is part 'o me pay."

Suddenly Mapes was pummeled with whatever the girls had handy: scarves, makeup brushes, combs, and shoes. Clearly shocked by their reaction, he strode out of the dressing room, but not before goosing one of the girls as he passed.

For the first time, Clarissa felt a part of the group. As everyone collected the items they'd thrown and settled back to the mirrors, she remained standing. "Thank you. I appreciate your support."

They brushed off her gratitude with comments about Mapes and his other attempted exploits.

At least she wasn't alone.

For once she wasn't alone.

After an afternoon spent riding with George, Tilda was exhausted but invigorated. He was such a nice boy, and was so kind to give her attention.

But there was no time to rest. It was time to dress for dinner. So many changes of clothes in a day. Tilda had already gone through the extent of her new wardrobe.

Dottie wiped dust from the toe of Tilda's shoes. "You really should wear different shoes for riding than for inside, Miss Cavendish."

"I'm afraid I only have the one pair."

Dottie shrugged. "Then don't worry about it none. I'll make sure you look presentable."

It was the height of luxury to have such help, and a larger luxury to have each day open before her to use as she wished, without a care. Tilda was used to cleaning houses six days a week. Having free time was as foreign as having someone else make her meals, which were served on prettily painted china instead of on chipped and mismatched pottery. Was it possible her working days were over? Would the Westons allow her to stay at Summerfield?

"May I ask you a question, miss?" Dottie asked.

Tilda was brought back to the present. "Of course."

"What do you think of Miss Farrow?" Dottie finished tying the first shoe around Tilda's ankle.

"She seems very nice. Not pretentious at all."

"Rats."

"Why do you say that?"

Dottie shrugged, then added, "I'm very happy for his lordship and the family, but I say 'rats' for my sister's sake."

Molly. Molly was Dottie's sister. "Why should she care?"

Dottie finished the second shoe, but didn't rise from the floor. "Molly and his lordship loved each other once — before he was a viscount."

Tilda put two and two together. "So that's why she left?"

Dottie nodded and rose. "They was gonna marry til the family secret came out and ruined everything — love-wise that is."

Tilda stood and adjusted the cuffs of her dress. "So Molly *and* Clarissa left the manor because of broken hearts?"

"They did."

Tilda thought of Molly, being back in the house, seeing the man she loved marry another woman. How heartbreaking.

As Tilda moved to the door to leave for dinner, Dottie added, "Don't let Molly know that you know, all right?"

"I can keep a secret."

Dottie nodded at the door. "You're a bit early to go down, miss."

"That's all right. I'll find something to do."

Out in the hallway, Tilda saw that Dottie was right: no one was around. Hearing no voices she decided to make good use of the time to do a little exploring.

Clarissa's old bedroom beckoned. Tilda looked both ways to check for witnesses, then went inside. As expected, the room was larger than her guest room. The furniture was adorned with intricate carvings and there were lovely pastel floral fabrics on the seat cushions and at the windows.

It was the bedroom for a beloved daughter.

Who'd run away from home.

Tilda whispered to the room, "If you were my room, I'd never leave."

She strolled past the vanity table, and picked up a perfume bottle of pink swirled glass. She pulled out the stopper and held it under her nose. A heady floral scent made her eyes close in pleasure. She moved to rub it against her wrists, but thought better of it. Someone would notice the scent and know where she'd been.

She spotted a jewelry box and after a moment's hesitation, opened it. Seeing the necklaces, bracelets, and earrings made her wish she hadn't had to sell her stash of stolen jewels to buy the dresses she'd brought with her to Summerfield. She lifted a bracelet with bronze-colored stones towards the evening sunlight. The stones held markings that made each one unique. She palmed the bracelet and slipped it into the pocket of her skirt.

At that moment, Tilda decided that this room would be her private haven, a treasure trove of all things . . . daughterly.

But the room wasn't done revealing its treasures. She opened an inner door and entered another room that was heaven itself. Lining every wall were dresses, bodices, and skirts. On an upper shelf were a myriad of hatboxes, stacked just-so. And on another shelf unit, were dozens and dozens of shoes and boots for every occasion. Tilda chose a pair of silk slippers adorned with violets. She remembered passing a dress of the same fabric and returned to the racks to find it.

There it was. She pulled out the dress of sheer voile, the sleeves offering a flirting hint of bare arms while the bodice was adorned with parading vertical tucks. The drapery of the skirt was drawn back to the bustle, with each layer edged in a satin cording that accented the lilac color. Tilda couldn't resist and held it against herself, checking her reflection in the full-length mirror.

"Broken heart or no broken heart, how could you ever leave all this behind?"

Hearing her own voice reminded her that she needed to move along. Reluctantly, she returned the items to their original places, and left the room.

For now.

Walking past the White's bedroom, Tilda heard loud voices. With a look in both directions, she leaned her ear against the door.

"But we've got to do it soon!" Mrs. White said. "They're not going to let us stay here forever."

"Have another headache," her husband said.

"I'll give *you* a headache," she yelled.

Fearing others would hear, Tilda rapped on the door. The talking stopped and Mrs. White pulled the door a few inches ajar. "Yes?"

Tilda pushed her way inside and shut the door. "I can hear you in the hallway."

Mrs. White's eyes grew large. "What did you hear?"

"Enough to know that you're up to something." She remembered another conversation. "What 'business' do you have here at the manor?"

"It's nothing," Mr. White said.

Tilda shook her head. "It's something, a very big something from the way you're acting."

"It's none of *your* business."

She pointed towards the door. "I will make it everyone's business unless you tell me."

Mr. White moved to the window, glanced out, then looked at Tilda. "I was a coachman here at Summerfield Manor."

"Don't tell her that!" his wife snapped.

He sat on the window seat. "She deserves to know. She's the one who got us here. If she hadn't told us the news of Morgan's upcoming marriage, we never would have vied to be her chaperones."

"You didn't *vie,* we chose you."

Mrs. White shook her head. "We campaigned for it."

They had. They'd been very solicitous and eager. The other couple Tilda and her guardian had interviewed had seemed blasé about the assignment.

Tilda pulled a chair close to Mr. White and sat. "Tell me everything."

With a deep sigh he continued. "I was a coachman here over twenty years ago."

The image of the first gathering in the parlor surfaced. "So that's why Mrs. Weston said you looked familiar."

He nodded.

"Why didn't you say something to them?"

"I did not leave on good terms."

"You were fired?"

"In a way."

Mrs. White threw up her hands. "If you're going to tell her, tell her."

He waved a hand, giving her the floor. Mrs. White faced Tilda, her hands busy in front of her bosom. "Mrs. Weston — Ruth — wasn't married to Frederick back then. He was wooing both Ruth and Fidelia."

"The earl's late wife."

"Only she wasn't the earl's wife then, of course. She was the daughter of a wealthy family who lived nearby. But Ruth wanted Frederick to choose her. So . . ." with a hand, she gave the story back to her husband.

"So Ruth hired me to seduce Fidelia — who was rather free with her affection — and it was arranged that Ruth and Frederick would walk in on us."

Tilda couldn't believe it. "Mrs. Weston seems a proper lady. She wouldn't be a part of such a thing."

"She was the instigator of such a thing," he said. "It went as planned, Fidelia was shamed, and Ruth got Frederick. The scandal of it got so bad around the village that Fidelia's family moved to London, where I think they had some financial difficulties and lost everything."

Mrs. White snickered. "That's why she married Jack when he was a mere shopkeeper."

"But he's the earl now."

"Now," he said, "But Fidelia died before he became earl, so she never knew. Ironic, don't you think?"

"Enough of that," his wife said. "The point is, from his age it seems that Morgan was born soon after Fidelia left Summerfield, so . . ."

Tilda let her thoughts follow the logical conclusion. "So he's your son?"

Mr. White looked to the floor.

"He is," Mrs. White said with a definitive nod. "Which means he is *not* the heir."

Not the heir? The entire Weston family would be turned end over end.

"Our plan is to talk with the earl and his brother and offer our silence in return for compensation."

Tilda blinked at the full implication. "You're going to blackmail them?"

The Whites exchanged a nod. "That's why we can't leave just yet."

"But you can't do that. They're nice people. What have they done to you?"

"They haven't done anything to us, girl. It's what they can do for us that we care about."

"But—"

There was a knock on the door and Mrs. Weston asked, "Mr. and Mrs. White? It's time for dinner."

Tilda moved to answer, but Mrs. White grabbed hold of her arm. "Silence. Understand?"

Tilda nodded and opened the door. "Good evening, Mrs. Weston," she said, pasting on a smile.

Mrs. Weston looked surprised. "Tilda." She looked past her to the Whites. "Are all of you ready to dine?"

Tilda didn't feel much like eating.

So much for spending her days as she wished without a care.

Chapter Seven

"Molly!"

Mrs. Weston rushed towards her, arms outstretched. Although it was totally inappropriate, she gave Molly an embrace, right there in the corridor near the back stairs. "How good to see you! The manor grapevine hinted you were here helping your mother, but with Miss Cavendish and the Farrows arriving . . . how is your mother?"

She offered her stock answer. "She is progressing."

"Very good. More importantly, how are you?" Before Molly could answer, Mrs. Weston drew her to a duo of chairs in an alcove and beckoned her to sit. Molly was again struck at the impropriety. A servant never sat in the presence of her mistress.

But I'm not a servant any more. She let that fact ease her nerves so she could answer the question. "I am well, ma'am. I have been working in a millinery shop in London."

Mrs. Weston nodded. "You always were good with hat design. Do you enjoy the position?"

"Very much." She took advantage of their familiarity, wishing to hear Mrs. Weston's take as to what was going on at the manor. "If I may ask, how are you and the family? You've endured enormous changes."

"We have," she said, pinching the piping that edged the drapery of her skirt. "But actually the demotion—as it were— from countess to the Honourable Mrs. Weston has suited me. You know better than I that being the lady of the house was beyond my comfort."

"At first perhaps, but before I left you'd come into your own and were doing a marvelous job of it."

"Marvelous no, adequate perhaps." She looked down the passageway and the vast manor house that loomed beyond. "I learned a very important lesson after the secret was revealed."

"What's that?"

Her smile was full of contentment. "God knows what He's doing."

It was a simple statement, yet shocking, for Molly's response to the same secret and its outcome held only discontent. "We can only hope so."

"We know so." She put a hand on Molly's knee. "We must acknowledge as much for the sake of our own happiness."

Molly looked to her lap. She wasn't sure what happiness was anymore. The only happiness she'd known was in Morgan's arms.

"You're thinking about Morgan, aren't you?"

"I heard he is betrothed."

"He is."

She sought Mrs. Weston's eyes, needing to see the truth. "Is he happy?"

"He will be."

"Is the girl nice?"

"I don't really know, as we've only just met her. But she seems very sincere and unassuming. On the other hand, her mother is quite the opposite and is all ambition and pretention." She let out a small laugh. "Listen to me, gossiping in my own house."

"I'm glad to hear the news. I miss hearing about the family."

Mrs. Weston's eyes grew sad. "I miss seeing all of *my* family."

Molly knew she was talking of Clarissa, but she'd made a vow of secrecy she would not break. "You haven't heard from your daughter?"

"Not a word. She initially went to stay with friends in London, but last we heard they were traveling in Europe somewhere."

Traveling in Europe? "I wouldn't worry. Even though she was brought up at the manor, she is a very capable woman, able to be out in the world." She immediately wondered if Mrs. Weston would take offense.

She obviously did not.

"I pray for my daughter every day. I just wish she would send a letter or a note saying she is well."

Molly was tempted to tell Mrs. Weston that Clarissa *was* well, but to do so would ignite a bevy of questions she could not answer.

Suddenly, her eyes lit up. "Molly! You're just the person who can help us."

"Anything, ma'am."

Mrs. Weston blinked, suddenly uncertain. "Oh dear, I'm not certain if I should ask. I'm sure it could be horribly awkward . . ."

"Please ask. At least ask."

Mrs. Weston fueled herself with a fresh breath. "Mrs. Farrow has requested that her daughter have her own lady's maid. They brought a maid with them from New York, but only one, and your sister is busy helping Miss Cavendish."

Molly guessed the direction of the conversation and leapt to fend it off. "Surely Albers could help?" Bridget was Mrs. Weston's lady's maid.

"If she were even five years younger I would agree with the assignment, but alas, Albers is getting on in years and in her ability to serve. As head housemaid Gertie is the logical choice—but we fear she is too brash and bossy and would overwhelm dear Genevieve. So the next logical choice is one of the other housemaids, yet Prissy and Sally have never . . . progressed, shall we say?"

Molly wished she could turn back the last five minutes, and veer right when she had veered left, avoiding this meeting. "I'm sorry, Mrs. Weston, but I am here to help my mother."

"I know you are, and I wouldn't impose but for the fact that you were the best lady's maid, and were so kind and understanding during my hard times."

"Thank you, but—"

"I do understand the awkwardness of the situation what with Genevieve marrying Morgan. Truly, I do."

At least she acknowledged it.

"But we are in great need here. And I think Genevieve needs someone her own age to talk to. Coming here from across the pond has got to be overwhelming. You are just the woman who can make her feel at ease."

The whole idea was preposterous and presumptuous. Besides, Molly wasn't a servant anymore. She was a milliner.

"I know what I'm asking you to do is above and beyond, as you have risen above and beyond the difficult situations from your past. To think that now you've found your calling as a milliner."

"I don't know that it's a calling, but I am good at it."

"I'd simply consider this detour an extreme favor until we hire a new lady's maid." She drew in a breath. "Only a woman of strength and character could serve the victor of love's battle."

Battle? Love was a battle?

More like a war.

Then Molly heard herself saying, "I'd be happy to help."

Mrs. Weston rose. "Thank you, Molly. I'll speak to Mrs. Camden right away and let her handle the details." She took Molly's hand between hers. "Once again you come to the rescue."

Then why did Molly feel as if she was the one needing rescuing?

Dottie stood in the doorway of their mother's bedroom, while Molly led Ma up and down the hallway that bisected the servants' rooms on the third floor.

"For my own information," Dottie said. "When a lady goes to tea at the dowager's cottage, what should she wear?"

"A day dress, not too fancy," Molly said. "She should have a parasol." Then she asked, "Is Miss Cavendish going to tea?"

"Miss Farrow is, but I don't know if the younger lady is invited. I'm just curious."

Molly was glad Dottie was serious about learning the intricacies of being a lady's maid. Serving the colonel's goddaughter was a good place to start.

Ma was beginning to groan, so Molly let her stop and rest. The timing was good as they heard footsteps on the back stair.

Dr. Peter appeared. "Well, well, look at you!" he said to Ma.

"She's getting stronger every day," Molly said. She looked to her mother and said, "Shall we show him what you can do?"

Ma nodded, and carefully Molly let go, leaving her to stand alone.

The doctor applauded. "Bravo, Mrs. Wallace!"

Ma beamed, but she nodded towards Molly. "She hepp."

"I know she helped," he said, "She's been a great help. You would not be standing here today if not for your daughter's diligent work."

"Hey!" Dottie said.

"Daughters." But he gave Molly a wink. "Let's get her back in the room and I'll check her out."

When they got Ma settled in bed, Dottie said, "I'd better see if Miss Cavendish needs anything."

"I'm afraid I also should go," Molly said.

"You're assisting Miss Cavendish too?" he asked.

"Actually Mrs. Weston asked me to act as lady's maid for Miss Farrow, the viscount's fiancée."

Ma's eyebrow rose. Molly hadn't told her yet.

"But you're not a lady's maid anymore," the doctor said. "I don't know the full measure of manor house order, but isn't she being a bit bold to even ask?"

Ma nodded for her. "Yes," Molly said, "she is. But I felt I couldn't say no."

"Mor-un," Ma said.

Molly hoped Dr. Peter didn't understand what she was saying and made her exit.

Molly knocked on the bedroom door, her stomach as fluttery as if this was her first day on the job.

"Come in."

Molly entered and offered a nod. "Good afternoon, Miss Farrow. I'm Molly Wallace. Mrs. Weston asked—"

She raised a hand, stopping the explanation. "She asked because my mother asked. I don't see the necessity of bothering someone else with my needs. But Mamma prefers having Jane all to herself and what Mamma wants . . ."

Molly was surprised at her admission.

Miss Farrow continued. "I'm very sorry to impose like this. I know you *used* to be a lady's maid and were merely here visiting. How is your mother feeling?"

Molly was taken aback. "She just walked up and down the hall, and she can stand alone." Why was she venturing beyond her normal answer?

"That's marvelous. Evidence of your fine help, I'm sure." Her face grew sad and she looked to the floor. "My father suffered a heart attack and a fit of apoplexy, but he didn't recover."

"I'm so sorry, miss."

Miss Farrow quickly rallied. "I am the one who should be sorry for mentioning such a thing when you are worried about your mother's recovery."

"I'm not much worried anymore. She'll be fine. It's just a matter of time and work."

"Good for her." She stifled a yawn. "Excuse me."

"A long day already, Miss Farrow?" Molly asked.

"Not because of exertion of the physical kind as much as effort of the social kind. I am a loner of sorts. At home there was only my parents and then just my mother, so I had most days to myself unless I wanted to see friends."

So what did you do all day?

Miss Farrow smiled. "I bet you're wondering what I did all day?"

Molly was impressed. "If you wish to share."

She began to remove a necklace and Molly rushed forward to help.

"Up until I was ten, we were very working class. Then for years we had a housemaid who helped both of us dress. Now, here . . . having my own lady's maid is new to me. You know more about the process than I do."

Molly held the necklace by its ends. "Where would you like this, miss?"

She pointed to a jewelry box on the dressing table. "Perhaps you can teach me how things work in that regard?"

Molly had never met anyone of Miss Farrow's class who was so candid and self-deprecating. "I'll do my best."

"And what would you like me to call you? I hear it is a British tradition to call lady's maids by their last name. Shall I call you Wallace?"

Molly remembered the Farrows referred to their maid by her first name. "Molly will be fine, miss."

"Well then, Molly. On to my other need. What am I supposed to wear to tea with a dowager countess, in her cottage?"

Miss Farrow's genuine nature was going to make this easier than expected.

And so much harder.

Morgan and Genevieve approached the cottage, arm and arm. They were greeted by the dowager exclaiming, "There you are!"

Colonel Cummings came out of the house and offered a smile and a wave.

"Are you ready for this?" Morgan whispered to Genevieve in their final moment alone.

"Of course," she said, though she wasn't at all sure of it. "They don't bite, do they?"

"Only on Tuesdays."

The dowager met them with a kiss on the cheek. It was then Genevieve noticed what she was wearing — or rather, not wearing. "I'm terribly overdressed," she said, referring to her bustled skirt, feathered hat, and parasol.

"Yes, you are," the dowager said, "But not through any fault of your own. Your maid, Miss Thompson is it?"

"Actually, Miss Wallace is helping me, as my mother needed full use of Jane's time."

"Molly is acting as your lady's maid?" Morgan asked. There was an odd hint of panic in his voice.

"Your aunt arranged it." She could tell by the looks on their faces that there was more to Molly's assignment than she understood.

But the dowager recovered nicely and moved on. "You are dressed very appropriately for tea. It is I who have rankled convention by choosing to wear more comfortable attire here at the cottage." She held her skirt away from her body and made a circle. "I had Albers make me some simple skirts and blouses."

"At my suggestion," the colonel said.

"At his suggestion," she said with a nod. "One of the many changes I made when we married and moved here."

The colonel snickered. "She needed some stirring up after living forty years as mistress of the manor."

She put her hands on her hips. "And a good mistress I was too!"

He raised a hand, deferring to the truth of it.

"Yet living here more simply, with the man I love . . ."

She winked at him and he winked back, which made Genevieve want to sigh in appreciation. She hoped she and Morgan could share such a sweet love someday.

"Anyway," the dowager said, slipping her hand around Genevieve's arm as they walked towards the door. "I soon acquiesced to function over frills."

"Her fashion choice is quite the scandal," her husband said.

"But you don't care," Morgan said.

"Oh, she cares," the colonel said, "But she pretends not to."

"Oh, pooh. It's not like I don't dress to the nines when need be. Come inside now and I'll show you how to make a perfect cup of tea."

"And we also have carrots and squash," the dowager said to Genevieve as she showed off their vegetable garden.

"My wife has developed a green thumb."

"I'm learning. Have you ever gardened, my dear?"

"Can't say as I have."

"There is much satisfaction in the full task. I used to only know the eating part."

Genevieve smiled. "I know and enjoy that part — probably more than I should."

"Nothing wrong with having a good appetite," the dowager said. "The surprise is admitting it."

Genevieve sucked in a breath. "I shouldn't have said that."

"You may speak plainly with us, Miss Farrow," the colonel said.

The dowager plucked out a weed, then turned to Genevieve. "I wonder if you possess the special qualities of being down-to-earth and candid because you're American."

The statement surprised her. "As I've only been an American, I don't know what those roots entail that's especially . . . special."

They all chuckled. Then the dowager said, "My best advice to you, Miss Farrow, is to be yourself, as your *self* is quite delightful."

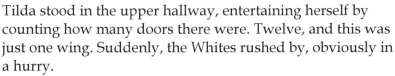

Tilda stood in the upper hallway, entertaining herself by counting how many doors there were. Twelve, and this was just one wing. Suddenly, the Whites rushed by, obviously in a hurry.

"What's going on?" Tilda asked as they passed.

Mrs. White stopped and leaned close. "We're doing it. Now."

It had to mean the blackmail.

Mr. White ran a shaky hand through his hair. "I asked the earl and Mr. Weston if we could speak to them and they said yes. We are to meet them in the study at three." He shook his head. "I can't believe we're actually doing this." Then he turned to his wife. "Maybe we shouldn't."

She grabbed his arm roughly and pulled him towards the staircase, where they descended in a flurry.

Tilda's stomach clenched. Although they'd implied they were going to confront the male Westons with their demands, to have the moment imminent made her want to hide in her room. Or run and warn the earl and his brother.

Yet they wouldn't appreciate being confronted with the news about Morgan. Would they blame her for bringing the Whites into the house? Would they hate her and send her away?

Unfortunately, there was no time for her to ponder her choice. Curiosity won out over nerves and she followed the Whites downstairs.

The couple was already in the study when Tilda turned into that corridor. The wide hallway was set apart from the main pathways of the house, so it was the perfect place to eavesdrop.

Tilda leaned over and untied one of her high-top boots. Then she squatted down, ready to take up the tying if someone were to come by. And then . . . she listened.

The pleasantries were accomplished and she heard the earl say, "So, what can we help you with, Mr. White?"

The man cleared his throat. "I . . . it seems I used to . . ."

Mrs. White took over. "Here's the gist of it, gentlemen. My husband used to work at Summerfield Manor as a coachman."

Mr. Weston responded. "Why didn't you say something? Forgive me if I didn't recognize your name: White?"

"At the time you called me by my first name: Warren."

There was a moment's hesitation, then Tilda heard a gasp.

"Yes," Mr. White said. "That's me. I was the one."

"The one what?" the earl asked.

Tilda heard Mr. White expel a breath. His wife answered for him. "The one who had relations with your wife, Fidelia, when she was being courted by Mr. Weston."

"I don't think dredging up the past has any place here," the earl said.

Mrs. White ignored him. "You know it's true. Right, Mr. Weston? You and your wife — before she was your wife — walked in on them."

Mr. Weston responded. "A horrible business, that. A regret that my wife and I share."

"But what you may not know is that it was your wife who hired me to do it."

There was a short pause. Then . . .

"I know," Mr. Weston said. "She told me. She was desperate to win my hand and mistakenly thought I was seriously considering marrying Fidelia."

"What does any of this have to do with now?" the earl asked. "I didn't know about this love triangle when I met my wife. I only learned of it a year or so ago, and regret that this *tête-à-tête* you speak of was instrumental in causing her family to leave Summerfield and lose their position in society."

"That wasn't the only cause of their downfall," Mr. Weston said. "Fidelia's father was involved in shady bank dealings which caused them to lose their standing and their fortune."

"Agreed," the earl said. "But her disgrace, being found in the barn with you, Mr. White . . . it caused great harm."

"Actually," Mr. White said, "I do regret my part—"

Mrs. White interrupted. "The reason we asked for this meeting is for one very important fact not yet mentioned."

"And what might that be?" the earl asked.

"The fact that my husband is the father of your son, Morgan."

At that moment a maid walked down the corridor. Tilda began tying her shoe in earnest until she passed.

But when she was gone, all Tilda could hear was silence coming from the study. Had she missed something?"

"That's absurd," the earl said.

"It's the truth," Mrs. White said.

"My wife was not pregnant when I married her."

"Prove it."

Tilda was impressed by her audacity and for the first time realized the truth didn't really matter.

She heard the sound of chair legs against the floor as someone rose. "What do you want from us?" Mr. Weston asked.

"Five hundred pounds," Mrs. White said. "Pay and we'll be on our way."

After a pause the earl said, "We could have you arrested for extortion."

"Go ahead and try. We'd be happy to share the core of the issue—and we *will* share it with all of Summerfield and beyond if you choose to ignore us, or refuse to pay."

"I am sorry about all this," Mr. White said. "I—"

"Shush!" Mrs. White said.

Mr. Weston spoke next. "Who else knows of this lie?"

"No one," she said.

Except me.

"We don't have that kind of cash lying around," the earl said.

"We'll give you some time," she said. "We quite enjoy the hospitality of the manor."

The earl's voice was strained. "But the wedding is imminent. Can't all this wait until after—?"

"Ah . . ." Mrs. White said. "There you see the true issue at hand. Will Miss Farrow still want to marry your son if he's not your heir?"

More silence, which allowed Tilda to take in the immensity of the situation. Poor Miss Farrow. Poor Morgan.

Finally the earl said, "You told us to prove Fidelia wasn't pregnant when I married her. I say to you, prove that she was."

"The point is, your lordship," Mrs. White said, "I don't have to. All I have to do to ruin the wedding is imply that the Viscount Weston is really the son of a poor coachman. The illegitimate son."

"You're despicable," the earl said.

"I prefer 'enterprising.'"

Another person rose. "We'll get you your money, but you must promise that no one else learns about this. Especially Morgan and Miss Farrow."

"I think we can do that," Mrs. White said.

Tilda heard movement coming towards the door, so she scurried down the corridor, into the foyer.

A few moments later, the Whites appeared. Mrs. White was beaming, but her husband was as white as the marble floor. "How did it go?" Tilda asked.

"Perfectly."

Mr. White looked towards the stairs. "I believe I have one of your headaches, wife. Let us retire."

"As you wish."

They ascended the stairs and disappeared down the upstairs hall. Tilda felt the need to be as far away from them as possible—as far away from everyone as possible—so she rushed outside to the gardens.

She wound her way around the carefully manicured flower beds, avoiding the gardeners, seeking a place where she could be alone. She spotted a bench on the other side of an arbor and made it her destination.

Tilda fell onto the bench and pressed her hands against her ears. If only she could forget what she'd heard, if only the words of blackmail and threats were a dream that could be erased by the simple act of waking up.

If only the Whites hadn't been her chaperones, none of this would be happening. She would have arrived at Summerfield, been welcomed into the manor, and been enjoying a ride with George right now instead of worrying about the fate of the family and whether they'd blame her for their troubles.

Maybe I should apologize to the earl and Mr. Weston, and assure them . . .

What could she assure them? That she wasn't a part of the blackmail scheme even though she'd had foreknowledge and had brought the Whites here in the first place?

Tilda covered her face with her hands. "Why didn't I stop them? Now everything is ruined."

"Tilda?" Tilda looked up to see Miss Farrow standing on the other side of the arbor. "Are you all right?"

Tilda sat erect and ran a shaky hand through her hair. "I'm just feeling a bit overwhelmed."

"May I?"

Tilda scooted to the side. Miss Farrow sat, and drew in a fresh breath. "I understand your feeling. I feel the foreigner here, in more ways than country."

Tilda marveled at how Genevieve made her feel at ease with just a few words. "We are both foreigners in this world. And though it can be rather scary, I do like it here. A lot. Don't you?"

"I hope to."

"You don't like it here yet?"

"I'm not saying that, it's just very different from New York."

"I like your accent," Tilda said.

"And I like yours." Miss Farrow pointed to the extensive beds of roses. "We've just decided to use roses for the wedding."

Mention of the wedding forced Tilda's thoughts to return to the crisis at hand. "When is the wedding again?"

"In three weeks."

"So soon."

"The planning has been going on for months. Hundreds of invitations have gone out."

Hundreds of people who would spread the word about the scandalous Westons. "With the wedding nearly here there's no turning back."

"Why no, I suppose there isn't."

"But you just met him, yes? Met Lord Weston."

"That's true, but we've been corresponding for nearly a year."

"So you love each other?" *Please say you love each other so you'll marry no matter what.*

Genevieve laughed. "I've heard Americans accused of being direct. Are you sure you're not one of us?"

"Sorry," Tilda moved a pebble with the toe of her boot.

"Do you want to know a secret?"

Not really. "If you'd like to share."

"I would be happy for a much simpler wedding, one that would let Morgan and I concentrate on each other more than the lavish details."

If he's not the heir, you might get your wish. "You aren't excited about the fancy stuff?"

Miss Farrow shook her head. "I'm more the quiet sort. Slip in, slip out. Say our I-dos, be blessed, and move on with our lives." She stood and plucked an orange-colored blossom from a bush. "I'm totally unlike my mother. Being immersed in riches and titles makes Mamma ecstatic." She put the bloom to her nose, taking in the scent. "I'm sorry. That sounded very callous and unappreciative."

"But what if the wedding doesn't happen? Would you be terribly disappointed?"

Genevieve dropped the flower to the path, then stooped to pick it up. "Why yes, I would. Why do you ask?"

"No reason."

Miss Farrow looked towards the house. "I suppose I should be getting back. We are finalizing the wedding schedule today. I'll see you soon."

As she walked away, Tilda wished she didn't like her so much. She liked everyone at the manor and didn't want to see any of them hurt. The only people she disliked were—

"There you are." Mrs. White slipped through the arbor and took a seat beside Tilda before she could flee.

"I really need to get back to the house." She tried to stand, but Mrs. White held her back.

"You were talking to Miss Farrow."

"I was."

"You didn't say anything about . . ."

"No, no. Nothing."

"I assumed you were smart enough to realize that ruining our little plan wouldn't bode well for you."

"It what way?"

Mrs. White smoothed the skirt of her dress. "You would be guilty by association. We lose. You lose."

"But I don't have anything to do with your plan."

"You brought us here, didn't you?"

"You brought *me* here."

Mrs. White shrugged. "I'm not sure anyone cares who opened the gate, only the result."

Tilda leapt to her feet and moved away from the woman. "Why are you doing this? The Westons are nice people. What did they ever do to you?"

Mrs. White considered this a moment. "They have and we have not." Then she stood, backed Tilda against the arbor, and held a finger to her face. "You keep quiet or you'll regret it."

Tilda's mouth was dry. "Regret it how?"

Mrs. White removed her finger and grinned. "What would the Westons think if they knew you used to make your money in the pubs frequented by your father and his fellow soldiers?"

"What are you talking about?"

Mrs. White leaned close and whispered. "I don't think they would extend their hospitality to a whore."

Tilda gasped. "But I didn't—"

"Of course you didn't. But haven't you realized the truth doesn't matter? The rumor of it would be enough for them to send you back to Aldershot."

The thought of going back to that life where she would be all alone, where she'd have to go back to cleaning houses . . . "You're evil."

Mrs. White shrugged. "I'm resourceful and wise. I suggest you be the same."

Chapter Eight

Dottie, what are you doing?

Molly watched as Dottie ignored her usual place at the servants' breakfast table—sitting with the housemaids—and took a seat next to Molly and the other lady's maids.

The entire room froze as though a photograph were being taken.

As the head housemaid, Gertie was the first to speak. "Mr. Dixon?"

At the head of the table, the butler rose. "Dottie, you need to take your proper place."

Dottie settled in, putting a napkin in her lap. "But this *is* my proper place, isn't it? I'm a lady's maid now and I've deferred to Miss Albers, Molly, and even Miss Thompson."

Gertie intervened. "You are *acting* lady's maid to Miss Cavendish, Dottie. It is not a full position, only a temporary one."

"But it could end up being *my* position if Miss Cavendish stays on and likes my work." She turned to Molly. "Isn't that right, Molly?"

"Your sister is not in charge," Mrs. Camden said. "Mr. Dixon and I run this household."

"Speaking of Miss Wallace, why is she sitting up so high?" Gertie asked. "She's visiting her mother. She shouldn't sit up at the table, even if she *was* Mrs. Weston's lady's maid. That was ages ago."

"And that will be enough," Mr. Dixon said. He looked to Jane. "Please forgive the acrimony, Miss Thompson. I fear we've given your American sensibilities a rough example."

"Not at all, Mr. Dixon. I am here to work within this household and learn how things are done."

"An admirable example that should inspire everyone." He looked directly at Dottie. "Dottie you have been given an enormous opportunity to assist the family."

"I understand that, sir, and —"

He lifted a hand, stopping her words. "But . . . as has been stated, it is an extraordinary, unprecedented jump."

"Not so unprecedented," Dottie said. "Molly did the same thing years ago, jumping from housemaid to the countess's lady's maid."

Molly's stomach flipped. Dottie wasn't helping her cause. And the truth was, Molly had paid for her quick rise by being on the receiving end of harsh treatment from the other servants.

The butler gave Dottie a scathing look. "The core and very strength of an English household is the steadfast order that directs and guides us, that keeps our domestic government running smoothly." He looked to Mrs. Camden for affirmation, and she nodded. He continued, "The Wallace sisters have been asked by Mrs. Weston to assist Miss Cavendish and . . ." He looked at Molly. "Molly has graciously agreed to serve Miss Farrow."

There was a moment of silence, and Molly knew everyone longed to ask how she felt regarding the odd situation.

She didn't want to talk about it.

Luckily, Gertie pointed at Jane with her own concerns. "But why would Molly have to do that? They brought a lady's maid with them."

Jane defended herself. "Mrs. Farrow wanted me all to herself. Sorry for the disruption."

Mr. Dixon gave her a nod. "There is no need to apologize, Miss Thompson. It is not for us to determine the right or wrong of any decision made by the family, nor to disagree. It

is up to us to fully support and follow their wishes. To a tee."
He turned his attention to Dottie. "As for you, I suggest you
work especially hard in your new assignment above stairs.
But while you are down here below . . . a little more humility
would be preferred."

"Yes, Mr. Dixon." She turned to face the others. "And
everyone can all call me Dottie like you're used to. I've a long
way to go to earn the honor of being called 'Miss Wallace'."

"That's the spirit," Mr. Dixon said upon sitting. "Now,
let's get on with the meal. There is work to be done."

When Molly passed Dottie the stewed tomatoes she gave
her a smile.

Gutsy, but well played.

Dr. Peter closed his doctor's bag. "You're doing well, Mrs.
Wallace, but to get your dexterity back you need to practice
more clenching and unclenching of your hand."

Ma's brow furrowed. Molly doubted she knew what
"dexterity" meant. "So you can hold a knife and cut
vegetables again."

This, Ma understood. "I tye."

"I know you will." He moved towards the door, then
hesitated and turned back to Molly. "Would you like to get
out?"

"Out?"

"Of here. The manor. With me. When was the last time
you were in the fresh air?"

*The time I confronted Morgan about not telling me he was
betrothed.* She would love to replace that memory with
another. "It's been too long. I'd love to venture out with
you." She turned towards Ma. "Is that all right?"

Ma's grin was her answer. "Go."

They walked down two stories and out the main door to
the doctor's waiting wagon. He helped her into the seat, then
joined her, taking the reins.

The horse began an easy walk. With a glance back to the manor, Molly said, "That's the first time I've ever walked through the front door other than to stand in the drive with the other servants to greet an important visitor."

"Does that bother you?" he asked.

She thought of Morgan and how she would have been the Countess of Summerfield if she'd married him. "It is what it is."

"I applaud your good attitude," he said.

"It is neither good nor bad, it simply is what—"

"It is."

They pulled through the front gates and turned towards the village. "Are you making fun of me, doctor?"

He looked at her, his face serious. "Heavens no. I am also aware of the discrepancies and disparities of class. My father and I serve both manor and cottage, visiting both ends of the social spectrum while being a member of neither."

"Which means you are caught in the middle."

"Exactly."

"At least you are indispensable."

"So are you, Miss Wallace. What would your family do without you? You saved them from an awful fate at the hands of your father, and—"

"How do you know all that? You were off at school."

He grinned. "The Summerfield grapevine has a very long and winding reach."

"I know. I hate it." She wondered if he knew anything about herself and Morgan.

"I suppose a person's opinion of the grapevine depends on which side of the news they're on."

"I don't like being talked about."

"Understood. But in this case the village news divulged your good character. After your mother defended Dottie against your father . . . if you hadn't convinced the Westons to take all of them on as staff, who knows what would have happened to them."

It was disconcerting he knew so much about her family's business, but it was also satisfying to hear the acclamation in his words.

"Are you happy working in your father's practice here in Summerfield?" she asked.

"I am," he said with a confident nod. "City life is not for me."

"But don't you find us rather boring?"

"Not at all. I am kept just busy enough. And with each case comes new knowledge."

"But you're the one who's supposed to *have* the knowledge."

She saw him redden. "Socrates said it best, 'All I know is I know nothing.'"

"Who is this Mr. Socrates?"

He smiled "No 'mister' to it. He was an ancient Greek philosopher."

"He sounds wise."

"He was. And his words still apply, for I know so little. The entire field of medicine involves knowing a very little about a lot. I pray that someday it will know enough to truly help everyone in need. There is still so little we can do."

"I commend your humility."

"My humility is a necessity lest I think too highly of myself. No matter what little I can do to help, it still comes down to the Almighty having the ultimate power."

"Unfortunately," Molly said under her breath.

"What?"

"God and I often battle over what I want versus what He wants."

He chuckled. "Need I ask who wins?"

His question didn't require an answer.

"So what do you want that God denies?"

Morgan. "I'm afraid once again it comes down to 'it is what it is.'"

"You cannot use that twice in one conversation."

"I think I just did."

"Then perhaps you need to change *it*. Having a goal or a heart's desire is beneficial."

"That's not how it seems."

"'Delight thyself also in the Lord: and he shall give thee the desires of thine heart.'"

She looked at his face. "Is that also Socrates?"

"No. Those are the words of a king."

"I've rarely heard such inspiration from any monarch."

He smiled. "King David of Israel, a couple thousand years ago."

The words ignited her thoughts. "Wouldn't it be wonderful to say or do something that lingered on long after we die, like Socrates and King David?"

"Perhaps *that* should be your new desire — since the old one isn't working out."

What an interesting thought.

Dr. Peter stopped at an intersection. "I was going to check on Mr. Forbes who has a sprained ankle. Would you like to come along?"

She thought of her duties back at the manor. Ma was doing fine, and Miss Farrow? There were some ladies coming to tea later on, so she would need help getting dressed. But Molly had a few hours free. "I would love to."

It felt good to make her own choices again.

Genevieve approached the drawing room on the arm of her mother. Or rather, her mother was clutching *her* arm with extra vigor, her advice assaulting Genevieve's left ear.

"Be charming and sweet, and remember the names of the other ladies. And please address them by the correct title. Only eat one biscuit — if any, and check your bodice and lap for crumbs, and —"

"I won't have to play the piano for them, will I?"

"You will do what they ask you to do — with no complaint."

The dowager and Mrs. Weston were in the room when they entered. Mamma immediately eased her grip on Genevieve's arm and turned on her own dubious charm.

"Lady Summerfield. Mrs. Weston. We have arrived, ready to meet and greet your esteemed friends."

The dowager accepted Genevieve's kiss to her cheek and whispered, for her ears alone. "Remember to be yourself." She patted the place beside her and Genevieve was glad for her proximity. The dowager's one nugget of advice was of far more worth than her mother's stream of do's and don'ts. With a few breaths in and out the flips of Genevieve's nervous stomach settled.

A bit.

Mrs. Weston adjusted the crystals hanging from a candelabra on the piano. "Did we overwhelm you this morning with wedding plans, my dear?"

Genevieve had been glad to hear all the details of flowers and the schedule for the festivities. "Not at all. I am very glad you have things so well handled. I trust you completely." She looked at the dowager. "I wish to do things right, to fit in, and bring honor to your family."

Mamma took a seat nearby. "I have carefully trained and groomed her as to all things British."

"But shouldn't that be our job?" the dowager asked.

Genevieve rarely saw her mother blush, and quite enjoyed it.

They heard a carriage out front and Dixon emerged from that invisible place where he lingered in order to be at everyone's beck and call. As he answered the door, there was a faint tittering of women's voices coming closer. Genevieve began to stand.

The dowager put a gentle hand on her arm. "No, dear. We remain seated and let them come to us."

Mamma overheard and gave her own nod of understanding. That there was already a discrepancy in etiquette from what they were used to ignited Genevieve's nerves anew.

Dixon appeared at the exact middle point of the opened double doors. "Your ladyship, Mrs. Weston, ladies . . . the Baroness Colgrove, the Baroness Wyngate, and the Viscountess Gresham." He stepped aside and three women entered the room with a flutter and flurry of stunning day dresses, smart hats, and carefully contained curiosity.

They greeted the dowager first. Genevieve knew the dowager countess ranked above them all, though she did wonder how things would have proceeded if one of the guests was a Marchioness, or a Duchess — those of higher rank than countess.

"My dear Adelaide," the Baroness Colgrove said, leaning down to kiss both cheeks. She moved on to greet Mrs. Weston. The process was repeated twice more by the other ladies. They gave Genevieve and her mother a glance, but offered nothing more, as if the two of them were invisible until properly introduced.

Only then did the dowager speak. "Please be seated." The ladies each selected one of the chairs that had been gathered close from the large inventory of the room. Before the moment could be more awkward than it already was, she made the introductions.

"I would like you to meet Mrs. Farrow from New York City."

Genevieve could tell that her mother wanted to stand again and her right hand twitched a bit as though she wanted to shake hands. Instead, she smiled nicely and nodded. "It is ever so good to meet you, your ladyships."

It was Genevieve's turn. The dowager slipped her hand around Genevieve's arm, and drew it close. "And this wonderful girl is Miss Genevieve Farrow, my grandson's betrothed."

"I am very glad to be here in Summerfield," Genevieve said, "And very honored to meet all of you." Belatedly she added, "Your ladyships."

"The pleasure is ours," Baroness Colgrove said. She looked to the other two ladies, as if giving a signal for some plan to commence.

Baroness Wyngate accepted the signal with a nod and said, "We understand your father worked in a factory?"

Genevieve heard her mother's intake of breath, which unfortunately fueled her response. "He most certainly did not! My husband owned a factory, many factories, and was instrumental in equipping them with the newest and most up-to-date sewing machines in the world. If not for the ingenuity of men like my Oscar, there would be no ready-made clothing for sale in stores such as Macy's and Bloomingdale's."

Baroness Colgrove raised an eyebrow. "Readymade . . . mmm."

"How nice for him," the viscountess said.

"It was more than nice," Mamma said. "My husband was ingenious and hard-working."

"I imagine he was," Baroness Wyngate said.

The other ladies shrugged.

They might as well have slapped Mamma with a glove.

Mrs. Weston exchanged a look with the dowager. Someone needed to handle this.

The need for intervention was interrupted as the tea was brought in. Mrs. Weston poured and served while Mr. Dixon offered tea cakes.

Genevieve wondered if the slight would evaporate with her father undefended. She was just about to stand up for him herself, when the dowager said, "Mr. Farrow was a man of enterprise and industry. Two traits that deserve our respect."

The ladies acquiesced with a slight tilt to their heads. Their non-response made Genevieve's insides stir — and not in nervousness.

As if in a determined synchronicity, all five women held their teacups at chest level and sipped together. The sound of the cups returning to their saucers were like five staccato notes, marking a moment.

"If you'll pardon me," she heard herself saying, "I get the impression you believe 'work' to be distasteful."

"Of course not," the viscountess said. "It is just . . ."

"Necessary," the dowager said.

Spurred by her support, Genevieve continued. "My father started with practically nothing. His family were immigrants in New York City."

Three pairs of eyebrows rose.

She continued. "He was employed in a cotton mill when he was six. From there he worked his way up to a garment factory, then to selling sewing machines, then to designing a way for those machines to be adapted for factory work. And by doing so, he made millions." She leaned forward. "Millions."

"How American of him."

Her skin bristled. "Absolutely. How American. The industrious can-do spirit is what makes our country great. The United States is a land where anyone can rise to the top with determination and hard work."

As soon as she said it, Genevieve wished she could take back the last line. The world she was marrying into was a society of established aristocracy, with well-established walls defining its borders.

"We admire your family's history," the dowager said. "It is an inspiration."

Baroness Colgrove took a sip of tea, then said. "You mentioned they were immigrants? From where?" She looked to the other guests. "Farrow . . . what is your family's origin?"

Genevieve hesitated, for she had been warned of the tension between the English and Irish. But she couldn't retreat now. "Ireland." She looked to her mother. "Wasn't our name originally O'Farrow, Mamma?"

Mamma swallowed, then said. "Perhaps. Although *my* family emigrated from France."

By the looks on their faces, France was just a stitch better than Ireland.

But then Genevieve noticed that Mrs. Weston was avoiding eye contact and was taking far too many quick sips of tea.

I've gone too far. How can I make things right?

Then she remembered the dowager's advice to be herself. It was worth a try.

Genevieve set her tea cup on her lap. "Ladies, I must apologize for my defensive outburst. I am very nervous about meeting such esteemed women as yourselves. I am honored to be here in Summerfield and feel blessed to find myself on the verge of belonging to such a noble family as the Westons." She glanced at each face, then to her lap. "Yes, my family's beginnings were lowly but they rose to higher measures because of their desire to better themselves, help others, and live a respectable life under the Almighty's gracious direction. I feel in my heart *and* my mind, that I belong here, that marrying dear Morgan is but another step on the God-driven path of my purpose. I have much to learn, and if agreeable, I will look to all of you to guide and teach me how to be as good an Englishwoman as I am an American."

Genevieve knew she must have taken a breath during her monologue, but as she finished she found her lungs fully empty and had to breathe deeply amid the constraints of her corset.

She looked first to her mother, who was smiling and nodding, then to Mrs. Weston, who no longer found her teacup of interest. The dowager reached over and gave a pat to her knee. "Well said, my dear."

As for the others . . .

Each woman set their cup and saucer upon their laps, and with a quick glance, one to the other, Baroness Colgrove spoke. "This country can use strong women of spirit. So I will speak for all of us as we welcome you here, Miss Farrow. And best wishes on your upcoming marriage."

"Yes, best wishes," the viscountess said.

"Morgan is lucky to have you," Baroness Wyngate added.

The dowager gave them each a confirming look before saying, "Will one of you please tell me about the latest Paris fashion. I am horribly out of touch."

Genevieve let herself breathe, then allowed her mind to wander over the intricacies of bustles, skirt silhouettes, and sleeve length.

Tilda stood outside the drawing room, hiding behind a potted plant. She was happy for Miss Farrow. To be introduced to two baronesses and a viscountess would be divine. She was disappointed she hadn't been invited, but understood. They treated her kindly, but this was Miss Farrow's chance to shine.

Suddenly, Mrs. White came up beside her. "Envy is a sin," she whispered.

"So is greed."

"Touché, girl."

Mrs. White's presence was making it impossible to hear what was going on in the party. Tilda just wanted her gone. For good. "When are you leaving?" she whispered.

The woman huffed. "When we get paid."

"When will that be?"

"The earl asked for a few days. If he wants us gone sooner, all he has to do is belly up." Then she turned on her heel. "Happy eavesdropping."

Tilda was glad for her departure. It was hard to eavesdrop in the presence of an extortionist.

Clarissa was relieved there had only been a matinee today so she could enjoy her one evening off. She headed back to the flat and hoped to find that Agnes had scrounged up something halfway delicious for dinner. After that, she'd go to bed early. She longed for the escape of sleep, and the happier place of dreams.

Walking into her building, she spotted the little street urchin who always played on the stairs.

As Clarissa began to ascend, she noticed a glaring flash of white in the girl's hand. It was clearly a nice handkerchief. She backtracked a step. "Where did you get that?"

"I didna steal it."

"I didn't say you did. But where did you get it?" There was no way this homeless waif should be in possession of such a pretty handkerchief.

"The fancy rich lady gave it to me for my dolly before she went a visitin' upstairs. She was wearin' the prettiest lace shawl."

The dolly reference was quickly passed over, as the only doll the girl owned was a piece of wood on which she'd scratched the features of a face. But the mention of a lace shawl . . .

"What did she look like?"

"She was like you, with dark 'air, and dark eyes. When she smiled it looked like she meant it."

No, it couldn't be.

"Let me see that." The girl handed the handkerchief over, and Clarissa saw an *L* embroidered in one corner. *Lila?* "When was the lady here?"

"Yesterday."

Clarissa tried to remember yesterday. It had been a normal day, and Agnes hadn't mentioned a thing about a visit from Lila and— "Was there a man with her?"

"Nah. Just another lady, not dressed near as fancy."

"A maid?"

The girl shrugged, then said, "Can I 'ave it back? Dolly's cold."

Clarissa handed it over and rushed up the stairs. If Lila had come to call, Agnes had some explaining to do.

She unlocked the door and burst inside, "Agnes, why didn't you tell me Lila came to visit?"

In the small space it only took a moment to realize Agnes wasn't there. And then she noticed something odd. There were fewer clothes hanging from the pegs on the wall. In fact, none of Agnes's clothes were there at all.

128

Clarissa looked under her bed and saw that one of the suitcases was gone. She ran out to the hall and called down the stairs. "Girl!"

The girl moved to a place where she could look up the two flights. "Yes'm?"

"Did you see Miss Sheets leave?"

She nodded. "Right after you left today, she left."

Clarissa stumbled back into the room, closed the door, then asked aloud, "Why would you leave me?" Suddenly, she thought about the possibility of a note and looked around. There, on her pillow, was a piece of paper. And a turquoise and pearl necklace.

She brought the note to the window to read, and quickly sank to a chair when she saw that it wasn't from Agnes at all, but was from Lila:

> *Dear Cousin,*
>
> *I was ever so glad to see you again. You are a very talented actress and I wish you much success. You are also a very brave woman to tackle London alone. Please know that we miss you terribly and you are welcome back in Summerfield at any time. If you don't wish to go home straightaway, Joseph and I would be happy to have you stay with us at Crompton Hall.*
>
> *I wish you would have told us the truth about where and how you were living. I readily forget and forgive the incident at Harrods now that I see the conditions that led to your actions. We are family, Clarissa. We are willing to help.*
>
> *And so . . . on a whim I have left you one of our grandmother's necklaces. As you know, it is made from real pearls and turquoise from the 1850's. I know she would want you to have it. Use it in any way you deem necessary.*
>
> *May God keep you safe. Yours always,*
> *Cousin Lila.*

Clarissa mentally skipped over the polite niceties and focused on the mention of a necklace. As soon as she picked it up memories flooded back of the jewelry around

Grandmamma's neck, and of playing dress-up as a child. Clarissa had even worn the piece a time or two for parties.

She clasped the necklace around her neck and looked in the mirror. There were nine square medallions filled with small pearls and a solid circle of turquoise stones. The medallions were held together by five strands of silver chain, culminating in a medallion-clasp at the back of the neck. She pressed the piece against her skin. Two words flooded her mind: *Home. Family.*

But then Clarissa heard heavy boots in the hall. A loud banging on the door startled her. "Miss West, it's the landlord! I knows yer in there. I needs me rent now."

Clarissa held her breath. *Please go away.*

He banged some more. "I's tired of playing games. I's given you plenty of warnings. You get me all the rent in two days or I'll kick you out on the streets. You hear me?"

Her heart beat wildly and she froze until his footsteps receded down the stairs. Clarissa listened to her breath go in, then out. In, then out.

She stumbled to the bed and fell upon it, drawing her knees to her chest, clutching a pillow as if it could provide her with a new life.

One fact rose above all others. With Agnes gone, for the first time in her life, Clarissa was completely and utterly alone.

Chapter Nine

It wasn't fair.

Everyone was busy with something, leaving Tilda to spend time with the Whites or by herself.

The latter was the best choice. In a way, she had the entire house to herself, yet the one room out of dozens that held her interest was Clarissa's.

Making sure no one saw her, Tilda slipped into the bedroom. By now, she felt at ease in the space and had already chosen her favorite spot, a chair upholstered in rose-colored velveteen with a matching tufted ottoman. She retrieved the jewelry box on the vanity and plopped in the chair, put her feet up, and emptied the jewels on her lap.

She'd already snitched three pieces for herself—a different one to commemorate each visit, but they had been small pieces, not easily missed.

Today she felt emboldened. Was it the bite of jealousy towards Genevieve that spurred her to take a bigger risk? Or tension about the blackmail?

Whatever the reason, she plucked an emerald choker from the pile. She let it drape over her palm and admired the diamonds that separated each green stone. It was far more valuable than any piece she'd stolen back in Aldershot, or even here. But it wasn't the value that enticed her. It was the way the gem's facets reflected the morning sunlight, revealing a depth beyond their actual size.

She clasped the choker around her neck, feeling regal with the weight of it. For the full effect, she needed to look in a mirror. She was in the process of emptying her lap of the jewels to do just that, when the bedroom door opened.

"Oh!" said the head housemaid.

Tilda froze a moment, uncertain whether to yell at her to get out, or to act nonchalant. She chose the latter.

"May I help you?"

Gertie's eyes moved from Tilda's neck to her lap, to the jewelry box on the ottoman, to her neck again. "This is Miss Weston's room."

"I know that."

"That's her jewelry."

Tilda's stomach tightened, but she managed to keep the same tone. "I know that."

Gertie took three steps into the room. "Mrs. Weston would not like you touching her daughter's things."

"She's let me wear her clothes."

Gertie blinked once, then said, "Clothes ain't jewels." She pointed to the stash. "Those are worth a lot of money."

"I know that."

Gertie put her hands on her hips. "If I tell the mistress you'll get in trouble."

"No, I won't. I'm a guest."

"Guests ain't the same as family. And guests—proper guests—know their place and the limits of hospitality."

Tilda wasn't certain what to do. No one had ever caught her in the act. She offered a sigh, placed the jewels in the box, and set the box on the vanity. "If you'll excuse me, I think I'll go riding with Master George and leave you to your scrubbing and dusting."

But as she passed Gertie, the maid touched her arm. "The necklace?"

"I'm going to wear it back to my room to see if it goes with my green dinner dress."

It took all her self-control not to run down the hall. Even with her bedroom door closed Tilda didn't feel safe.

This wasn't good. Not good at all.

But then she got an idea.

She removed the necklace and slipped it into the waistband of her skirt.

Then she rang for Dottie.

"Do you really want to see where I sleep?" Dottie asked.

"I'm interested in everything at the manor." Tilda leaned forward, confidentially. "I know it's not proper, but doesn't that make it exciting?"

Dottie looked uncertain. "I suppose it won't hurt. Come on."

Tilda followed Dottie up the back stairs to the second floor above ground. There wasn't much to it but a long hallway bisecting the space with rooms on either side. There was a door at the end of the hall.

"Where's that go?"

"To the rooms of the female staff. These first rooms belong to the male servants. Mrs. Camden locks the door between us at night."

"Why?"

"So we're kept safe."

"From the men?"

She nodded.

"But certainly if you work with these fellows day after day, you can trust them."

Dottie's face lit up. "That's what I've always thought. The lockin' seems rather silly to me. Besides, we have to walk right past their rooms to get to ours, so if there was a bad one in the bunch . . ."

Dottie's face clouded, making Tilda wonder if she'd already suffered a bad experience. She was ready to commiserate. Being a housemaid in officers' quarters wasn't that different from being a maid in a manor. Men thought they could take liberties.

But Dottie didn't say any more, and moved on past the men's rooms, through the hallway door, stopping at a room on the right. "This is my room. And Molly's and Ma's are across the hall."

Now that Tilda was this far, she was truly curious. As expected there wasn't much to the room: a narrow bed, a dresser, some hooks on the wall, and a washbasin on a stand.

Dottie moved to the window. "At least I can see out now. When I was a tweeny, my room was in the attic with no window at all. But now that I was moved up to under-housemaid—"

"And lady's maid to me . . ."

Dottie smiled. "Prissy, Sally, and Gertie don't like my promotion much, but I don't care. I work as hard as they do, if not harder. It wasn't like I ever expected to act as a lady's maid. Your visit gave me that chance and I thank you for it."

Tilda nodded, discomfited by the word *visit*.

Then she remembered her reason for wanting to see the maid's quarters. "Since Gertie is the head housemaid, I bet she has a bigger room."

"Not really."

"It has to be bigger. Show me."

Dottie hesitated.

"Come on, it will just take a minute."

They returned to the hall and Dottie pointed to a door across the way. "That's it."

Tilda started to open the door.

"No! Don't!"

Tilda put a finger to her lips. "I'll just slip in and out in order to take a look. You stay here."

"But—"

Tilda didn't wait for more discussion, but entered the room, closed the door, retrieved the necklace from her waistband, and stuffed it under the mattress. *You tell on me, I'll tell on you.*

Then she slipped out of the room and was greeted by a very relieved Dottie.

"You being up here was a bad idea. We need to get you back downstairs, where you belong."

Tilda couldn't have said it better herself.

Genevieve's mother adjusted the veil on Genevieve's riding hat, her eyes intent on the task as though getting the veil just-right was imperative. Genevieve found it a bit disconcerting to be so close to her mother, face to face. She noticed a delta of lines at the outer corners of her mother's eyes, and a deep furrow bisecting her brows. A worry line? Was *she* the cause of that line?

Mamma felt her scrutiny and stopped the primping. "What?"

"You're quite pretty," Genevieve said. And it wasn't a lie. Her mother was the prettier of the two of them. Genevieve took after her father and had inherited his soulful eyes and skin that had a tendency to blotch instead of blush.

The fresh blush on Mamma's cheeks took years off her face. "Thank you, my dear." She finished the final adjustment to the veil and continued her instruction. "After you've been riding for a while, find a nice spot where you can stop and dismount. Morgan will have to put his arms around your waist and help you down. There's nothing more sensuous than those few moments when a man lifts you to the ground."

Genevieve couldn't imagine her mother in such a situation. "Does the thought of it bring back memories?"

Together they walked towards the top of the stairway. "Very good ones. And don't be fresh."

"I didn't know Father rode."

"He didn't."

Once again Genevieve was made aware of her mother's many suitors before she married her father. Yet they weren't suitors from society, but from the working class. What would Genevieve's life have been like if Mamma had married one of those men? Genevieve certainly wouldn't be off to ride with a viscount who soon would be her husband.

Whether born to it or not, her mother had been quick to take on all the rules and accoutrements of wealth. Those who knew nothing of her past would never guess the measure of her humble roots.

Genevieve missed a step and grabbed her mother's arm. "It's this veil. If I'm riding, shouldn't I be able to see clearly?"

"The horse sees so you don't have to."

A top hat, veil to her nose, earrings, gloves, boots, a tight riding jacket, stirrup pantaloons, and an asymmetrical skirt designed for riding sidesaddle. It was ridiculous.

And now the longer right side of the skirt slipped off its button loop in the center back. "Help me, Mamma, or I'll trip and tumble down the rest of the stairs."

Her mother reattached the knee-loop on the back button, making the hem even. "There you are. Can you reach back and unhitch it when it's time to ride?"

Genevieve held the railing for support and felt for the button. "I can manage." As they reached the foyer she changed the subject. "What are you going to do while Morgan and I are riding?"

"Apparently Mrs. Weston, the dowager, and I are going to speak to the cook about the wedding menu."

"Shouldn't I be here for that?"

"Heavens no. Your job is to secure your connection to the groom so this wedding plays out as planned."

Secure my connection?

Dixon opened the front door, and Genevieve drew her mother through it, stepping away from the butler's hearing. "I thought the arrangement *was* secure."

"Oh it is—as much as anything can be—but I'll feel better when he's madly in love with you."

Self-doubt perched upon Genevieve's shoulders and dug in with sharp claws. "What if that never happens?"

"Love is not a necessity, daughter. Just a preference." Mamma kissed her on the cheek. "Have a nice ride, dear. A productive ride."

"Here, let me help you down."

As if scripted by Genevieve's mother, Morgan put his hands around her waist and lifted her to the ground. Unfortunately, as her feet touched, the heel of her boot caught the hem of her skirt and she stumbled. She heard a ripping sound. He saved her from a fall, but she was so discombobulated by the moment that she didn't have time to enjoy the contact.

"This is the second time I've tripped today," she said.

"Are you all right?"

"I blame this stupid veil," she said, "Mamma said I don't have to see, that the horse will see for me, but it's the before and after the ride I have to worry about." She feared she'd said too much. "Have I impressed you yet?"

He smiled. "Tis the best comeback from near disaster I have ever witnessed."

She curtsied. "Why thank you, Lord Weston."

"Shall we take a stroll? There's a quaint stone bridge up ahead."

"I adore quaint stone bridges."

She dutifully fastened her skirt on its back button, making her chances of tripping again less inevitable. He offered her his arm and they let the horses graze.

"Are you finding the manor to your liking?"

"From what little I've seen of it."

"You wish to see more?"

"I wish to see all of it. Every room."

He laughed. "I'm not certain *I've* seen every room. Remember, I too am a newcomer."

She was glad for the opened door. "What was your life like before you found out you were the heir?"

He stopped walking. "Would you like to see the mercantile?"

By the sparkle in his eyes, there was no way she could refuse. "I'd love to."

As soon as they entered the Summerfield Mercantile, an older woman squealed and ran to Morgan, enfolding him in a warm embrace.

"Morgan! Dear boy!"

He kissed her forehead, then turned her to face Genevieve. "Nana, this is Miss Farrow from America. Miss Farrow, this is my grandmother, Mary Hayward."

The meat of the infamous story of Morgan's father came back to her. Mary Hayward was the innocent woman who raised Morgan's father in London after her husband stole him from the Summerfield woods. The Weston family had thought Jack drowned until the secret had been revealed, elevating Jack from shopkeeper to earl.

Mrs. Hayward bobbed a curtsy. "Nice to meet you, Miss Farrow. I'm ever so happy you're going to marry my grandson, for there's no finer man in all England."

"She says the same thing when my father is here—about him."

"You are both fine men," she said. "Being proud is my right and privilege."

"You have every right to be proud," Genevieve said. She looked around the store. "So this is the mercantile."

Mrs. Hayward scurried behind the counter. "This is it. Proud as punch I am of how it's doing too. I'd never run a shop before coming to Summerfield, but I find I like the position."

"And you're doing a fine job of it." Morgan straightened a display of tobacco tins.

Another woman appeared in the doorway that led to the back. "Morgan! How nice to see you."

He kissed her cheeks, then made this new introduction. "Miss Farrow, this is Rose Wilson, a dear family friend who's worked at the store with us since I was a child. She's like one of the family."

"I happily accept the designation." Rose's cheeks complemented her name. "Nice to meet you, Miss Farrow."

The easy pleasure shared between the three increased Genevieve's desire to become a part of their family.

"How is business?" Morgan asked.

"Steady. But enough about the store," Mrs. Hayward said. "I'm ever so pleased all my grandchildren are doing so well. Lila is happily married and now you are happily engaged." She looked to Genevieve. "How are the wedding plans coming along?"

"Much was arranged before my mother and I left New York. I expect my dress and trousseau to arrive from Paris any day. Mamma ordered gowns enough to last into the next century."

"She's obviously pleased with the match?"

"Of course." She thought of an oft-used tag line. "She says it's what my father would have wanted."

"*She* says?" Mrs. Hayward asked.

Genevieve kicked herself for creating doubt. "Mamma is the more ambitious of us two."

Morgan's eyebrows dipped. "But your father was very successful in business. Certainly that required a great deal of ambition."

Genevieve found the right words. "Mamma is the more *socially* ambitious of us two."

Rose laughed. "If not for women pursuing social interaction, men might never emerge from their work."

"We'd emerge," Morgan said.

"To eat," Mrs. Hayward said. After they shared a laugh she said, "I am happy for your mother's social ambition because my Morgan is in need of a good wife."

"You think every man is in need of a good wife."

"Only because it's true." She pulled a box from a shelf. "Could I interest you in an embroidered handkerchief, Miss Farrow? Or perhaps a few yards of ribbon?"

Absolutely.

"She loves you very much," Genevieve told Morgan as they rode back to the manor.

He nodded. "Love is her specialty. And humility. She keeps me grounded."

"To have one grandmother be the dowager countess and the other a shopkeeper . . . tis a good balance, I think."

"Indeed it is. I am one of the lucky few who have been able to experience both sides of society."

"Do you prefer one over the other?"

He rode in a silence a few yards. "Oddly each offers its own restrictions."

"Such as?"

"With my title comes opportunities to travel and to experience fine things, but also vast responsibilities. Many people rely on us to succeed in order for *them* to succeed."

"I never thought of that. But you're right. Summerfield provides employment and land to farm for so many."

He continued his explanation. "Being a part of the working class means a different sort of responsibility—the responsibility to survive and create a good life for one's family. Yet in some ways being a shopkeeper afforded me more freedom of choice."

"In what way?"

He glanced at her, then looked away as though avoiding the answer. "Look, there's my brother-in-law up ahead. I want to introduce you."

As they rode towards the meeting, the unspoken answer sped through Genevieve's mind. As a shopkeeper Morgan could marry Molly. As an earl, he could not.

Genevieve set her insecurity aside and forced a smile.

"Hello there, Joseph, I would like you to meet my fiancée, Miss Genevieve Farrow. Genevieve, this is my brother-in-law, Joseph Kidd."

She remembered the family tree. "So you're married to Lady Lila?"

"I am."

"I can hardly wait to meet her."

"And she you. Now that we are back from London, we shall make that happen."

"I'd like that very much."

He touched the brim of his hat. "It's very nice to meet you, Miss Farrow. We will arrange to have you and your mother to dinner soon."

As soon as Mr. Kidd rode away, Morgan said, "You'll like Lila."

"Will she like me?"

"Why wouldn't she?"

His certainty eased her doubts. At least for the moment.

Molly examined the ripped hem of Miss Farrow's riding skirt. She tried to ignore that she'd ripped it while riding with Morgan.

"Truly, Molly, you don't have to repair the hem," Miss Farrow said. "I'm actually quite a skilled seamstress. I can do it myself."

Of course she was a skilled seamstress. What talents did this woman *not* possess?

"It's all right," Molly said, draping the skirt over her arm. "It's part of my job." She moved to the door.

"But you don't have—"

Molly slipped into the hallway and shut the door on yet another instance of Miss Farrow being kind.

There was only so much kindness she could bear.

Clarissa staggered from the stage after the final bows. It had taken all her strength just to get through the performance as her mind wasn't on the production, but on the details of her situation. Eviction loomed, Lila had seen Clarissa's disgusting apartment, and her maid was gone. In addition, the memories elicited by her grandmother's necklace were insistent, speaking to her of better times.

Suddenly, Mapes grabbed her arm and pulled her aside. "Could you look any more angry out there? Yer supposed to be one of the 'rapturous maidens', yet you look sick and annoyed. What's wrong with you?"

"I've had an off evening. Let's leave it at that." She pulled free of him and strode towards the dressing room, wanting out of her costume and makeup.

Unfortunately Mapes followed her. "None of us care what mood yer in. Yer an actress. Act. You keep this up, and you'll never be the lead."

A sudden truth made her whipped around to face him. "You're never going to help me get the lead, are you?"

He moved close and pinched her breast. "You knows the terms."

Clarissa slapped his hand away. "And I reject them. Completely and utterly." She escaped into the dressing room and went to her place at the mirror.

Mapes made sure they had every eye by following her, standing behind her, and leaning in so his mouth met her ear. "You knows the other side to the condition. Do you really want me to tell everyone who you are?"

Suddenly, it didn't matter. Clarissa hadn't wanted her family to find her and feel disgraced by her choice of the stage. But now . . .

Since Lila and Joseph knew the need to keep the secret lessened.

She looked at Mapes in the mirror and hissed at his reflection. "Go ahead. Tell. See if I care." Then she raised her voice and added, "Do what you want, but I will never, ever sleep with you."

The other chorus girls stopped what they were doing. Some applauded and others called out, "It's about time" and, "You can't always get what you want, *Mister* Mapes."

Clarissa saw his jaw tighten and his face turn a mottled red. This was not going to turn out well.

"Shut yer traps, ladies—*if* any of you can be called that. From my experience none of yous is rapturous and certainly there's not a maiden among you."

"And you're no gentleman," Clarissa said.

"Speaking of gentlemen and ladies," Mapes said, walking behind the girls' chairs. "You wants to know the real identity of Clara West?"

If the truth was coming out, Clarissa wanted to be the one to do it. She stood and faced her fellow actresses. "My real name is Miss Clarissa Weston. My uncle is the Earl of Summerfield."

After a moment of silence, the same question was asked by more than one of the women.

"If you's a lady then whatcha doing here?"

The question hit her like a blow. She wasn't a star and was never going to be a star. "That's a good question."

"So what's the answer?" another girl asked.

The answer was simple. She slid out of her chair and faced Mapes, digging her finger into his chest. "I quit."

Accompanied by the applause she had always craved, she exited the dressing room and walked out the stage door into the alley. Her heart pounded and her mind flashed warnings. *What are you doing? You need the money. You can't quit!*

Mapes ran after her. "You can't leave with the costume."

She hadn't realized she was wearing it. Thoughts of her own clothes hanging on pegs in the dressing room flashed into her mind. Yet she didn't dare go back. Instead she called to Mapes over her shoulder and hurried towards the street. "Watch me."

"That costume is worth a lot of money!"

"So am I."

Ooh. Good one, Clarissa.

Miss Clarissa Weston.

Clarissa didn't walk towards home, she marched through the streets as if she owned the world. For the first time in months she felt as if she was in control of her own life.

Two men stepped directly in her way.

"Move!"

One ran a hand up her arm. "Well, well, pretty lady. I'll pay you for a spin."

Clarissa suddenly realized she was wearing the heavy makeup of the stage. Her hair was not pulled back neatly, but was puffed out in an exaggerated poof of the carefree maidens in the play. Her dress was worn without a corset and was almost Grecian in its flowing comfort.

She stood out. She looked carefree and easy.

Loose.

She tried to side-step the men, but they moved with her.

"Come on, lass," said the second man, pointing to his cheek. "Set some of that lip rouge right here."

"Let me by. I want to get home."

"We don't need to go to yer house. We can do it in that alley over there. I ain't picky."

That was it. With a surge of strength, Lila pushed them both away. One stumbled and landed on the cobblestones. "Do you know who I am?"

"I know *what* you are," the first man said with a laugh as he pulled his friend to his feet.

"I am Miss Clarissa Weston. My uncle is the Earl of Summerfield."

The second man poked the first in the ribs. "And I's the Prince of Wales. Bow!" He swatted his friend on the shoulder. "Come on now. Bow to me!"

The friend offered a purposely wobbly bow.

"You want one too?" the man asked.

"Na, she wants you to kiss 'er ring."

"I'll kiss her whatever. Just watch."

The man lurched close but Clarissa stepped away. Then she noticed an audience had gathered. Their laughs and jeers made the back of her neck prickle.

She had to get out of there. Now.

She stormed past them all, ignoring those who bowed low or curtsied, mocking her.

She walked quickly until their laughter died away, then once out of sight, she ran the rest of the way home. Up the stairs. Into her room. She locked the door behind.

But as Clarissa started to light the lamp she thought better of it. If the landlord saw the light . . .

She fell onto the chair, totally spent. Quitting her job, running the gauntlet of the tough streets of London, coming back to the threat of eviction . . .

She heard a quiet knock on the door and held her breath. She didn't dare answer.

Yet the meekness of the knocking wasn't the landlord's style.

"Lady?"

It sounded like the girl on the stairs. Clarissa went to answer it, but hesitated. "Are you alone?"

"Course I is."

Clarissa unlocked the door, and the girl eyed her up and down. "You look different."

"It's my costume from the play."

"You all right? You ran by me so fast . . ." The girl looked past her into the room. "Why you sittin' in the dark? I 'ates the dark."

The severity of Clarissa's situation collided with its absurdity. The wealthy girl who grew up with everything now had nothing, had given up everything for nothing. "Come in and I'll light it."

As Clarissa lit a lamp the girl tentatively came inside, her eyes wide. "My oh my, don't this beat all. This place is 'normous."

Surely she was joking. "It's a horrible place. All crammed together. No room to move around."

The girl ran her hand over the metal footboard of the bed. "More room'n I ever 'ad. I canna remember e'er sleepin' in a bed."

Clarissa felt her heart fall to her toes. Her throat tightened. "What do you mean you've never slept in a bed?"

She held a hand over the quilt to touch it, but drew it away. "Probably did when I was born, but the stairs a'been my bed since I can remember."

"Where are your parents?"

"I don remember having a da, and Ma 'ad enough of me and left." She stared at the pillow.

"Left you alone?"

Beth shrugged.

Clarissa had seen children running around on the streets but hadn't given much thought to how they got there. She assumed they had family. And she'd passed this girl day after day. She'd known she was alone, but had handily ignored that fact.

How had she ignored what was so obvious? Was she truly that shallow and selfish?

The full weight of shame made Clarissa clear her throat. "How long ago did your mother leave you?"

"A long time. Years."

"How old are you?"

"I dunno."

Clarissa tried another track. "How old were you on the last birthday you remember?"

"I don know my birthday for sure. But I might be twelve. Maybe. Do you know your birthday?"

"December sixth." The girl started to put her bare feet into a pair of Clarissa's shoes. Her feet were black with dirt. "Come here, girl. Let's see what's under all that grime."

Clarissa poured some cold water from a pitcher into the wash basin and wet a cloth, rubbing it on a sliver of soap. As she stroked the girl's face, she saw the perfection of creamy skin and the enormity of beautiful hazel eyes. "Well, what do you know. There's a pretty girl under here."

"Me ma was pretty."

"I'm sure she was. Now wash your hands and arms."

The girl did as she was told. When she was finished, Clarissa moved the basin to the foot of a chair. "Now your legs and finally your feet."

What the girl really needed was a full bath, but without Agnes to haul the water this would have to do for now.

Thinking of Agnes made Clarissa glance at the maid's bed. Suddenly Clarissa saw a way to assuage the apathy and selfishness of her past. It was as though a door had been opened before her and she had the choice to step over the threshold into a new and better place.

She took the first step. "How would you like to sleep in the other bed?" Clarissa pointed to Agnes' mattress. "It's not as big as mine, but you're welcome to it."

The girl's mouth gaped open, and she approached the bed as if it were a holy relic. "Really? I can sleep 'ere?"

Her past disgrace wrapped around Clarissa like a wool blanket in the heat of summer. Yet since she had passed over the threshold it was time to shuck it off and kick it out of the way. "Of course you can." Another shame tapped her on the shoulder. "I don't even know your name. I've passed you every day and I don't know your name."

"It's Beth."

"Beth what?"

"Just Beth."

Clarissa held out her hand to shake. "Hello Beth. I'm Clarissa."

"Clarissa what?"

"Just Clarissa."

She thought of the girl's other needs and went to the food shelves. There wasn't much there, only some bread and old cheese. "Are you hungry?"

"I's always 'ungry."

Of course she was.

There was barely enough for one, much less two, but as soon as Clarissa brought two plates to the table, she slid both portions onto one, and set it in front of the girl. "*Bon appétit.*"

Beth took a bite, then looked up. "Ain't you eating?"

"I ate at the theatre. It's all for you."

Clarissa didn't need to eat, for she was already full.

Clarissa didn't know what awakened her, but when she opened her eyes she saw the moonlight illuminating Beth, curled up on the other bed, her arms cradling the makeshift doll. She'd kicked off the covers, her dress pulled over her knees and legs against the chill. The thought of her sleeping like this night after night in some dark corner, ripped a hole in Clarissa's heart.

She quietly went to her, pulling the covers over her shoulder, tucking her in. Beth didn't awaken, but let out a soft mew of pleasure. Clarissa gently moved her hair away from her face and found herself doing something she'd long ago left behind.

She prayed. For her situation, for her family.

And for a little girl named Beth.

Chapter Ten

"You're doing very well, Genevieve," Mrs. Weston said. "Did you ride in New York?"

Genevieve tried to get comfortable on the side saddle. "Quite the opposite, I'd never even sat on a horse until your nephew and I started corresponding."

"How does the one bring about the other?" Morgan asked.

"In my mother's mind my possible betrothal to a viscount who lived on a country estate made riding lessons mandatory. But I'm supposed to pretend I've been doing this all my life."

Mrs. Weston laughed. "Your honesty is refreshing."

"You'll catch on quick enough," George said.

"I never rode much either," Morgan said. "My sister Lila is the horsewoman."

George grinned at his mother. "Come, Mamma. Let's race to the signpost."

And they were off. "Care to join them?" Morgan asked.

"I don't dare."

He laughed. Continuing to walk, they followed the curve in the road and saw Mrs. Weston and George talking with a trio of farm workers along the edge of a field. They trotted to catch up.

Mrs. Weston did the honors. "Gentlemen, I would like to introduce you to Miss Farrow, come all the way from America to marry my nephew."

The men bowed and offered greetings.

"It's nice to meet you too," she said.

Mrs. Weston turned the nose of her horse to leave. "Let us know if your wife needs anything when the baby comes, Mr. Dalton."

"Thank you, ma'am. You're very kind."

As they rode on, Genevieve asked, "Do you know everyone who lives in the area?"

"George does," Mrs. Weston said. "And I am doing my best to catch up. It will be part of your job too."

The vastness of the responsibility overwhelmed. "Is Mr. Dalton a tenant farmer?"

"He is."

"His wife makes the best blackberry pie," George added.

His mother laughed. "Horses and eating are my son's most avid interests."

"What's wrong with that?" he asked.

"Schooling. You're missing your autumn half at Eton so you can be of help with the wedding and Miss Cavendish. But you *will* go to Oxford one day."

"I'd rather be here. I'm not going to be the earl anymore. That will be Morgan's job."

Genevieve had never really thought about George moving down in status when his cousin Morgan moved up as heir.

"We have that in common," Morgan said. "I disliked book learning too."

"See?" George said to his mother. "At least he got out of it permanently."

"I'll hear no more about it." Mrs. Weston pointed towards the cottage up ahead. "I see the dowager and the colonel are out and about."

"They're holding fishing poles. I want to fish too." George rode ahead, calling out to his grandmother and her husband.

"Do you like to fish, Miss Farrow?" Morgan asked.

"I've never tried."

"Your mother didn't anticipate the need and get you lessons?" Mrs. Weston said with a smile. "Tsk-tsk. She missed the mark on that one."

"I'll make sure she knows about the deficiency." It would be enjoyable to have one-up on her mother.

"We're so glad you stopped by and can go fishing with us," the dowager told Morgan and Genevieve. "But honestly I am glad Ruth insisted on taking George back to the house. Just having the two of you here gives us more time to get acquainted."

Colonel Cummings came out of a shed, holding a basket and more fishing poles.

"Are you ready for this?" Morgan asked Genevieve as he tied up their horses.

"Of course," she said, though she wasn't sure of it. "At least I hope I am."

"You'll do fine," the dowager said. "The day will be a success even if we don't catch a thing."

"Really?"

The colonel nodded. "You must understand, Miss Farrow, that fishing is just as much about the act of trying as the act of catching."

She laughed. "Try, I can do."

The four of them walked away from the cottage, into the woods. Soon Genevieve heard the rushing of a river ahead. "Are we close?"

"Closer than most families, my dear," the dowager said with a wink.

Her wit certainly kept Genevieve on her toes.

They reached the river and the colonel showed her how to press a worm onto a hook.

"Does that disgust you?" Morgan asked.

The feel of the squiggly, slimy thing was awful. "I can do it."

"Now drop your pole in the water and when you feel a tug, yank up fast."

The four of them took positions close, but not too close, together. The sound of the river, the shade of the trees, the blue of the sky . . .

"You're enjoying this, aren't you?" Morgan asked.

"I—" Genevieve felt a tug on her line. She yanked upwards. "I got one!"

Morgan and the colonel came running and helped Genevieve get the fish to shore, off the hook, and dropped into the basket where it desperately flapped about.

"I can't believe I did it!" she said.

The dowager beamed. "You're fishing like you've been doing it your entire life."

"Are you certain you haven't fished before?" Morgan asked.

"Not once." She plucked another worm from the lot, and pressed it onto the hook.

Morgan laughed. "Look at her! Ready for another one."

Keep 'em coming.

"Fishing?" Mrs. Farrow said to her daughter. "You went fishing?"

Miss Farrow handed her riding hat to her mother and began to unbutton her habit. Molly stood nearby to retrieve it. "Don't make it sound as though I did something repulsive."

Her mother's nose crinkled.

"I even caught one."

"Ladies don't fish."

"Excuse me, Mrs. Farrow," Molly said. "The dowager didn't know how to fish either, not until she married Colonel Cummings. But now I hear she truly enjoys it."

"Exactly," Miss Farrow said, handing Molly her jacket. "I should have taken lessons, Mamma. It was a huge oversight on your part."

Molly didn't know if she was teasing until Miss Farrow gave her a wink.

Her mother missed the signal and took the comment seriously. "Who would have expected such knowledge was necessary? I tried my best to cover every angle."

Miss Farrow stepped out of her riding skirt and pantaloons, and into lace-trimmed pantalets, a petticoat, and a bustle. Then Molly carefully lowered an afternoon dress over her head, being mindful of her hair.

"Actually, Morgan says he's not much of a rider either. His sister is the one who likes to ride."

"That's right," Molly said. "Actually, Lady Kidd's courtship with her husband began while they were out riding."

"Really," Miss Farrow said.

"Well, aren't you a font of knowledge," Mrs. Farrow said.

Molly realized she'd inserted herself into a private conversation. "Excuse me, ma'am."

Miss Farrow put a hand on her arm. "It's all right, Molly. I'm glad to learn the history of Summerfield, so feel free to share at will."

Mrs. Farrow moved to the door. "Come downstairs when you're presentable. Mrs. Weston and I are going to talk about our gowns for the wedding." She turned back to Molly. "Since you presume to know so much, do you know when that awful White-couple is going to leave? I find their presence disconcerting."

"Why?" Miss Farrow asked.

"I don't know exactly. But why are they even here? They are not actually guests of the Westons. They were chaperones for that girl. Shouldn't they be gone?" Mrs. Farrow looked to Molly.

"I'm sorry, ma'am. I don't have an answer for you."

"Hmph. How convenient."

What did that mean? But as soon as she left, Molly apologized again. "I'm sorry for being so forward, Miss Farrow."

"Not at all. I need a friend of the family to guide me through the maze that is Summerfield, and I feel very lucky to have you as that friend."

Wonderful. Simply wonderful.

If only Molly could hate her.

Molly's thoughts consumed her as she headed towards the back stairs. She didn't want to be Miss Farrow's friend. To think that Miss Farrow was heading downstairs to talk about the wedding . . . Every mention of the marriage added salt to Molly's wound. If only —

Molly pulled up short when a bedroom door opened directly in front of her and Morgan came out.

"Oh. Molly."

She didn't know whether to bob a curtsy or speak to him plainly, as she used to do. "I was just helping Miss Farrow after her outing. Your outing." How awkward.

"Remember when you and I used to go fishing?"

"If I remember correctly, we didn't do much fishing."

His eyes sought hers. "It was quite enjoyable — if memory serves."

Molly felt herself blush. "It does. It was."

He looked up and down the hallway, then said, "You're an extraordinary woman, to serve Miss Farrow like you're doing."

She took a step towards him, lowering her voice. "I am not extraordinary. I don't want to serve her. It kills me to hear about your marriage."

He reached out and touched her arm. "It kills me to have you so close, yet so far away."

The deepness of his gaze was intoxicating.

Yet this was getting them nowhere. Molly looked away then bobbed a curtsy. "If you'll excuse me, Lord Weston. I must check on my mother."

She tried to calmly complete her walk towards the back stairs, but when she reached the steps, she lifted her skirt and ran up. When she entered her room, she was out of breath and felt as if she would burst. She paced along the length of the bed and back again, her gait failing to keep up with her thoughts.

In spite of all logic, she still loved Morgan. Surely it was a punishment from God that she'd been placed in the position to serve his fiancée.

She stopped pacing as the time-worn inner reprimand began its chiding: *If you'd said yes to him the first time he proposed, you would have been married when he discovered his father was the earl. It would have been too late. Your hesitation cost you your happiness.*

"Stupid girl. Stupid, stupid girl!" She picked up the water pitcher and hurled it across the room. It crashed against the wall and broke into a hundred pieces.

"Mah?"

It was her mother, calling from the next room.

Molly left the mess where it was and went to her.

It was just one mess among many.

My, my, the plot thickens.

Upon hearing Molly and Morgan's voice down the hall, Tilda had ducked out of sight, into an alcove.

Molly's angry words still hung in the air: *I am not extraordinary. I don't want to serve her. It kills me to hear about your marriage.* Thanks to Dottie, Tilda knew Molly and Morgan had loved each other and had been close to marriage. That Molly still held feelings for Morgan was an interesting twist. And by all appearances, he had feelings for her too.

Tilda started when she heard the sound of some crockery crashing to its death overhead. She looked to the ceiling, and decided it could have come from Molly's room.

Now *that* was upset.

There was another noise in the hall, and Tilda glanced out to see Mrs. White, who surprised her by ducking into the alcove with her. "Interesting, isn't it?" she said.

She'd overheard Morgan and Molly too? "It certainly is complicated."

"Or not."

"Why not?"

Mrs. White offered a dramatic sigh of exasperation. "You stupid girl. Don't you see that you could use Molly and Morgan's love to your advantage? Don't you see that breaking up his engagement to Miss Farrow is to your advantage?"

"How?"

Mrs. White poinged Tilda's forehead with a finger. "If our blackmail is successful and Morgan isn't the heir then who is?"

Tilda thought a moment. "I don't know how these things work."

"If he's not the heir apparent then Mr. Weston is the heir presumptive, and when he dies, his son." She stared at Tilda. Waiting. "George?"

The knowledge hit her like a fist. "George would be the earl?"

"And since you and he are the same age and since you've taken a liking to him. . ."

I could marry him and . . . "No! I can't be a countess."

"Why not? This family is full of strange situations. A smart girl would play into them."

Just as she and Mrs. White moved into the hallway, Miss Farrow came out of her bedroom. "Miss Cavendish. Mrs. White. Did you see Miss Wallace go by?"

Tilda considered her answer, but only for a moment. "I did. She seemed very upset. Is something wrong?"

"I am not sure what I said or did, but I get the distinct feeling Miss Wallace doesn't like me."

Tilda's mind raced with everything Mrs. White had said. If Tilda was to marry George, it would makes things easier if

Miss Farrow and Morgan *didn't* marry. But before she could decide what to say, Mrs. White said it for her.

"If you don't mind me saying so, Miss, I think there are still feelings . . ." Mrs. White nodded towards Morgan's room.

"What are you talking about?"

Suddenly Gertie appeared in the hall. "Excuse me, Miss Farrow, but your mother wishes to speak with you."

Miss Farrow nodded once, then said to Tilda. "We will continue this discussion later?"

"Of course."

Tilda was left with Gertie glaring at her and Mrs. White egging her on.

She had much to ponder.

Clarissa woke to the sound of sweeping. She turned over in bed, "Agnes, can't you wait until I go to work?"

Then she remembered: she had no job, Agnes had left, and . . .

She sat upright and saw Beth, busy with the broom. "You don't have to do that."

"I don mind." Beth swept the dust onto a piece of newspaper before dropping it into the waste bucket.

Clarissa looked to Agnes's bed where Beth had slept. It was neatly made. "Did you sleep well?"

"Better'n I can e'er remember." She pointed to the shelves. "I was gonna make you somethun to eat, but couldn't find anythun."

"What say you and I go out and get something for breakfast?"

Beth nodded with enthusiasm.

"Let me get dressed." Even as Clarissa got out of bed, she was trying to remember how much money she had. It wasn't much. If only she'd gotten paid before quitting.

"'Ere, I'll 'elp you," Beth said.

With Beth's help Clarissa got dressed and was brushing her hair, when Beth pointed to the stack of hat boxes. "What are those?"

"I'll show you." What little girl didn't like to play dress up? Clarissa opened the first one and put it on. "What do you think?"

"Tis beautiful," Beth said with an awed voice. "I ne'er seen anythun so pretty."

"You try one." Clarissa opened another box and pulled out a pink bonnet with silk roses along the seam of the crown and brim. She hesitated just a moment before placing it on Beth's head, thinking of the effects of her filthy hair on the silk, but did it anyway. She tied the satin ribbon under her chin, slightly to the side and nudged Beth towards the dappled mirror on the wall. "Look at you."

The hat was too large, but seeing Beth's big blue eyes peering out from under the brim brought back memories of her own childhood. She'd had a child-sized hat for every occasion, frilly dresses with lacy petticoats and bloomers, and freshly polished boots and silk slippers worn with silk stockings.

"Try this on too." Clarissa got out Grandmamma's necklace and held it around Beth's neck.

"Ooh," the girl said.

"The proper jewelry makes an outfit."

Beth laughed. "I think this one's a bit too fancy for what I's wearing." She handed it back to Clarissa. "But I would like to try on another hat."

As Clarissa pulled out the third hat, there was a loud pound on the door. "Time's up, Miss West. Pay up or yer out."

Clarissa put a finger to her lips, warning Beth to be quiet.

But their silence was too late. "Break her down," the landlord yelled, and before Clarissa could pull Beth to safety, a man broke through the door and the two men were inside.

"Get out of here!" Clarissa yelled. "You can't be in here."

"Law says I can." He stepped aside so a third man could enter, "Get it all out but the furniture—that's mine."

A man gathered Clarissa's dresses from the hooks and piled them across his arms. "Put those back!" she yelled.

"He'll not put 'em back," the landlord said, and pulled her towards the door. "I warned you more'n once. Get down to the street, or I'll have Jed here carry you down."

"You canna take 'er things!" Beth yelled.

The landlord pointed to the girl, and the third man plucked Beth from the floor and took her outside, towards the stairs, with Beth kicking and flailing all the way.

"You leave her alone!" Clarissa yelled. She was torn between staying in the flat to protect her things and running after Beth. She chose the latter, getting outside in time to see the man drop Beth on the street.

"Are you all right?"

"I's fine," Beth said, though she rubbed her arm.

Suddenly, all Clarissa's possessions were on the street, tossed about as if they were rags. She wanted to cry, or hit someone, or . . .

Then a woman ran up to the dresses and pinched one, running away with it. "Hey! Stop that!"

But there was no stopping it. There was a feeding frenzy over her possession, and all Clarissa recovered were two hat boxes.

Clarissa saw Beth playing tug-o-war with another hat box, but she lost the battle when a boy slugged her in the side. Clarissa ran to the girl, helping her up. "Are you hurt?"

"I's all right." But then Beth lunged after another little girl carrying away a hat. The ribbon tore from the crown, with the thief winning possession.

Beth started to run after her, but Clarissa called her back, pulling her close. "Let it go."

When everything was gone, the landlord came out, fingering through Clarissa's jewelry box. Clarissa let go of Beth and snatched her grandmother's necklace away from him. "Give that to me."

He lurched for her, but Beth got in his way. "Gimme that," the girl said.

"Don't get in the middle of this, lass. I'll keep what I like. It's rightfully mine now."

Two men from the neighborhood ambled towards them. "How's it feel to be out on the streets, yer highness?" They mocked her with a low bow. "Dincha know her uncle is some earl?"

The landlord's eyes lit up. "Earl, is it?"

It was the wrong thing to say, for now the landlord wrapped his arms protectively around the jewelry box. "If yer uncle's the earl, whatcha doing here?"

"None of your business," she said.

"Wanna bet she's the black sheep?" one of the men said.

Beth pointed to an alley, "Look! There's one of yer dresses!" She ran after it.

A crowd gathered. All Clarissa wanted was to be away. She held the necklace in her palm and ran away with the two hatboxes.

"Want me to go after her?" she heard one of the men ask the landlord.

Clarissa ran faster, not daring to look back.

Clarissa wasn't certain when the notion to go home to Summerfield came about. But sometime between the chaos of the eviction and finding herself blocks away and winded from running, the notion of *home* invaded her thoughts and enveloped her entire being. It was as visceral and real as needing air in her lungs. Suddenly, she knew that in order to survive, she needed to breathe the life-giving air of home.

As soon as that knowledge took over, she became consumed with making it happen.

She stopped to regroup, leaning against a building. She had no money for a train ticket and no friend with a wagon or carriage who could give her a lift. She set the hatboxes on the ground and wiped the sweat from her brow. Only then did she realize she still clutched her grandmother's necklace.

She stared at it, seeing it as more than a piece of family history, but as a means of escape.

There was a pawn shop a block or two back; she remembered seeing its window of wares, and backtracked to its door.

Clarissa had never been in such a shop before, and was immediately assailed by the smells of age, dust, and desperation. There was little room to move, as goods were stacked high on either side of a small walkway, and hung from the ceiling, making her feel she was entering a lair of the precious and mundane. For the goods ranged from an iron pot that had seen much wear, to a red velvet cloak she could imagine worn to an opera.

"Help you, miss?"

The voice came from a man who blended in with the goods surrounding him. He too was a mixture of old and new, his wrinkled face being the former, and his jaunty blue cap, being the latter. His age was indeterminable. Somewhere between forty and dead.

"I do hope you can help me," she said. She set the hat boxes on the floor and draped the necklace from her hand.

The man's eyes lit up for a briefest of moments until he forced the excitement away for the sake of the deal. "Aye. Tis a nice enough piece, this is. May I?" He lifted it up, his fingernails crusted black, and his hands looking as though they hadn't met soap and water in a year. Suddenly, the realization that he was holding her grandmother's jewels, a necklace that brought back memories of the woman's darling face, her smile sparkling every bit as much as the gems . . .

Clarissa snatched the necklace back. "I'm sorry. I've changed my mind."

The look of anger that crossed the man's face made her want to leave as soon as possible. Yet she had to get money for the train.

She lifted the two hatboxes into the narrow opening that served as a counter. "Here. These. I want to sell these."

The man didn't even try to act pleased at the switch from jewels to hats. He knocked the lid off one, and peeked into the other with a sneer. "Don't have much call for fancy clothes."

She pointed at the cloak. "What about that cape over there?"

He grunted. "I took that in as a favor."

At his words, Clarissa changed the direction of her method. She offered him her best smile. "I would be ever so appreciative of you bestowing a favor upon me. I assure you the quality of the hats are beyond compare. They were handmade especially for me at Madame Lupine's. Surely you know the reputation of that millinery establishment?" She could see that he didn't know ostrich plumes from egret. "How much will you give me for them?"

He peered into the second box again, but Clarissa could tell it wasn't for the sake of seeing, but for the sake of buying time while he came up with a number. Finally, he dropped the lid into place and said, "A shilling."

"But I paid ten times that much—for each."

He shoved the boxes forward an inch. "Then take them back to the shop that made 'em."

Clarissa did her own calculation. "One pound."

"Two shillings."

"Thirty bob."

"Three and six."

This was absurd. "Twenty. For them both. Please."

He looked at her over his crooked glasses. "Yer tearing me heart out. Ten. And that's me final offer."

Weary of the whole thing she nodded, accepting the pitiful amount.

Money was exchanged, and Clarissa was eased of her bulky burden. But more importantly she still had Grandmamma's necklace and would soon be home.

As the train neared the Summerfield station, the word *home* that had spurred Clarissa to a decision in London suddenly grew less distinct and less inviting.

The thought of seeing her parents and her grandmother again overwhelmed. She'd told them so many lies, defying them all by going on the stage when she'd promised she wouldn't. They thought she was traveling through Europe with the Duvalls. Father approved. He'd sent her a small stipend every month for expenses.

But she'd only stayed with the Duvalls for six weeks, finding their frivolity grating upon constant contact. When they'd gone off to Europe Clarissa had taken the opportunity to get her own flat in London.

The surge of independence had been exhilarating, like standing on the top of a mountain and feeling that everything that could be seen was hers for the taking. She would have loved to share her elation with her parents but they would have ordered her home. Single women did not live alone — and having Agnes with her didn't count as a proper chaperon.

She had planned to contact them after she was a star on the stage. But then, in a surge of celebration, she'd overspent the money Father sent, fell into debt, owed rent, and she and Agnes had been forced to move to a cheaper place. Her humiliation — and location far from the bank where her father sent her drafts — led her to live on the income *she* created.

Her first job at the Jolly was humiliating. It was a deplorable dance hall, and Clarissa never did get used to the way the men in the audience hooted and leered at her. Getting a part at the Savoy — even if it was only in the chorus — was a huge step up.

But of course that hadn't turned out well either.

The point of her mental discourse was that she'd not accomplished a single positive thing in London. She'd lied, connived, and dived from the position of fine lady to woman of disgrace. She owned only the dress on her back, and one very fancy necklace. She couldn't show up at Summerfield Manor and expect to resume her life as it was. They had all moved on.

As had she. She was not the same spoiled, naive girl who'd left home. The spoiled part was still partially intact, but her naivety had abandoned her the moment she'd first received a bill she could not pay. Of course that had not stopped her from ordering new hats.

Old habits were very hard to break.

Since I've made such a mess of things perhaps I should stay on the train and head back to London.

Her impulsive thought was quickly discarded, as there was nothing for her there.

As there was little more for her in Summerfield.

Clarissa ran a hand across her brow, the confusion and need for a decision causing her head to ache. All she wanted tonight was something to eat, a bath, and a soft bed.

Suddenly, the memory of Lila's note came back to her: *You are always welcome at Crompton Hall.*

No. It was a ridiculous notion. Lila was her nemesis. She was sweet and kind, humble and caring. Clarissa had yelled at her at Harrods's, publicly accusing her of stealing Clarissa's husband, family, and even her future.

Her headache intensified, yet she had to go to Lila's.

"What other choice do I have?"

The man in the seat across the aisle looked at her. "Miss?"

"Never mind."

The train slowed for the station. Her time for weighing her options was up.

Her last decision had to be played out.

So help me God.

It was nearly dark as Clarissa followed the row of trees bordering the drive that led to Crompton Hall. She'd walked from the train station, not daring to hire a wagon or carriage lest she be recognized.

Clarissa could honestly say she had never in her entire life walked from the village of Summerfield to Crompton Hall. It was a distance that tested a woman's soles and perseverance. Clarissa's entire torso was sore from the rubbing of her corset against her seriously tested lungs.

Upon reaching the front door she knew she couldn't walk another step. It took all her strength to knock. At this point all shame was gone. She didn't care who answered, as long as her journey could finally be over.

The door opened and the butler looked her over, his face revealing his shock. "Miss Weston?"

Her mouth was completely dry, but she managed. "Is Lila here?"

"Yes, Lady Lila is at home."

Normally, the correction would have annoyed her, but in her weariness she didn't have the energy to be annoyed. "Could you ask her if she'd see me, please?"

He nodded once, then opened the door for her to enter. "Please wait in the drawing room."

Clarissa fell into the first chair she came to. The last time she'd slept—just last night—seemed weeks ago. Had she really awakened this morning with Beth in the room with her and—

"Beth!" Clarissa burst out of the chair, spurred by the memory of the little girl. The last time she'd seen Beth, she was running after one of Clarissa's dresses. Clarissa sank back in the chair with the added weight of guilt. "I left her. I left her behind."

The fact she hadn't thought of Beth before now damned her. Her mind began to make excuses: she'd needed to flee the landlord and the taunting men, she'd needed to sell her hats to get a train ticket, and she'd needed to sort through the decision to go home or to Crompton Hall.

Yet to have no thought of the homeless girl she'd left behind . . .

"Clarissa?"

With difficulty Clarissa rose from a chair. "Surprise."

Lila went to her, kissing her cheek. "You're here."

Clarissa couldn't meet her gaze. "That, I am."

There was an awkward moment that hung heavy with questions. Clarissa sighed and got it over with. "I was evicted and was left with nothing but the clothes on my back. I quit my job. And Agnes left me."

Lila led her to sit with her on a settee. "How horrible for you."

"Yes, it was. Quite."

"I'm so sorry for your troubles, but I am very glad to see you here."

"It seemed the best alternative as I don't want to go back to Summerfield Manor. Not yet."

"Of course. You are very welcome here."

Clarissa could only nod. It was humiliating to come like a beggar off the streets. Yet that's just what she was.

"I'm sure you're hungry. Please come join us for dinner."

The thought of sitting down with Joseph and Lord Newley was beyond bearable. "I don't think so," Clarissa said. "I know I look a fright and I also know what an imposition this is."

"It's no such thing, I'm glad you came," Lila said. "But I will abide by your wishes." She moved to the bell pull to call for the housekeeper. "I'll let Mrs. Crank get you settled in upstairs. Would you like a tray of dinner brought up?"

"That would be nice." She remembered promising Beth to go out to breakfast, and had given the girl her portion of their meager dinner the night before. Her stomach roiled at the lack of food.

Mrs. Crank appeared in the doorway and did a double-take at seeing Clarissa. "Would you please take Miss Weston to the west bedroom and see to it she gets anything she needs, including a dinner tray."

"Of course."

"What I'd really like is a bath."

Mrs. Crank looked her over, and her eyebrows rose in distaste.

"Then a bath you will have," Lila said. "And bring Miss Weston some of my clothes."

"I'll see what I can do, your ladyship," Mrs. Crank said. With a sniff, she looked to Clarissa. "Come with me."

As Clarissa followed the housekeeper to the stairs, she paused in front of Lila. "Thank you. For everything."

She was weary enough to be totally sincere.

Clarissa ate every bite of her dinner. She remembered many a meal at the manor where she'd picked at her food, turning her nose up at Brussels sprouts and even potatoes if Mrs. McDeer didn't cook them the way she liked. There would be no more of that.

Her hip bath had been emptied and cleared away, and the covers of the bed folded down. Clarissa was just about to blow out the candle when there was a knock on the door. "Come in."

It was Lila. "Have all your needs been met?"

"You've been very kind." She climbed into bed. "Only one need left: sleep. I don't think I've ever been so tired."

"You've been through so much."

Clarissa snuggled into the pillow, her eyes heavy.

Lila blew out the light. "I'll see you in the morning then. Sweet dreams."

But before Lila left there was one more thing Clarissa had to say, "Lila?"

She turned back from the door. "Yes?"

"I don't want my family to know I'm here. Not yet."

Lila nodded. "But I thank God you *are* here. Safely here."

"Me too."

Before the door could click shut, Clarissa fell asleep.

Chapter Eleven

Clarissa stood at the window of the drawing room at Crompton Hall enjoying the view of the winding drive and the gardens nearby. Just looking out a window was an odd sensation. During the last awful months in London she'd purposely kept her gaze within the safe confines of her room—repulsive as it was. Even if she'd wanted to see out, the one small window had been grimy with the soot and smoke of poverty.

The expanse of the Summerfield countryside made her want to run outside and twirl in a dance of freedom and fresh air.

Yet, she wasn't ready to be confronted by her family regarding the truth of how she'd mishandled her life since leaving them. She didn't want them to know how she had suffered because of her own mistakes. No one outside the confines of Crompton Hall could know she was back.

At the sound of someone clearing their throat. Clarissa turned. Mrs. Crank stood in the doorway. "Is there something I can do for you, Miss Weston?"

"Nothing, thank you."

Her lip curled the smallest bit. "Will you be staying long?"

Subtle. "Am I too much trouble for you?"

"Of course not, miss. I didn't mean to imply —"

"Of course you did."

They shared an awkward pause, then Clarissa turned back to the view. Insufferable woman. Back home, if Mrs. Camden had ever been so rude to a guest she would have been dismissed on the spot.

Hearing movement behind her, she said with a sigh, "Mrs. Crank, really, I'm staying and there's nothing you can do—"

"I'm glad you're staying," Joseph said.

Clarissa spun around. "I'm sorry. I thought you were the housekeeper."

"Is she being difficult?"

Nothing I can't handle. "She seems as cranky as her name."

He entered the room, glancing behind himself as if to check to make certain the woman wasn't lurking close by. "She's had free rein of the house since my mother died and doesn't take well to guests or any disruption to the status quo."

"So I've noticed."

He traced the back of a chair with a finger. "Actually, she doesn't take too well to anyone. I'm scared to death of her."

It felt good to laugh.

"Lila wishes for me to extend her apologies this morning. After breakfast her stomach felt a bit unsettled."

"Is she all right?"

"Perfectly."

She felt the need for her own apology. "And I must apologize for sleeping so long and missing both of you at breakfast."

"Did you receive a tray?"

She put a hand on her midsection. "I am very properly fed."

"Capital. Now please sit and tell me how you're faring."

They sat across from each other, with a short expanse of Aubusson rug between. "I'm very thankful you've taken me in."

"Our door is always open to you."

"You're very kind."

He removed a piece of lint from his trouser. "Lila is the kind one."

"So you weren't keen on me being here?"

He smoothed his trouser. "You and I did not part London on agreeable terms."

The seduction. Oh. That. "Please forgive me for my misguided actions. I'm embarrassed to remember it."

"As am I."

His candid words added to her discomfort and she rose, feeling the need to cross the stage of this drawing room before she said her next lines.

Lines. Stage. So was the root of the problem.

She stood in front of the fireplace and faced him. "Would you like to hear an awful truth?"

"If you'd like to tell me."

"During the past year it feels as though I've been living in the midst of a never-ending play. It's as though each movement, each bit of dialogue, each setting and prop, was a predetermined portion of a theatrical performance. I've been an actress in my own production."

He smiled. "'All the world's a stage, and all the men and women merely players'?"

"Indeed. It appears Shakespeare was correct."

"Was *your* play successful?"

"Not really." She might as well state it plain. "Not at all."

His smile faded. "I'm very sorry to hear that."

There was pity in his voice, yet instead of decrying it, she embraced it. "I made a mess of things, Joseph. Nothing turned out as I expected or hoped."

"I'm sorry."

Her need for pity quickly evaporated. She turned towards the high mantel and placed her hands upon the heavy molding, leaning her forehead against it. "If only we'd married."

She'd expected some sympathy for her words, so was surprised when he said, "We would have made each other miserable."

She whirled around to face him. "You think so little of me?"

He stood. "It has nothing to do with you or even with me—on our own. It's the combination that was wrong. Chocolate and lamb are good on their own, but together . . ."

"Which am I? The chocolate or the lamb?"

He offered a smile. "The down-to-it is that I would not have been enough for you, and you would have been too much for me."

She let this sink in but a moment. Then she laughed. "I do believe you're right."

The tension left the room like smoke out a chimney, allowing Clarissa to return to her seat. She drew in a fresh breath and looked up at the painting above the mantel. "That's your mother, is it not?"

"It is."

"She was beautiful."

"I wish I'd known her. She died of childbed fever soon after I was born."

"How tragic."

"For all of us."

The talk of a birth made Clarissa think of Lila. "Are you eager for your own children one day?"

"Eager. And petrified."

"Why the latter?"

"I don't know how to be a father."

"No one does. And your father didn't know how to be a father when he was left alone with you. But he did it. Seems to me you turned out well enough."

"Why thank you." With one last glance at his mother's portrait, he said, "Lila will be a wonderful mother. She's giving and kind, thinking of others over herself."

The fact those qualities could never be said about herself, made Clarissa cross. Lila had the good attributes, the man, the house, *and* the promising future.

Life was not fair.

"Would you like to see the nursery?" Joseph asked.

"Nursery? Is Lila—?"

"Not yet. But since she was used to working at the mercantile every day, she found this new life of leisure quite boring. Longing for a project, we decided to make a room ready for the time when God graces us with a child."

"Lila is always the optimist."

He gave her a stern look as he walked out of the room. "You might try it some time."

"Tis a lovely space," Clarissa said, looking across the room that would one day house Lila and Joseph's children.

"I take none of the credit," Joseph said. "Lila has taken it upon herself to make the choices. I offered her the use of a designer from London, but I think she feels more comfortable running the ideas past me alone."

"And you are willing to do whatever she wants."

"And more."

His blush was precious but made her jealous. She'd spent most of her life able to make people do her bidding. But had they done so willingly or only because of her coercion?

They heard footfalls in the hall.

The village carpenter Timothy Billings walked in. His eyes grew large.

"Miss Weston! You're back!"

Clarissa pressed down her initial rise of panic. "Hello, Mr. Billings. And I am not back. Not really."

Joseph rushed to explain. "Miss Weston has returned from London, but prefers to stay with us at Crompton Hall until she determines the right time to make her return known to others."

Although he had been tactful, Clarissa added her own addendum. "I'm hiding from my family until I feel brave enough to face them."

Timothy's eyebrows rose. "My lips are sealed."

She changed the subject. "So, Mr. Billings. What are you doing here?"

He raised the box he was carrying. "I brought some drawer pulls for Lady Kidd's approval."

Clarissa looked around the room with new clarity. "You built all these cabinets and furniture?"

"My father and I did. As per Lady Kidd's design."

The butler appeared at the door to the room. "If you'll excuse me, Mister Kidd, your father would like a word with you regarding a business matter."

"I'll be right there." Joseph nodded to the pair. "I'll tell Lady Kidd you're here, Mr. Billings. If you'll excuse me?"

"Of course," they both said.

There was an awkward moment of silence and Clarissa realized it wasn't proper for her to be left alone with a man, even if he was just Timothy.

"Perhaps I should come back later?" he asked.

So he'd realized it too. The notion of making him go seemed ridiculous. During her year away, propriety had taken a backseat to survival. "May I see the pulls?" she asked, if only to create a segue.

He opened the box and pulled out shiny brass pulls with ornamental back plates. "Do you think Lady Kidd will like them?"

"I can't imagine why not." She crossed the room. "Talk with me, Mr. Billings. Give me the news of the village."

"I'm afraid our meager news pales when compared to your adventures."

She drew in a breath. He knew about her life?

He ran a hand across the top of the dresser as if testing its grain. "How were the great capitals of Europe?"

Oh. Those adventures. "Old, crowded, and full of people I couldn't understand."

He laughed. "Sounds like Summerfield — but for the crowded part."

She ran a finger along a piece of molding. There was no dust. "Actually, I've been in London for quite a time." She looked at him and added, "On my own."

He covered his look of surprise, "Did you enjoy it?"

"I did not." She strode to the window and pulled the lace curtain aside. "In truth, I made quite a mess of things." The time seemed right to ask another question. "How is my family?"

"Haven't you kept in touch?"

"It's hard to do so while traveling."

He nodded, then said, "You do know your cousin is getting married, yes?"

Lila *was* married — to Clarissa's old fiancé.

"The viscount?" Timothy said.

It took her a moment. "Morgan? Who is he marrying?"

"An American heiress."

An American? How odd. Yet considering that Morgan had once been in love with a maid, an American heiress was certainly a step in the right direction. "Why an American? How did they ever meet?"

"I'm sure I don't know. But she has arrived with her mother. The wedding is in a few weeks."

The thought of her own mother, planning the wedding of her nephew, was bittersweet. An eon ago she was looking forward to planning Clarissa's wedding.

"There's another visitor at the manor too. The goddaughter of Colonel Cummings."

"I didn't know he had a goddaughter."

"Apparently, no one did. Her name is Tilda Cavendish. She's an orphan. Her father served in the army with the colonel."

Clarissa's thoughts returned to the orphan she'd left behind, then scurried back to the present. "How long is she staying?"

"No one knows — at least no one in the village."

"How old is she?"

"Sixteen or so. About the same age as Master George."

Clarissa put two and two together. Or rather one and one. "I bet she'd love to put her hooks into my brother."

Timothy shrugged. "I wouldn't know anything about that."

"Speaking of . . . how is George?"

"He's grown a foot and is still focused on horses."

George had always been more interested in horses than people. Although their interests had been disparate, she felt a twinge of wistfulness at the thought of her little brother.

"Do you miss them?" he asked.

"I haven't let myself."

"Until now?"

He was very perceptive. She'd spoken more words to Timothy during this one meeting than she had in their entire lives.

"If I may ask about the secrecy? I know your family would be ever so pleased to see you."

She ignored his question and sat in an oak rocking chair. "This nursery . . . I've never felt very maternal. I always thought I'd have children because it was expected of me, but I have never experienced motherly feelings." She added under her breath, "Never experienced them as a recipient much either." At his look of surprise, she waved a hand. "I *am* in a confessional mood, aren't I?" She took a deep breath. "Must be the fresh air."

She stood and unrolled a carpet a bit with her foot. It was woven with pale green and gold colors that complemented the walls perfectly. "It's time I ask you a few personal questions, Mr. Billings."

"Tit for tat, is it?"

"'Tis only fair."

He nodded. "Ask away."

He was so charming she hesitated. Yet she wanted an answer. "Isn't it awkward working here when you were in love with Lila?"

"No," he said, but immediately changed his answer. "Actually, yes, it is hard. But I believe things happen for a reason. Lila and Mr. Kidd were in love even before they knew she was the daughter of an earl. They loved each other in spite of an impossible situation, until God made it possible."

"You act as though God has this grand plan for everyone's life." *There* was a new notion.

"Perhaps not grand in the world's sense, but a plan? Yes."

"Really, Mr. Billings. So God planned for me to go to London and muck up my life?"

"No. You did that."

She laughed.

He lifted a finger, wanting to continue. "God allows us free will to choose His way or reject it."

"Are you implying His plan did not involve me living the life I led?"

"All I know is that He will use whatever has happened for good."

"You make it sound so destined."

"I don't believe in destiny as if we don't have a choice. I believe in purpose. We each have a unique God-given purpose. The trick is to find out what it is."

"Some trick."

"Not really. Coming home is always the right road towards your purpose. You can't branch out until you return to your roots."

She snickered. "My family may think otherwise."

He shook his head as if he knew another truth. "When the time is right you *can* go to them and make everything right."

"You make it sound so simple. As if they'll forgive me for going against their wishes, wasting their money, lying to them, and causing them disgrace." His eyebrow raised, yet he seemed to sincerely care. For that reason she continued, "I was an actress. I performed on the stage."

He nodded once. "I'd heard you had that interest."

"A forbidden interest."

"Were you successful?"

"No." That one word could sum up her career. Yet it also provided some release. "There is no future for me there."

"All the more reason to come home and start again. You've not disgraced your family. You've gone after a dream. That it didn't work out as you planned is not shameful. Trying took courage."

She loved how he seemed so certain. "You have my life figured out better than I do."

"I have little figured out, but I know God does. He puts people in the right place at the right time and links them together so they can move forward and find out what might come next."

Next was all she had.

Tilda peered down from the upstairs railing and saw the Whites in the foyer — with their baggage.

"Mrs. White!"

She knew it wasn't ladylike to call out like that — as confirmed by the disapproving look from Mr. Dixon — but Tilda didn't care. She raced down the stairs.

"You're leaving?" Tilda asked. She watched through the open door as Mr. White put their luggage in a carriage.

"We are." Mrs. White touched Tilda's cheek. "We achieved what we wanted to achieve here.

Tilda read into her words. "It's done?"

"Yes, our visit is done," Mrs. White said. She kissed Tilda's cheek. "Take care of yourself, girl. And best of luck in your own . . . endeavors. And you're welcome."

"What for?"

She smirked and leaned close. "You can thank me for planting the seed of discontent in Miss Farrow's mind about Morgan's feelings for Molly. If you end up winning George, I expect an invite to the wedding."

And then they were gone. Meaning the money was paid.

"Is there something I can help you with, Miss Cavendish?" Dixon asked.

"Not a thing," she said.

The next step would be hers alone.

Morgan paused on the back stairway, leading below stairs. "I'm not sure we should venture down here."

"It is a part of *your* house," Genevieve said, though it did feel like a foreign place. Looked like it too. The stairway was utterly plain compared to the extravagant carved and carpeted staircase at the front of the house.

He stood on a step and faced her. "You say this is my house, but it doesn't feel like it. It's not a house at all. It's a museum. I showed you all twenty-five of the bedrooms. They're all pristine, untouchable, and fancy."

For some reason his last word struck her as humorous. "I believe 'elegant' might be a better word."

"Either way this house is a museum."

"A museum where a family lives. Your family."

Eventually our family.

He glanced towards the bottom of the stairs where sounds of a busy kitchen could be heard. "Is it possible to enjoy something and despise it at the same time?"

She could tell it was really bothering him. "You tell me."

A deep sigh was his answer. "Well, come on then. Let's go explore the dungeon."

Two housemaids walked down the long passageway, chatting. When they saw Morgan they put their backs to the wall and lowered their eyes.

"Good morning, ladies."

They bobbed a curtsy. "Good morning, my lord. Miss."

Morgan and Genevieve walked past a series of rooms that looked to be offices, a small sitting room, some storage vestibules, and a laundry where great steaming vats were manned by one woman, while another wrung fabric dry, and another ironed a sheet. Again, the ladies stopped their work and nodded. Genevieve couldn't imagine the constant washing and ironing that was involved in such a house.

They passed a dining room containing a long, but simple table with chairs. "This must be where the servants take their meals," she said.

Suddenly, a bell rang nearby. Along the wall a series of bells were mounted, each one marked with a title: Dining,

Study, Morning Room, Drawing Room, Music Room, Library, Foyer, and all the bedrooms.

"I'll check," came a voice. Then Molly came out of the kitchen, and upon seeing them, pulled up short. "Morgan," she said. "I mean, my lord. Miss Farrow."

Oddly, Morgan blushed. "Molly." He looked at her, then away.

The moment that passed between them made Genevieve's insides contract. She felt the immediate need to break the moment. "Were you aware that Miss Wallace has kindly agreed to take on the job as my lady's maid?"

"So she told me."

For the first time Molly looked at Genevieve, then back to Morgan. "I am enjoying getting to know Miss Farrow. Congratulations on your engagement, my lord."

Morgan's face turned bright red. "Yes, well . . ."

A bell on the wall rang again and Molly looked to see which one. "If you'll excuse me." She stepped into the kitchen. "Miss Albers, it's Mrs. Weston ringing for you."

An older lady's maid came out of the kitchen, eating a cookie. She put the food behind her back, greeted them, then hurried to answer the call. Molly followed her towards the back stairs.

Morgan just stood there, his eyes staring at nothing. Genevieve wasn't sure what to do or say. Finally, she managed, "It's all quite interesting."

Her words brought him out of his daze. "What?"

She pointed to the row of bells. "It's quite interesting, all this."

He nodded, then led her into the kitchen.

Quite interesting indeed.

☙

Molly burst into her mother's room, causing Dottie to spill Ma's tea.

"I'm leaving!" she proclaimed.

"Leaving where?" Dottie asked.

"Leaving Summerfield Manor. I'm going back to London."

Ma shook her head. "No."

Molly forced herself to calm down. She sat on the bed and took her hand. The words she needed to say stuck in her throat, yet the emotion behind them expanded and forced them out. "I'm sorry, Ma. But I can't be here any longer and watch Morgan and Miss Farrow. It's too much to bear."

"Nee you."

"You don't need me anymore. You're making fabulous progress and you have Dot here. And Dr. Peter even mentioned you going down to the kitchen in a week or so."

Ma shook her head. "Say."

"I can't stay. I have to go."

"When?" Dottie asked.

The direct question forced Molly to make a decision. "Now." She kissed her mother, then stood. "Right now."

Dottie stood too. "But Mol, we just got you back. We don't want to lose you to London again."

"You won't lose me," she said, her hand on the doorknob. "I'm not hiding this time. This time you'll all know where I am, I'll visit, and maybe you can visit, and . . ." It came down to this. "I have to leave this place for my own sanity. I'll send a letter telling you I arrived home safely."

"But this is your home."

Molly swirled around to face her sister. "No, it's not. Never will be. Never can be."

With that, she left her mother's room and went next door to pack.

Tilda did a double-take. Molly Wallace was leaving with a suitcase? Out a side door?

Suddenly, the implication of her departure pushed forward. Molly couldn't leave. She was a key player in the plan that could be playing out this very day, in this very manor.

Could be. If Tilda pursued it.

Or could not be, if Tilda left it alone.

Without further thought, Tilda ran outside after her. "Miss Wallace!"

Molly stopped, and a flash of annoyance crossed her face before she applied a polite smile, "Yes, Miss Cavendish?"

"You're leaving?"

"I am. My mother's health has improved and I—"

"You can't leave."

Molly studied Tilda's face. "Can't?"

Tilda's heart pounded with the knowledge of what she was about to say. The notion that she could stop before she started came. And went. She looked around for prying ears. "Come with me." She led Molly to the far side of a row of tall bushes.

"Really, Miss Cavendish. I want to catch the afternoon train and I don't have time to waste."

"You don't have time to listen about a plan that will allow you to marry Morgan Weston?"

Tilda took pleasure in the initial shocked expression on Molly's face. She was disappointed as Molly's shock turned to indifference. "Why would I want to do that?"

"Because you love him."

Molly fiddled with the handle on her suitcase. "How can you say such a thing?"

"Because I have eyes." Tilda paused a moment. "And ears."

Molly looked up then away. "Tis none of your business."

"It's too complicated to tell you everything right now, but the point is, it is my business. And yours."

Molly shook her head and began to walk away. Tilda grabbed her arm and lowered her voice. "Morgan is not the earl's son. Mr. White is his true father."

Molly's brow furrowed as she shook Tilda's hand away. "What are you talking about?"

And here we go . . . Tilda gave a shortened version of the facts, ending with the extortion of the Whites.

"Are the earl and Mr. Weston paying?"

Tilda nodded. "The payoff was this morning. The Whites are already at the station, heading home."

Molly looked towards the station and Tilda could see her mind at work. Then she looked back at her. "If the payment's been made and they're gone, then no one will ever know the truth—if it is the truth."

"Oh, it's the truth," Tilda said.

"Which remains a secret *because* of the money paid."

"It doesn't have to remain a secret."

"What are you talking about?"

"The truth could still come out, which would mean Morgan stops being the heir. Which means Miss Farrow would *not* gain a title if she did marry him, so she and her mother will head back to America, where they belong. Leaving Morgan free."

"To marry me." Molly's words were said in a whisper. Her eyes were unseeing as if trying to comprehend the full picture. Finally she blinked. "Why would *you* want the truth to come out? You don't know me."

Tilda took a breath to provide a long answer, but lacking the right words ended up condensing it into a single statement. "George."

To her credit, it only took Molly a few moments to fill in the blanks. "You'd be a viscountess. You. A viscountess."

"And eventually the countess."

Molly shook her head. "But you're an orphan. A soldier's daughter."

Tilda's throat was dry. "I am the goddaughter of Colonel Grady Cummings who is the husband of the Dowager Countess of Summerfield."

"It's still highly unlikely."

Yes, it is. What am I doing? But pride forced her to say, "I would make it work." Tilda looked back towards the house. "I'm making it work already."

Molly moved the suitcase to her other hand. "When are you going to implement your plan?"

Good question. "Not for a little while. I have some preparations to make before then." She took a fresh breath.

"I'm asking for time, Miss Wallace. If I'm not successful, you can leave. But it would be tragic to go back to London before you've made every attempt to win back the man you love."

Molly took in a breath, then let it out. "I suppose I can stay. I really don't want to suffer any more regrets in my life."

"Exactly." Tilda understood regrets. She only hoped today's actions wouldn't be added to the list.

After luncheon, the men dispersed to work on the business of running the estate, leaving Genevieve to spend time with her mother and Mrs. Weston.

Or not.

She'd retired to her room saying she had a headache — which was not a lie. The turning point that changed the morning from good to bad had been when Morgan ran into Molly. It had been very obvious that flowing beneath the generic conversation was a rushing stream. A whirlpool of emotions. As such, Genevieve's instincts had been set on full alert

She glanced at the bell pull, tempted to call Molly so she could ask questions.

And yet . . . did she really want to know the truth about her fiancé and her lady's maid? If there *had* been a connection, clearly the family had broken it, for Molly had been in London for a good length of time. Had she been sent away? Or had she gone voluntarily?

Genevieve's gaze fell upon the vases of flowers that adorned her room and were replenished with regularity. They brought her great pleasure, but . . . perhaps they could serve another purpose.

She armed herself with two of them and set out.

"Miss Farrow," the cook said. "You're back."

"I am," Genevieve said, nodding towards the vase in her hand. "If you could . . ."

The cook removed one flower arrangement from her arms and Genevieve set the other on the large table that spanned the length of the kitchen.

"These are lovely," Mrs. McDeer said.

"Which is why I'm here. Since I arrived there have been six arrangements in my room."

"Don't you like them?"

"I do, very much. But six vases of flowers is too much for one person to enjoy and it seems a waste for them to be seen by only me. And so . . ." She grabbed a new breath. "I thought all of you might enjoy them."

"Ooh," said a kitchen maid, leaning close to smell them. "I never seen such pretty flowers below stairs."

Mrs. McDeer shooed her back. "This is very kind of you, Miss Farrow, and we appreciate your generosity."

Suddenly, Genevieve realized the conversation was nearly over and she hadn't learned a thing about Molly. Yet how to begin?

Mrs. Camden came into the room and did a double-take. "Miss Farrow?"

"Look here, Mrs. Camden," said the cook. "Miss Farrow's brought us some flowers to brighten our day."

A crease formed between the housekeeper's eyes before she smiled. "How nice of you."

"It's the least I can do. You have all made me feel so welcome."

"I'm very glad. How is Molly working out as your lady's maid?"

This perfect opening made her pray for the right words. "I am very pleased with Miss Wallace. I hear she was gone from the manor for many months and no one knew where she was?"

Mrs. McDeer and Mrs. Camden exchanged a glance. "Her sister knew of her whereabouts."

Genevieve plucked a wilting stem from the vase. "Why did she leave?"

Silence fell between them.

Mrs. McDeer moved back to the stove. "Excuse me, the stew."

Mrs. Camden led Genevieve out to the passageway, her voice low. "Apparently Miss Wallace had a longing to make hats. I hear she's very good at it."

Genevieve couldn't let it stop there. "She could have made hats here in Summerfield."

"Summerfield does not offer the same opportunities as London."

She had to press the issue. "But she was the lady's maid to Mrs. Weston, when she was the countess. That's a very esteemed position."

Genevieve could see a battle going on in Mrs. Camden's mind. "Much changed at the manor when the dowager's oldest son was found alive and was elevated from shopkeeper to earl. His younger brother had to step down and his wife was no longer the countess. Perhaps Miss Wallace did not like her own step down." She checked her watch pin. "I'm sorry, Miss Farrow, but I have some things that need my attention. If there's nothing else?"

So much else.

So much she didn't know.

On the way upstairs, Genevieve heard voices in the hall leading from the drawing room to the morning room, and recognized one of them as Dottie's. She held back to listen.

"Come on, Dot," came a male voice. "You being a hoity-toity lady's maid means it's time for you to give me some well-deserved attention, don't you think?"

Dottie did not answer verbally, but Genevieve heard groans and a scuffle.

She stepped out, making her presence known. Nick, a footman, stepped away from Dottie, who he'd pinned against the wall.

"Good day, Miss Farrow," Nick said.

She ignored him and looked to Dottie. "Are you all right?"

"I's fine. Now." She glared at Nick. "He and the others are jealous cuz I got promoted and they didn't."

"I don't need to be jealous of you. I am first footman."

"Which means you're below me, a lady's maid."

Nick looked like he wanted to lunge at her, so Genevieve intervened. "I was needing you upstairs, Dottie. If you please?"

Dottie bobbed a curtsy and fled. Genevieve turned to the footman. "I'd appreciate it if you'd leave her alone, Nick is it?" She wanted him aware that she knew his name.

"Yes, Miss Farrow." He did a neat turn and walked away.

As Genevieve walked to her bedroom to speak to Dottie, she found her hands shaking. Some mistress of the manor she'd be if such an encounter shook her up.

Upstairs, she found Dottie waiting for her, just inside her bedroom door. "Sorry, Miss Farrow," Dottie said. "I know I shouldn't a said that bit about me being above 'im, but they're all treating me so bad about it."

"You should be proud of following in your sister's footsteps."

"I am. Me getting the chance with Miss Cavendish is like what Mrs. Weston did for my sister years ago."

The more Genevieve learned about the history of the family, the sooner she'd understand the current situation. She sat down. "Tell me."

Dottie glanced towards the bedroom door, as if she considered escape.

"Please, Dottie? I'm new here and feel the need to catch up on all that's gone before."

"Well then . . . it was six or eight years ago, when the old earl died, making Mister Weston the earl and Mrs. Weston the countess. Mrs. Weston didn't take to it well and started to stay in her room all the time. She had a French lady's maid who thought she was being wasted serving a recluse who didn't care nothing about fashion, so she quit. Molly was a housemaid, but like me, she was given the chance to help.

She did a good job of it too, and became a real lady's maid until she had to leave because — "Dottie slapped a hand over her mouth.

"Why did she have to leave?"

Dottie's eyes darted frantically, as if seeking the right answer.

"If you're going to be a lady's maid, Dottie, there needs to be an element of trust between you and the family — and I'm nearly family. It's all about trust and honesty. I need you to help me understand the Westons so I can marry Lord Weston and be a good wife to him."

"But that's the reason Molly left," Dottie said. "She and Morgan were in love. But then he found out his pa was the earl and he was the heir, and . . . everything was a mess so Molly ran away to London."

Genevieve's worst fears were realized. She tried not to let it show, and rose from her chair. "Thank you for telling me. I appreciate your candor."

Dottie's face pulled in panic. "I shouldna told you. Molly will be furious with me."

"Then let's not let Molly know that I know. Will that make it better?"

"Oh, yes, Miss Farrow. I like the sounds of that."

After Dottie left, Genevieve leaned against the door. The attraction she'd sensed between Morgan and Molly was real — and still present. Which only meant one thing.

She would have to work even harder to make Morgan fall in love with her.

Chapter Twelve

Tilda listened at her bedroom door. Not hearing anything she stepped out in the hallway in her nightgown and wrapper. Down in the foyer, the clock struck three.

She gave one last look both ways, then tiptoed down the dark hall to Clarissa's room. She slipped inside and closed the door with a subtle click.

"Tilda?" A voice came out of the shadows.

Tilda put one hand to her heart and the other protectively into the pocket of her wrapper. "Mrs. Weston. You scared me!"

"Sorry. I couldn't sleep, and felt the need . . ."

Even in the moonlight, Tilda could see she'd been crying. She went to her and knelt beside her chair. "Are you missing Clarissa?"

Mrs. Weston nodded and wiped her eyes with a handkerchief. "It strikes me at odd times." She took a ragged breath and peered around the darkened room. "Only in this room do I feel her presence." She offered Tilda a crooked smile. "I miss her so."

Tilda's heart melted. "I'll be your daughter — until she returns."

Mrs. Weston turned towards her, and touched her cheek. "You are such a dear girl." She stood, drew Tilda to standing, and began to stroll towards the door. Then she stopped. "What brought you here in the middle of the night?"

Tilda nearly panicked, then thought of a feasible excuse. She pointed at the window seat. "I couldn't sleep either and remembered the wonderful view of the gardens from Clarissa's window. With the full moon so bright . . . I hope you don't mind."

"Not at all." Mrs. Weston said. "You go have a look at the moon." She raised a finger. "But not too long. Perhaps . . . perhaps you and I could spend some time together later today?"

"I'd like that."

"Good night, Tilda."

"Good night, Mrs. Weston."

Tilda paused long enough to let her heart return to a normal rhythm. What a piece of luck.

What a close call.

Not daring to press fate any further, Tilda made a beeline for the jewelry box and emptied her pocket of its bounty.

She'd awakened in the middle of the night with the knowledge that all her progress to ingratiate herself with Mrs. Weston and George could be ruined by a stupid housemaid's tattling. There was a proper time to enjoy the lark of snitching a bracelet or two and there was a proper time to be smart about it. The fact that Gertie had caught her stealing the emerald choker changed much.

Of course that issue was taken care of, for that necklace was still stuffed under Gertie's mattress, ready to be found in case she made a stink.

Beyond that, with the Whites paid off and gone, and Molly as her ally, Tilda wanted to avoid unnecessary risks. Her deed accomplished, she took a lingering look at the jewels that had been hers for a short time. Sacrifices had to be made towards the larger cause.

Someday, she'd get all this—and more.

Especially since Mrs. Weston seemed open to thinking of her as a daughter.

Tilda closed the lid on the box and retraced her steps to her room. Once in bed, an easy sleep returned, allowing her dreams to be filled with happy expectation.

On the morning after her talk with Tilda about the secret of Morgan's parentage, the last thing Molly wanted to do was spend time with Genevieve Farrow. She considered asking Mrs. Camden to assign Prissy or Sally to the task, or even Dottie, but her sudden withdrawal from her duties would make people curious. And right now — as Tilda had said — what Molly needed most was time. Time to think about all Tilda had told her; time for Tilda to set in place the big reveal.

Molly stood behind Genevieve, pinning her hair for breakfast. They both looked up when Mrs. Farrow swept into Genevieve's room. "Come, come, daughter. Let's go down for breakfast. You know I hate lukewarm eggs."

Unwittingly, Molly must have made a face for Genevieve said, "I'm sure you find helping me tedious. Do you miss your shop?"

"It's not my shop."

"Do you miss making hats then? Using your creative talents must have been very rewarding."

"Yes, I guess it was."

Genevieve turned around on the dressing table bench. "I certainly don't want to keep you from it. Is your mother getting better?"

Her sudden interest seemed suspicious. "A little."

"How wonderful." Genevieve turned back to the mirror and powdered her cheeks.

Molly was torn. Maybe it would be better to just leave all this intrigue. Morgan was all flirtation and folly. She had no proof he was strong enough to go against his family's wishes. And when the secret came out that he wasn't the heir . . . would he truly come running back into her arms? Surely it would be more complicated than that.

So why was she staying at all?

Mrs. Farrow fumbled through Genevieve's jewelry box and pulled out a long string of pearls. "Here. This will be perfect with your dress."

Molly thought they were too much for a day dress — and by her sigh, so did Genevieve — but she put them on anyway. The string, even when strung double over her head, hung nearly to her waist. It was a show of excessive opulence. At least in Molly's opinion.

As soon as they left, Molly sank onto the stool, her head hung low. "Why am I staying here?" she asked the room.

As if in answer, there was a tap on the door, and Dottie opened it. "Come on. Here's a tray for Ma's breakfast."

Molly rose with little enthusiasm. Genevieve, Morgan, Ma, Tilda . . . too many people claimed a piece of her. If only she could lock herself in a room for a week, sleep, and think. And not think.

"What's wrong?"

Molly sighed. "What isn't?"

Dottie came in the room with the tray, and closed the door with her foot. "Is it about Miss Farrow? I'm sorry, Mol. I didn't mean to tell her."

"Tell who what?"

Dottie blinked a few times. "Aren't you upset with me telling Miss Farrow about you and Morgan?"

Molly's heart flipped. "What did you tell her?"

"That you were engaged once. That you loved each other. That you left Summerfield when he found out he was the heir."

Molly set the notion that Genevieve knew their history against her recent suggestion that Molly return to London. One plus one equaled . . .

"She wants you out of the way, doesn't she?" Dottie asked.

"I imagine she does."

"She must think Morgan still loves you. He doesn't, does he?"

It was the question of her life.

Clarissa awakened with one thought and one thought alone: *I am bored.*

Being back in the country, away from the hubbub of London, away from the theatre . . . who would have thought she would ever miss working?

There was a knock on her bedroom door and the maid Annie, asked, "Are you ready for me, Miss Weston?"

"Come in." What else did she have to do but get dressed to go to breakfast? Beyond eating three meals and teatime, she had no plans for the day.

Clarissa let Annie help her out of bed and used the chamber pot while the girl turned her back. She handed it to Annie, who put a towel over it and set it aside.

Then Clarissa took up the damp towel to wipe her face and arms, the act making her think of bathing a child.

Beth. She was the only child Clarissa had ever bathed, ever cared for. Clarissa had been seven when George was born, but had done her best to ignore him, and had certainly never held him beyond the requisite as his sister. When he'd turned five, she had thought he would prove to be an enjoyable playmate, but once he'd seen a horse his need for human companionship had evaporated. Clarissa hated the stables with their horsey smells. It was worse than any stench she encountered in London. She much preferred indoors to out.

Clarissa sat at the dressing table and let Annie fuss with her hair. She enjoyed seeing her full face in a mirror that was clear and had kept its silver. The ones in her flat had been horribly mottled, forcing her to choose which portion of her face to inspect. Now, her eyes were looking a bit haggard, but that should be expected considering her awful ordeal.

When her hair was accomplished, Annie opened the large armoire. "Beggin' your pardon, Miss Weston, but Lady Kidd had me bring in these outfits for you to wear. She said there is more where they came from if these don't suit."

Clarissa pretended not to care, but she was happy to see the pretty clothes. In London she'd had to sell many of her nicer ensembles to pay the bills and been left with little that could be deemed fashionable. Plus, walking about in her neighborhood in a la-di-da outfit would have been a good way to get assaulted. Whatever she'd kept was now long gone, probably prettying up some whore or barmaid.

The image of Beth running after one of her gowns intruded.

To erase it, Clarissa let her fingers walk along the fabrics, finally choosing. "I'll wear this one today."

"Very good, miss." Annie laid it on the bed, then retrieved fresh pantaloons and a camisole, Clarissa's own corset, stockings with garters, a petticoat, and a bustle.

Finally, she was ready for the dress. The bodice and pleated skirt were green mousseline de laine, broken up by a peach overskirt creating a lace-edged drapery to the knee, culminating in a soft bustle in back. The long-sleeved bodice was bisected from hip to neck with small ruffles, with matching cuffs. Two centered bows—at neck and hip—made Clarissa feel like a pretty package. Perhaps that's all she was.

"Tis a little too big for you, miss."

Clarissa was glad for that. Lila's origins from shopkeeper obviously made her more beefy than lean. "I have always kept my waist at twenty inches."

"I can see that, miss," Annie said as she finished buttoning the back. "Your waist is the tiniest I've seen. If you'd like I could make alterations for next time."

If there is a next time. "We'll see."

With her toilette complete, Clarissa descended downstairs in time to eat.

When Lila saw her, she did a double-take. "My, my. You look far lovelier in that dress than I ever did."

Of course I do.

"Doesn't she look lovely, Joseph?"

He sipped his coffee and nodded. "Lovely."

She mentally disparaged his lack of effort. "So," Clarissa said, as she filled her plate from a buffet resplendent with eggs, ham, scones, and stewed tomatoes. "What is the plan for today?"

193

She saw Lila and Joseph exchange a glance. Then Lila said, "I thought you might help me quilt some blankets for the poor."

Goodie. "I'm not sure I can handle such excitement." She took a seat at the table.

Joseph took offense. "If Lila's plans don't suit you, then I suggest you go home."

My, my he was testy today. "And bother my own family? Is that what you're suggesting?"

He turned his hand over in the air with a gentle sweeping motion.

"Now, now, you two," Lila said. "You both mean well, and it is true that my activities must seem boring to a woman used to the excitement of London. I admit that I am a bit bored myself."

"Lila, you shouldn't say such things," her husband said — even though he'd admitted as much to Clarissa the day before.

"You know it's true, darling. You were raised to the aristocracy. I am new to the position. I am quite unused to free time and having others do for me what I am used to doing for myself."

A footman came in and whispered something to the butler, who stepped away from the buffet. "Mister Kidd, your father has requested your presence."

"Where *is* he?" Joseph asked. "We expected to see him at breakfast."

"Apparently, there is some issue with a tenant? I believe he is outside."

Joseph dabbed at his mouth with a napkin, then pushed himself away from the table. "Pardon me, ladies. If you will excuse me?"

Clarissa was glad for his departure, for she was curious about something. "Tell me, Lila. Did he ever gain a seat in Parliament? I know when he and I were engaged, that was something my father was supposed to help him secure. Of course, since our betrothal fell apart . . ."

Lila did not bite. "He has not gained a seat," she said.

Clarissa felt satisfaction in that. Joseph should suffer some consequences for spurning her.

"Although your father still offered to help, I encouraged Joseph to decline the offer."

Her satisfaction quickly transformed into anger. "Father was still going to help?"

Lila nodded and took a sip of coffee. "Joseph is family."

"But not a son-in-law."

Lila motioned for Dowd to pour more coffee. "Joseph declined the offer because of my preference. I am not a city girl, and the thought of spending three or four months in London every year when Parliament is in session, and attending Ascot, court balls, parties, regattas . . ." She sighed. "It's too much. Besides, it would cause us to be away from the beauty of the countryside in the summer and keep us in the heat of the city. Where is the logic in that?"

"You wouldn't have to go with him to London."

"We do not wish to be apart."

For a man to give up his ambition for the love and preferences of his wife was alien, and ignited something in Clarissa's belly: a longing for such a love.

Yet that was ridiculous. In her current situation, love was impossible.

"Joseph does not approve of me staying here," she said. "Is it because I was on the stage?"

"It is because he knows how much your family misses you."

There was more to it than that. "I shan't go back until I sort through my predicament. To lose everything . . ." She put the napkin to the corner of her eye. Eliciting sympathy often came in handy.

"Did you manage to save our grandmother's necklace that I brought you?"

It was still hard for Clarissa to hear "our grandmother." She changed the subject. "How did you find out where I lived?"

"I inquired at the theatre. The necklace . . .?"

"I have it. Thank you for bringing it to me."

"I was glad to do it." Lila looked to her lap as if seeking strength in the weave of the tablecloth. "Did you find the money I left of good use?"

Clarissa felt her mouth grow slack. "Money? What money?"

Lila set her napkin beside her plate. "I left you twenty pounds. Agnes assured me she would get it to you."

Clarissa tried to think back to the day she found out that Lila had made a visit. Then it hit her. "Agnes was gone when I got home. I saw your note and the necklace, but there was no money."

Lila whispered, "Oh my. She stole it."

Clarissa pushed back from her chair, needing to pace. "That no good, unfaithful . . ." She stopped at the end of the table near Lila. "She knew how much I needed that money. Twenty pounds would have paid off the landlord and I never would have been evicted."

Lila blinked once, then said softly. "If you'd had the money to pay off your landlord, you never would have ended up here, back in Summerfield."

True. But . . . "So you're saying it's good Agnes stole from me?"

"Perhaps it is God's doing."

Clarissa returned to her seat. "I think you put too much confidence in God's interest in me."

Lila shook her head. "You are not confident enough. God does have a plan for you."

Clarissa laughed as she placed her napkin back in her lap. "You've been talking to Timothy."

"Timothy?"

Her surprise seemed sincere. "Timothy already talked to me about God's plan for my life, my purpose, and how everything happens for a reason."

Lila nodded with enthusiasm. "All good points. And good for him." Lila also replaced her napkin and resumed eating. "When did you speak with Timothy?"

There was the slightest hitch in her voice, as if . . . "Are you jealous?"

"No!" Lila glanced at Dowd and lowered her voice. "Of course not. I simply was not aware that you'd spoken."

Clarissa eased her mind. "Joseph was showing me the nursery when Timothy arrived with some drawer pulls."

Lila nodded once this time. "He is a very skilled woodworker." After a fresh breath she added, "And a very fine man."

"You say that almost as a warning."

Lila shrugged. "He is a dear friend whom I would not want to see hurt."

"There is more to it than that." Clarissa also lowered her voice in confidence. "He still loves you."

She expected Lila to deny it. Instead, she said, "I know."

"If you know then what are you going to do about it?"

"There is nothing to *do*. I have chosen a man I adore, and I pray Timothy will also find true love." She nodded towards Clarissa's plate. "Would you like some more scones?"

Lila could change the subject, but it did nothing to truly change the issue at hand. Clarissa had a thought and found herself saying it aloud before it could be stopped. "Why are you so nice to me? Don't you understand I hate you?"

Lila's fork stopped in midair. She set it down gently. "I don't particularly like you either."

Clarissa let out a laugh. "Finally some honesty!"

Lila stirred sugar into her coffee. "We don't have to like each other to forgive each other."

"Forgive? What do I have to be forgiven for? You're the one who stole Joseph from me."

"I did not steal him."

"He was my fiancé. Then he wasn't."

The spoon went round and round in Lila's cup more times than necessary. "I am sorry you were hurt, but not sorry he is my husband. It was God's plan."

"There you go again, acting as though God were in charge."

Lila's spoon ceased its circling. "If not Him, who?"

She was so naïve. "I am not God's pawn to move around."

"You are God's child and are given the ability to choose which square you land upon." She sighed deeply. "Life is too short to hate, Cousin. If it were easy to love, it wouldn't mean half as much. We are family now. Our lives are linked forever. Can't we forget the past and work towards our future?"

"Our future? What future do I have? I have lost everything."

"That's not true."

It certainly seemed true.

Everyone was busy with something. Genevieve had seen the men talking business outside, her mother was off reading a book, Tilda was everywhere—the girl constantly popped up in the most unusual places, and George was off riding. Genevieve wandered around Summerfield Manor.

She had enjoyed the tour with Morgan and her foray into the servants' stronghold in the basement, but had been warned by her mother that such visits were simply not appropriate.

She was stuck in a twenty-five bedroom mansion with a dozen common areas, yet had nowhere to go. She'd even taken to opening stray doors. In doing so, she had found caches of linen, china, wine, and other supplies.

Actually . . . the only room she hadn't visited was the study. It was the bastion of the men of the house, the place where they conducted their daily business.

But since they were all outside, the room was empty . . .

Now was her chance.

Genevieve entered the passageway leading to the room and was glad it was devoid of servant or family. She hesitated but a moment, nervously playing with her pearls. She hurried towards the door—which was blessedly open. She tapped on the door jamb with a knuckle, "Hello?"

When there was no answer, she slipped inside. With a single scan of the room she immediately felt as though she was home, back in her father's study in New York. There was a large oak desk with two facing chairs and one massive leather chair behind. The walls were paneled in walnut, with fluted half-columns dividing the vertical space into sections six-foot wide. An intricate parquet floor and coffered ceiling made it a massive wooden box. Heavy velvet curtains puddled on the floor, with hefty braids and tassels pulling them aside enough to let in a modicum of sunlight. A scattering of chairs edged the room, with a four-paneled screen in the corner sporting paintings of figures representing the four seasons. Other gilt-framed paintings of fox hunts, battles, and seascapes hung from brass wires, an unnecessary reminder that this was a male habitat, *women keep out*.

Papa had never made Genevieve stay out of his office. Some of her best memories were playing in the leg space under his desk or sitting on a stool near his chair playing word games with him and drawing pictures. He could draw a dog better than anybody.

Caught in the memories, she moved to the leather desk chair and sat down. She leaned her head back and stroked the well-worn arms, thinking of Papa and how much she missed him. Would he approve of her being in Summerfield, ready to marry a man she barely knew? Would he be angry they were spending the money *he'd* earned to buy her the title of viscountess, and eventually countess?

Actually, the answer was probably yes. He was a man of ambition. He'd had to be. To rise from a worker in a garment factory, to the president of a sewing machine company, took hard work, drive, and a vision. Unfortunately, the hard work and long hours had taken a toll on his health, and he'd died at forty-five from a heart attack. She'd been the one to find him, on the floor in his study, his face contorted, his breathing strained. He couldn't talk, could barely move, and had died a week later, leaving her alone— with her mother. Alone.

Genevieve pressed her fingers against her eyes, forcing the tears away. He'd brought her up to *not* be a crier. As his only child she'd received the attention and instruction he had to share for both a daughter *and* a son. As such, she was usually tougher than she looked.

She removed her hands and took a cleansing breath, letting the memories of Papa return to the cozy place in her heart and mind where he resided.

She spotted a bronze statue of a spaniel by the fireplace. Her thoughts shifted to their dog, Digger. She rose to see it more closely and knelt before it. It was nearly life size.

As she picked up the hollow statue, she heard male voices in the foyer. She held her breath and listened. They were getting closer.

As she set the statue down, her long pearls got caught beneath an ear, shattering the strand. Beads tittered across the floor around her, white beacons against the richness of the wood floor. She scrambled after them, hearing footsteps in the passageway.

They were coming to the study!

She couldn't be found here! It was too late to escape without them seeing her. She scurried to the corner and slipped behind a screen just as the earl and his brother entered the study. She hoped they wouldn't stay long.

She heard the squeak of the leather as they each took a chair, and then the sound of a match as they lit their cigars. Genevieve would have to stay put. She looked around and found herself truly in a corner. With a careful step back she leaned against the wall. It offered some relief.

She was totally unprepared for the discussion that began with the earl. "I hated when he spoke of Fidelia having 'a bun in the oven' when I married her."

His brother, Mr. Weston, hesitated. "Did she?"

"No!" His voice backed down. "At least not that I know of. Though Morgan *was* born just seven months after we married." He quickly continued, "But he was small and we thought him early. We assumed so. I had no reason to think otherwise."

"Fidelia didn't say . . .?"

"No. Nothing. She didn't even tell me her real surname until after we married. She'd taken on her mother's maiden name, being ashamed of the scandalous recognition 'Breton' would ignite."

"Scandal because of her supposed indiscretion with Mr. White?"

"No, no. More than that."

What were they talking about? Morgan's mother and Mr. White? Bun in the oven?

The earl continued. "Her father was in banking and lost his investors millions."

"Ah yes. That would take down a name."

"Which I now know is the reason she was so intent on marrying me. She wanted to be out and away from her parents. She was quite cowed and desperate. She needed to be saved."

"Forgive me, but I find it hard to imagine Fidelia cowed and desperate."

"She was. Then. At least for a short while."

"But . . ." Mr. Weston cleared his throat. "Could she have been so intent to marry you because she was with child?"

He hesitated, but said, "I don't believe that. You were there. You and Mrs. Weston walked in on them. What did you see?"

Mr. Weston puffed on his cigar, sending aromatic smoke Genevieve's way. "You're asking me to recall a memory from twenty-five years ago. All I remember is seeing the two of them lying in the straw, a flurry of petticoats and embarrassment as they stood upon seeing they were discovered. I saw nothing . . . tangible."

"Then why was there a scandal at all?" the earl asked.

"Because the coachman bragged and embellished. Word spread round the village and Fidelia's reputation was ruined. She lost her chance to marry any man of position, much less me."

"Her reputation was ruined in spite of the truth *then*," the earl said, "and *now*, in spite of the truth, Morgan's future is at stake. Life is very unfair. Truth should prevail."

"It can prevail, but it doesn't always matter." He puffed on his cigar. "At least the Whites are paid off and gone."

Genevieve *had* noticed them leave the day before. What did Mr. Weston mean "paid off"?

"George will be unhappy that we had to sell some of his beloved horses."

"He will survive."

"As I mentioned, we could have asked Mrs. Farrow for the funds."

Mr. Weston answered, "You couldn't have done that without telling her the reason. Just the hint of scandal might have sent them back to America. The Farrows are paying us for a title and a family legacy, not a public indignity."

The earl sighed. "I do like Genevieve. She is a sweet girl, self-deprecating, and eager to please."

"And her mother?"

"She is . . . otherwise."

"Do you think Morgan loves her?" Mr. Weston asked.

Genevieve desperately wanted to hear the answer, putting a hand to her mouth. Unfortunately she found them still full of pearls. Realizing too late, one dropped to the floor with a subtle *ping.*

The room went silent. Did they hear? Did they see it roll towards the foot of the screen?

"I think he wants to love her," the earl said.

The seriousness of the subject regained their attention.

"The arrangement often comes before the attachment," Mr. Weston said. "Give them time."

"Time is what we've just paid for. But . . ."

But?

"But I'm fairly certain if Morgan knew he wasn't the heir, he would wish to marry Molly."

"He still has feelings for the girl?" Mr. Weston asked.

"I'm afraid so. He came to me yesterday, worried about it. He is very fond of Genevieve but . . ."

"First love dies hard. Maybe you should send Molly away. Surely her mother is well enough."

"I thought about it," the earl said. "Yet apparently she has taken on the task of being Genevieve's lady's maid. It will be suspicious if we force her to leave."

"It might be harmful if we allow her to stay. And surely it's not easy for her to serve Miss Farrow."

"But hasn't she has been at Summerfield since she was a child?"

"She has," Mr. Weston said. "And she is loyal to a fault."

"Loyal enough to do the right thing and leave?"

Genevieve found herself praying the answer was *yes*.

Mr. Weston answered. "She must not find out about the White's allegations or she will never leave."

Genevieve heard the scrape of a chair against the floor. "We have paid for the secret to remain so, and with the Whites gone, it has left with them. Let's push that awful couple and this entire nasty business out of our minds."

Easy for you . . .

She heard footsteps coming towards her corner. She held her breath as Mr. Weston plucked the fallen pearl from the base of the screen. "Mrs. Weston must have dropped this." He walked away. "I will see you at luncheon."

"Wait, I'll walk with you."

The fading sound of footsteps followed by the silence of the room told Genevieve the coast was clear. Only she couldn't move because her entire future had fallen to the floor around her, as scattered as the pearls.

The fact Morgan might not be a blood heir didn't mean that much to her. The point was, he deserved the position. The family needed him to carry on. They needed her to help him.

But if the truth came out, Genevieve would lose him to Molly. Then what? Summerfield would suffer and she would return to New York in shame. Mrs. Astor, Mrs. Vanderbilt, and all the other matrons of New York's elite Four Hundred, would make good use of the story, embellishing it beyond the truth just like the coachman embellished his conquest of Fidelia. Money or no money, who would want to marry a girl who was spurned for the love of a maid?

And her mother? Genevieve would pay for this folly—for it would be deemed *her* folly—for the rest of her life. She would probably end up an old maid, living with her mother in their cavernous house on Fifth Avenue, eating dinner in out-of-date gowns, having nothing to talk about but their health, the weather, and what might have been.

"I have to make Morgan love me. I have to!"

Hearing her words said aloud spurred Genevieve to move. She slipped out from behind the screen and tiptoed to the doorway, snatching an errant pearl from behind an andiron as she passed. She checked at the door and finding no one in the passageway, hurried to the foyer, then up the stairs to her bedroom. Once inside, she emptied her hands of the pearls, dropping them in the back of a drawer.

Only with her hands emptied did the tension of the morning catch up with her. She fell to her knees, leaning forward until her forehead touched the side of the bed. Her breath came in small gasps that turned into sobs. She clasped her hands and prayed fervently for God's guidance and mercy.

And a miracle.

Tilda hesitated in the doorway of the sunroom. Mrs. Weston was sitting on a wicker chair among the potted plants, some needlework in hand.

The woman must have sensed her presence, for she looked up and smiled. "Tilda. Right on time. Come in and join me." She pointed to a nearby chair.

Tilda entered, hoping Mrs. Weston wouldn't expect her to know how to sew.

She decided to make her limitations clear. "I never learned anything about sewing and such."

"Your mother didn't teach you?"

"My mother ran away from Papa and me soon after I was born."

"Oh. Was there . . . was there a problem at home?"

Tilda took a seat and shrugged. "Me."

"You?"

"I was too much for her." She had the thought that Mrs. Weston's sympathy might be advantageous. "Her leaving broke Papa's heart and he never forgave me."

"Forgave you? You were a baby."

She shrugged again. "I can't blame him really. To be saddled with a baby and no woman to help. Course there were women. Nanny types. And other types too. But they were more interested in gaining Papa for a husband than keeping care of me. The last one, Mrs. Smith, was the best of them because she was old and didn't think of such things."

"Did you go to school?"

"A few days I did. But then Papa was reassigned to a different town and we had to leave. I learned my alphabet and sums from a neighbor lady. But then she moved away." Tilda wondered if the story sounded pathetic enough—not that she was lying about any of it. "I grew up knowing more men than women, as Papa and his soldier friends liked to drink and gamble and . . ." She shrugged, letting Mrs. Weston fill in her most blatant fear for a young girl.

It must have worked because she gasped. "I'm so sorry you had to endure such things, my dear."

Suddenly, Tilda felt the need to qualify her story. If Mrs. Weston thought she was tainted in a sexual way, she might not allow her to marry her son. "It wasn't as bad as you're thinking. They all cared for me in a fashion. In ways I was lucky to have a dozen papas."

Mrs. Weston let out a breath of relief. "Well then. Let us make up for lost time. A proper girl knows how to do fine needlework."

Tilda let Mrs. Weston show her how to thread the needle and work in the ends as she made stitch after diagonal stitch. She found the entire act of it incredibly boring.

After a half hour, Mrs. Weston noticed. "You don't enjoy it, do you?"

"Sorry, but no."

"Is there any pastime you enjoy? Any affinity?"

Tilda wasn't certain what 'affinity' meant, but somehow it did make her think of something she liked to do. "I like to draw."

"Paint?"

"Draw. With a pencil."

Mrs. Weston rose from her chair and pulled the bell rope. Mr. Dixon arrived. "Yes, madam?"

"Would you please bring Miss Cavendish a stash of paper and some pencils?"

"And erasers," Tilda added.

He nodded and left to accomplish the task. While she was up, Mrs. Weston picked up a small side table and set it in front of Tilda. "It's not a proper easel, but it might do for today."

Tilda was moved by her interest, and the way she was attending to Tilda's needs.

Mr. Dixon returned with supplies in hand. "I wasn't certain what constituted a 'stash', but I hope this will suffice."

It was more than enough. In fact, "I have never had more than three pages at a time. These dozen are like a treasure trove to me." She looked directly at the butler. "Thank you, Mr. Dixon."

"Just Dixon, miss."

But he smiled. He actually smiled.

"There now," Mrs. Weston said. "Now . . . draw something. How about that tree out the window? Or the fern over there?"

Tilda shook her head. She knew exactly what she would draw. "Sit still please."

Mrs. Weston put a hand to her chest. "Me?"

"You must be still . . ."

She *was* still and Tilda's pencil flew across the page. She hadn't drawn since Papa died, as her time had been taken with her housekeeping work. But the connection between her eyes, mind, and hand freely returned, as if her talent was something that could be ignored but not denied.

She noticed Mrs. Weston fidgeting. "I'm nearly through."

Within a couple minutes, she was. Tilda took one long look at the drawing, smudged a shadow a little more, detailing the crook of her model's neck and let out a long breath. "There. It's done."

"May I see?"

Tilda felt a bevy of nerves when she handed it over. She *thought* she was good, but was she?

But by the look on Mrs. Weston's face, her question was answered in the affirmative. "Dear, dear girl. You have much talent. It's beautiful."

"As is my subject."

Mrs. Weston beamed. "I insist you draw a portrait of each member of the family. Will you do that for me?"

"Of course."

"They will be so pleased."

They. The family. Not *we*.

Someday *we*.

Chapter Thirteen

"A dinner party at Crompton Hall?" Tilda asked.

"Yes, dear." Mrs. Weston opened Clarissa's closet and walked in. "It's time you meet Morgan's sister, Lila, and her husband, Joseph. That's why we have to choose a gown for you." She began perusing the bodices and skirts that hung on hooks, then moved to the first set of deep drawers. She pulled out the bottom drawer to reveal gorgeous silks and satins.

"Ooh," Tilda said, without meaning to.

Mrs. Weston smiled and pointed at a cream colored dress. "This one?"

Tilda shook her head, her eyes locked on the object of her desire. "The blue one."

Mrs. Weston removed the dress from its resting place and held it up. "Ah yes. I remember this one. Clarissa wore it many times. It was a favorite." She leaned close. "She always received scads of compliments when she wore it." Then she held it in front of Tilda. "I think it might fit."

It had to fit.

Dottie adjusted the hang of the skirt, then stepped back. "Whoo-ee, Miss Cavendish. You are a vision." She pointed towards the full-length mirror. "Go see."

Tilda felt a stitch of apprehension as she stepped towards the mirror. When she'd first seen this royal blue dress she'd thought it the most beautiful dress she'd ever seen. When she touched the ribbed texture of the faille fabric she marveled at its soft richness. And the lace . . . from the stand-up lace collar to the waist were white batiste tucks, outlined with ruffles made of wide cascading lace. It was the most elegant dress she'd ever seen — much less ever had on her body. She felt like she'd just been introduced to the dress of all dresses, that she *had* to wear.

That it fit was fate. "Ooh," was her summation.

"You bet your bonnet, 'ooh'," Dottie said. "You'll turn some heads tonight, that's for sure. Too bad it's just family."

Family was fine. Family was quite enough.

Tilda touched the bow at the shoulder as if it could break. Was this really her? Little Tilda Cavendish who was given neighborhood castoffs because her father didn't want to waste money on her? "I look grown up."

"That, you do. How old are you — if you don't mind me asking."

"Sixteen last March."

"Old enough."

Tilda caught Dottie's reflection in the mirror. "Old enough for what?"

"For being fully growed. For being able to have a suitor and . . . you know."

Tilda didn't *know*, but she could imagine. And there was only one family-member she wanted to be "growed" for tonight.

If this dress didn't get George's attention, she might as well return to Aldershot on the morning train.

Genevieve was at the foot of the stairs, heading up to dress for dinner.

"Miss Farrow?"

She turned to see the earl coming towards her. "Yes, your lordship?"

He fished something from his pocket, and when he opened his hand, she saw one lone pearl. "I believe this might be yours?"

Her mind was a jumble. How much did he know? Should she lie? Was he truly observant enough to remember her wearing the strand of pearls earlier in the day?

Yet one fact rose above the rest: *he's your future father-in-law.*

"Yes, I believe it is mine," she said, plucking the pearl from his palm. "Thank you." She lifted the hem of her skirt to go upstairs.

"I found it in my study."

She froze, then faced him. "Oh?"

"Was there a reason you were in my study?"

Genevieve knew her mouth was open, yet she could neither make it close nor find any words.

"Miss Farrow?"

She glanced around the foyer, then said softly. "I was just familiarizing myself with the manor and saw all the books and the lovely paneling in the room, and went in." She thought of a detail to ease her offense. "It reminded me of my father's study and brought back some bittersweet memories." She hesitated, wondering if she should just tell the full of it. With a sigh and an extra beat of her heart, she did. "When I heard you and Mr. Weston coming I didn't want to be caught snooping so I . . . I hid behind the screen." She held up the pearl. "And my necklace broke."

His jaw tightened, and she knew he wanted to ask what she'd heard.

"I know I shouldn't have been there. I will not enter uninvited again."

"You have the run of the house, but you should have made your presence known. I . . . we . . . "

Although she'd made a likely excuse, she might as well finish it. "I heard everything."

He took a half-step backward.

She hurried to say, "Is there something I can do to help?"

The earl's jaw dropped. But then he recovered and asked quietly, "You don't wish to back out of the marriage?"

"Of course not." She was shocked by his assumption.

"But if people believe he isn't who we say he is, that he's not the heir . . ."

"He is both. No one can take that away from him."

"The Whites would like to try."

She had to make her position clear. "Whether it's true of not, I want what's best for this family and for your son. I care about all of you. And selfishly, I also want to be a part of Summerfield's future—whatever that may be."

The space between his eyes dipped, and she knew he was fighting for composure. "My dear girl, there's not a selfish bone in your body."

Genevieve felt herself blush. "I thank you for the compliment, but it's not true. Not true at all." *At all.*

He touched her arm. "Morgan is very lucky to have you. As are we all."

She wanted to ask him what they were going to do about the Whites and paying the blackmail, but if he trusted her, she needed to trust him.

"Dixon has rung the gong so we best get ready for dinner," he said. "Can I lead you upstairs?"

She took his arm and they ascended the stairs, parting at the door to her room. "I don't need to say anything, but . . ." he put a finger to his lips.

"Agreed," she said. "You need not fear anything from me."

He nodded once and left her to dress.

Oddly, she felt better that he knew that she knew. Yet, where would it all end?

It took three carriages to carry the Westons and Farrows to Crompton Hall for dinner. Mr. and Mrs. Weston and the earl were in the first carriage, with the carriage carrying the dowager, Colonel Grady, George and Tilda following behind.

In the third carriage Genevieve was happy for the close proximity of Morgan seated beside her, with her mother and Nana seated across.

"I fear I'm a bit nervous to meet your sister," she said.

"You have nothing to fear from Lila," Morgan said.

"None whatsoever," his grandmother said. "She is the joy of my life." She nodded to Morgan. "As is her brother."

"I have no jealousy against her," Morgan said. "Her accolades are well-deserved and exceed mine by half."

Out of the blue, Mamma asked a question of Morgan's grandmother, "What shall I call you? Your last name is not the same as your son's?"

Genevieve looked to her lap, hating the question, which was nothing if not rude. Her mother knew very well the complete story of Morgan's grandmother.

"You may call me whatever you'd like," Nana said. "Mary, or Mrs. Hayward. And what shall I call you?"

Touché.

"Mrs. Farrow."

Genevieve stifled a smile, and saw out of the corner of her eye that Morgan was smiling too.

If Mamma would allow herself to think of it, she probably had more in common with Mrs. Hayward than she did with the titled Westons. For the Farrow money also existed because of selling goods. But Mamma would never admit the roots were at all similar. In her mind's eye, she considered herself titled but for the pesky fact that such ranks did not exist in America.

"Here we are," Morgan said as they reached a drive edged by two manicured rows of trees. "Crompton Hall is near."

The manor house was red brick, and was less imposing than Summerfield Manor, though in many ways more charming. Ivy covered the sides, giving it a sense of permanence and history as well as making it seem one with the land. A lush flower garden with bursts of brilliant color greeted them on their right as they neared the entrance. A gazebo sat in the middle of it, and Genevieve could imagine nothing more enjoyable than spending time there, perhaps reading a good book.

As soon as the carriages arrived, a dark-haired woman came out of the house, her face radiant and welcoming. Two men accompanied her. Genevieve's first impression was that Morgan's sister was a beautiful woman in temperament and countenance. She glowed.

The coachmen unfurled the carriage steps and helped the ladies out. As greetings commenced, Lila approached, taking Genevieve's hands, and kissing her cheeks. "It is so wonderful to finally meet you, Miss Farrow."

"Genevieve. Please. And I am so happy to meet Morgan's sister." Belatedly she added, "Lady Kidd."

"I will have none of that, for I will be your sister soon," Lila said. She kept hold of Genevieve's hands and said softly. "I have always wanted a sister."

"So have I." Their bond was locked into place.

Lila slipped her arm through Genevieve's and led the Summerfield Manor contingent into the house, where a butler and two liveried footmen made quick work of hats, wraps, and gloves.

Lila's husband Joseph, and his father, Lord Newley, gave their welcome, and the group moved into a drawing room as dark and masculine as Summerfield Manor's was light. The visual weight wasn't just caused by the template, but by the weight of the heavily carved furniture and drapery.

The dowager noticed Genevieve taking it all in and stepped close. "You are looking lovely tonight, my dear. Your cheeks are flushed—with anticipation for the nuptials, I assume?"

"Of course," she said, praying there would be nuptials. She saw that the earl and his brother had overheard and exchanged a look of concern.

Her mother broke the moment as she took Lord Newley's arm and pointed to the painting above the fireplace. "Was this your wife, Lord Newley?"

"It was."

Genevieve didn't hear more explanation, as Lila led her to share a settee. "Tell me all about the wedding plans. Has your gown arrived yet?"

"Any day now. I can't wait to see it."

"Morgan told me he's planned a wedding trip through Europe."

Genevieve knew very little about the plans which had been made as part of the negotiations between her mother and the Westons. Mamma wanted her to be seen in all the great cities of the Continent as the new Viscountess Weston. Traveling on the Farrow dime, of course.

"Did you and Mr. Kidd have an extended honeymoon?" she asked Lila.

"A long trip, no. I fear we are both hopeless homebodies." She grinned a bit wickedly. "But I assure you, after nearly a year of marriage, the honeymoon is far from over."

Genevieve felt herself blush.

Lila lowered her voice. "I'm sorry. Have I embarrassed you?"

"It's just difficult to even imagine . . . we don't know each other all that well as yet. I don't even know if Morgan has true feelings for me." She'd probably said too much. "Forgive me. They are silly fears. He is a wonderful man and I grew to love him through his letters."

"As he grew to love you."

"Really?"

Lila seemed surprised. "Surely he's told you and has shown you." She looked at her brother. "If he hasn't I'll get after him straight away. Morgan? Come here."

"No!" Genevieve said under her breath. But it was too late. Morgan walked towards them.

"You called, sister?"

She took his hand. "Are you making our dear Genevieve feel at home in Summerfield?"

He cocked his head to the side and addressed Genevieve. "Am I?"

"Of course," she said, not knowing what else to say.

"You need to show her every nook and cranny of our village. Has she seen the mercantile yet?"

"She has, though I was thinking I would go again tomorrow. Nana said she's expecting a shipment of flour and other goods, so I told her I'd help unload." He smiled at Genevieve. "Would you like to join my little excursion, Miss Farrow?"

"What's with this Miss Farrow-business, Morgan?" Lila asked. "In a matter of weeks she's to be your wife. I think first names are appropriate."

"Very well. Genevieve," he said with a bow to his head.

She smiled. "I would love to go with you, Morgan," she said. "I want to see every part of your world, as it will soon be my own."

His smile revealed that he liked her answer.

The laughter of Genevieve's mother tittered off the dining room chandelier before sprinkling over the assemblage like an annoying drizzle. It was clear she thought herself terribly charming, but on more than one occasion, Genevieve caught the others exchanging glances that said their opinions were otherwise.

Except for Lord Newley. He seemed enamored by Mamma's exuberance. His cheeks were flushed from their exchanges, and his own deep laughter rumbled as the natural accompaniment to her mother's breezy storm. Or hurricane, depending on opinion. The two attended the dinner in their own private world, oblivious to the rest of them.

Others might suggest the two were flirting, but Genevieve had no doubt. Since finding the earl unaffected by her charms, it was only natural that Dorcas Farrow set her sights on a new titled man; a widowed viscount. Genevieve imagined her mother had already determined how marvelous it would be if both mother and daughter would marry and gain a viscountess title, two for the price of one. How terribly . . . American.

"Oh, Lord Newley," came her mother's voice above the rest. "You are simply too-too."

Whatever that meant.

Genevieve's eyes met Morgan's, and they shared a silent laugh. Mrs. Weston also smiled, and said to Genevieve, "I admire your mother's *joie de vivre*. Has she always enjoyed life so exuberantly?"

Genevieve hesitated to find the right words. She couldn't share the truth, that her mother's normal mood was more peevish than pleasant.

"She is quite carefree," Morgan said.

"Mamma has the philosophy that worry begets worry, so she might as well ignore the entire process."

The earl overheard. "Oh, to be without troubles," he said.

The laughter at their end of the table faded. "Are you troubled, Papa?" Lila asked.

"Of course not," he said.

Lila turned to Tilda. "You look enchanting tonight, Miss Cavendish. That royal blue brings out the auburn in your hair."

"It's Miss Weston's dress," the girl said. "I'm borrowing it."

Mrs. Weston chimed in. "It is doing no good stuck in a drawer in Clarissa's room."

"The lace looks to be Belgian?" Colonel Grady asked.

The dowager patted her husband's hand. "I think he cares nothing for fashion and then he notices such a detail."

"Always eager to surprise, wifey."

Wifey. The endearment was incredibly precious.

Genevieve looked towards Morgan and he gave her a wink. It gave her the immense hope that someday he would call her *wifey*.

Clarissa stepped away from the upstairs railing, leaning against the wall of the hallway for support.

They'd gone on without her! The sound of her mother and father, Grandmamma and Colonel Grady . . . their voices made her chest tighten. And to hear her little brother's voice of deeper tenor . . .

She heard Lila say, "You look enchanting tonight, Miss Cavendish. That royal blue brings out the auburn in your hair."

Royal blue? Clarissa knew exactly what dress Tilda was wearing. She was wearing *her* dress! The royal blue was a favorite. And yes, the lace was Belgian, hand-chosen in Paris. The girl was getting Clarissa's compliments!

Who was this Miss Cavendish anyway? Lila had mentioned Colonel Grady's goddaughter was staying at the manor, but for some reason Clarissa had assumed she was much younger, certainly not old enough to wear *her* clothes.

Then she had a sudden, awful thought. Was the girl staying in *her* bedroom?

The desire to get home *now* drowned her like a wave and nearly sent her rushing down the staircase into the dining room. No entrance on stage could rival the drama that would ensue.

Why not do it? The entire family was present.

She moved to grab the railing, needing a moment to calm her breathing. She ran her hands over her hair, smoothing the strays. *You can do this. You must do this.*

Before she could move, she felt a hand upon her shoulder.

She spun around to see Mrs. Crank. "You scared me," she whispered.

The housekeeper took a step back. "You will not go down," she said. Her eyes strayed to the stairs.

"Whyever not? It's my family."

"You will not disrupt Lady Kidd's dinner party."

Clarissa did not like being told what to do. "Being here in secret is my choice. If I want to reveal myself . . ."

Mrs. Crank shook her head slowly, back and forth. "This is not the way. Not the place."

217

Was she right? Clarissa's imaginings of going home were quite different. They involved walking up the long drive of the manor and having Dixon open the door. The look on his face would be priceless. She would simply say, "Good day, Dixon. Is my family at home?"

And then they would all come running, along with Mrs. Camden, Nick, and Gertie. Even Mrs. McDeer would come up from the kitchen. Their faces would beam with utter delight, and then Mrs. McDeer would scurry back to her realm to cook Clarissa's favorite meal of mutton and mash, with an apple tartlet for dessert. Grandmamma and the colonel would be called up from the cottage to join them, and Clarissa could enjoy a second homecoming within her grandmother's arms.

To go down now would provide a few moments of pleasurable spectacle, but revealing herself to everyone, all at once, meant it would be quickly over and done.

Besides, she hadn't completely figured out what she was going to say to them. She'd come up with a few pages of dialogue, but the best words, said for the best effect, were not solidly memorized. She needed more —

"You need more time, miss," Mrs. Crank said.

With a nod, Clarissa accepted the housekeeper's directive as her own. "You are right. Thank you for stopping me."

The woman returned the nod. "Would you like your dinner tray brought up to your room now, Miss Weston?"

Why not? Dissecting the logistics of a homecoming had given her an appetite.

It was surreal.

Although Tilda had enjoyed — and endured — many meals at Summerfield Manor, this was her first true dinner party complete with seven courses, wearing a real gown, and listening to the exchange of two families of high society.

George leaned over from her right. "Do you like quail?"

So that's what it was. "Not much meat on it," she said.

"If only we could pick it up." He grinned and moved his hands towards the bird. "Want to?"

"No!" she whispered, looking around to see who might have seen and heard their exchange.

Uncle Grady subtly raised a finger in warning.

George put his hands in his lap. Not that he actually would have done such a thing, but she was happy that he'd invited her to be a part of it.

Tilda remembered what her guardian Miss Smith had once told her: "Teasing is a form of flirtation, and flirtation is the first step to courting."

"Are you teasing me, Master George?"

"Absolutely yes. Should I stop?"

"Absolutely no."

Suddenly, the surreal quality of the evening became very, very real.

***

The carriages pulled away from Crompton Hall.

"So," Morgan said. "What do you think of my sister?"

"I find her quite delightful," Genevieve said, with a final glance at the mansion. "And — " She leaned forward, her gaze drawn by a single upstairs room, lit with light. A woman stood at the window, half hidden by lace curtains. "Does anyone else live there?" she asked.

"No," Morgan said.

"I'm sure they have a team of servants," her mother said, "Though certainly not as many as work at Summerfield Manor. All in all, Crompton Hall is a much smaller place and — "

"Not a servant," Genevieve said. "See? Up there."

But when the others turned to see, the woman was gone.

"It probably *was* just a servant, turning down a bed," Morgan's grandmother said.

Probably.

***

219

"Come in."

Lila entered Clarissa's room.

Clarissa put down the book she was reading. "Is the evening over already?"

Lila nodded towards a tray nearby. "Did you get enough to eat?"

"Enough," she said. She pointed at the window. "I saw my family leave."

Lila swallowed. "Yes?"

"Mother let that girl wear my dress."

Lila's eyebrows rose. "You overheard all that?"

"I listened from the upstairs hall."

"You could have come down."

"I will admit that hearing their voices made me miss them. Mrs. Crank had to stop me from racing downstairs and making my entrance right then and there. She said I was not to disturb the party."

"The party would have been better for the reunion."

Clarissa shrugged. "Perhaps. But it was also the first time you met the Farrows and—" She thought of another memory. "My, Mrs. Farrow is talkative. Whatever comes into her head is said aloud. Is that an American trait?"

Lila laughed. "Not distinctly American," Lila said. "My mother also lacked the ability to filter her conversation."

Clarissa shook her head, needing to return to the original subject at hand. "I want a homecoming to be on my terms, at the time of my choosing, in my home."

Lila nodded. "Whenever you'd like to reveal yourself, I would be happy to arrange it."

"I'll let you know." Clarissa opened her book, dismissing her.

Molly stood at the foot of the bed while Dr. Peter attended her mother. "I feared I was making her do too much too fast," she said. "And after dinner, when we were walking, she stumbled and hit her head on the bedpost."

Dr. Peter examined the large knot on Ma's forehead. "I'm glad you sent for me. Swelling like this is not unusual as head injuries swell quickly. And getting ice for it was the right thing to do." He gave Ma a look. "Do you feel all right otherwise, Mrs. Wallace?"

She nodded. "Cumsy."

"You are not clumsy, Ma. You are doing very well."

"Indeed you are. For now, just rest and begin fresh tomorrow."

There was an intense rapping on the door. "Dr. Peter? Dr. Peter!"

Molly answered it, and found Barry, the hall boy. He was out of breath. "A note came. Mr. Dixon told me to run it up. You're needed, Dr. Peter."

Peter read the note. "It's Mrs. Hopkins."

"What's wrong?"

"Her baby is coming."

He closed his medical bag. "My father is in London. I have to handle it."

"Have you delivered many babies, doctor?" Molly asked.

"This will be my first."

"I helped deliver my sister and brother."

He paused at the door. "Would you care to assist me, Miss Wallace? Your gentle, authoritative hand would be most welcome."

Molly looked to Ma, who waved a hand at them. "Go."

"All right," she said. "I'll send Dottie up to be with Ma."

A few minutes later she sat beside Dr. Peter in his wagon. It brought back memories. "Here we are again."

"Indeed," he said. "I can think of no one else I would rather have by my side, Miss Wallace." Catching the more personal implication, she glanced at him and saw his blush. "You know what I mean."

She did. Yet the other meaning, combined with his delightful blush . . .

He was actually quite charming.

Chapter Fourteen

Genevieve slipped her hand around Morgan's arm as they
walked from the manor towards the village. She was glad to
be away from the house, as it was veiled in the ever-present
threat that the blackmail secret would come out, and then all
would be lost.

Morgan would be lost.

"It's nice you agreed to go to the mercantile with me,
Genevieve. Nana needs my help to get new shipments
organized."

"I'm glad to come along, for it will give me the chance to
get to know her better."

"It's not going to be an entertaining outing, for I'm going
to have to work."

She hated that he thought her so shallow. "I will be
happy to work right alongside you, Morgan." She squeezed
his arm. "I will always be happy and willing to work
alongside you."

He stopped walking and his eyes lingered a long moment
on hers. "I believe you."

"You should."

The way he studied her face made her want to look away,
but she forced herself to return his gaze. "You're
embarrassing me," she said.

He looked to the ground, then back to her face. "You
fascinate me. You exude such a strong sense of honor as
though I can completely trust you."

She wanted to say, "You can", but considering the tenuous situation, she couched her words. "I will always do my best to honor you and your family."

"I'm glad you agreed to *walk* to the village," he said, taking her arm and setting the pace. "I just can't get used to the idea of taking a carriage to the store. It seems . . . presumptuous."

"I enjoy the walk. Especially in such fine company on such a fine autumn day."

"You always know just what to say to make me feel right about my decisions."

I try.

As they passed a man herding sheep down the lane, Morgan stopped to talk to him. "Mr. Deals, good morning to you."

"Morning to you, your lordship." He tipped his hat at Genevieve.

Morgan did the honors. "Mr. Deals, I would like you to meet my bride-to-be, Genevieve Farrow, come all the way from America. Miss Farrow, Mr. Deals."

"Nice to meet you, miss," he said, offering another tip of his hat.

"Nice to meet you, Mr. Deals." The sheep surrounded them, an undulating mass of softness and black noses. Genevieve giggled and raised her arms high above them. "I can honestly say I would never have had this experience in New York."

"Get!" Mr. Deals said, using a stick to prod them away. "I apologize. Sheep is dumb animals and take no heed of decorum."

"Nor should they."

She and Morgan moved through the herd, with the animals quickly filling the space behind them.

"Nothing fazes you, does it?" Morgan asked as they resumed their walk.

"Actually, most things overwhelm me but I'm good at hiding it."

"Name something. Anything."

Put on the spot, her mind went blank. She could only think of something that encompassed the whole of it. "I don't know how to be a wife, much less a viscountess."

"And eventually a countess," he said.

"Don't make it worse!"

He laughed. "I admire your candor. But fair being fair, I admit the same to you. This whole title thing has been thrust upon me too."

"And the husband-thing?"

Once again he stopped walking and peered at the ground a moment before looking at her. "I will admit it was not my idea. I will also admit that your family's money is very necessary to the future of the Summerfield estate and manor. It's unfortunate that our match was made with such mercurial terms attached, but I am also a businessman. I grew up knowing about expenses and revenues from the time I could add one plus one."

"That is an asset in itself."

He smiled, but raised a hand, wanting to continue. "I am not a romantic but a pragmatist. If a problem needs to be solved, I look for the answer, and . . . and . . ."

"My family's money is that answer?"

His hand moved towards hers, and their fingers skimmed each other. "You are the answer. For this would never have worked with just any American heiress."

"It could have. After all, money is money."

He shook his head. "You are right. It *could* have. But the fact we have developed an affinity for each other . . ."

She was moved by his admission. "It does make it easier," she said. "Like-mindedness is a great beginning to any marriage, but especially one that holds a greater responsibility to a title, an estate, and all those who work there."

His smile was genuine and she saw a glimmer of moisture in his eyes. "This *will* work, won't it?"

It was a question, not a statement. She made the transition to the latter. "This *will* work."

He pulled her hand to his lips, ending the kiss with a smile and a nod.

"Where would you like these pots, Mrs. Hayward?"

"Over here, Genevieve," Nana said. "And call me Nana, remember?"

"Of course." It was hard to be so familiar. Her own grandparents had died when she was little, so she had no habit of address to guide her. Yet Nana *was* a nana, not a grandmother, or grandmamma, and certainly not Mrs. Hayward. Everything about the woman encouraged an aura of comfort and family.

Genevieve set the pots and pans on a shelf and arranged them nicely. She watched as Morgan came in from the back, a huge sack of flour on his shoulder. His shirtsleeves were rolled up and his face glistened with sweat. He was as handsome as she'd ever seen him.

He dropped the load and caught her looking at him. She felt herself redden. "Quit lollygagging and get to work," he said with a smile.

"Yes, sir!" The pots arranged, she noticed a blue bit of sewing on a chair behind the counter. She held it up and saw it was a young girl's dress. "You're making this?" she asked Nana.

"I am. The daughter of a friend needed a new dress and I offered to make it."

"It's all hand-sewn?"

"Is there any other way?"

"Actually, if you remember, my father was in the business of sewing machines. My very own machine should be arriving any day. You are welcome the use of it."

"I wouldn't know how."

"I'll teach you. I used to sew all my dresses. And Mamma's."

Nana's eyebrows rose.

"We weren't always wealthy, you know. Besides, I enjoy it."

Genevieve caught Morgan studying her—but not in a bad way. "What?" she asked.

"Nothing."

But it *was* something, and it made her glad.

All morning Clarissa had sensed Lila was nervous about something. Finally, when they were walking in the garden, she confronted her. "What's wrong? You're acting as if something horrible is going to happen and you don't want to tell me."

Lila nodded as she plucked a flower from the garden and held it to her nose.

"Something horrible *is* going to happen?"

Lila drew in a breath. "Not horrible, but it will upset you."

Clarissa's imagination took the situation to its worst level. "Just tell me!"

"Our Grandmother is coming over this afternoon to work on the quilt."

Clarissa let out the breath she'd been saving. "Is that all? That's not horrible."

Lila hesitated. "Tilda's coming with her."

She felt her ire rise to the surface like a teapot boiling over. "Why did you invite her?"

"I invited her before you came home. After all, Tilda is the colonel's goddaughter."

"If she's his goddaughter, then why is she living at the manor?" Clarissa knew she was being petty and peevish, but couldn't help herself. She plucked her own flower from the garden and spun it between her fingers before tossing it away.

"You know the practical answer," Lila said evenly.

Clarissa sighed. Yes, her grandmother's cottage was small. "When are they coming? I'll be sure to be properly hidden away."

"At two. You *can* join us, you know. I'd like your help on the quilt."

"I'll think about it."

And she would. Too much.

Clarissa paced from her bed to the window and back again. Downstairs Grandmamma had arrived with Tilda. Clarissa had watched them drive up, and could imagine them in Lila's morning room, stitching away. And with each stitch, Tilda was securing her position in the family.

You could have helped Lila with the quilt. She offered.

"It's not about the quilt!" she told the room.

There was a knock and a housemaid came in with a tray of tea and biscuits. "Pardon me, Miss Weston, but Lady Kidd thought you might enjoy some refreshment."

She flipped her hand at it. "Take it away."

The maid nodded and began to leave.

"Wait!"

"Yes, miss?"

"I do need something from you. A favor."

"Of course."

"I need you to go see what's going on with the quilting."

Her forehead furrowed. "Going on?"

Did she really need it spelled out? "What's being said. Just stand outside the door a few minutes, listen, then report to me."

"Mr. Dowd and Mrs. Crank won't take to me listening when I shouldn't."

"Then don't let them see you." She opened the bedroom door fully, then whispered. "Go on now. And hurry back."

As soon as the girl left, Clarissa felt a wave of guilt. And shame. So it had come to this?

She sat on the window seat and waited.

Five minutes later, the maid rapped on the door and entered.

"You weren't gone long," Clarissa said.

"Mrs. Crank saw me and sent me on my way."

Clarissa sighed dramatically. "So did you hear anything?"

"Not much. It sounded like her ladyship and the dowager were teaching the girl how to quilt."

"That's it?"

"There was some laughing involved. But then Mrs. Crank—"

Clarissa dismissed her. "Thank you. That will be all."

The girl bobbed a curtsy and left.

Oddly, it wasn't the quilting lesson that bothered Clarissa the most. It was the laughter. For laughter meant they were getting on well and were at ease in each other's company.

Laughter meant Tilda was becoming one of the family.

Laughter meant it was time for Clarissa to go home.

As Molly started to leave her mother's room, Ma took her hand, stopping her. "Wheh go?"

Molly considered fibbing by saying she had things to do for Miss Farrow—especially after coming back late from helping Dr. Peter deliver a baby boy. But as a fib formed in her mind, the truth came out. "I'm going on a picnic with Dr. Peter."

She did not expect her mother's smile. "Guh."

"Good?"

Ma nodded. "He guh mahn."

"Are you trying to match us together?"

"Uh-huh."

"It's just a simple outing, as a thank you for me helping with Mrs. Hopkins' delivery."

Her crooked grin was exasperating.

"Keep this up and I won't tell you a thing about it."

Ma put a hand over her mouth. Molly kissed her on the forehead and left to spend time with Dr. Peter—who *was* a very good man.

Molly looked down at the tablecloth, smoothed upon the grass. Dr. Peter placed a basket on one corner, anchoring it against the autumn breeze.

"Quick!" he said. "Let's sit down before it blows away."

He held her hand as she sat at one corner, him sitting fully across from her, with the basket on a corner in between.

He began unburdening the basket. "I've brought some ham sandwiches—made with Mrs. Keening's fine brown bread, some apples, some wine, and two pieces of pound cake."

"Also thanks to Mrs. Keening?"

"Actually father's cook is quite adept at making sweets." He patted his midriff. "Too adept."

"When will your father be back from London?"

He handed her a napkin and a sandwich. "I'm not sure. I think he's enjoying himself. He's reconnected with old friends. Plus . . ."

"He has you taking care of business here."

He shrugged. "When I moved here I didn't think I would be on my own quite so much or so soon."

"You handled the birth of Mrs. Hopkins' son very well."

He smiled. "I was shaking in my shoes the entire time. Babies will be born whether a doctor is there or not. I'm just glad there were no complications. I'm going to check on her later today." He pulled the cork from the wine bottle and poured two glasses. "You handled your part in the birth quite well too, Miss Wallace."

"I'm glad to have been there. Seeing a new life begin is rather extraordinary."

He raised his glass. "To new life and new beginnings."

They clinked their glasses across the tablecloth.

"Now that your mother is doing better—save for the bump on the head—what are your plans? Are you staying on in Summerfield?"

She had no answer.

"If you don't wish to tell me . . ."

"My hesitancy is due to my uncertainty. I am torn."

He adjusted the ham within his sandwich. "Because of Lord Weston?"

She drew in a breath. "Why do you say that?"

He shrugged. "Your mother mentioned that you and he once loved each other."

"My mother can't talk."

"You are not the only one who can decipher her words. And when she has something to say she can be very determined to say it."

Molly stood, leaving her sandwich behind. "She had no right to tell you that. It's in the past and—"

"Is it?"

Molly stared down at him. "What are you implying?"

To his credit he held her gaze. "Love cannot be shut off like water in a spigot."

The truth in his words calmed her anger. "No, it can't." She lowered herself to the ground. "But neither can love overcome all boundaries."

"Unless you have magical powers to breach the bastions of the titled."

"There might be a way."

His eyebrows rose. "For you to marry Lord Weston?"

She'd said too much. "Never mind. There is no way. No way at all." She stopped herself from saying more by taking a bite of sandwich. "Good bread."

He ignored her pitiful attempt to change the subject. "It must be hard for you to serve Miss Farrow."

She bought time by chewing. Yet his perceptive statement deserved an answer. "Unfortunately, her kindness and gracious nature makes it hard for me to hate her."

He let out a laugh. "I appreciate your honesty."

His statement emboldened her. "Since we're being honest, I must admit that I waver between wanting to do whatever needs to be done to win him back, and running back to London, vowing to forget him."

"Is there nothing in between?"

She didn't understand.

"Is there not a choice to let him go and still stay in Summerfield?"

Until he'd said the words, she truly hadn't thought of this option. "And what would I do here? Be a lady's maid at the manor and see Morgan and Miss Farrow happily married?" She shook her head adamantly. "I can't do that."

"Then don't do that." He took a bite of an apple and chewed a moment. "You could assist me. You've already shown an aptitude for it."

"I know nothing about medicine."

"And I know a little. Together we could attend to the people of Summerfield. With Father away, I need help, and I'm sure I could convince him to offer you a nurse's wage."

Molly stopped eating... stopped being present at the picnic at all. Her mind swirled with the thought of staying at Summerfield, near family, being a nurse.

"Of course if that does not spark your interest . . ."

She forced herself back to the present. "It *is* interesting," she said. "I'll have to think on it."

He beamed. "I can wait." He raised his glass again. "To patience and wise decisions."

"You're leaving?" Lila asked, as she attempted to fold a completed quilt.

She was getting it uneven, so Clarissa helped. "It's time."

"What made you decide *now* was the time?"

"I could make up an excuse, but my mind is too much of a jumble to lie."

"So the truth is . . .?" Lila asked.

"I hate the idea that that girl, Tilda, is taking over my life."

"I doubt that is true."

"She wore my dress and she was here today with Grandmamma."

"What are you going to say to your family about what you've been doing the past year?" Lila asked.

"I'll think of something."

"The truth might be best."

Easy for her to say. "I will deal with that in the moment. I am good at improvisation."

"I'll say a prayer that you find the right words."

Amen to that.

Tilda sat on the sunporch doing a sketch of Mr. Weston. She was having trouble getting his chin just right. It was a little too pointed.

Dixon came in with a look on his face that Tilda had never seen before.

Excitement.

"Yes, Dixon?" Mrs. Weston asked.

"There is someone to see you, both of you."

"Tell them to come back tomorrow," Mr. Weston said without moving the position of his face.

"I'm afraid that won't be —"

Suddenly, a young woman swept into the room. "Never mind, Dixon. Hello, Father. Hello, Mother. I'm back!"

Clarissa?

The portrait was forgotten as mother and father rushed to embrace her. They spoke over one another, and Mrs. Weston began to cry. It was quite moving.

Except for the fact that Clarissa's sudden arrival changed everything.

When Mrs. Weston stopped hugging her daughter to retrieve a handkerchief from her waistband, Tilda was remembered. "Oh. Tilda. Come meet our darling Clarissa, back home again. Clarissa, this is Tilda Cavendish, the colonel's goddaughter."

Clarissa stepped forward, her hand extended. "Tilda."

It was a friendly gesture, yet Tilda saw a spark in Clarissa's eyes that was anything but.

"Sit everyone, sit," Mrs. Weston said. She turned to Dixon. "Please bring us some refreshment. I'm sure our daughter is hungry."

"That won't be necessary," Clarissa said. "I've been eating quite well at Crompton Hall."

"Crompton Hall?"

The question propelled Clarissa through some long, drawn-out story of staying with the Kidds after she was evicted, some maid leaving, and being fired from her job as an actress. The last, was the most interesting. For even Tilda knew no woman of good breeding ever went on the stage.

"But what of the Duvalls?" Mr. Weston asked. "When did you have time to be in the theatre when you were traveling with them in Europe?"

Tilda caught a glimpse of fear in Clarissa's hesitation, but being a good actress, she covered it quickly. "I didn't go with the Duvalls to Europe. Actually, I've been on my own for quite a while."

"But you said—"

"I lied." She rose from her chair and moved behind it, gripping its back, making Tilda think it was a bit of stage direction she'd used before. "I apologize to both of you, to the entire family. It was selfish of me to ignore your wishes, but I simply had to see if I could make it in the theatre."

"Did you succeed at all?" her mother asked.

Her father stopped the answer with a hand. "I don't want to hear about so-called success on the stage. Any success you may or may not have achieved is countered by your deception."

Clarissa moved to him, kneeling beside his chair. Again, Tilda had the feeling she'd been in this position before. The progression of events seemed staged, as if by sinning, confessing, then asking for forgiveness, Clarissa gained the most dramatic effect.

"I'm sorry, Father. I know you trusted me."

"What happened to all the money I sent you?"

"At first I used it for frivolous things, but when the Duvalls left on their travels and I was on my own, I used it for rent and food, and by then I didn't have a respectable address for you to send money to, and I'd already lied about going with the Duvalls." She let out a dramatic sigh. "It was gone too soon and I had to work to survive."

Tilda let a *harummph* escape.

Clarissa looked in her direction, her eyes searing. "You find that amusing, Miss Cavendish?"

"Only that most people have to work to survive."

Clarissa stood to her full regal height and smoothed her skirt. "Well, I never had to do such a thing. But now, having had that experience, I am better for it."

"Was your life very difficult?" her mother asked.

"More than you know." She touched her mother's hand, then returned to her chair. "I am the prodigal son, returned home."

Tilda remembered that story from Mrs. Smith. The prodigal son lived a wild life, then returned home where his father welcomed him with open arms and a celebration.

While the good son who had loyally remained at home was ignored.

Tilda didn't want to be ignored.

Mrs. Weston clapped her hands together. "I have a splendid idea. I'll contact all your friends and give a dinner in your honor. Nothing elaborate. Just a small soiree amongst close friends. I know they'd love to see you."

"That would be grand," Clarissa said.

Apparently prodigal daughters also got parties.

Clarissa sat at the window seat in her old bedroom, dressed for bed, taking it all in. She had not planned to answer her parents' questions with total honesty, yet one truth had led to the next until her sins lay scattered across the floor, ready to be trod upon and kicked away by forgiving hearts.

Reluctantly, she had to admit that Lila's suggestion that the truth might be best had proven itself correct. The fact her parents' happiness at having her home muted their anger fed well into the scene. The entire homecoming — with her father sending for George, who joyfully wrapped his strong arms around her, making her tear up — could not have played out better. Well done. A standing ovation please.

Actually, it felt good to have most of the details of her time in London in the open. Her confession left her free to enter her old life without fear of the past demanding its due. The old adage that "confession was good for the soul" rang true.

Letting that freedom fill her, she stood and stretched her arms to the coffered ceiling, reveling in the space and luxury of her room.

It was of great relief that it appeared untouched since she'd left. The small desk by the window was still adorned with the two Derby porcelain statues of an eighteenth-century man and woman that she had played with as a child. And the large canopy bed awaited her slumber.

She moved to her dressing table and sat on the bench, picking up the sterling-backed brush and mirror. She began to brush her hair, remembering the countless days when Agnes had done the honors.

But Agnes was gone. With Clarissa's money.

Good riddance.

She opened her jewelry box and was immediately buoyed by the familiar pieces. She took the box to the cushion on the window seat and dumped it out, arranging each piece in a long-specified order.

But . . . where was the emerald choker? Every other piece was accounted for but that one.

Tilda.

Clarissa knew the girl had been borrowing her clothes. She wouldn't put it past her to help herself to some jewels.

Yet surely she'd had no reason to wear such a glamorous choker around the manor.

Clarissa was halfway to the door, on her way to her mother's room, when she heard the clock on the mantel strike midnight.

Accusing Tilda Cavendish would have to keep until morning.

Chapter Fifteen

Clarissa awakened when the sun suddenly fell across her face. "Agnes! What are you doing?"

But another voice, not Agnes, answered, "Sorry, Miss Weston, but I assumed you would like to get up in time to have breakfast with your family."

Clarissa pushed herself to sitting, squinting against the morning light. "Good morning, Albers." It was her mother's lady's maid, who used to be Grandmamma's lady's maid. Albers was ancient.

Albers adjusted the drapery so the light wasn't so glaring. "Good morning, miss. Would you like me to choose a dress for you this morning?"

"As you wish."

Clarissa let her feet hang from the edge of the bed and stretched, enjoying the delicious ache that came from her muscles accomplishing their own awakening.

"What's this?" Albers said, moving towards the jewels on the window seat. She picked up the jewelry box and began to put things away.

Clarissa jumped off the bed to stop her. "Leave them."

"But such precious gems shouldn't be left out. The housemaids will be in here to clean, and . . ."

"You don't want them to steal anything?"

"It's best not to test temptation so blatantly."

Clarissa couldn't have set up the situation any more perfectly.

She pointed at the jewels. "It turns out I am missing an emerald choker and was going to speak to Mother about it this morning."

Albers's eyes scanned the necklaces, bracelets, and earrings. "Are you certain it was here?"

"Positive. I had little use for such an extravagant piece when I left to live with the Duvalls."

"Oh dear. This will not do. Will not do at all."

Her plan to bring down Tilda Cavendish began. "Hasn't my room remained untouched in the time I've been gone?"

Albers nodded. "The maids have dusted and such, but no one . . ." She drew in a breath.

"What?" Clarissa forced herself not to smile.

"Miss Cavendish. She has been in here to borrow some of your dresses."

"She borrowed my clothes?"

"With your mother's permission. The girl came here with very little and she is nearly the same size as you, and . . ." Albers shook her head. "But she wouldn't steal. She's Colonel Grady's goddaughter."

"Whom he hasn't seen for many years."

Albers blinked. Repeatedly. "Oh dear. This will not do. Will not do at all."

Actually, it would do quite nicely. "Is my mother dressed yet?"

"Yes, miss. I helped her before I came in to you."

"Will you go get her for me, please?"

Mother peered at the array of jewels on the window seat. "You're right. It's not here."

Clarissa kept her impatience in check. "Someone stole it."

Mother put a hand to her chest. "I can't imagine. All the staff has been with us for years. They have all proven themselves trustworthy."

"Then who is new in the house — beyond the Farrows, of course?" *Come on, Mother . . . make your own deduction.*

She drew in a breath. "No. It can't be."

"Can't be whom?" Clarissa feigned ignorance, catching a look from Albers.

But Mother didn't say it aloud, and only shook her head. "I should not accuse until I—"

"But it's my choker!" Clarissa said. "And it belonged to your grandmother, yes?"

"Yes, it did. It means as much to me as it does to you, but—"

"But what? If you have suspicions, voice them. I want that choker returned."

Mother glanced at the clock on the mantel. "Perhaps we should address this after breakfast. I wouldn't want to upset the staff's schedule."

Really?

"Come dear. I don't do well with confrontation on an empty stomach."

Mother did not do well with confrontation, period.

Something was up.

Although Tilda had braced herself for an aggravating breakfast featuring the new star of the house, Clarissa, she had not expected to feel tension.

After the initial it-is-so-wonderful-to-have-you-home-again comments from the family, conversation died, only to be punctuated by awkward "Well then's" from the earl and smiles from Mr. Weston.

Finally, Mrs. Farrow broke the silence. "What is going on this morning? I expected a jolly breakfast and find this odd . . ." She waved her hands in little circles.

"I find it odd too," Mr. Weston said, putting down his fork. He looked at his wife. "What is going on, my dear? I see the looks you and Clarissa are exchanging. Everyone sees."

Mrs. Weston took a deep breath and set her napkin beside her plate. "Clarissa has found a necklace missing from her room."

"A very precious necklace in both worth and sentiment," Clarissa added.

Tilda's stomach flipped. After returning Clarissa's jewelry to her room, she'd forgotten about planting a necklace in Gertie's room.

"Stolen?" the earl said. "Are you positive?"

"Very," Clarissa said. She looked directly at Tilda.

What did she know? Tilda rushed in to deflect the attention. "How horrible. It must have been one of the maids."

"You shouldn't automatically think the staff was involved," George said.

"Who else but staff?" the earl said.

"The Whites were here," Mrs. Weston said.

The earl and his brother exchanged a glance. "Their involvement is totally possible."

With a nod Mrs. Farrow buttered a roll. "I didn't like that Mrs. White at all. Mr. White was nice enough, but his wife . . ." She made herself shudder. "There was something dodgy about her."

There was a moment of silence, as if everyone was trying to define "dodgy."

"I can't imagine they would dare leave with anything stolen and risk us sending the law after them," Mr. Weston said. He looked at his brother.

"Nor, can I," the earl said.

Mr. Weston continued, "But I suppose we must do our due diligence and make inquiries within the house."

The earl nodded and motioned the butler close. "Dixon, would you please ask Mrs. Camden to join us? And perhaps as head housekeeper, Gertie should be here as well."

"Absolutely, your lordship."

Mrs. Farrow rose to get another helping of eggs. "I knew there was something going on this morning. I am very attune to changes in the atmosphere." She returned to her chair, letting Nick help her move close to the table. "There was a distinct vibration in the air this morning."

"Mamma . . ." her daughter said.

"I was right, wasn't I?"

Morgan exchanged a look with Miss Farrow. "Perhaps we should leave and let this be handled with as much discretion as possible."

"I agree," the earl said. "George, you too. And Miss Cavendish, you can be excused also."

Thank goodness!

"No!" Clarissa said. "I want her to stay. Mother?"

Mrs. Weston hesitated, then nodded. "I think it best." But she nodded to Morgan and Miss Farrow. "You two go on. And Mrs. Farrow? If you please?"

Mrs. Farrow was caught with a forkful of food in her mouth, but she dabbed her mouth with her napkin, and left the room with the others.

Wait for me!

Tilda felt her heart beat in her chest. This was not going well. If only's plagued her.

Mr. Dixon returned with Mrs. Camden and Gertie. They stood in a row in front of the buffet. "We are gathered, Lord Summerfield."

The earl looked a bit confused, as if he wasn't certain how to proceed. Theft was obviously not something oft encountered at the manor. "Well then. It seems in Miss Weston's absence, a certain necklace has gone missing from her bedroom."

"How awful," the housekeeper said. She turned to Gertie. "Are you aware of this?"

"No, Mrs. Camden." But suddenly she glanced at Tilda, took a fresh breath, and said, "I did, however, see Miss Cavendish trying on Miss Weston's jewelry."

With all eyes on her, Tilda wanted to sink beneath the table. Should she admit to trying them on? Or deny it completely?

Mrs. Weston came to her defense. "I have allowed Miss Cavendish access to Clarissa's closet—with my blessings as she came to the manor with only a few dresses." She smiled at Tilda.

Clarissa huffed. "Although I must admit I find the idea of my things being used by another distasteful, I acquiesce to Mother's decision. But the item missing is an emerald choker." She glared at Tilda. "A very precious emerald choker."

Tilda managed to swallow, then shook her head. "I have never seen it."

Gertie let out a soft, "Hmm", which was enough to gain everyone's gaze.

"Gertie?" Mrs. Camden said. "Do you have something to say?"

The direct question made the maid look panicked. Her hesitation caused the earl to say, "Out with it, please."

Gertie's face blotched with red. "A week or so ago, I entered Miss Weston's room to check to see if Prissy had dusted yet, and found Miss Cavendish with all of Miss Weston's jewelry dumped out on her lap. I do believe she was wearing an emerald choker."

Once again, all eyes turned towards Tilda.

"Is this true, Miss Cavendish?" the earl asked.

Yes or no. Partial truth or a lie . . .

"No," Tilda heard herself saying. "I wouldn't go through Miss Weston's things. I was very grateful to be able to wear a few of her dresses, but jewels . . ." She shook her head no. "I wouldn't dare touch such valuable possessions."

Everyone's gaze turned back to Gertie. "She's lying! I saw her! She even left the room with it on."

Tilda pushed back from the table. "You accuse me of stealing from a family that has been nothing but kind to me?" She looked at each face. "If you don't believe me, search my room. But only if you search hers too!"

Gertie's right eyebrow rose.

"I'm sure that isn't necessary," Mrs. Weston said.

"I think it is necessary," Clarissa said. "Father? Uncle Jack?"

The men stood, clearly annoyed by the disturbance in their day. "Dixon and Mrs. Camden, would you please see to the search? I would like this wrapped up as soon as possible."

"Not without me and mother," Clarissa said.

"Very well. Go now. Get this done."

Tilda began to follow Mrs. Weston, but Clarissa turned on her. "Not you."

"Since I have been wrongfully accused I have a right to be there."

"She does," Mrs. Weston said. "Come now, Tilda."

"Do her room first," Tilda said, pointing at Gertie.

The maid looked at her, incredulous. But then her eyes gained a nervous mien.

"To your room, Gertie," Mr. Dixon said.

Clarissa pushed ahead to walk next to her mother. Tilda was fine being the last in line.

For now.

It was crowded in the hallway bisecting the servants' bedrooms. Mrs. Weston, Clarissa, and Tilda stood outside with Gertie hovering nervously near the door, while Dixon and Mrs. Camden searched her room.

"It will be all right, Gertie," Clarissa told her. "I know you didn't take it."

Gertie looked surprised at the support and glanced at Tilda.

Which solidified Clarissa's opinion that Tilda was to blame. The only thing she couldn't figure out is why Tilda would suggest their rooms be —

"Found it!" Dixon said, dropping the mattress back on the frame.

"What?" Gertie entered the room. "I . . . no . . . I didn't put it there!"

"Gertie, Gertie," Mrs. Camden said, shaking her head.

"I'm telling you, I didn't put it there." She looked at Clarissa. "I didn't take it, miss. I swear to God, I didn't take it."

Tilda spoke up. "Then why is it under your mattress?"

Gertie lunged at the girl, knocking her into the wall, her hands on her shoulders. "You put it there! You set me up!"

In a flurry of hands, Gertie was pulled away. Yet her accusations continued.

"You little imp! I'm the one who caught *you* with Miss Weston's things. You wore the choker out of the room. You did this."

Clarissa was appalled to see her mother take Tilda in her arms, comforting her.

Dixon yanked on the bottom of his vest and smoothed his coat. "I am sorry, Gertie, but your services are no longer needed at the manor."

"But I've worked here for ten years! I don't have anywhere else to go!"

"Come now," Mrs. Camden said, leading the maid back in her room. "Collect your things."

Dixon offered the ladies a bow. "I do apologize for this, Miss Weston, Mrs. Weston. I don't know what got into her, but let me assure you, theft will never be condoned at Summerfield Manor. This will never happen again."

Mother nodded and led Tilda down the stairs to the family's floor.

"I don't feel very well," Tilda whined.

"Of course, you don't," Mother said, stroking her hair. "You've had a distressing morning. Why don't you rest, and later, maybe you can go riding with George."

Tilda nodded, and kissed Mother's cheek as she was left off at her room. Before entering she looked directly at Clarissa and said, "I'm glad you found your necklace, Miss Weston. I believe Dixon when he says such a thing won't happen again."

Clarissa blinked, trying to read the secret meaning of her words. Was it an innocent comment, or was Tilda saying that *she* wouldn't steal again?

As Clarissa and her mother reached the top of the stairs leading them to the public floor, her mother said, "At least the necklace is returned and all is well."

Clarissa held back her mother's progress. "It is not well. Don't you see that Tilda is the one who stole it?"

"No, she isn't. It was found in Gertie's room."

"But what would a maid do with such a necklace? She'd have a hard time selling it."

"Maybe she just thought it was pretty."

Clarissa was incredulous. "What has that girl done to you? To this family?"

"Done?"

"Don't you see? She's tried to take my place—and she was nearly successful. You had her wearing my clothes and you've let her draw your portrait."

"She came with very few—"

"Dresses. I know. But as she's the colonel's goddaughter why isn't she staying with him and Grandmamma?"

"There's hardly room for her at the cottage."

Clarissa got to the core of her complaint. "There's hardly room for her here at the manor—not as your daughter. I am your daughter. Your only daughter."

Mother cupped Clarissa's cheek with a hand. "Yes, you are. And I thank God for bringing you back to me." Then she slipped her hand around Clarissa's arm and began to descend the stairs. "What should we do this morning, you and I?"

Clarissa's mind was blank.

Genevieve heard the crunching of wheels upon gravel, and the uneven sound of horses' hoofs. Through the drawing room window she saw a wagon coming up the drive with two men on board. A delivery. Nothing out of the—

"They're here!" She burst through the front door to greet the wagon.

Dixon followed close behind, and the driver looked confused as to whether he should address the girl or the butler.

He chose the latter. "Trunks came on the train for a Miss Farrow?" he said.

But Genevieve was already at the back of the wagon, checking the number. Three. Yes, that was right. "Those three are mine from New York," she said pointing them out.

The driver came round to look. "That other trunk is yours too."

"I don't think so. I've never had an ivory trunk."

He climbed onto the bed of the wagon and checked a tag and read, "'Miss Genevieve Farrow, care of Summerfield Manor.' That's you."

"That's me."

"Who's it from, man?" Dixon asked.

He looked again. "House of Worth, Paris."

Genevieve gasped. "It's my wedding dress! That one first, please!" She hurried back inside and called out, "Mamma! Mrs. Weston! Ladies, come quickly!"

Mrs. Weston appeared from the vicinity of her morning room. "What's wrong, my dear?"

Clarissa and Tilda appeared at the top of the stairs. "Someone get hurt?" Clarissa asked.

Genevieve realized she'd been totally unladylike in yelling out like that. "My wedding dress has arrived! Come see!"

One man carried in the ivory trunk. Mrs. Weston instructed him, "Up to the third bedroom on the left, please."

Dixon led the driver inside and with the other man's help they soon had the three other trunks in the foyer. "Where would you like these, Miss Farrow?"

"The tan one goes in my mother's room and the other two in mine." She remembered to add, "Thank you."

She rushed upstairs after them and heard Mrs. Weston say to Dixon, "Call Molly to Miss Farrow's room, please."

Genevieve suffered a fleeting thought: *It's going to be hard on her to see my wedding dress.* Her excitement outweighed her sympathy. She and mother had spent months sending drawings and stipulations back and forth to Paris. In spite of their effort, they had to trust Monsieur Worth in the final fabric choices and details.

She was the last to enter the room. "Where is my mother?"

"I do believe she's out," Mrs. Weston said. "Come now, Genevieve. Open it."

Her heart raced as she lifted the lid and removed the top tissue.

"Oooo."

The other ladies echoed the sound, as if there was no other.

Genevieve laid a hand upon the ivory satin, afraid it would disappear with more contact.

Molly entered the room and pulled up short, hesitating. Clarissa said, "Molly, help us get the dress out."

Molly just stared at the ivory dress in the ivory trunk.

"Molly?" Mrs. Weston said. "Please help us. You've unpacked dozens of gowns for me. Help us do it correctly."

She stepped forward and gently stopped Mrs. Weston from pulling it up by the shoulders. "We need to remove the side tissue first and lift it at the bust-line so as not to risk stretching the shoulders." Once the tissue was removed, she did the honors, carefully lifting the one-piece dress from the box, letting the neckline flap over her hands.

The dress kept coming, revealing a four-foot train edged with accordion pleats.

"Shouldn't an angel chorus be singing?" Genevieve asked. "Because it's heavenly."

The moment was shattered when Clarissa looked over and said, "Strip, Genevieve."

"Clarissa!" her mother said.

Clarissa sighed. "She can't very well try it on until she takes off what she has on, can she?"

With Molly busy holding the dress, Genevieve turned to Tilda for help. "Can you undo my back buttons?"

Mrs. Weston studied the dress. "It's impeccably made. Look at the beautifully finished seams and the built-in slip."

"That was mother's idea," Genevieve said. "That way the slip would fully match the cut of the dress." She glanced towards the door. "Where is she?"

Genevieve stepped out of her dress and removed her bustle and petticoats. She carefully stepped into the wedding dress as Molly held it, while Mrs. Weston steadied her with a hand.

Once on, Molly carefully moved the train to the side so she could reach the buttons that paraded up the back. The long sleeves were adorned with ruffled lace cuffs, her bodice lined with flat lace, culminating in a V at her waist. The slim skirt was covered with yards of scalloped lace, while a row of pleats edged the bottom of the dress and train. Over her hips were drapings of satin, and parading across the front of the skirt was a garland of white silk flowers, repeated in a corsage on her bodice, and as a crown for her scalloped veil.

Genevieve wasn't near a mirror yet, so couldn't see the full effect, but by Mrs. Weston's teary eyes and the hand pressed against her chest, she suspected the gown was as beautiful as it felt.

"It fits perfectly," Clarissa said. She addressed Molly, "Are you about done back there?"

"Almost."

Just then, Mamma burst into the bedroom, wearing a riding habit complete with leather gloves, veiled hat, and riding crop. Her face fell. "Why didn't you wait for me?"

"We didn't know where you were." Her mother's outfit confused her. "You were riding?"

"I was. At Crompton Hall." She offered a wicked smile. "Lord Newley is quite the horseman." She smacked the crop against her palm.

Genevieve was embarrassed, and checked the faces of the others to see if they too were shocked.

"I didn't realize you were spending time with Lord Newley," Mrs. Weston said.

"We've been seeing quite a lot of each other since the dinner the other night." She removed her hat and gloves, and thankfully set the crop aside. Then she smiled and moved towards her daughter. "Well look at you."

"Isn't she gorgeous?" Mrs. Weston said. Molly spread the train behind.

"I haven't even been able to see yet." Genevieve moved carefully towards the full-length mirror. With one look she matched Mrs. Weston's hand to her breast. "It takes my breath away."

Mrs. Weston leaned close. "*You* take our breath away."

Only then did Genevieve look at her own face. Although she'd mentally braced herself to see the image of a rather ordinary girl wearing an extraordinary dress, she was happily surprised to see a girl who was . . . pretty. Mrs. Weston was exaggerating towards the positive, but only to the same extent as Genevieve had expected the negative.

Her mother came close and fluffed the lace at the neckline. "It's a bit smashed."

Clarissa made a face. "What do you expect, traveling hundreds of miles in a trunk?"

Mamma ignored her and examined the back. "I was expecting a bit more *oomph* in the bustle area."

Molly spoke up, "If you please, Mrs. Farrow, once it's had time to rest and I press it, it will be revived."

Genevieve looked over her shoulder at Molly, offering her a smile. What must she be thinking and feeling right now?

"How do you feel in it?" Mrs. Weston asked.

She took a moment to find the words. "The dress makes it . . . real."

"That it is," Mamma said. "Soon you will be the Viscountess Genevieve Weston."

"Just the Viscountess Weston," Clarissa corrected. "Or Lady Weston, but not Viscountess Genevieve Weston. She loses her first name to all but family."

Mamma flipped her hand. "I do have trouble keeping all these titles and forms of address straight."

"Considering you bought the title for your daughter, perhaps you should try harder," Clarissa said.

"Clarissa, really!" Mrs. Weston said.

But Genevieve agreed with her. "You're right, Clarissa. It is our duty to know these things and we *shall* try harder."

Clarissa shrugged and moved to leave. "You look very pretty, Genevieve. Honestly. Now if you will excuse me?"

"Me too," Tilda said. It seemed odd the girl had said nothing.

"Now then," Mrs. Farrow said. "Let's try on the veil."

Out in the hallway with Clarissa, Tilda said, "She looked so pretty."

Clarissa stopped her progression towards the stairs. "Are you talking to me?"

"Well . . . yes. I was just saying—"

Clarissa stepped close enough to make Tilda long to step away—but she held her ground. "I do not wish to hear anything that you have to say, Miss Cavendish. Do you understand?"

Tilda found her throat completely dry. "I was just agreeing with what you said about the dress."

"I don't need or wish for your agreement, your presence in this house, or for you to have anything to do with my family."

Tilda felt her anger rise. "But I'm the colonel's goddaughter."

"Then go live with him."

"I can't. I have to live here."

Clarissa's index finger rose between them. "Your logistical problems are not my concern. If you want to continue to live in this house, you must remember one thing."

"What's that?"

"There is only one Weston daughter here."

Tilda's heart beat in her throat, but she couldn't back down. She thought of something. "Actually, two. Soon Miss Farrow will be a Weston too."

Clarissa's eyes grew large and Tilda could see her nostrils flare. Then Clarissa flicked the tip of Tilda's nose. "I know you took my necklace. So watch yourself."

Clarissa's warning did not have its desired effect.

Tilda was more determined than ever to win her place at the manor.

"Psst! Molly!"

Molly paused at the foot of the back stairs. Her heart leapt at the sight of Morgan coming towards her.

She bobbed a curtsy. "Yes, Lord Weston?"

"Don't Lord Weston me, Mol."

Every time he said her name, a part of her melted. "What do you want?"

His grin was the one she remembered fondly. "You know the answer to that."

A sudden thought interrupted her memory. "The wedding dress came today."

He cleared his throat. "Ah."

"Ah? Your bride's dress arrives and all you can say is *ah?*"

"How nice?"

She smacked his arm, then stepped back, appalled by her reaction. "Sorry. Your lordship."

He lowered his voice. "Oh, Molly, I know it's awkward for you. It's awkward for me too."

"Then do something about it!" she whispered. "Call off the wedding."

He looked to the floor. "If only I could."

She drew in a breath, feeling it fall to her toes. There it was. The full truth of it. "I thought . . . from what you've been saying to me . . ."

"These things are set in stone. As the heir I have to . . . You know that."

The secret tapped her on her shoulder. Hard. Then harder. "But what if you weren't the heir? Would you marry me then?"

His face pulled back. "What do you mean not the heir?"

"In theory. If you were free to marry me, would you?"

He leaned close and whispered in her ear. "Of course. This very minute."

They heard feet on the stairs and stepped apart. It was only Dottie, but Morgan quickly said, "Thank you, Miss Wallace" and walked away.

"How did he answer your question?" Dottie asked.

"You were listening?"

"I couldn't hear his answer. If he was free would he marry you?"

"Yes—not that it matters because he can't." She didn't want to talk about it anymore. At least not to Dottie. "Where is Miss Cavendish?"

"In the sunroom, I think. Sketching Mr. Weston."

Tilda was off the hook for the moment.

From her position at the bottom of the back stairway, Genevieve heard Molly and her sister talking one floor above.

And more importantly, before hearing the two women, she'd heard Molly and her Morgan.

Her Morgan. How ridiculous. It was clear he still loved Molly. Though she hadn't heard his answer to the question about whether he'd marry Molly if he were able, the fact he'd whispered his answer was an answer in itself.

The fact there was a chance he *wasn't* the heir and *would* be available to marry Molly . . .

As Dottie and Molly parted and headed down the stairs, Genevieve hurried out of sight, rushing down the hall, entering the nearby morning room in a rush.

"Genevieve?"

She turned to find her mother sitting at Mrs. Weston's desk. "Mamma. What are you doing in here?"

"Writing some letters. Why are you out of breath?"

Without warning, Genevieve burst into tears. Her mother was quickly at her side, leading her to a sofa. "Gracious sakes. What's wrong?"

She was so emotionally exhausted that she lost the ability to hedge. "Morgan doesn't love me. He loves Molly!"

"Miss Wallace?"

She nodded and dabbed at the tears. "They've loved each other for years, and I virtually heard him say that if he wasn't the heir, he'd marry her." And then, before she could stop herself, she said, "And he may not even be the heir at all."

When her mother didn't say anything, Genevieve looked up from her tears, *hoping* she hadn't heard the last of it.

"What's this about Morgan not being the heir?"

Genevieve took a deep breath, wishing she could backtrack thirty seconds. "It's not true, it's only a rumor."

"I haven't heard such a rumor and I am keen on gossip."

Yes, you are. "Forget I said anything."

"I will not forget anything." She took Genevieve's arm, none too gently. "I insist you tell me everything."

Reluctantly, Genevieve told her about the Whites and the blackmail.

It didn't take long for Mamma to make her assessment. "If Morgan isn't the heir, then he will marry Molly and you will not get your title."

"That is my fear."

Mamma took a deep breath. When she let it out, it was accompanied by one word. "Men!" She rose and began to pace. "It's just like men to be interested in some maid when they have a real lady waiting for them. And if that Mr. White hadn't seduced Morgan's mother . . . I have a mind to pack up and move back to New York."

"No!" Genevieve popped out of her seat and grabbed her mother's arm. "Don't even think such a thing."

"But if he isn't the heir . . ."

"He may be. It's just the White's story saying he isn't."

"If their story comes out the truth won't matter. People will talk and the Weston name will be sullied. I don't want us connected with such a scandal."

"It won't come out. The Whites have been paid. They're long gone."

Mamma moved away from Genevieve, pulling a lace curtain aside to look out the window. "Then there is the other problem. If Morgan doesn't love you . . . I assure you, you don't want to marry a man who's going to have some floozy on the side from the very start."

There was the slightest hint she was speaking from experience. Yet surely Genevieve's father had been faithful during their marriage.

She couldn't think of such things now. She had to concentrate on her own predicament. "I love him. I love Morgan."

Mamma gave her an unbelieving look. "Please."

"I do," she said. "Perhaps I didn't when we came here, but since then . . ."

"Since then, he's swept you off your feet while making goo-goo eyes at a maid."

When she said it that way . . . "He's been very sweet. I like the good man he is, as well as the better man he will become."

"When he's not being unfaithful."

Genevieve stomped a foot upon the carpet. "Then I have to make him love me! Only then will he forget about Molly."

Mamma held her gaze. "Then do it. Make him love you."

Genevieve laughed. "How? How do I do that?"

"You make him kiss you. One kiss — one good kiss — and you will be on your way."

"But I shouldn't, we shouldn't."

"Balderdash. Young people do it all the time." She returned to the desk. "When you aren't a striking beauty you have to use other means. Gracious, daughter. Sometimes you are far too proper and naïve."

Genevieve was offended. "You brought me up to be proper. You hounded me with the rules of propriety and etiquette. And now you want me to set that all aside?"

"It's just a kiss, girl. I'm not asking you to have relations with the man."

"Mamma!"

She swatted the air with a hand. "Being so tightly laced can be extremely tedious, my dear."

It sounded as if her mother wanted her to be un-laced. Genevieve suffered a shudder. She would never go so far. Not for any gain. She took a few breaths, trying to calm herself in spirit and voice. "All right. How do I get him in a situation where he will kiss me?"

"You're a bright girl. Think of something."

"But—"

"Go on now. You've burdened me enough for one day. I have letters to write and notes to send."

Genevieve walked through the manor, her mind desperately trying to think of a way to get Morgan's attention. Wafting up from below stairs was the smell of dinner. Fish.

She got an idea.

Chapter Sixteen

While the family was down at breakfast, Molly opened one of Miss Farrow's trunks for unpacking. Beneath the top layer of tissue, her gaze fell upon the most beautiful and delicate lace neckline.

"Ooh," Dottie said. "What is it?"

Molly pulled it free from the trunk. "It's a wrap to go over a nightgown."

"It's fancy enough to be a ball gown."

That, it was. The robe connected with a hook and eye at the neck and bustline, but otherwise hung free. A mantle of lace created a capelet that extended over dropped shoulders and was edged in six-inch, ruffled lace trim. The skirt and sleeves were the finest lawn cloth, culminating in a wide, lace-trimmed ruffle at the bottoms. Adorning the lace bodice was a garland of pink silk roses with green satin leaves.

Next in the trunk was a matching nightgown with narrow straps at the shoulders. The set was exquisite. "It's for the wedding night," Molly whispered.

"How do you know?"

"I know." *And it kills me.*

Dottie dug through the rest of the trunk, laying the multitude of undergarments on the bed. "Look at this corset." She held it in front of herself and moved to the mirror. "I've never seen a pink corset adorned with flowers."

It too, was exquisite. But Molly turned practical. "The outline of those flowers might show under some of her bodices."

"Who cares?" Dottie said, holding it tight against her apron. "I can't imagine wearing something so pretty when no one will see it."

Was her sister that naïve?

Dottie must had sensed her thoughts, because she added, "Oh, I know Morgan will see it, but still . . ."

That's the rub. Morgan will see it. See Genevieve in it.

Dottie touched Molly's arm. "I'm sorry. I shouldn't have said it so plain."

The truth was always plain. Speaking of truth, and speaking of marriage and Morgan, Molly had arranged to meet with Tilda at ten. It was nearly that now.

She quickly moved to the last trunk. Inside, instead of clothes there was a sewing machine.

"Crikey," Dottie said, peering in the trunk. "I've never seen one of those. Have you?"

"At the hat shop we had one."

"So Miss Farrow can sew too?"

Molly didn't feel up to discussing Miss Farrow's talents. "Can you finish up in here? I have to speak with Miss Cavendish."

"What about?"

A secret. "None of your business, sister." A secret about a secret. Would Molly's life ever be free of them?

Molly found Tilda on the bench beyond the garden arbor, sketching the house.

"Can I see?" she asked.

"I don't have all the chimneys right yet."

"It's very good," Molly said with all honesty. "You have talent."

When Tilda shrugged she looked younger than her sixteen years. Suddenly the idea of having this girl—this immature girl—be in charge of Molly's future seemed ridiculous. And rash.

NANCY MOSER

Tilda set aside her drawing and pencil. "What did you want to talk to me about?"

Molly looked around to make certain no one was nearby. "I need the secret to come out *now*."

"Now?"

"Soon. Very soon. The wedding dress and trousseau have arrived. Soon they will be married and it will be too late."

"I can't just blurt it out," the girl said. "And the information can't come from me."

"Then figure out a way." She needed Tilda to understand the urgency. "If you think it doesn't matter to your plans if the information comes out before or after the wedding, it does. Afterwards the earl and his brother might do something drastic to contradict the information. They wouldn't want to discredit Morgan's marriage to an heiress — whose money they desperately need. *After* is too late."

Tilda looked confused. "But how could they contradict any of it? Mr. White said —"

"Mr. White is a blackmailer and can't be trusted. Besides, his silence has been purchased. Don't you think he would change his story and deny any of it is true if he were paid *more* money?"

"I never thought of that."

"You need to think of it. You need to realize that the secret only benefits the two of us if it stops the wedding from ever happening." Molly took a fresh breath. "Besides, if you wait until after the wedding I get no benefit from the secret at all. And if I lose you lose."

"What do you mean by that?"

"I mean that if I lose my chance with Morgan, I will not idly sit by and watch you go after George."

"How . . . how are you going to stop me?"

"I can let the family know that you were a part of the blackmail."

"But I wasn't!"

"You knew what the Whites were doing and did nothing to stop them."

"Yes, but—"

"And I will also inform Mrs. Weston that you stole Clarissa's necklace, and arranged for Gertie to take the blame."

"Gertie told you that?"

Actually Dottie did. "Gertie didn't have to. With all those things said against you it won't much matter if the colonel is your godfather. You will be sent away, back where you came from."

Tilda bit her lower lip, her eyes on the flowers nearby. She collected her art supplies and stood. "All right."

Molly was surprised she agreed so quickly. "When will you do it?"

"I'll set it in motion today."

"How will you do it?"

But Tilda simply walked away. It was unfortunate Molly had been forced to threaten the girl, but she had little choice.

Now to wait.

Even though they lived in the same house, Genevieve sent Morgan a note: *Meet me at the river at half-past one, at the place where we went fishing. I long to see you.*

It had taken many drafts to get the note the way she wanted it. The actual invitation-part was easy, but the last line . . . she had decided on the word "long" because it implied passion and was a bit . . . risqué? Yet if her assessment of its definition was correct, there was the chance he would expect something of her beyond the one kiss she was willing to give. She would have to risk it and trust his status as a gentleman.

Driving the pony-cart, Genevieve arrived at the riverside early, needing time to take her plans from vague to specific.

She'd carefully chosen her dress to be one that would not be ridiculously heavy when wet—and one she did not care about if it was ruined. She wore her oldest slippers and a hat that was far from a favorite and had only made the trip across the ocean because Mamma had designed it herself.

She stood before the river and assessed the best access to the water. The safest access — for the point was not to drown, but simply need saving.

Some trees that had long-ago fallen in the river created a small pool of water that was slightly apart from the current. Along the shore there were some rocks . . . perhaps if she walked upon the stones, it might be logical that she could slip and fall into the pool.

But timing was everything. She couldn't very well be in the water when he arrived, for then it would be clear that — though wet — she was in no danger. Morgan had to see her fall, hear her scream . . .

Genevieve nodded, solidifying the plan, though she felt queasy about her ability to follow through.

Her worries were interrupted when she heard a horse approach. There was no time to second-guess or gain courage. She hurried to the stepping stones and began to walk upon them, as if whiling away the time until Morgan's arrival. When she heard his horse stop, her heart skipped a beat.

Almost . . . hold on . . . just a moment longer . . .

"Hello there, Genevieve," he called out.

She pivoted on a rock to greet him, then leaned towards the pool, her time to fall upon her. But her courage — and acting abilities — betrayed her, and realizing she was not going to able to pull off a proper accidental fall, she jumped in. The scream was a bit tardy, weak, and insincere. But it was too late to try another one.

Though the water was not cold, her sudden immersion up to her eyes was still a shock.

"What are you doing?" Morgan asked.

"I fell in."

"You did not. You jumped. Don't you know my father was thought drowned in this very river? You shouldn't pretend like that."

As the skirt of her dress billowed towards the top of the water, she pressed it down. She was a fool. "Are you going to help me out, or not?" She extended a hand towards him.

He managed to pull her to shore, only getting one boot wet. Standing there, dripping and soggy, he took a step back.

"I don't understand," he said. "You ask me to come here and I find you jumping in the water? Whatever would compel you to do such a stupid thing?"

She pushed strands of wet hair away from her face, trying to capture a smidge of dignity. "If you must know, you are to blame."

"Me?"

Her skirt and petticoats weighed a thousand pounds as she leaned down to wring them out. "Yes, you."

"What did I do?"

Genevieve knew she was at a crossroads. Either she sidestepped the issue that stood large between them, or she just . . . "You still love Molly."

Morgan opened his mouth to speak as if he too was at a crossroads. "I can't help whom I love."

Genevieve was stunned. "At least you could pretend and deny it."

He retrieved her soggy hat from the shallows with a stick. "I wasn't the one who brought her up. And that still doesn't explain why you hurled yourself into a dangerous river."

"I did not *hurl,* I stepped in. And if I know the story correctly, your father did *not* get swept away. He was stolen by your grandfather."

"That's neither here nor there. Anyone can see it's dangerous. Whyever would you jump in?"

"Again I say I didn't jump in, I stepped in."

"Because . . .?"

She looked down and realized the bodice of her dress was clinging to her body. She could make out the bow at the top of her chemise. She pulled the fabric of the dress away, then crossed her arms to attempt some coverage. "May I have your jacket?"

He seemed to come-to. "Of course." He removed it and handed it to her. *You could have at least draped it over my shoulders for me.* Since nothing was turning out as she planned, weariness and resignation fell around her as heavily as a sodden blanket. "If you insist on knowing the reason I stepped in, it's because I wanted you to pay attention to me."

"Haven't we gone riding and fishing? Didn't I take you to the mercantile on more than one occasion?"

"Yes, but—"

"I have made time for you every day since you arrived."

"You make it sound like an imposition."

"In a way, it is. For I have work to do around the estate. You may think of my father, my uncle, and I as men of leisure, but I assure you we work very hard to keep this place running. Hundreds of people depend on us for their very survival. Don't you think *that* is of more importance than spending time flirting with each other?"

"Of course it's important. And I don't want to spend time flirting,"

"Don't you think feigning a fall in the water is flirting?"

She had no defense.

He slapped his riding crop against a log. "I believe you and your mother came to Summerfield expecting the high life of parties, soirees, and recognition. But this is not New York City with your elite Four Hundred, with parties and dinners every night among people of like mind and money. This is a hard working estate and—"

She felt her anger ignite. "Do you truly think so little of us? And don't you dare speak of hard work. My father began with nothing. Hard work is the core of the story shared by the majority of those you look down on within the Four Hundred. Hard work, having a dream, and making something from nothing is the American way. We attained our position in society because of determined work, not because we were born into a title that required nothing of us but a lofty bloodline."

"Decrying our titles makes you a hypocrite. You wanted one so much you found a way to buy your own."

"That was my mother's idea."

"You went along with it."

"Obviously, a foolish decision."

"Foolish?" he shouted. "Foolish, you say?"

She'd gone too far.

He pressed her hat into her hands, his eyes flashing, and his face red. "If our way of life is so foolish and abhorrent to you, and if you do not find my attention enough for you, then perhaps we should both reconsider our arrangement."

Even as she mentally shouted *No!* she heard herself say, "Perhaps we should."

The air vibrated between them, and Genevieve immediately longed to take it all back. She was on the verge of saying as much when he pointed to the pony cart.

"You need to get back to the house and into some dry things. I'll ride with you."

The thought of riding up to the manor, soaking and rumpled, made her shudder. "I prefer to go alone, thank you."

"Suit yourself."

To her dismay he mounted his horse and rode off, leaving Genevieve on the shore.

What had just happened?

Her emotions crashed together like water rushing over rocks in a rapids. She sank onto the riverbank. "All I wanted was a kiss."

As she watched the water flow past her, the life she'd expected flowed with it. In one moment of impulse, she'd brought up the subject that should never have been mentioned: Molly. She'd forced Morgan to admit he still loved her.

The entire American versus British argument was prideful hyperbole. Morgan was right. *She* had sought and chosen this life in Summerfield. She was shooting herself in the foot by defaming that life.

"Perhaps we should both reconsider our arrangement." Had those words truly come out of his mouth? And had she truly agreed?

Shame weighed upon her and she lowered her head. "God, please . . . I've ruined everything. All I wanted was a kiss, some affirmation that Morgan cared about me, and now . . . help me!"

She let the tears come. The ones that were caused by embarrassment sped quickly down her cheeks. But the ones that were borne of her fear of the future lingered and stung.

Molly was surprised to be called to Genevieve's room in the middle of the day. The next time she should have been needed was to dress for dinner.

She was shocked by what she saw.

"Miss Farrow! What happened to you?"

"A little mishap in the river," she said, unbuttoning the front of her bodice.

"Here, let me." Molly took over, and helped her peel away the damp blouse, heavy skirt, and petticoat.

"I'm afraid they may be ruined."

Probably. The ladies in the laundry would have a conniption over the mud and muck.

Molly helped her into new underthings, finishing with a silk wrapper that tied at the neck "If I may ask, miss, what happened?"

"A stupid mistake, a stupid plan."

"Plan?"

Genevieve shook her head, dismissing the question. She sat at the dressing table and Molly began to pluck the displaced hairpins out of her coif.

"I'm just glad you're all right. The river is very dangerous. You know the earl was thought drowned as a child and—"

"I know, I know." She stopped Molly's hand with her own. "I also know you and Morgan loved each other."

Love each other.

She knew that Genevieve knew — thanks to Dottie. But to have her state it so bluntly was disconcerting. What had happened to bring this about?

They captured each other's gaze in the mirror. "Yes, we did," Molly told Genevieve's reflection.

The next obvious question would have been, *"Do you still?"* but Genevieve only nodded once. Then she broke their gaze and began to fiddle with a perfume bottle.

Molly didn't know what to say. To admit more would make Genevieve's defenses rise, and worse, Molly would be ordered to leave the manor. Leaving of her own volition was far different from being forced out.

And so . . . Molly lied. "We don't love each other anymore."

Genevieve's hand stilled, and relief washed over her face like sunlight breaking through clouds. "I understand how you loved him. He is an easy man to love . . ."

Molly only nodded and took a brush to Genevieve's hair.

Tilda didn't like being rushed, but rushed she was. Molly had made it very clear she wouldn't wait forever. When they'd talked, Tilda had acted as if she already had a plan to reveal the blackmail-secret.

She had only the vaguest of ideas. Though involving George did seem to be her best option.

Not knowing what else to do, she sought him out at the stables.

She did not find him riding, currying a horse, or talking with the workers as she expected. She found him in a tugging match with a man who was astride one horse and was leading away four others.

"You can't take them!" George yelled, lunging towards the reins.

"Come now, Master George," said the man on the horse. "The duke bought them fair and square."

"But they weren't for sale!" Two stable men rushed to restrain him.

The man looked confused. "The duke wasn't the one who came to the earl. 'Twas the other way around, and they's been bought and paid for. Now let me get on here. The duke don't take well to waiting."

The man rode off, taking five horses with him. George shucked off the restraints of the men and they backed away. Staring after his beloved horses he looked as though his legs would give out beneath him. Tilda stepped close. "They've been sold?"

"Father and Uncle sold them. Sold *my* horses."

"Did they say why?"

"Only that it was *necessary*. Whatever that means." He pointed after them. "Friar Tuck, Alan a Dale, and three others. They were mine!"

An opening was laid out before her, but it was one she needed to enter amid privacy. She slipped her arm in his and drew him away from the workers. "I'm so sorry, George. I know how much they meant to you."

"As if it mattered."

"I . . . I think I know why they were sold."

George pulled his arm away and faced her. "Then tell me!"

Her heart pounded. Could she do this? Did she have a choice? "It's because of Mr. White."

"That man who brought you here?"

She nodded.

"What about him?"

She had second thoughts. To have this conversation would be opening Pandora's Box. She would never be able to retrieve what escaped. Or undo it.

"Never mind. I don't know anything. I'm just so sorry —"

He lifted her chin. "You tell me what you know. All that you know."

Tilda's stomach wrenched and she hoped the words would come out in logical order. "When the Whites were asked to be the chaperons on my journey here, they were very excited about the possibilities in Summerfield."

"Possibilities? What does that mean?"

She ran the toe of her shoe through the dirt. "Apparently Mr. White was once a coachman here and had some intimate doings with . . ." Now, was the tricky part.

"With?"

This was awful. If only she'd kept quiet.

"Tilda? Answer me."

She looked to the ground. "Intimate doings with the earl's wife — before she was the earl's wife."

George blinked. "Fidelia?"

Tilda nodded.

"What do you mean by 'intimate doings'?"

She knew it wouldn't be ladylike to state it plain. At her age she wasn't supposed to know of such things — and certainly should never speak of them. "I didn't understand what the Whites were talking about, but it seemed as though they might have wanted to get money from your father and the earl to keep the encounter quiet?" She shrugged. "I don't know if that's what happened, but . . ."

George grabbed her hand and pulled her with him. "I'm going to find out exactly what happened. Right now."

"But I don't want . . . I don't need to go too."

He stopped walking. "Is what you say true or not?"

Her mouth was dry. "It's true."

"Then I need you there."

Tilda desperately needed to be anywhere else.

This was it. Tilda and George sat in the earl's study, facing his lordship and his brother, Mr. Weston. The only thing that would make it more dramatic was if Morgan joined them.

Was Morgan aware of the blackmail deal — the blackmail secret? Or was he oblivious to all that had been done to save his title?

"I don't like your tone, son," Mr. Weston said to George.

"And I don't like having five of my best horses sold without my knowledge or permission."

Mr. Weston exchanged a look with his brother. "We do not need your permission. And we told you, it was necessary."

George glanced at Tilda. "That's only a half-answer."

"It's the only answer we have."

George shook his head back and forth. "It's not good enough."

"Excuse me?" his father said.

George let out a long breath, and it seemed clear that he was not used to questioning his father and uncle's authority. "Did Mr. White blackmail you?"

Both men jerked their heads back, as if the words had slapped them. "Who told you that?"

At the question, Tilda wanted to flee, but it was too late. "Tilda."

The men glared at her. "What do you know about all this?"

A thousand words scrambled around her. Finally a few fell into order. "I know that Mr. White used to work here and he . . ." She looked to George, wanting to be rescued.

"He knew your wife, Uncle Jack." George leaned forward and directed his question to his father. "Does this have something to do with Mamma too? Because she knew Fidelia, and they both wanted to marry you. Isn't that right, Father?"

After a hesitation, his father nodded. "Yes, on both counts."

They shared a moment of silence and Tilda feared the entire thing would be dropped. Maybe that would be for the best. She was tempted to keep the discussion going yet dreaded the thought of it.

"Father, please tell me the truth. I deserve that."

Mr. Weston stood at the window a moment, as if contemplating the past. Then he turned to face the room. "Yes, it is true that the horses were sold to pay for Mr. White's silence."

"Was the past so awful?"

"Not at all," Mr. Weston said. He and his brother seemed to speak between themselves with only their eyes. "The truth is, all this happened long before Jack even knew Fidelia, when we were all very young."

The earl continued the story. "I was living in London with Nana and my ersatz father—the man who stole me from the woods. I was working in a store there, learning what would become my trade."

Mr. Weston offered his side of it. "Fidelia and Ruth were both gentried girls in the county, both in contention for my hand. They were as different as two young women could be. Your mother was sweet and elegant and dignified."

"And Fidelia?" George asked.

"Fidelia was brash and a bit wild."

"It seems no contest."

"It wasn't. But I was at fault for not making my feelings clear. Your mother felt desperate to win me—though she already had my heart. She paid Mr. White to get Fidelia in a compromising situation, one that she and I would interrupt. And so it happened. Fidelia was disgraced and your mother and I were married."

"I can't believe Mother did that."

"Neither can she. She feels badly for going to such drastic measures, but we have found peace between us."

The earl added, "We didn't want Mr. White to stir up the distant past that is so personal to the family and of no consequence to anyone else. So we paid him off."

"If it was of no consequence, then why pay him?" George asked.

There was a moment's hesitation. "Perhaps we shouldn't have," Mr. Weston said. "But at the time it seemed the best choice."

Tilda was confused. They spoke of Mrs. Weston arranging for the intimate meeting, but neglected to mention that Mr. White *had* seduced Fidelia--fully. Without that fact there could be no mention of Morgan's paternity. Had the Whites been lying about that?

"I hardly think such a secret needed to be squelched at the expense of my horses," George said.

"It is regrettable, but at the time we felt compelled to get such a detestable couple out of our lives."

This couldn't be all they would say! George was only hearing one-tenth of the truth. Before Tilda could stop herself, she heard herself saying, "But Mr. White implied there was more to the secret than just that."

The men gave her a scathing look. "There was not more to it," the earl said.

"But—"

Mr. Weston took a step towards her. "Miss Cavendish, are you questioning the authority and honesty of myself and my brother?"

Yes. But no. "I'm sorry. Perhaps I was mistaken."

"Indeed."

The earl rose, dismissing them. "We are sorry for the way this had to play out, George. But please be assured that we handled this deplorable situation with careful consideration."

"Can I get some more horses to replace them?"

"Eventually."

That was it? George was appeased by the pathetic half-answer and the promise of more horses?

After he and Tilda left the study, George said, "I will miss Friar Tuck and the rest. They were good—"

Tilda stomped her foot on the floor of the foyer. "That's all you can think about? Your stupid horses?"

The rise of his eyebrows indicated he did not appreciate her tone or her words. She hurried to replace her anger with a smile. "Sorry. I didn't mean that."

"If you'll excuse me. I have work to do." He left her standing alone, her hopes for the future as cold and unyielding as the marble of the floor.

Genevieve wanted to fade into a teacup. During afternoon tea Morgan didn't even look at her, taking an odd interest in stirring his tea, as if he was required to study it before tasting it.

There was also some bit of tension between the earl and Mr. Weston, with the latter dabbing his napkin upon his mouth far more often than a drip of tea or a crumb of biscuit deserved. Clarissa kept playing with her hair—which seemed lopsided towards the left. And Tilda and George seemed to be at odds with one another, though it was clear by Tilda's frequent glances towards the boy that he was the one who was most perturbed and she was desperately wanting to make amends.

Genevieve knew exactly how she felt.

Leave it to the mothers to get to the bottom of the tension.

"What *is* going on this afternoon?" Mamma finally asked.

"I would like to know that too," Mrs. Weston said. "Everyone is silent and quite out of sorts. Has something happened we should know about?"

"Nothing," her husband said.

"I'm merely thinking about my party tonight," Clarissa said.

"I'm just tired," Morgan said.

George shrugged and Tilda's teaspoon rattled on her saucer as she set it down.

"How about you, Genevieve?" her mother asked. "Enliven the conversation by telling us about your outing to the river."

"It was soggy," Morgan said, under his breath.

His words drowned her, causing a desperate need for air. She stood and set her teacup to the tray with a titter of china against silver. "If you'll excuse me, I'm not feeling well."

Her mother also stood, her face confused.

"I'm fine, Mamma," Genevieve said. "All I need is a rest. Hopefully all will be well."

She paused a moment and made a point of looking at Morgan, but he did not return her gaze.

Clarissa wore her previously-stolen choker to her party. In her opinion, a point had to be made.

Her second point against Tilda was that the girl was *not* invited to tonight's gathering. This was Clarissa's homecoming party and she didn't need some nothing whippersnapper drawing the focus from herself.

Clarissa checked out the arrangement of the music room. It had been her choice to forgo the dining room and a formal dinner for something more modern and young: an array of savory and sweet dishes spread upon a serving table. She'd asked for two tables to be set for cards, and now went through the piano music to make certain no one chose something too dismal. Lively pleasure was the order of the evening.

Dixon entered with Nick close behind, carrying an undulating bowl of punch. "Set it here," he told the footman. Then he addressed Clarissa. "Does everything meet with your approval, Miss Weston?"

"It does. Thank you for creating the perfect atmosphere on such short notice."

"It is a pleasure," he said. "We are all so glad to have you back home where you belong."

She did not miss his emphasis on the last three words. "And I am glad to be here."

They both heard the sounds of a carriage.

It was show time.

The music room was aglow with light, music, and witty conversation—though many of those present who thought they were witty, were not. Just as many who took a turn showcasing their talent by playing the piano or singing would have done everyone a service if they'd remained silent.

Clarissa had purposely refrained from singing, biding her time, waiting to be asked.

Currently, the notes Fanny played were fumbled more than fingered and her voice was flat in tone and tune.

Julien slid to Clarissa's side and whispered, "Painful, isn't it?"

Clarissa didn't nod, even though he was right.

He leaned close a second time. "Allow me to put us out of our misery." He plucked a feather from a vase, strode to the piano, and tickled Fanny's ear.

She immediately stopped playing—which was a relief.

"I believe it's time for our hostess to take a turn. Miss Weston? If you would grace us with a song?"

If you insist.

Clarissa sat at the piano and began a rendition of "May Day". The text was from one of her favorite plays, "Sylvia" and when she sang the verse that spoke of lasses and their lovers meeting, she made certain each male guest caught her gaze. She had no romantic interest in any of them, but it made for a better party if they thought otherwise.

When she finished, the applause was more sincere than dutiful. But then Julien said, "That's not the right song for you, Miss Weston."

"And what is the right song?"

He nudged her away from the keys and sat down himself. With only a chord of introduction, he sang, "'Landlord fill the flowing bowl, until it doth run over. For tonight we'll merry, merry be. Tomorrow we're hung-over.'"

Everyone tittered, most behind closed hands.

What would have been an amusing song in parties past, now seemed an obvious dig.

Julien grinned at her, his eyes more malicious than mischievous. "Isn't that a more appropriate song for Miss Clara West of London showgirl fame?"

"Ha!" said Hugh in a loud expulsion of air. He quickly put a hand to his mouth. "Sorry."

Clarissa felt her cheeks grow hot. They knew of her life in London? She wanted to ask Julien questions, but feared for his answer.

"Who else would like to sing?" she said. "Or how about a game of Whist?"

"I saw you performing at the Jolly," Julien said. "Quite the costume you had—or lack of one."

"Oooh," Daphne said. "Was it very scandalous?"

"Very," Julien said, making a low-cut motion at chest level before running his hands up his own leg.

Clarissa could hear her *tsk-tsk* even though no sound was made. "I cannot believe you stooped so low, Clarissa. The stage . . ." Fanny offered a shudder.

Clarissa's throat was dry. "I was not at the Jolly long, but moved to the Savoy. I was appearing in *Patience* there." She thought of something to add. "The Kidds saw the play when they were in London and commended me on my performance."

Fanny's shrug showed her disappointment that the scandal was lightened.

"Where did you live in London?" Boyd said.

"In a flat."

"Alone?"

"My father says no well-bred woman would ever live in London on her own."

"I was not alone. I had my lady's maid with me." Clarissa strolled to a table and began to shuffle the cards. "It was quite exciting living so. Mother and Father were proud of me for my achievement and independence."

"That's not what I heard," Fanny said. When Fanny realized she had everyone's eyes, she explained. "My mother said your mother was appalled and embarrassed by the horrible living conditions that became your lot."

Thank you, Mother.

"Is that why you came home?" Boyd asked. "Life became unbearable?"

That he'd hit upon the truth caught Clarissa off guard. Would it be to her advantage to tout her conquering of adversity, or to make light of it?

One image came to mind . . .

"Actually, there was a young girl who lived on the stairs of my building."

"Lived? On the stairs?"

"She was an orphan without a home. She slept on the stairs at night, and played with a doll that was no more than a scrap of wood during the day."

Five pair of eyes blinked at her, as if she'd described the life of an undersea monster. "She was a sweet girl, and slept in my apartment one night. She loved to try on my hats."

"You let her touch your things?" Daphne asked.

"The poor in London have two problems." Clark said. "Number one, they are poor."

Titters.

"And number two, they're all so dirty."

Clarissa felt her ire rise. "They're dirty because there is no running water and the sewers are often open."

Fanny made a face — which actually helped her appearance. "The stench must have been disgusting. Clarissa, how could you have ever chosen to live in such a place?"

It was a good question.

Daphne took a seat across from Clarissa, with Julien and Boyd filling the other two spots at the card table. Clarissa began to deal. She dealt the last card up. "Hearts are trump," she said.

As the others looked at their cards, with the other two gazing on from behind, Daphne said, "I heard Father say that no lady of bearing would ever appear on the stage or live on her own, no matter if her uncle is an earl or not."

Clarissa froze. So that was how it was going to be.

She laid her cards face-up on the table and stood. "Since I did appear on the stage and did live on my own, I assume you can no longer tolerate my presence. And honestly, the feeling is reciprocated." She stepped away from the table and swept a hand towards the door. "Thank you all for coming."

With a nod to Nick, the servant moved to the door of the music room and opened it.

They all filed out, with Julien the last. "I do apologize for mentioning the theatre."

"Not at all," Clarissa said. "Did you enjoy my performance?"

He let a smile escape. "Very much."

"Good evening to you, Mr. Darlinger."

He gave a smart bow and left.

Good riddance.

Clarissa expected the knock on her door, and finished setting the stage by smoothing the bedclothes over her legs and torso. "Come in, Mother."

She entered, worry evident on her face. "Your friends left early."

"I told them to go."

Mother came to her bedside. "Things did not go well?"

She shrugged. "They went as expected."

Mother thought this over a moment before saying, "I had hoped they would be more forgiving."

Clarissa remembered Fanny's mention of their mothers talking. "I had hoped *you* would be." She slid down the pillow and turned on her side. "Good night, Mother."

"It will get better, dear."

No, it won't. Thanks to you.

Chapter Seventeen

Genevieve had never felt so alone.

Sleep alluded her most of the night, the tick of the mantel clock in her bedroom an element of torture, chiding her for staying another second in this awful land of uncertainty.

When the night lifted enough for her to see the outline of the furniture in her room, she moved from bed to window seat, drew her knees to her chest, and pulled her nightgown over her legs and under her toes. She watched the sky turn from black to pink and blue beyond the row of trees on the horizon.

Her whispers broke through the silence of the coming day. "Red sky at morning, sailors take warning; red sky at night, sailors delight." She sighed at the realization that the saying predicted bad weather. But why not? It would follow her mood.

She leaned forward against her knees, squeezing her eyes shut, putting all her focus in her desperate prayer. "God, please show me what to do. How do I get Morgan back? I'm sorry I tried to force things to happen. I ruined everything."

As she took a breath, two words slid into her mind: *Trust me.*

With only a moment's hesitation she nodded at the directive, for it *was* her best choice. Actually, her only choice.

For whom else could she trust? She had no confidantes at Summerfield Manor. Mrs. Weston was a nice woman, but Genevieve didn't want her to know something was amiss. Clarissa was distant, intent on her own drama. The dowager was too intimidating, Tilda was too young, and Molly . . . Molly was too involved.

Her mother was the obvious choice, yet Mamma had a way of over-simplifying things. Look how her instruction to "Get Morgan to kiss you" had turned out. That Genevieve had made a mess of that . . . she wasn't up to a lecture. Or more bad advice.

Which meant there was no woman she could talk to. No one who might understand and —

Lila!

Morgan's sister had dealt with the complications of love. Perhaps she could provide some insight. But before Genevieve moved ahead with her plan, she paused and looked heavenward. "Lila?" she asked.

She wasn't sure what she waited for: a thunderclap for *no*, a ray of clear sunrise for *yes*?

A soft laugh escaped at the notion. And with the laugh a feeling of peace.

"Lila it is."

Genevieve knew it wasn't proper to arrive at Crompton Hall unannounced. Yet she felt if she went through the proper procedure of sending a note to ask for a meeting time, the delay would send her nerves into an even higher state of distress. Making the excuse of wanting to drive the pony cart into the countryside to explore, gave her the transportation and cover she needed.

Pulling up to the front door of the Kidd residence, Genevieve knew she needed to talk with Lila as much as she needed air to breathe. Stopping the pony, she took a moment to take a fresh breath. "If this is wrong, stop me," she prayed under her breath.

She walked to the front door, her heart beating double time. "Help me," she whispered as she rang the bell. The door opened and the upward angle of the butler's right eyebrow indicated she had indeed breached a bastion of British protocol.

Too late now.

"I was wondering if Lady Kidd was free to have a visitor?"

"Please come in, Miss Farrow and I will check."

She was led into the drawing room, where she purposely returned to the chair she had sat in before, as if finding a familiar place would make the moment pass with more ease.

Suddenly, she felt a wave of panic wash over her as surely as the water of the river had drenched her the day before. *What will I say to her? She's Morgan's sister and will be on his side. I'm the stranger here. Perhaps she doesn't even want me to marry —*

The butler appeared on the edge of the room. "Lady Kidd will see you. Please come with me to the morning room."

As she followed the butler, Genevieve continued to suffer second thoughts. She'd met Lila once. There was no reason she should feel at ease confiding in her. *Is this the right thing to do? Stop me, Lord, if it's not. If it is, give me the right words.*

Genevieve entered a room that appeared too heavy with dark furniture to have the "morning room" designation.

"Miss Farrow," Lila said from her desk. "How wonderful for you to visit." Lila rose and moved towards some chairs near the windows which were bathed in light. "I like this spot the best. The result of having there be no mistress of the hall for over twenty years is that the house is far too masculine. I have plans for some lighter pieces in here, but that will be a future project. Please have a seat and tell me everything that is happening at the manor."

Genevieve felt her face grow warm. And when her face grew warm, she knew it became a blotchy mess.

"Are you all right?" Lila asked.

"Yes, I'm . . . actually no." She decided an apology was the first order of business. "I am so sorry to disturb your morning. I had the impulse at dawn—after barely sleeping all night—and proceeded without the proper protocol. But I'm in dire need of help. I stewed all night and then prayed and thought of you. I felt peace about coming here." She cocked her head. "Then I felt nerves, and . . . I now realize how inappropriate it is for me to bother you at all." She took a cleansing breath.

Lila reached across the space between the chairs, took Genevieve's hand, and gave it a friendly squeeze. "I am happy for the company. Soon we will be sisters. I have never had a sister, and I long for us to be close."

"I do too."

"So then, release your nerves and let your fears go. It is good you are here. Now tell me what is wrong."

Genevieve put a hand to her mouth, stifling a cry of relief. "You make it sound so easy."

"It is." Lila pointed at Genevieve's forehead. "You have a worry line etching its way into your pretty face. I will do my best to make it disappear."

Genevieve pressed a finger to her forehead, feeling the crease. "My mother has always chided me for having a transparent face. What I feel is shown and known to the world."

"I think that is better than the opposite."

"Perhaps."

"So," Lila said. "What caused that worry line? And remember, since your face *is* so transparent, you might as well just state it plain."

Genevieve shot one final arrow of prayer towards heaven: *Guide me. Guide her.* "My worry is that Morgan doesn't love me and still loves Molly."

Lila's head pulled back. "My. That is indeed a worry."

Genevieve's slim hope plummeted. "I was hoping you would tell me I was mistaken."

"I'm afraid I've taken on candor as a trait I embrace. Yet I don't mean to hurt you."

"I am already hurt. I just want to know what to do about it."

Lila nodded once. "My brother has not been rude to you, has he?"

"Not until yesterday."

"What happened yesterday?"

Genevieve shared — with full detail — the fiasco at the river. "It was my own fault. I am not good at playing the part of damsel in distress."

Lila's smile was one of amusement *and* compassion. "And *you* brought up the subject of Molly to him."

"A soggy slip of the tongue."

"By opening the subject, you allowed him to visit it."

Genevieve rose from the chair, pacing in front of the window. "I ruined everything. If only I could have kept my mouth shut. But I'd seen their attraction, and with Molly as my maid, I see what a lovely person she is."

"Which makes it even more difficult. But it's not generally wise to encourage the enemy. Or fraternize with them."

She threw her hands in the air. "I know!"

"And it's not right that you and Molly have been put in this situation."

"Mrs. Weston was the one who arranged it."

"She should have known the difficulties. Molly was her lady's maid when Morgan proposed to her."

Genevieve's legs gave out but she managed to reach the chair before she collapsed into it. "They were engaged?"

"I assumed you knew."

"I knew they had a romance, but I never knew it had gone so far."

Lila raised a finger. "Only as far as the proposal on Morgan's part. She never accepted. And then the situation changed completely when Papa was discovered to be the rightful earl, Morgan the heir, and . . ."

"That's when Molly left."

"It is. No one has known where she was except her sister." Lila smoothed the fabric of her skirt. "She broke my brother's heart."

As he is about to break mine. If Genevieve had been required to rise and walk, she would not have been able.

"Dear Genevieve. I know what it's like to love a man and have the situation skewed against a happy ending."

"That's why I'm here."

"I needed a miracle, and received one. Our marriage is like coming home. Joseph and I are meant to be."

"But I don't know if Morgan and I are meant to be." Lila hesitated. "Is there *any* affection between you?"

"More on my side, than his. But I do care for him. I might even be able to say I love him. I certainly fell in love with the man who sent me letters all those months. When the marriage was arranged, I too thought that God had sent me a miracle. I planned to live happily ever after."

Lila spread her arms, palms up. "Then you will. Happiness cannot be forced, but I believe it can be interwoven with a sense of purpose. It can be a goal, as well as a state of mind."

"I'm trying. I'm praying."

"Which is all you can do. Unfortunately, love takes two, and you have little control over the other person."

Genevieve smiled. "So I can't knock him over the head to make him love me?"

"You can be your loveable self and make yourself open to his love."

"But what if my*self* isn't enough for him?"

Lila put a hand to her lips, deep in thought. Finally she spoke. "I believe life should be lived in a delicate balance of working as if everything depends on us, yet trusting God as if everything depends on Him."

"I like that."

"God is not surprised by this situation. There is a good purpose for all of it."

Genevieve wasn't so sure. "There is a purpose amid my confusion?"

"Even in that."

Clarissa found her mother in the sunroom, lounging in a wicker chair, her eyes closed. She hesitated in the doorway, uncertain whether to approach.

Mother opened her eyes and looked in her direction. "Clarissa, come in."

"Are you sleeping or brooding?"

A crease formed between her mother's eyes. "Neither." She pointed to a chair close by. "Come tell me how you're doing. I am so saddened your friends didn't treat you with more respect."

"They treated me as they've been taught to treat all people who are not just like them."

"The rules by which we live are tightly wound."

"To the point of strangulation."

Mother turned her gaze to the vista of the lawn. "Why do you think I withdrew to my room for all those years?"

Because you were a coward. Clarissa left that truth behind and said, "Because Grandmamma intimidated you and you were overwhelmed with your new responsibilities as countess."

Mother nodded. "Although I spent my girlhood learning to be the mistress of a huge estate, although I was groomed to be the wife of an earl by your grandmother, the reality of the responsibilities and the title only emphasized what I lacked."

"Which was?"

"Gumption." Her mother angled herself towards Clarissa. "Above all else, *you* have gumption. In fact, it's what I admire the most about you."

The notion her mother admired anything about her was surprising. "I don't know what to say."

She took Clarissa's hand and held it in the space between them. "Then listen to me. Yes, you went off to London, and yes, you defied the family by going on the stage. You suffered a life far more dire than any of us could imagine."

Where was she going with all this?

"But . . . you *lived*. You jumped into your dream with both feet. You courageously tried something new and outside the boundaries of the life you were expected to live. You had gumption." She squeezed Clarissa's hand. "I am proud of you for that."

Clarissa's hand was released, yet it hung in the air. "I . . . I don't know what to say."

Mother chuckled. "That's a first."

Clarissa sat back, trying to let her mother's words settle around her. She'd sought her out with the intent of making her feel bad, but now . . .

Another issue demanded mention. "I may never make a decent match. My friends care little for my gumption, and have no tolerance for my so-called courage."

"And of course, I wish for you to marry. Yet it *is* good you recognize the limitations of your current friends."

She remembered their chiding last night. Were there any among them she could truly call a friend? "Perhaps I need to find new friends."

"Good friends who admire you for who you are."

Clarissa laughed. "No one has ever admired me for who I was."

"I do. Now I do."

Clarissa felt tears threaten, and suddenly Mother was out of her chair, kneeling beside her, drawing her into her arms. "I am so sorry for abandoning you for so many years during my seclusion. I am so sorry for never giving you the support you deserved. I am so glad you are home again."

Clarissa began to sob like a child. Although it was embarrassing, it was the release she'd needed since London—since many years before.

Clarissa walked to the village, her arms swinging with joy, her face raised towards the sunlight. All was right with the world. Never, ever, would she have thought her mother could be the cause of such happiness.

To know Mother was proud of her, and even admired her for who she was . . . she couldn't help but smile.

Entering the village of Summerfield, she greeted everyone she met, and was greeted in return—though many looked confused at her very presence. It made sense. She'd revealed herself to her family but not to the world.

On a whim, she entered the mercantile. There, to her surprise was Gertie.

"Good morning, Miss Weston," Gertie said from behind the counter. "How can I help you today?"

It took Clarissa a moment to find words. "You're working here?"

"I needs to work somewhere." She nodded towards Mrs. Hayward and Rose, who came out from the back of the store. "These ladies were kind enough to give me a job *and* a place to stay."

Mrs. Hayward looked a bit embarrassed. "I hope that's all right, Miss Weston. I know Gertie left the manor under awkward circumstances, but—"

"I was set up and fired without cause," Gertie said.

"Hush now," Rose said.

"Actually, I agree that the circumstances were unfair," Clarissa said. Then she got an idea. "I just might be able to speak with my mother and get you your old job back. Would you like that, Gertie?"

"Not really."

"What?"

She straightened a stack of tooth-powder pots. "I kinda like it here. I like not wearing no stupid uniform, and not having to get up at the crack a dawn, overseeing the making of beds and the emptying of chamber pots."

"That will be enough, Gertie," Mrs. Hayward said.

But Gertie wasn't through. "Getting fired was the best thing ever happened to me. Begging your pardon, Miss Weston. I do appreciate all the years your family gave me work, but . . ." She shrugged and smiled. "Everything happens for a reason."

"She is a good clerk," Rose said. "Unless you really need her back at the house, we'd like if she could stay and work with us."

Gertie offered a nod and a smile.

"As you wish," Clarissa said.

"Was there something we could help you with, Miss Weston?" Mrs. Hayward asked.

Clarissa was no longer in the mood to shop. "Not today, thank you." She left the mercantile, pleased for Gertie, yet surprised by the swiftness of her defection to shop girl.

Gertie's words followed her out: *Everything happens for a reason.*

The vast array of her life's circumstances attempted to fall into place. Up until this morning Clarissa had never expected to feel at ease with her choices to go to London and appear on the stage. Yet now, could she—like Gertie—feel as if she was finally in the right place, that indeed everything had happened for a reason?

So intent was she on her musings that she nearly ran into a man turning a corner.

"Miss Weston. So sorry."

"Hello, Mr. Billings," she said. She hadn't seen Timothy since their talk in Lila's nursery.

"I'm glad to see you again," he said. "All set free from your self-imposed prison?"

"I am not one to remain hidden away too long."

"No, you're not."

She looked at him sideways. "Do not presume you have me figured out, Mr. Billings."

He grinned. "I wouldn't dare." He took a deep breath of the country air. "Are you missing London?"

"A bit."

"If you ever wish to visit, let me know. I go to London quite often for supplies. In fact, I'm going this next Saturday."

"I will keep that in mind."

They said their goodbyes with a nod and the tip of a hat. The mention of London . . . there was nothing for her there.

But then the image of Beth appeared in her mind. Her big blue eyes, her innocent face.

An innocent living in a tainted world. Was Beth all right? Unfortunately, there was no way to know.

Molly paused outside the door of the library to listen. Hearing no sound, she tentatively entered. She'd finished reading *Pride and Prejudice* to her mother and was now in need of a replacement.

She returned the book to its shelf and perused her other options. She wasn't in the mood for another Jane Austen. The happy ending of *Pride and Prejudice* had pleased her mother, but had rankled Molly's nerves. The Bennet sisters had found true love, but real life was far more complicated than the lives shown in books. People didn't cooperate as neatly as characters did.

Yes, Morgan and Genevieve were at odds. Molly had sensed as much when Genevieve had come back to the manor soggy from the river. She'd even heard servant gossip about how they weren't speaking.

"Good," she said to the shelves.

Her own fairy tale ending was still a possibility. Morgan had told her that he was willing to marry her—if he was free to do so.

Which he wasn't.

At least not until Tilda spilled the beans about his real father.

But putting her trust in a girl she didn't know did not give Molly comfort. She plucked a random book from the shelf, sank into a chair, and sighed. "Why can't I ever be in charge of my own destiny?"

"How about now?" A voice came from the other side of the room as Morgan suddenly rose from a reclining position on the sofa.

Molly sprang to her feet. "I didn't know you were here."

"I'm hiding, taking a catnap."

She held the book to her chest. "You should have made your presence known."

He grinned and moved towards her. "Isn't that what I just did?"

"I . . . I don't know whether I should flee or . . ."

"Fall into my arms?"

"I wasn't going to say that."

"Weren't you?" He moved closer. "I know what my choice would be. You wanted to be in charge of your own destiny? Go ahead."

There it was. Her chance to fully tumble into the past, take charge, and make something happen.

His dark eyes were so inviting. Taunting actually. As if he dared her to make a move.

She suffered an internal plea for help. *Help me choose!*

Before she could let the logic of her choices gain a voice, she found her feet moving towards the door. "If you'll excuse me. Ma is waiting for me to bring her a book."

Morgan quickly sidestepped in front of her and snatched the book from her bosom. "She's waiting for *The Innate Properties of Agricultural Finance?*"

Molly felt her face grow hot. "She's waiting for me." She left the room.

Morgan called after her. "As am I, Molly. As am I."

Molly ran down the passageway and out a side entrance, feeling as if her lungs would burst from the pressure. Once outside she put her hands on her hips and drew in one fresh breath, then another. What a catastrophe.

And yet . . . Morgan had given her the opportunity to go to him. For that one moment *she'd* been the one in control. Why hadn't she taken that chance?

As soon as she spotted Tilda walking towards the stables from the front of the house, she knew the reason for her hesitancy.

"Miss Cavendish!"

Tilda stopped walking. Her look revealed that she was not pleased to be accosted by Molly. She reluctantly walked towards her, not speaking until they were close. "I'm trying, all right?"

"So you haven't . . .?"

"Obviously not. You would have known. Everyone would have known." She looked at the manor. "I tried to get the earl and his brother to speak up about what Mr. White told them, but they skirted around it. They never mentioned that he claims to be Morgan's father."

"So now what?"

"Now I go to the stables and see if I can dig up any proof among the workers."

"What would they know about it?"

"Mr. White was working there when it happened. I've heard there's still an old man around who may know something."

No one would know anything. Or if they did, they wouldn't share. The cause was lost.

Tilda started walking. "I need to go. George is angry at me, and that, above all else, has to be fixed." Tilda rushed away.

This would never work. None of it.

Tilda scanned the stables for George, but he was nowhere in sight. That was probably for the best because she had another task to accomplish. She stopped the first stable-boy she saw. "Excuse me, I need to speak to Mr. Hiram?"

The boy looked surprised. "He's in there," he said, pointing to a thatched hut. "But he don like no visitors. Don like to be disturbed neither."

Her heart flipped. She'd hoped Mr. Hiram was a kindly old man, eager to talk about the past. But friendly or not, she had to speak with him.

As she approached the hut she noticed smoke weaving its way from the chimney. Somehow, that sign of warmth gave her courage.

Her knock upon the door seemed to test its meager hinges.

"Who's there?"

"Tilda Cavendish, sir."

"Who?"

"May I speak with you? Please?"

Suddenly, the door was yanked open, and she was faced with a man shorter than herself, though his height may have been effected by his leaning heavily on a cane. He adjusted his glasses upon his nose, but they immediately slid back to their original position. He gazed over them. "Who's you?"

"I'm Colonel Cumming's goddaughter."

"Who?"

Was he so isolated he didn't even know about the colonel? "Colonel Cummings married the dowager countess?"

His head jerked back. "When did this happen?"

She had no idea. "A while ago."

"Hmm," he said. "I canna keep track of it all."

It wasn't the recent past she was interested in. "I was wondering if I could talk to you about something that happened ages ago."

"What kind of ages?"

She tried to guess Morgan's age. "Twenty-five years or so?"

"Now you're talking." He pointed his cane at a narrow bench outside the hut. "I needs to sit."

"Of course." She stepped aside, ready to rescue him if he fell.

He sat on the bench with a loud *whooph.* He set his cane between his legs and leaned in its knob. The layers and depth of his wrinkles made Tilda long to sketch him. He squinted at the sun and motioned Tilda to stand so she became his shade. "Now then, miss," he said. "Whatcha want from me?"

Suddenly faced with the question, she hesitated. The earl and Mr. Weston had obviously not been keen to reveal the truth about Mr. White, so was it wise for her to pursue it?

"Come on. I gots things to do."

Tilda looked right, then left, making sure they had their privacy. "I was wondering about the incident involving a coachman and the earl's late wife, Fidelia?"

His chin pulled back. "Why?"

She brought forth her excuse. "As I'm part of the family now, I am curious about its history."

"Well that's history, all right, though it's history I'm bettin' they'd rather forget."

"But I'd like you to remember."

He raised a hand. "My past is all I got to talk about, and far too few e'en care."

"I care," she said.

"So you do." He took a deep breath, his face raised to the sky as if the past was waiting there. "I may not have eyes now, but I had eyes then. And ears. The coachman that was caught in the hay with Miss Fidelia Breton—White was his name—told everyone the extent of his conquest. Twas quite a coup, a man like him having a go at a gentrified lady like her."

Tilda was surprised that Mr. White had been telling the truth. "He . . .?"

"So he said. Course he was egged on by the lot of us."

"So he didn't . . .?"

Mr. Hiram pointed a finger at her. "Youse much too young to know about such things—much less ask."

"I'm older than my years."

His eyebrows rose. "I's sorry to hear that, girl."

She appreciated his compassion, but had to nudge him back to the story. "So Mr. White and Miss Breton . . .?"

"That's how I remembers it. Whatever happened it were more than enough—enough for her and her family to run away to London in shame."

"Was she . . .?"

"I wouldn't be surprised."

It was time for *the* question. "I wonder how long after the earl married Miss Breton that their son was born. . ."

The man's rheumy eyes widened. "You don't think . . .?"

"No, of course not."

His head shook back and forth, back and forth. "Aye aye aye. We best keep our mouths closed about any such thought. You may not know about the wagging tongues of Summerfield, but I do, and if even the hint of such a thing got out . . ."

Suddenly, George rushed forward and grabbed her arm, the horse he had been leading forgotten.

"Ouch!"

He yanked her away. "Sorry, Mr. Hiram, but Tilda is needed elsewhere."

"Master George. Sorry if I said—"

George didn't wait for the rest of the man's apology. He pulled Tilda across the yard and behind a shed, where he spun her around to face him. "What are you doing? What other mischief are you trying to stir up? I thought you cared for me and my family. But this is the second time I've witnessed you trying to destroy it."

"I'm not trying to destroy it. I'm trying to save it—for you, George. I'm doing it for you. If Morgan isn't the earl's blood son, then you will be the heir."

George stared at her. "You're ruining everything."

"No I'm not! I'm fixing everything. I'm giving you back your title!"

"Maybe I don't want a title. Did you ever consider that?"

No.

He raised a finger to her face. "You leave my family alone. Or else."

She knew she shouldn't say the words, but they came out anyway. "Or else what?"

He shook his head as if the sight of her disgusted him. Then he retrieved his horse, mounted in one swift motion, and rode away.

"George! Come back!"

He ignored the gate and hurled the horse over the fence.

And fell.

"George!"

Tilda was not alone as she ran towards him.

But she was alone in her guilt.

Clarissa was just coming downstairs when Tilda burst in the front door.

"What do you think you're doing?"

But then she saw her brother being carried in by two stablemen.

"What happened?"

"He fell off his horse," said a man. "I've sent for the doctor."

"But Doctor Peter is here with Mrs. Wallace." She pointed to a footman. "Go upstairs and fetch him."

Dixon had arrived, giving instructions to the men. "Take Master George upstairs. Second door on the right."

Clarissa led the way, glaring at Tilda. "Get my mother and father. The morning room and study. Hurry!"

Clarissa rushed ahead of the men, preparing the bed for her brother. The men eased him down carefully. He had blood on his head and his arm was crooked oddly. Sally came in and Clarissa motioned to the table, "Get some fresh water, and cloths."

Mother and Father arrived at the same time, rushing to the side of the bed. "What happened?" Father asked.

One of the men answered. "He jumped the fence and missed."

The other man said, "His horse was lame to begin with. He wouldn't a made it no matter who was riding 'im."

"So why was George riding him?" Clarissa asked. "He knows better."

The men looked to Tilda.

She was involved. "What did you do?" Clarissa asked her.

The girl just stood there, shaking her head.

Sally returned with water and a cloth. Mother dabbed at the blood on her son's head. "Where is the doctor?"

At that moment, Dr. Peter rushed in. All others moved back, giving him room. He lifted George's eyelids. "He fell from a horse?"

The details were explained again.

Clarissa noticed Tilda backing towards the door and grabbed her arm. "Oh, no you don't. What did you have to do with this?"

"I think you'd better answer, girl," Father said.

"I . . . we were arguing."

"About what?"

Her eyes flit from Clarissa, to her father, to her mother.

Stupid girl. Clarissa expelled a sigh of exasperation. "She's the cause of George's fall. It's her fault!"

Morgan entered the room with the earl. Then Genevieve and her mother.

Dr. Peter pointed towards the lot of them. "Please. Out." With a look to Mother, he added, "You may stay, but the rest must go. And send for Miss Wallace to assist me."

As Father herded them out of the room Clarissa hissed at Tilda. "You'll pay for this. I promise you that."

Tilda had every reason to look scared.

Chapter Eighteen

Tilda ran from the manor, needing to get away from the accusing eyes — and her own guilt.

Only when her lungs burned did she stop and gasp for air. And forgiveness.

She fell to her knees and leaned forward until her head touched her hands upon the ground. "I'm so sorry. Please let George be all right. Please!"

"Tilda?"

She looked up and saw her godfather rushing towards her. "What's wrong? Are you all right?"

The notion of standing and sluffing it off came — and went. She sat back on her heels, her head shaking. "It's a mess. An awful mess."

"Now now," he said, helping her to her feet. "It can't be as bad as all that."

"Worse," she said.

"What you need is a cup of tea. Come home with me."

Tilda hadn't realized how close she was to the cottage. As they approached she saw the dowager weeding the garden. "Matilda, how nice of you to visit."

Tilda saw the colonel give his wife a look. "Tilda is upset."

"About what?"

"Wifey, please. Let me get the girl inside. Will you make her some tea please?"

The thought of a dowager countess making her tea seemed very wrong. "I don't need tea," she said, then quickly added, "Thank you."

"Then sit down," the colonel said, leading her to a chair near the fire. "Tell us what's wrong."

The truth pushed forward, each fact waving an insistent hand.

"Out with it," the colonel said. "You'll never be free until you say it aloud."

"You're assuming the girl came here to confess something, Grady," the dowager said as she sat close by.

He stood by the fireplace and gave Tilda a steady gaze. "Didn't you?"

Tilda let the truth escape unchecked: the Whites, their true motives, the blackmail, her talk with Mr. Hiram, and even her hopes of marrying George and being countess someday.

The dowager expelled a long breath. "You. The countess."

Embarrassment became Tilda's prime emotion. "I'm sorry. I know how ridiculous that sounds. But when I came to the manor and everyone was so nice to me. . ." She thought of something to add. "I had a difficult life with Pa. He didn't want me and I never knew my mother."

"Excuses are like too much pepper," the dowager said. "They make the truth inedible."

"I don't disagree," the colonel said. "But her father *was* a difficult man. And he did think of himself before all others."

"If you knew this," the dowager said, "you should have taken Matilda away years ago."

"I had nothing to offer her. I was in India much of the time, I had duties to queen and country."

Although Tilda was glad someone else was in trouble, she hated seeing the colonel take the blame. "He's not at fault, Aunt Adelaide. He's been ever so kind to me." She looked to her lap. "Everyone's been kind. Well . . . almost everyone."

"Who isn't kind?"

Tilda thought of Clarissa's threat. It might behoove her to have allies. "Clarissa. She hates me."

"I am certain that's not true," the dowager said.

The colonel shrugged. "It could be true. You know Ruth was treating Tilda like a daughter."

"Women," the dowager said. "More complicated than any species on earth."

"I'll agree to that statement," the colonel said.

She pointed a finger at him, but Tilda could see it was only in jest. "I'll have a talk with Clarissa. Now then, as for the other . . ."

Then suddenly, Tilda remembered a detail she had left out. "George caught me talking to Mr. Hiram, and got mad."

"Understandably, as you were trying to disrupt the entire balance of family and title," the dowager said.

Tilda stood, realizing her omission would look as horrible as it was. "George was mad, and rode off on a lame horse, tried to jump a fence, and fell."

The dowager looked to the barn and back at Tilda, "Is he all right?"

"He was carried up to the house."

"Carried?"

"Dr. Peter is there, but when I left, George hadn't woke up."

The dowager bolted from her chair and out the door, as if one motion was indelibly connected to the other.

"Oh dear," Tilda said. "I should have mentioned George first. I can't even get that right."

The colonel pointed at her. "Don't. This is not about you."

"I know."

"Do you? By conniving and manipulating and keeping the truth from a family who have loved you and taken you in as their own . . . you've made a fine mess of things, girl."

"I didn't do it. The Whites were the ones—"

"The blame is yours as much as theirs, for you knew what they were up to and let their plan move forward for your own purposes. You saw evil and let it have its way. You hurt a family who cared for you." He looked to the ceiling, shaking his head. "The good book says we are to 'Depart from evil and do good; seek peace and pursue it.'" He looked at Tilda again. "You did just the opposite."

"I didn't mean for it to turn out so wrong."

"Then make it right."

"How do I do that?"

He took her arm and pulled her to standing. "I have no idea. But for now, we're going up to the manor to check on George and we're going to pray each step of the way." He paused at the door. "We're going to pray for George, Tilda. We'll get to you later."

Clarissa paced up and back in the hall outside George's bedroom. With each step her contempt for Tilda grew. Clarissa had only been home a few days and already that girl had been responsible for Gertie being fired and her brother's accident.

"Stop pacing," Morgan said. "You're making us nervous."

Uncle Jack agreed, "Please, Clarissa."

With a sigh she took a position beside her father, who stared at the carpet, his hand to his mouth. He mumbled something under his breath that sounded like, "He can't die. He can't. He can't."

Clarissa needed him to stop. "Surely you don't think he's going to die."

"I hope not."

Suddenly, Grandmamma appeared at the end of the hallway. "He is not going to die. I will not allow it."

It was typical for her grandmother to assume she could fix everything, but this time . . .

"I am afraid not even you have that power, Mother."

"Certainly none of us have that power standing out here in the hall." She strode into the room before anyone could tell her that Dr. Peter had requested they wait outside.

With the door opened the family in its entirety poured in like water through the break in a dam. Dr. Peter looked aghast at the flood of Westons. He stood beside the bed and gave a bow to the dowager and the earl.

"So?" Grandmamma asked, with only a glance at Mother at one side of George's bed, and Molly on the other. "How is he?"

"His heartbeat is strong, your ladyship."

She surveyed the area around George and pointed at a bowl of bloody water in Molly's hands. "Blood?"

"Superficial cuts, my lady," Dr. Peter said. "They are of no lasting concern. I initially thought his arm was broken, but it appears to be all right, just sprained."

She sat beside her grandson, taking her hand in his. Patting it. "Come now, Georgie. Wake up now. You have horses to ride."

Clarissa wasn't sure mentioning horses was such a good idea.

George did not awaken.

Clarissa heard someone arrive at the bedroom door, turned, and saw Colonel Grady with Tilda.

"She's the cause of all this!" Clarissa said, striding towards the girl. Tilda took refuge behind the colonel, but Clarissa caught the sleeve of her dress and pulled her into the open. "You're to blame! Why don't you go back where you belong and leave my family alone!"

"Clarissa!"

Grandmamma strode towards her. "Yes, she *is* to blame, but now is not the time."

"But I know—"

Her grandmother gave her a glare that had quieted many a grown man. "Not. Now." Then she spoke to all present. "George must be our first concern. I will stay with him now. The rest of you go."

Clarissa brushed past Tilda, out the door. "I'm not through with you yet."

"Leave me," the dowager told Dr. Peter. "Give me some time alone with my grandson. Come back in a half-hour."

"As you wish, my lady."

Dr. Peter nodded to Molly and the two of them left the room.

Molly was glad the upstairs hallway was vacant of worried family. There was enough worry between herself and Peter.

Peter took a deep breath and ran a sleeve over his brow. "I do hope he awakens soon."

"What are his chances of a full recovery?"

"We know so little about the brain. But the sooner he wakes up, the better." He pointed to the back stairs. "I need air. Care to join me?"

"That sounds perfect."

They took the stairs, then exited a side entrance and strolled into the garden. Peter inhaled the autumn air. "The good thing about a crisis is seeing a family band together."

"That's what happened with my family too." She pulled up short when she realized they'd reached the bench by the arbor—the bench she used to share with Morgan during their clandestine meetings.

"He wouldn't look at me," she whispered.

"Who . . . ?" Then Peter said, "His lordship? Morgan?"

"I'm in the room with George, not three feet away, and all of them look right through me, as if I'm not even there."

"Families always see family first."

"I suppose."

"I see you, Molly."

She looked into his eyes. They were the palest blue, the exact opposite of Morgan's deep brown. The pale color inspired images of fresh air, clear sky, and freedom.

He brushed his fingers against hers. "I will always see you for who you truly are. And love you for it."

Love me for it?

Molly felt her mouth go dry. He was declaring his love for her?

"I . . . I . . ."

He put a finger to her lips. "Shh. Don't say anything until you can tell me what I need to hear." He looked back to the house. "I'd better go in."

As she moved to follow him, he stopped her. "Take a moment, Molly. I'd like you to fully consider what I said. Will you do that for me?"

She could only nod.

He touched her chin, then left her.

Molly stared after him. Peter loved her? He wanted her to love him?

But she loved Morgan.

Didn't she?

She closed her eyes and thought about Morgan. Yes, there he was. Teasing her in the study. His smile, his brown eyes. She waited to be embraced by a warm rush of feelings.

That didn't come.

Molly opened her eyes and looked at the arbor and the bench where she and Morgan had cuddled and kissed. Then she turned towards the manor house. The Morgan of the arbor and the Morgan of the manor house were as different as tin was to gold. Her Morgan—the Morgan she'd loved and who had proposed to her—was gone forever, captured by his new station, held prisoner in a decadent jail. There was no escape for him. She could not set him free. He was living out a life sentence, apart from her. Separated from her by centuries of tradition and protocol.

Was he happy in his gilded cage?

What was there to be unhappy about? He had a title, a vast estate, his family, and was betrothed to a wonderful American girl. His future was bright.

Unless something happened to ruin it.

"No!"

Molly hurried back in the house and stopped Mrs. Camden in the corridor. "Have you seen Miss Cavendish?"

Molly received a questioning look. "I believe she's in the sunroom. Is there something I can help—?"

"No. Thank you." Molly hurried towards the back of the house. *Please be alone, please be alone.*

She paused at the doorway and scanned the room. It was empty. But then she heard a sigh and saw Tilda sitting in a wicker chair, her knees drawn to her chest.

"Ahem," she said.

Tilda glanced her way. "Oh. It's you."

Molly rushed towards her, needing to say her piece before they were interrupted. "I wanted to make sure you don't say anything to anyone."

"About what?"

Really? "You know very well about what."

"Oh. That," the girl said. "It's too late. The dowager and Colonel Cummings know. And George."

Molly's stomach flipped. "How do they know?"

"George overheard me talking to Mr. Hiram, and I told the other two."

"You what?"

Tilda set her feet to the floor with a clop-clop. "That's what you wanted me to do."

"Yes, but now. . . if they know, it's all a mess."

She nodded. "Completely and utterly."

Her dismissal was maddening. "If they all know, then why hasn't everything come out? Why isn't the manor abuzz with it?"

"George's accident." Tilda pulled her knees back to her chest. "It'll come out as soon as he's better. I know it will. And then you'll have your chance to marry Morgan."

"But I don't want to marry Morgan!"

Silence fell between them, as if the very air was surprised by her declaration.

"Since when?"

A few days ago? Five minutes ago? "I'm not sure."

Tilda's head shook back and forth. "They won't even let me in to see George," Tilda said. "I need to tell him I'm sorry."

"How much does he know?"

"Everything." Tilda glared at her. "Actually, this is all your fault. You wanted me to get the truth about Morgan out in the open. That's what I was doing when George overheard and told me he doesn't even want to be the heir. He was so mad he rode off and fell."

"No you don't," Molly said. "I will not take responsibility for the accident. You wanted the truth out as much as I did."

Tilda shrugged. "What does any of it matter now?" There was a sound and they both turned and saw Dixon standing in the doorway.

How much had he heard?

"Yes, Mr. Dixon?"

"I'm sorry to disturb. I was looking for Mrs. Weston. The dowager countess is requesting all the family," he cleared his throat, "all the family to meet in the drawing room immediately."

"Of course," Tilda said. "If I see her, I'll tell her."

As soon as he left, Tilda began to cry. "This is the end. The dowager knows the truth. She's calling the family together—and it's very clear I'm not included. She's going to tell them about Morgan, Mr. White, and my part in all this."

"Do you really think that is what—"

Tilda jumped to her feet. "I have to go!"

"Go where?"

Tilda rushed past her; away.

Molly stood alone in the sunroom. She had not been alone in this room since she was an under housemaid and had to dust and sweep the carpets.

A short distance away, the Weston family was gathering. Soon they all would hear that Morgan was not a true Weston, not the son of an earl, and not an heir.

Which means he'll be free to marry me.

Yet what had she just admitted to Tilda? *I don't want to marry Morgan.*

But what if he was truly free?

That question and her need for an answer spurred Molly to walk out of the sunroom, towards the front of the house.

She was not invited to the family meeting, but that didn't mean she couldn't listen in.

Tilda rushed up the back stairs on her toes, trying to make as little sound as possible. She paused at the far end of the hall leading to the bedrooms and saw Mrs. Weston exiting George's room, heading towards the front stair.

"Good bye, Mrs. Weston," she whispered.

When the coast was clear, she rushed to her room and retrieved a carpet bag from beneath her bed. She stuffed it with clothes—just the clothes she'd arrived with. Nothing more. She would not be accused of stealing again. Ever.

As soon as she was through, she took one final look at the room, knowing she would never see it again. She checked the hall a second time, and began to retrace her steps, when she paused.

She tiptoed down the hall to George's door. She pressed a hand against the glowing walnut and whispered, "I'm so sorry, George. Please wake up. Please forgive me."

Then she ran down the back stairs, out the side door, and hurried off to the village.

To the train station, and beyond.

Chapter Nineteen

"Mother, really," Mr. Weston said, as the family settled into the drawing room. "You call a meeting now? When George is upstairs, suffering?"

"He is in good hands with Dr. Peter. I call a meeting now because he *is* suffering. Because of the cause of his suffering."

"Ha," Clarissa huffed. "Tilda is the cause of that."

"Where is she?" the colonel asked, looking around the room.

"What does it matter? She is not family, Colonel," Clarissa said.

"No, she is not," the dowager said. "And as such I did not tell Dixon to invite her here."

At her comment Genevieve's nerves rattled and she raised a tentative hand. "I am not family either."

"Oh my dear," the dowager said. "We are getting twisted by semantics. You are like a daughter already. Speaking of . . . where is your mother?"

As if in answer, they heard someone at the front door.

The dowager sighed. "I detest interruptions."

They heard Dixon answer the door and then he appeared at the doorway to the drawing room. "Lord Newley is here to see you, your lordship."

"If you could ask him to come back another time—or wait in my study."

"He insists on seeing you immediately. He says it's important."

The earl looked to his mother. "May I? I will make it short."

She flipped him away. "Go on then. Another minute will not matter."

Matter in regard to what?

The earl followed Dixon out of the drawing room. As Genevieve's attention was pulled in that direction, she saw her mother scurry past the doorway, moving towards the stairs.

Considering Mamma did *not* scurry, she knew something was afoot. Genevieve rose from her chair. "If you will excuse me a moment. I saw my mother . . ."

"Bring her in," the dowager said. "I have a need to get this done."

"Done?" Clarissa said. "You're being very mysterious, Grandmamma."

"The mystery will be gone soon enough."

Genevieve caught up with her mother at the foot of the stairs. "Come into the drawing room. The family has gathered."

But Mamma's face was ashen as she shook her head. "I cannot." She began ascending the stairs.

Genevieve took hold of her arm, stopping her. "Mamma? What's wrong?"

Her mother bit her lower lip and looked in the direction of the earl and Lord Newley who were talking in a corridor on the other side of the foyer. "I did something dreadful. I said too much."

Genevieve saw both men look in their direction. She lowered her voice. "What did you say?"

She shook her head. "I'm so sorry, Genevieve. I didn't mean—"

But then the earl came towards them. "Genevieve, Mrs. Farrow. I think it's best we all go into the drawing room."

Genevieve wanted to ask questions, but dared not. She took her mother's arm and found it shaking. They went into the room and to Genevieve's surprise, Lord Newley came too.

The dowager put her hands on her hips. "Jack? We were having a family meeting here. I'm sorry, Lord Newley, but—"

"It's all right, Mother," the earl said. "After speaking with Newley, I have guessed the content of this gathering. And after what he just told me . . . he too has business being here."

The dowager threw her hands in the air. "Gracious. Why not invite the entire village?"

The colonel put a calming hand upon her arm. "Continue, wifey. Perhaps you should get to the point."

"That would be preferred," the earl said, settling into his seat. Lord Newley stood nearby, and Genevieve's mother sat next to Genevieve, her hand gripping her daughter's as if it were a lifeline.

"Very well then," the dowager said. She pointed at the earl and then his brother. "You two should know what this meeting is about, because you were the ones who were blackmailed."

"Blackmailed?" Mrs. Weston said. "About what? Who?"

The dowager motioned to the earl. "I shall let you answer both questions, Jack."

"This isn't necessary," Mr. Weston said with a glance to his brother. "We paid him off. It's over."

"It is necessary," the dowager said. "Because the information involved has already leaked out and damage is being done."

The earl nodded towards their guest. "That is why Lord Newley is here. He was told of the blackmail."

"Told?" the dowager asked. "By whom?"

Lord Newley pointed at Genevieve's mother. "Mrs. Farrow told me all about it this morning."

Genevieve turned towards Mamma and whispered. "How could you?"

"Will someone please tell us what's going on?" Morgan asked.

The dowager faced her grandson. "Mr. and Mrs. White had ulterior motives beyond accompanying Matilda to Summerfield Manor. Extortion was their game."

"What did they have to extort?" Morgan asked.

Genevieve's thoughts sped to the men's study, where she had overheard the entire transaction. To realize that in mere minutes the entire family would know Morgan was not the heir . . . . She put her free hand to her stomach, trying in vain to calm it.

The dowager continued. "It turns out that Mr. White was once a coachman here at the manor, and he had an . . . encounter with Fidelia, before she was Jack's wife, when she was still being courted by Frederick."

"I never courted Fidelia," Mr. Weston said. "She imagined and exaggerated our attraction."

"Be that as it may," the dowager said. "Mr. White claimed that he and Fidelia had relations, to the result of having a son."

"I have a brother?" Morgan said.

"I'm afraid not."

The room was silent and Genevieve could see that people were processing the statement.

The dowager made it plain. "Mr. White claims to be your father, claims that you are that child."

Morgan's mouth gaped open, then he bolted from his chair. "I don't believe any of this!"

The earl moved to comfort him. "I don't either. Yes, I married your mother soon after the scandal with Mr. White, but she was not with child at the time. I know it."

The dowager sighed. "Unfortunately, only Fidelia knows for sure, and she is no longer with us."

Mrs. Weston put her hands to her face. "It's all my fault! I was the one who paid the coachman—this Mr. White—to get Fidelia in a compromising situation. I wanted to discredit her in Frederick's eyes. I was a stupid, desperate girl. I am the cause of all this."

"Nonsense," the dowager said. "You may have lit the flame, but the other players made their own choices about participating. As for what really happened? How far it went? I agree with Jack and Morgan. I do not believe Morgan is the result of that dalliance."

"Then why did you pay off the Whites?" Lord Newley asked.

"To buy their silence."

"That didn't work very well, did it?" he said. He looked to Genevieve's mother. "Apparently silence — and discretion — is a rare commodity."

Mamma looked to her lap and Genevieve felt both pity and anger. "Mamma?"

She shook her head. "I apologize. I shouldn't have said anything."

The dowager crossed the room to face her. "Why would you spread such a rumor? If it got out and people believed it, then the marriage between Morgan and your daughter would be at risk."

"She wanted to marry me," Lord Newley said. "*She* wanted to become a viscountess."

The room suffered a multitude of gasps. Genevieve didn't want to believe what she was hearing. Yet knowing her mother's ambition . . . the situation *was* believable. "You would ruin my chance of marriage and a title, for your own?"

Her mother raised her chin and stood. "I'm truly sorry, but I can't endure this any —"

"Sit!" the dowager pointed at her chair. "I will deal with you later."

Mamma sank to the chair and seemed to fold into herself. Genevieve felt a sad satisfaction in her humiliation. Her mother had pressed her own ambitions once too often.

The dowager continued. "Ignoring the detour into Mrs. Farrow's lack of loyalty and confidence further focuses on the real issue at hand. The truth will not matter to those who prefer a ripe story. They will only care that the heir to the earldom of Summerfield might not be a Weston at all."

Mrs. Weston raised a finger. "If Morgan is no longer the heir, then Genevieve will not become a titled lady."

The dowager nodded. "That is true."

Morgan stood beside Genevieve, his face heavy with regret and shame. "I am so sorry for all this."

She reached out and brushed his fingers with her own. Then she felt a deep stirring. A nudge. A strong prodding to speak up. It was in her power to make things right and offer hope in this awful situation.

Buoyed by this knowledge and feeling of a courage far beyond herself, Genevieve stood to make her proclamation to all. "Another truth that must be shared is that I don't care whether I gain a title or not. I still want to marry Morgan."

Mrs. Weston put a hand to her chest. "Your family is giving us a good portion of your fortune. You are entitled to be more than simply a missus."

At the mention of money, Genevieve suffered a wave of embarrassment. "My mother wanted the title for me — and apparently for herself. But it means little to me. I fell in love with the man I first met through his letters. A man who spoke of his family, his land, and its legacy with passion. I did not fall in love with a title."

For the first time since her humiliation, Genevieve's mother looked up. "But Morgan loves Molly."

Genevieve stared at her, mortified. She couldn't believe her own mother had said those words aloud.

The earl stepped towards his son. "I know you did once, but . . . is she correct?"

Morgan's face flashed with a myriad of emotions. "It's true, I loved Molly."

Mrs. Weston raised a finger to make a point. "If you are not the heir you would be free to marry her."

Morgan stood fully erect, as if needing the strength of his stance to proceed. Genevieve braced herself for his public declaration.

He glanced at her, then faced the room. "Yes, I would be free of my title and status, but not of my heart and mind." With a sweeping gesture that made Genevieve startle, he knelt beside her and took her hand. "I am so sorry for how I have acted since your arrival. I admit I haven't been fair to you. I admit I have made things difficult and complicated and have dealt with the situation poorly."

Genevieve felt everyone's eyes. Up until now her humiliation had been private. For him to admit his true feelings and his hurtful actions for everyone's ears . . .

He bowed his head and let his thumb travel over the top of her hand. "With Molly's return, I dabbled in feelings from the past. I played with love as if it was a game. I acted like an immature boy instead of a gentleman and a man of character."

She waited for the "but" when he would tell them he could not deny his feelings any longer.

He looked up at her, meeting her gaze. "Will you forgive me, my sweet and patient Genevieve? Will you still agree to be my wife?"

She couldn't trust that she'd heard correctly. "What did you say?"

He smiled. "Will you marry me, Genevieve?"

Expecting one thing yet hearing another gave her pause. Once she fully realized what was being offered to her, Genevieve surprised herself by remaining silent. Although Morgan's confession and declaration seemed sincere, she knew she was at a crossroads. For once in her life *she* was in control.

It was her decision.

Amid this freedom came a calm assurance, an inner affirmation that her instinctive choice, the one that sprang from her heart *and* mind, was the right one. Genevieve reached out and touched his cheek. "I will marry you, Morgan Weston. You, not the title."

He leaned close enough to touch his lips to hers. It was unconventional that their first kiss was in front of the entire family, but somehow it seemed appropriate.

He stood and drew her up beside him, linking her hand around his arm. "So then. What is the family's position on the scandal now?"

Genevieve heard the others discussing a united front, but had no ear for any of it. Her ears, her eyes, her breath, and her heart were tuned to the man beside her. Her man.

Will you marry me, Genevieve?

Molly fled her eavesdropping perch and ran upstairs two flights. She burst into her mother's room.

Ma put a hand to her chest, her eyes wide. Molly ran to her. "Ma. I'm sorry. I didn't mean to scare you."

Ma took a few deep breaths. "Wha wong?"

Molly sank onto the bed. "I've been a total fool. Morgan acted like he still cared for me, but he didn't. Not really. I need to go back to London. I never should have stayed so long."

Ma shook her head vigorously. "No! You and Pe-uh. He luh you."

Molly hesitated, and thought about acting surprised, but chose otherwise. "I know."

"And you luh him?" Ma raised her eyebrows, waiting for her answer.

Molly stood and paced by the bed. She wanted to be able to say she loved Peter, but it was too soon. "I'm not sure if I love him. I think I *could* love him."

"Guh 'nuf."

"Is it good enough? To expect love to come?"

Ma reached for Molly's hand, then patted it. "Luh in this," she pointed to her heart, "but also in this." She touched her head, then wove her fingers around Molly's. "Join togethuh." She smiled. "Then en-joy."

The most telling moment for Molly was when she found herself smiling at the thought of Peter, and the two of them loving and enjoying each other. Although she'd relished snippets of such thoughts before, the memories of Morgan had hung like a cloud above her, promising sun, but threatening rain.

She let the image of Peter's face take center stage.

She felt her smile widen.

Molly kissed her mother on the forehead. "He's the one. I know it."

"Teh him."

Molly nodded. She started to leave for George's room, but decided against it. This was not something said over a sickbed. She'd wait until Peter went home. Then she'd go to him and say all that was in her heart.

Tilda stood at the ticket booth at Summerfield's railway station. "One to Aldershot, please."

The man eyed her suspiciously. "Does the colonel know you're leaving, Miss Cavendish?"

Tilda longed for the anonymity of Aldershot. "Yes, of course. I'm just going home to visit a family friend."

"Hmm," he said, as he slipped her a ticket. "The train from Aldershot just left. Won't be one going back for a couple hours."

"That's fine," she said. But as she sat upon a bench on the platform, she regretted the delay. Surely the family would discover her gone and come after her.

Wouldn't they? Or would they say good riddance?

She moved to the bench furthest from the ticket booth, accepting its small increase of privacy.

She had just settled when she heard a familiar voice. "Tilda?"

"Mr. White?" Tilda looked past him, expecting his wife to barrel forward. She kept her voice low. "What are you doing here? You shouldn't be back here. The earl could have you arrested."

"If he so chooses, I'll take my licks." He patted a valise he held close to his chest. "But I'm hoping he'll think otherwise after I return the money to him."

Tilda couldn't help but gawk. "You're bringing it back?"

"I had to. The guilt of it was like a guillotine ready to slice through me."

It was hard to comprehend. "But what of Mrs. White? Surely she didn't agree—and where is she?"

He stood tall and tried to make his chin strong. "I've left her."

She didn't know what to say.

"For once in my life I stood up for what I believed and didn't let her bully me into doing things I oughtn't. And for that, I thank the guilt, for it made me grow a backbone."

Tilda let a chuckle escape. "Good for you."

He glanced at her carpet bag. "Are you going somewhere?"

Not anymore. She stood and linked her arm through his. "Shall we go to the manor together?"

As they walked, she thanked God for second chances. Undeserved chances.

Morgan would not release Genevieve's hand from his arm— nor did she want him to do so. The way he looked at her now . . . things had changed. The strength she had found to stand up for herself and for their love garnered immediate rewards, as if her declaration had afforded Morgan the strength to take his own stand.

He chose me!

"Would you care to go riding later?" he asked her.

"That would be delightful."

Genevieve spotted Mamma as she made her way out of the drawing room. Her head was down and her eyes glanced furtively like a mouse afraid of a cat.

The dowager called after her, "Remember this, Dorcas Farrow: if you weren't the mother of the bride, I would send you back to America immediately. Loyalty and trust is as essential to our family as air, and you showed evidence of neither."

Mamma nodded. "I'm so sorry, Lady Summerfield." She looked towards the stairs, then gave Genevieve a plaintive look.

Reluctantly, Genevieve said to Morgan, "If you could excuse me? I think Mamma needs me right now."

He glanced at her mother and nodded. "She was very wrong," he said, loud enough for her to hear.

"I know." Genevieve removed her hand from his arm. "I'll be back shortly."

Morgan let her go and Genevieve rushed to Mamma's side, reaching her as she tripped on the first step. "Come now. Let me help you upstairs."

Genevieve led her mother into her bedroom, where her maid was busy mending a seam. Jane immediately stood, her face questioning.

"If you'll leave us, Jane? Perhaps go fetch some tea?"

As soon as they were alone, Mamma climbed onto the bed and drew a pillow to her chest.

Genevieve wasn't certain what to do. Other than consoling each other while grieving Genevieve's father, she had never been in a position to offer Mamma comfort. Mamma was the strong one, the one who let nothing faze her.

She sat on the edge of the bed. "How can I help?"

"You can't," her mother said into the pillow. "I've done myself in quite well on my own."

Genevieve took advantage of the opening. "Why did you tell Lord Newley the secret? I told you about the blackmail in confidence, and you assured me you would keep it so."

Mamma suddenly sat upright. "I'm a bad person. That's all there is to it."

Genevieve was almost relieved to witness her mother's familiar drama. "You are not a bad person, but you did a bad thing by talking too much about private matters. Again I ask, why?"

Her mother swung her legs off the side of the bed, looking like a child with her feet inches from the floor. "When Lord Newley showed interest in me . . . I had not received male attention like that since . . ."

"Since Father."

"Since never."

Genevieve didn't understand. "Surely Father courted you and showed you special attention."

She shook her head adamantly. "We had affection for each other, but I married him because I wished to be married. And he married me because he wanted a partner."

"There is nothing wrong with those reasons."

"There is something terribly wrong when they are the only reasons. There was no love."

Oh.

She looked at Genevieve with a directness saved for a woman to a woman. "When you had the chance to gain a title, I pounced on it."

"I know status and position in society have always been important to you."

"Too important." Mamma left the bed and strolled to the fireplace. The drapery of her bustle was skewed to the side, but Genevieve did nothing to fix it. "Beyond New York society I have always been fascinated with kings and queens, and all things noble."

"Our roots are British."

"Our roots are poor Irish," she said, running a hand along the intricate carved columns that held up the mantel. "To be here at Summerfield Manor, to know that a title was in your grasp . . ." She gave her daughter her full attention. "I am ashamed to admit it but I was jealous of you."

"Of me?"

"I have always been jealous of you. For your father loved you far more than he loved me. I'm prettier and more witty and interesting, yet he preferred you."

Genevieve let the insults pass. "But Father did love you. I know it."

Mamma shook her head. "He loved you more." She waved a hand, moving on. "So when you told me the secret that Morgan might not be the heir, meaning that you might not become a viscountess, I thought perhaps I could be the one to gain a title. I could have something you did not."

Genevieve was speechless. She sank onto a chair. "We are not in competition, Mamma. I've never felt in competition with you."

"But I have, with you." She rushed to her daughter, taking her hands. "Please forgive me. I've been horrible to you, to the Westons, and to Lord Newly. I've shown them the very worst of myself. If you forgive me, I am hoping they will follow suit."

The feeling of power returned, but Genevieve pushed it away. This was not about the chance to wield power in order to rise above. This was a chance to wield power to come alongside and bring about closeness, forgiveness, and love.

She brushed a stray hair from her mother's face. "Of course I forgive you, and I'm sure the family will do the same."

"And Lord Newly?"

"I can't speak for him."

Her mother nodded and kissed Genevieve's hand. "You are a beauty, my dear. In so many ways."

Genevieve accepted the compliment with a nod, and more than that, with confidence that what her mother said was true.

Tilda stood at the entrance to Summerfield Manor, Mr. White by her side.

The man took a deep breath, slowly letting it out. "I'm nervous."

"So am I," she said.

"I don't know what will happen, but it's got to be better than the guilt of it."

Tilda wasn't so certain.

Before they could knock, Dixon opened the door. "Miss Cavendish? I didn't know you were gone." He glared at Mr. White. "Sir, you are not welcome here."

Tilda rushed to explain. "He's here to make things right, Dixon. Please let him in."

Dixon hesitated. "I will let you in, miss, and I will announce Mr. White."

With a final look at her companion, Tilda left her carpet bag outside and entered the manor. She stood aside while Dixon went into the drawing room to announce him.

The earl and Mr. Weston appeared. "Tilda? What's this about Mr. White being here?"

As they'd obviously not noticed her absence it was too long a story to explain. "He's here to make amends."

"I find that to be quite impossible," Mr. Weston said.

"He has the money with him," she said.

The eyebrows of both men rose. "Send him in, Dixon."

Mr. White entered the drawing room. He removed his hat. "I'm sorry to disturb you."

Uncle Jack stood shoulder to shoulder with his brother, protecting the rest of the family, seated behind. "What are you doing here, Mr. White?" the earl asked. "State your business."

"Mr. White held a valise towards the earl. "Here's the money you paid us. All of it."

Mr. Weston opened the bag, "You're giving it back?"

"I am, sir. Your lordship."

"Why?" Aunt Adelaide asked.

The brothers parted, allowing the rest of the family in on the conversation.

"Because I was wrong to take it. We were both wrong to take it."

"Speaking of 'we' . . . where is your wife?" the colonel asked.

"I don't know and I don't care. We have parted ways."

"Probably a good choice," Mrs. Weston said.

"I'm not just here to bring back the money," Mr. White said. "I've come to clear things up."

"Well then." the dowager said. "Out with it."

Mr. White turned his hat in circles. "I'll start at the end and work back, if that's all right with you."

"Just get to it, man," Mr. Weston said.

"The main thing I have to say is that I . . . I am not Lord Weston's father." He looked at Morgan. "The earl *is* your father."

There was a communal intake of breath. Morgan looked at him, "Are you certain?"

"I am." He stared at the floor. "I never . . . Fidelia and I never . . ."

Mrs. Weston piped in, "But you told everyone otherwise."

"Bragging. Pure and simple." He looked from Mrs. Weston to her husband. "You two walked in and broke up whatever might have . . ." He looked to the rest of them. "Nothing happened."

"Thank God for that," Aunt Adelaide said under her breath.

The earl addressed Mr. White. "I speak for all of us when I say that we appreciate you returning to Summerfield."

"The scene of the crime," Mr. Weston said.

The earl shut the valise, but held it at his side. "We appreciate you making things right, and clearing the air of this awful lie."

Mr. White gave the earl a bow. "Again, sirs, my lady, ladies, my deepest apologies."

When he left, he touched a hand to Tilda's shoulder. Dixon saw him out.

"I'm glad that's over," the earl said.

Morgan let out a sigh. "The thought of that man as my father makes me cringe."

"But he wasn't," Mrs. Weston said. "So it is over."

Clarissa stepped towards Tilda, a finger pointing. "What about her? She knew all about it and was trying to use it against us."

Tilda stepped back, but Colonel Grady took her arm and pulled her forward. "It's time you confess, girlie."

Here it was. The moment she'd wanted to avoid.

Mrs. Weston looked confused, her forehead tight. To confess would mean hurting her.

"Now, girl," the dowager said.

Tilda stepped forward, yet kept her distance from the others. She focused her eyes on the air, the guilt preventing her from meeting the gaze of those she'd hurt. She confessed everything. Each sin, each lie, each manipulation. When she spoke of her argument with George and his fall tears demanded release.

She regretted hurting Mrs. Weston most of all, but finally forced herself to look at her.

Mrs. Weston shook her head incredulously. "You wanted George to be the heir so you could marry him and be the countess?"

Tilda nodded. "At first I wanted the title."

"You wanted the title most, you mean," Clarissa said.

Tilda adamantly shook her head. "At first, I said. But then that mattered less than the fact that marrying him would mean I could stay here and truly be a part of the family."

She looked at Mrs. Weston, needing her to understand. "I loved having someone care about me like a mother. It sparked something in me I never knew was there. "

The woman's face softened.

Clarissa stepped in to put a stop to the sentiment, "That doesn't negate your actions."

They heard heavy footsteps, running down the staircase. Dr. Peter burst into the room. "He's awake! Master George has awakened!"

Everyone raced upstairs.

Tilda was the last to leave the drawing room. She glanced at the front door. Her bag was outside. She could still leave.

"Tilda?" The dowager and the colonel called to her from the foot of the stairs. "Are you coming?"

She left thoughts of escape behind.

At least for now.

Tilda stood in a corner of George's room beside a tall dresser. His family hovered over him, exclaiming, crying, touching his head and hands.

She leaned against the dresser and closed her eyes, letting the hum of relief pulsate around her.

And then she found herself doing something very rare. *Thank you for saving him, God. Thank you for making him all right.*

As her first prayers were released, others followed.

Thank you for letting the truth come out. I'm sorry for trying to manipulate everything. I made a mess of things. Let them forgive me. Please forgive me.

Gratitude, contrition, and then . . .

Somehow make it all work out. Please handle it. Will you? Please?

Surrender.

Uncle Grady approached. "Found yourself a corner, I see."

"Since I can't be invisible, it's the next best thing."

"You did well down there. Honesty has the power to cleanse."

"It doesn't erase the bad things I did."

"But it does soften the sharp edges."

He held out his arms and she found solace in his warm care.

As dusk settled over the village Molly stood outside Peter's house, her hand poised to knock. She pulled it back. *What am I doing?*

She retreated a step, staring at the door without seeing it.

What could she say to him? *I've broken all ties with Morgan and I love your eyes?*

Lost in thought, she was surprised to hear a knock on the door — from the inside.

Not knowing what else to do, she simply said, "Hello?"

"Can I come out?"

She laughed. "Of course."

Peter opened the door, then leaned against the door jamb, grinning. "I saw you through the window. What's made you so hesitant to knock, Miss Wallace?"

A thousand answers sped through her mind, yet none was strong enough to linger. "I can't say."

"You could say. I'd like you to say. There's obviously not an emergency with Master George, or you wouldn't hesitate. We left him in good spirits and in the loving care of his family."

"He's fine," she said.

"And your mother?"

"She's fine." *She sent me.*

"Then your reason to be here has to be personal."

She felt herself redden.

"Would you like to come inside?" he asked. "Or should I come out?"

As his house and office were just off the square she said, "Inside, if you please."

She remembered the last time she had been inside the house. She had come to see his father, Dr. Evers, but had been led to take a sharp turn to the right, into a room used for examinations.

Peter led her to the left, to a small parlor. She was grateful to sit.

"Would you like some tea?"

"No, thank you." She knew a tea cup in her hand would titter against its saucer, revealing too much.

He took a chair opposite, his grin replaced with genuine concern. "Please, Miss Wallace, tell me what's wrong. Forgive me for teasing you at the door. I can see you are upset."

"I am upset. But not at you. At me. And . . ."

"And?"

"And Morgan." Suddenly, the words spilled out like tea from a pot. "Ever since I returned to the manor he's been acting as though he still had feelings for me."

"Did you have feelings for him?"

"I didn't think I did, but then when he was so . . . encouraging." She shook her head sharply, not wanting to digress. "The truth is, I didn't—and I don't—have feelings for him. I think of him fondly, and my memories are pleasant, but even when I was told there was a chance we could be together, I—"

"Isn't he engaged to Miss Farrow?"

"He is. She is a wonderful girl, and though I've tried to hate her, I can't."

"So you want them to marry."

It was a question heavy with countless emotions. "It doesn't matter what I want. They *are* going to marry."

"Do you think they will be happy?"

She'd never thought of their happiness. "Actually, I do."

Peter rose. "And what would make you happy, Molly Wallace?"

He strolled towards her as if he had all the time in the world, as if the world they shared only consisted of the two of them. When he came close, he held out his hand. And then she knew exactly what would make her happy.

She placed her hand in his and let him draw her to standing. "You," she said. "You would make me happy."

His kiss sealed the moment forever.

Clarissa hated the silence of the night. In that silence she became aware of the voices in her head. Angry voices.

To distract them, she got up, lit a lamp, and brought her jewelry box over to the bed, dumping the pieces upon the soft billow of her down comforter. As was her habit, she organized them by color: the blue sapphires and lapis lazuli, the red rubies and garnets, the green peridots and emeralds.

Unfortunately, the jewels provided no pleasure or distraction. Instead, they made her remember that Tilda had touched these same jewels. The usurper.

The usurper who was forgiven, her position in the family strengthened in spite of her sins. Tilda was happy.

Mother was happy.

Genevieve and Morgan were happy.

Father and Uncle Jack were happy.

Grandmamma and Grady were happy.

George would be happy as he recovered.

Lila and Joseph were happy.

Was Clarissa happy for them?

She gathered the jewelry with a swipe of her hand and returned the pieces to their box, slamming its lid.

Everyone had someone who cared about them. Everyone had someone to care *for*.

"Everyone but me. I'm all alone. I have no one."

That's not true.

Clarissa started at the thought. It *was* true. Her family was quite content. They didn't need her.

"And I don't need them."

Someone needs you.

To interrupt the confusing thoughts, Clarissa returned the jewelry box to its place. But at the last minute she changed her mind and took out Grandmamma's necklace, the one Lila had left for her in London. The one little Beth had tried on.

And there it was. Beth. Beth needed her. Beth was Clarissa's someone.

Her heart beat double time. But where was the girl? How could Clarissa ever find her?

Timothy's voice came to mind. *"If you ever wish to visit London, let me know. I go to London quite often for supplies. In fact, I'm going this next Saturday."*

Clarissa clutched the necklace to her chest and bounced on her toes. "And I am going with you."

Chapter Twenty

Tilda quietly opened the door of her bedroom. She didn't expect anyone to be about at this late hour, but wanted to check just the same.

She tiptoed down the hall to a door, took a deep breath, and rapped on it gently. If no one answered, she'd go back to her room, but if some —

The door cracked opened. Mrs. Weston peeked out. Upon seeing it was Tilda, she opened the door. "Tilda," she whispered. "What are you doing up?"

"Can I talk to you?"

The woman hesitated a moment, then invited her inside. The room was dark but for the light of the moon. Mrs. Weston moved to light a lamp.

"Please don't," Tilda said. "Can we just sit in the moonlight?"

"As you wish." She beckoned Tilda to a window seat that offered a view overlooking the front gardens, retrieving a shawl on the way. "Here now. You'll freeze in your nightgown."

Only then did Tilda realize she'd left her room without a proper covering.

They angled towards each other as they sat, their knees nearly touching. "I'm sorry you've had a hard day," Mrs. Weston said.

Her kind words were like knives. "Don't be nice to me. I hurt your family. I tried to manipulate things for my own benefit. You should hate me."

"But I don't."

Tilda jerked her head back, incredulous. "Why not?"

Mrs. Weston took Tilda's hand between her own. "Because I love you, Tilda."

Tilda pulled her hand free and stood. "After all I've done, how can you?"

She shrugged. "I love unconditionally because *I* need to be loved unconditionally."

Tilda didn't understand.

"Don't you remember?" Then the woman nodded. "That's right. You weren't in the room when I offered a confession for *my* manipulation."

"Your . . . ?"

"Before I married my husband, I manipulated the *tête-à-tête* between Mr. White and Fidelia. I arranged the entire thing to achieve the results I wanted — to make Fidelia look bad, so I could get the man I wanted."

"Mr. White told me you hired him."

"Of course he did." She took a new breath. "I know something of guilt and shame. And regret. For many years I let those emotions isolate me. Did you know I stayed to my room for five years? I pulled myself away from my husband and children as my own self-imposed penance."

"I didn't realize that."

"Do you want to know what allowed me to come out of my prison?"

Tilda nodded.

"Confession."

Instead of merely being a statement, Mrs. Weston's words seemed like a directive. Tilda needed to finish her confession to this wonderful woman who'd taken her in. "I'm so sorry for everything I've done. You were kind to me and I used that kindness against you. I wish I could take it all back and start over."

Mrs. Weston moved close, putting a hand around her shoulders. "You can. Right this minute."

She let her hands fall away. "I can?"

"Do you wish to be forgiven?"

"I do." She hastened to add. "Please forgive me."

"I do forgive you—as I have been forgiven. And God forgives you too. He has washed your sins away."

"Really?"

"If you ask Him to."

Tilda thought back to the few times in her life she'd considered God and Jesus and faith and all that it entailed. Until yesterday she'd only had fleeting thoughts, in her mind one moment and out the next. Until yesterday she'd never let them linger and take root.

"I want all that."

"Then so you will have it. An open heart and mind is the first step."

"The next step?"

"Letting Him in," she whispered.

"How do I do that?"

"You've already done it. Now, just listen for Him. Day after day, minute after minute."

"He talks?"

Mrs. Weston's laugh was kind, and she gently pressed her fingers against Tilda's chest "He talks in here, using a still small voice."

That sounded absurd, but Tilda didn't want to say so. "How will I know it's Him?"

"Practice."

It sounded difficult. "Why would God speak to *me*?"

"Because you're His child and He loves you and wants what's best for you." She looked directly at Tilda's eyes. "As I love you and want what's best for you."

Tilda's new tears were different from any she'd shed before.

"So, Clarissa," Lila said. "What brings you back to Crompton Hall?"

Clarissa smoothed the fringed trim of her overskirt against her lap. "I need a reason?"

"Need a reason? No. But I am guessing you have a reason." Lila poured them both a cup of tea.

Clarissa sighed and let the steam from the tea warm her face. "Your intuition is far too keen. You will be a good mother someday."

"Mmm. That is my hope."

At her slight hesitation and her smile . . . Clarissa studied her face. "Are you . . .?"

"I'm hoping that too." She put a finger to her lips. "Don't say anything."

"Not a word." The subject of Lila and Joseph as parents was the perfect segue to the subject that demanded discussion. "I plan on being a mother myself soon."

Lila dropped a teaspoon to the carpet. "You're not . . .?"

"No!" Clarissa feigned surprise, enjoying the drama. "Do you think so little of my character?"

Lila's expression battled a moment, "Of course not. I just . . . you need to explain yourself."

"It's quite simple really," Clarissa said, though she knew it was far from simple. "I am going back to London to find Beth."

"Beth?" Then Lila took in a breath. "The little girl on the stairs."

"She's the one."

"I can't get her out of my mind. The sight of her running after a thief who'd stolen some of my clothes, the knowledge that she would have come back to find me gone. What must she have felt to know that I abandoned her like that? And how could I do that to her? How could I leave her in that awful neighborhood, living on a stairway, eating from the garbage?" Clarissa's eyes grew warm with tears. She retrieved a handkerchief from her pocket.

"You are righting a wrong," Lila said.

"But what if it's too late? What if something's happened to her? I'll never forgive myself. What kind of person leaves a child to such a life?"

"A person with her own problems."

Clarissa was glad for the acknowledgment, but didn't dare let it linger. "My problems were easily solved. I lost a job, a home, and my possessions, but I still had family. I had a place to go. I had you. Beth has no one. What if I can't find her?"

"We'll pray that you do." Lila set her tea aside. "Would you like Joseph to go with you? You cannot travel alone."

"I traveled here alone." Knowing that would not put Lila's mind at ease, she added, "Actually, I ran into Timothy the other day and he said he was going to London. I'm going to ask if I might go along."

"Timothy is a good man. Totally trustworthy. But it's still not seemly for a single woman to travel alone with a single man."

Clarissa waved the issue away. "In this issue I care little for being seemly, I only care for the security that a man's presence will afford me in London."

Lila nodded, taking it all in. "What are you going to do with Beth once you bring her back?"

Clarissa had been waiting for this chance to shock her. "I'll raise her at Summerfield Manor."

"Raise her as your child?"

She felt her ire rise. "Do you question my mothering skills?" *Because I have enough questions of my own.*

"I commend you for your charity."

Leave it to Lila to look for the good in it. "It's not charity, it's penance."

"Bringing the girl home with you can be an act of penance, but that act must be sustained for the rest of her life. She cannot be discarded when your guilt is lifted."

She knows me too well. "That's a rude thing to imply."

"Perhaps."

"And it just so happens to be an honest concern." Clarissa set aside her teacup and stood, taking a position behind her chair. "I know my weaknesses and the aspects of my character that need improvement. And I also know I will make mistakes with the girl. But surely my well-intentioned missteps will afford her a better life than the one she has now."

"Of course it will." Then Lila asked the other question that loomed in Clarissa's mind. "What about your family? What will they say?"

"Hopefully, they'll say 'welcome, Beth.' If they can take in Tilda and treat her as family, they can do the same for my Beth."

Lila smiled. "Your Beth?"

It felt good to state it so. "Absolutely."

"I'm just curious," Lila said. "Did you come here to gain my approval?"

Why had she come here?

"Do you need my approval?" Lila asked, rising from the chair.

"Not really."

"Then what do you need?"

It was difficult for Clarissa to say it, but she forced the words to be said aloud. "I need your prayers."

"That, you will have." Lila kissed her cheeks. "Godspeed, Cousin."

Tilda knocked on the door to George's room.

"Come in."

She entered tentatively, but her heart was beating wildly. Of all people, George knew the most about her bad intentions—and had suffered because of them.

"Tilda."

She couldn't determine his mood from the one word. "How are you feeling?" she asked as she moved to his bedside.

He ignored her question. "I know everything," he said. "Father told me."

She hung her head. "I'm so sorry."

"Did you only pretend to like me and my horses because you wanted a title?"

She hesitated, then said, "Partly. At first."

He surprised her by responding with a nod. "I know it may be hard to understand, but when Uncle Jack became the earl I was glad I wasn't the heir anymore. I was glad to just be the son of the Honourable Mr. and Mrs. Weston. I'm content with who I am and my place in the world." He took her hand, "You need to find your contentment, Tilda."

She didn't know what to say. She'd never thought about being content. Not one minute of her life.

"I've stumped you, haven't I?"

She was relieved to see his smile. "A little."

He tried to sit upright so she adjusted the pillows to support him. "I know people may say it's easy for me to be content amid all my blessings. After all, I live in a great manor house and have servants, good food, and horses to ride for pleasure. But it's not just for pleasure. It's become my vocation. I wish to do something with all I have. I'm not certain what I'll do yet, but I'm becoming the best horseman I can be so I'll be ready when an opportunity arises."

George's talk of opportunity and contentment were foreign concepts. "Your life is very different from mine."

"From what yours *was*. But you're here now. From the first day you came you had a new life among people who cared for you. Why wasn't that enough for you?"

She let out a puff of air. "I'd prepared myself for you being angry with me."

"I am angry," he said. "A little. But beyond that, I want you to be happy here. Yet I fear you'll never truly be happy until you accept what *is,* right now."

Her throat was dry. "Right now I'm just getting out of trouble. I feel horrible for all I did."

He tossed his hands in the air. "Good. You did wrong."

"I told your mother I was sorry and she forgave me. Do you forgive me?"

He held out a hand to her. "Of course I do."

She placed her hand in his, then gave him a hug.

With George's warm arms giving her comfort, Tilda felt as though she was getting another embrace, from everlasting arms.

And with that embrace she felt content.

The housekeeper was the first to notice it.

Mrs. Camden passed the plate of biscuits around the table in the servants' hall, and said, "Miss Wallace, what has happened to you? You seem almost gleeful."

All eyes fell upon Molly and she felt herself blush.

Nick pointed at her from across the table, crumbs falling from his mouth. "She's in love. Look at her."

There was instant tittering from the maids and sculleries.

"That will be enough," Mr. Dixon said. "Miss Wallace's personal life is not our business. She is not in our employ."

Dottie whispered to her. "Is it true? Did he . . .?"

Molly needed to stop all hints of a relationship between herself and Morgan. She didn't think anyone beyond Dottie knew of it, but didn't want to take that chance. "Actually, I *am* in love."

"With who?" Jane asked.

Mrs. Camden intervened. "If Miss Wallace wishes to share, she will."

"I am in love with Dr. Peter. Dr. Peter Evers."

There was a communal gasp and a dozen questions. Among them, the most prominent was "Are you engaged?"

"Not as yet."

Sally nodded. "He's been helping yer Ma, hasn't he? Is that when ya fell in love?"

As the floodgate was open, it would be hard to close it.

"I have seen Dr. Peter at work and respect his ability to help people."

"She's even helped him deliver a baby," Dottie offered.

"Is this true, Miss Wallace?" Mr. Dixon asked.

"It is. I have accompanied the doctor on several occasions where I could be of assistance."

"She helped with Master George," Dottie said.

Fanny, a scullery maid, held up her forearm. "I burned my arm in boiling water. Can you make it better?"

Suddenly others brought forth their aches and ailments, forcing Mr. Dixon to intercede "That will be enough. Miss Wallace is *not* a doctor. If you have health issues you will come to me or Mrs. Camden and we will see you get the proper attention." He pointed to the table set before them. "Now finish your tea. We all have work to do."

Molly drank her tea quickly and rose to leave. Dottie did the same and caught up with her in the corridor.

"You love Dr. Peter?" Dottie whispered. "Why didn't you tell me?"

Molly drew her further down the hall. "I didn't know it myself. I was so intent on Morgan."

"What does *he* say about all this?"

Molly thought back to the family meeting when she'd heard Morgan propose to Genevieve. "He is promised to another."

Dottie looked down the hall, waiting until Prissy and Sally passed them and went up the back stairs. "That didn't stop him before."

She was right. "He was wrong to lead me on."

"But—"

Molly put a hand on her arm, stopping her argument. "Let it go, Dot. For the first time in my life I am free to share the fact that I am in love. When I was a lady's maid I couldn't openly love Morgan because of my position at the manor, and now that he's the heir, I can't openly love him because of *his* position here."

Suddenly, Molly saw her past for what it was.

"What's wrong?" Dottie asked.

"I just realized that my romance with Morgan has always been blocked. Was that God's way of guiding me, of telling me it's not His plan for my life?"

"I don't know. Maybe."

Molly's mind cleared. "I'd thought that God brought me back to Summerfield Manor to be with Morgan. But maybe I was brought here to meet Peter."

Dottie bit her lower lip. "Then Ma's fit of apoplexy was a good thing. If she hadn't gotten sick you'd still be in London."

"And I never would have met Peter."

They let the weight of this revelation settle.

When Mrs. Camden approached they had to step apart. "I know Molly's news is very exciting, ladies, but there is work to be done."

And a new life to be lived.

"Miss Weston," Timothy said, when Clarissa entered the carpentry shop. "How nice to see you." He came towards her, brushing the sawdust from his clothes.

He missed a spot, as a spray of chippings clung to his hair. Clarissa reached up and brushed them away. "You may not think it's so nice when I finish talking."

His face clouded. "Is something wrong?"

"Very. Yet thankfully it can be rectified--with your help. May we sit?" He led her to a bench, brushing it off with his hand. "The other day you mentioned you were going to London."

"Tomorrow."

"I wish to go with you."

His blond eyebrows rose. "Of course. May I ask why?"

"I would expect you to." Clarissa looked around the shop, and though the other two men were busy working on some spindles she lowered her voice. "I left London very quickly, having lost my job, my flat, and all my belongings."

"I remember."

"I left behind something very precious."

"Do you think it will still be there after all this time?"

"I hope so." She swallowed. *I pray so.*

Chapter Twenty-One

Clarissa did not expect to feel sentimental when she returned to her old London neighborhood. "This doesn't make sense," she said aloud to Timothy, as they rode through the narrow, crowded streets in the hired hack. Clarissa had insisted they not bring Timothy's wagon and risk it stolen.

"I experienced nothing but hard times here, yet I'm feeling quite emotional."

"Hard times do not always mean bad times," he said. "You lived on your own, yes?"

"With my lady's maid—who left me, taking with her the money Lila had gifted to me."

"You had employment."

He was ignoring the negative, so she let herself go along. "I had a job. Although I never had a lead role, I enjoyed being on the stage." She looked at his eyes. "I was good at it."

"I can imagine you were." He looked straight ahead. "But you were let go?"

So much for ignoring the negative. She raised a finger to make a point. "I quit. There was a stage manager who pressed me to . . ." She sighed. "If I didn't do what he wanted, he would tell everyone who I really was."

He looked surprised. "You weren't using your real name?"

"In hindsight I should have. Perhaps it would have helped me gain those good parts. But even as I disobeyed my family's demand that I never go on the stage, I didn't want to bring our name into it. To the theatre world I was Miss Clara West."

"That was thoughtful of you."

This surprised her. "Really?" *Me thoughtful?*

"You were thinking of them. That's thoughtful."

"Hmm." She shook the notion away and continued her story. "One night I was in no mood to endure the man's pressures a moment longer, so I quit. I walked out, still wearing my makeup and costume." She pointed to the street ahead. "I lived up ahead. A little girl from the neighborhood stayed with me that night and we played with my hats." She let herself smile. "I am afraid I had an addiction to hats, spending my wages foolishly."

"A lesson learned?"

"Perhaps. I knew I was being imprudent but couldn't seem to stop myself." Images of the eviction played out in the air before her. "I suffered the consequences of that imprudence. The morning after quitting I was evicted, all my possessions thrown into the street."

"Your landlord could have used more discretion."

She sighed, feeling the memory purged with her breath. "I deserved it. I was weeks behind in my rent. His methods were unkind, but as a businessman, I gave him little choice."

Timothy stared at her. "That's very forgiving of you."

She let out a laugh. "Me, *thoughtful?* And me, *forgiving?* Who would have thought it possible?"

"Me," he said quietly.

This one word offered another surprise. She found it quite pleasing to know that Timothy expected good things from her. How extraordinary.

She rapped the roof of the cab. "Stop here, driver."

Timothy helped her to the street, and paid the man a coin. Then he took her arm and led her towards what used to be home. They stepped around a drunk passed out in the gutter. "You keep saying you'll tell me what precious thing we've come for, but I never expected it to be in such a questionable neighborhood, or to find that you once lived here."

Seeing it separate from that time of her life made her view it with fresh eyes. The building looked abandoned, with window panes cracked or missing, bricks splashed with the muck and mess of the street. Trash thrown from upper windows blew around her feet, the breeze carrying foul odors, both human and animal. The place reeked of decay and poverty.

Clarissa's new observations were brushed away, as memories of her mission rushed forward. Her heart beat wildly. "My precious item should be right inside that door."

Timothy lifted his hat and ran a hand through his hair before returning it to his head. "I don't understand. Anything of value that was left in this place will be long gone."

Hopefully not.

Please let Beth be here. Please let her be here.

Timothy opened the door for her and they entered. It took a moment for their eyes to adjust to the dim light of the narrow foyer. But within moments, Clarissa could see too well that Beth was not on the stairs.

"Beth? Beth!"

"We're here for a girl?"

Clarissa ignored his question and ran up the stairs, calling her name. Various tenants cracked open their doors to peer out. "Have you seen Beth? The little girl who lives on the stairs?"

No. No. Not for a few weeks.

Finally the woman who'd had a flat across from Clarissa's came fully out in the hall. "Miss West. You back? Cuz the landlord's looking for someone to fill your space."

"I'm not back. I'm looking for Beth, the little girl who lived on the stairs."

"Sweet one, she was."

"Was?" Her stomach flipped.

"A man came through and grabbed up vagrant kids."

Her heart dropped. "Grabbed up? Where did he take them? What was his name?"

The woman bit her lip, her eyes scanning the ceiling for a memory. "Berndo? Somethun like that. He looked to be a nice man. Not some thief or hooligan."

Clarissa shuddered. "But how do you know he was a good man?"

She shrugged. "He wore nice clothes."

Clarissa knew that trait held no guarantee of good character.

Timothy took her arm. "Come now. Let's see if we can seek him out."

Clarissa and Timothy hurried down the stairs and out to the street. The swell of people around them—none of them friends—made the task of finding Beth daunting. "I don't know where to start."

Timothy took over, stopping various people to ask, "Do you know a man named Berndo?"

He received no's all around.

Clarissa spotted a constable. She rushed towards him and asked the question.

"Berndo? Can't say as I do." But then his eyes brightened. "Barnardo maybe?"

"Maybe."

"Thomas Barnardo comes round every so often and picks up destitute kids."

"For what purpose?" Timothy asked.

"Oh, he's a good 'un, he is. He takes him to his orphanages. There's one for boys at Stepney Causeway and the girl one is in Barkingside."

Timothy and Clarissa exchanged a look. "Where is that?"

"Northeast. Ilford. Essex." The constable looked in that direction. "A far piece."

Clarissa's hopes deflated.

"Thank you, constable," Timothy said. Then he pulled Clarissa's hand around his arm. "Let's get going."

She stopped him. "But you need to get home. To travel there and find Beth might take a few days."

"I'm not leaving her behind. We've come this far, so let's finish it."

Clarissa was incredulous. "You would do that for me?"

"For you. And for your precious item."

"You are proving to be quite precious yourself, Mr. Billings."

Clarissa tried to get comfortable on the seat of Timothy's wagon. But riding all the way from Summerfield to London in it, and now from the mill where he'd purchased supplies all the way to the northeast end of London . . .

"I should have brought along a cushion to make you more comfortable," he said as he noticed her wiggling. "And are you certain you wouldn't want to stay the night at an inn? It's already been a terribly long day, with lots of traveling."

She shook her head and forced herself to stop squirming. "My mind is focused on Beth and I will not sleep until I find her."

He chuckled. "Add *determination* to your list of qualities."

"I most certainly will," she said, "though *it* is not a new trait. I have always been determined to get my own way."

Their laughter came easily.

"May I offer you a compliment, Mr. Billings?"

"I wouldn't refuse one."

"I have never felt so at ease with anyone. The conversations we've had on this trip and back at Crompton Hall . . . you bring out a depth to my nature I didn't know was there."

"It was always there, Miss Weston. Though I'm not sure why I was the first to tap into it."

He said it with mirth in his voice, but she responded in all seriousness. "You are the first. And the only."

He looked away from the road, meeting her eyes. "Then I say shame on the lot of them."

At that moment, the wagon hit a rut in the road, jarring them. Clarissa instinctively grabbed Timothy's arm.

When the road smoothed, she left it there.

The Girls' Village Home at Barkingsale was shocking. Clarissa had expected it to match the image of "orphanage" she had in her mind, the image conjured up by the novels of Dickens: dark, spare, filthy rooms, skeletal children, and evil adults.

They passed through a gate onto a large green surrounded by dozens of neat two-story cottages. Girls from childhood to near grown ambled along the perimeter, all nicely dressed, laughing and chatting. Some worked in the center gardens tending the flowers and plants.

"May I be of assistance?" a woman asked.

"I am Miss Clarissa Weston and this is my friend, Mr. Timothy Billings. We have come all the way from Summerfield seeking a child I knew in London. Her name is Beth."

"Family name?"

Clarissa's ignorance was embarrassing. "I don't know."

"Age?"

"Eleven or twelve?"

The woman's eyebrow rose. "We have six hundred young girls here. I really would need more identifying information."

It was appalling how little she knew about the girl. "She has light brown hair and blue eyes."

"And what relation is she to you?"

"None whatsoever."

"Then why are you here?"

Timothy tipped his hat to the woman. "Miss Weston is the niece of the Earl of Summerfield. Her father is the Honourable Frederick Weston. She comes with the best of intentions."

The woman nodded. "I mean no disrespect, Miss Weston, but the girls in the Village are here to save them from difficult lives and people who harmed them."

"I would never harm Beth," Clarissa said. "I'm sorry I don't have the information you need. But if you'll let me see the girls who were brought here during the last month, she will know me. I promise you that. We were friends. Please let us see each other and she can prove to you that she is as glad to see me as I am to see her."

A man came towards them, and offered a smile. "I am Dr. Barnardo. If I may be of assistance?"

This was the man who'd taken Beth in the first place. Clarissa made her own introductions, then said, "You rescued a young girl in the West End? She was living on the stairs of a tenement, and probably had a pitiful doll with her, one made of wood yet wrapped in a fancy handkerchief?"

He smiled and nodded. "Beth Wharton. Of course. A sweet girl indeed. How do you know her?"

Finally! "It is a long story, unnecessary to this moment," Clarissa said. "But I used to live in that building and befriended Beth. But when I had to leave in haste, she was left behind, and . . ." She sighed, deciding to lay it out plain. "I left in a hurry because I was evicted, and all my things were thrown into the street. The last time I saw Beth she was trying to save some of my possessions. I fled to save myself, not thinking about saving her. It was a shameful thing I did, leaving her behind to such a life, and the guilt has dogged me." She took a fresh breath. "I am here to make right what was wrong. To find Beth and bring her home with me, to give her a life of plenty when she has lived a life of poverty."

Dr. Barnardo clasped his hands in front of him, nodding, taking in her words. "I appreciate your candor, Miss Weston, as well as your change of heart. But just because you come from a life of grandeur does not necessarily mean Beth will be better off with you than she is here."

Timothy spoke up, "I can assure you, sir, the Westons are the finest of families, honest, caring people who would take Beth in as one of their own."

The doctor looked to Clarissa. "So your parents and uncle have agreed to take her in?"

Why had Timothy said such a thing? But it was too late to lie. "They don't know I'm here. They know nothing of Beth. I am only lately reconciled with them, and . . ." Frustration fell on her like a heavy weight. "I have done wrong in my life, Doctor. I have been selfish and manipulative. I have acted spoiled and willful, and . . ." He was smiling. "You find my confession amusing?"

"On the contrary, Miss Weston," he said, replacing his smile with sincerity. "I find your confession refreshing and genuine. Such qualities give me great pleasure. Forgive me if you mistook my commendation for disdain." He turned to the woman. "I will take over from here, Mrs. Dinsdale." To Clarissa and Timothy he said, "Let me show you what we do here at the Village."

"You'll take me to Beth?"

"I will."

"I'd like to see her now."

Timothy put a calming hand on her arm. Yes, yes, she must be patient.

"Forgive me. Please show me all you have accomplished."

They dismounted the wagon and he led them towards the center of the square, turning towards the perimeter. "Eight years ago, I received Mossford Lodge as a wedding present." He pointed to a large brick mansion to the north. "I had a fifteen year lease. When it was coming due, I heard that some nuns wanted to buy the house and twenty-six adjoining acres for their charity." He gazed upon the house as if remembering. "Their plan spurred my own. I raised over seven thousand pounds and built thirty cottages for the girls, each with a live-in guardian and gardens outside so they could enjoy the benefits of fresh air and family living they so direly need."

Clarissa looked upon the cottages. Each one exuded hospitality and a feeling of home.

He led them towards the center of the green. "The girls are taught a trade, with many going into domestic service. Our girls are sought after for their upbringing and skills."

"How commendable," Timothy said.

"Hope is the key," the doctor said. "Without hope for a better future, there is no reason to live."

Clarissa knew this to be true and was about to comment, when—

"Beth!"

The girl turned around and with instant recognition, ran towards them. Clarissa knelt down and let her run into her arms. "You found me! I prayed you'd find me!"

Clarissa put a hand on the back of Beth's head, holding her close, letting tears fall. "I'm so sorry I left you. It was so wrong of me. Can you ever forgive me?"

Beth pulled away and swiped a thumb over the track of Clarissa's tears. "Don cry. You found me. And I found you. Tis all that matters."

Clarissa couldn't have said it better herself.

Thank you, God.

"Careful now," Molly told her mother as they exited the manor house. "One step at a time."

Ma was breathing hard, leaning heavily on Molly, concentrating on each step. Molly led her into the garden.

"See the beautiful autumn flowers? The chrysanthemums are stunning. Which color do you like the best?"

As hoped, Molly's question pulled Ma's attention from her feet to the flowers close by. "I ligh gold."

"Those are my favorites too." Molly stopped. "Rest a moment. Take a deep breath. You're doing very well."

Ma did as she was told. "It is good to get ouh of my room after all these weehs. I love smell of air and leaves."

"I do too. Autumn is my favorite time of—"

Molly heard something to their right and saw Morgan approaching. "Come now, Ma. Let's move along. There's a bench up ahead."

As they slowly made their way towards that destination, Morgan hurried towards them. "Molly. Miss Wallace. Please. Stop."

She had no choice but to obey. Morgan caught up with them, and Ma suffered an awkward curtsy. "My lord."

"Mrs. Wallace. How good to see you up and about."

"Than you, your lorshih. Is due to my dear daugh-er an Daher Peher."

"Indeed. You've been in very good hands." He looked to Molly. "May we speak a moment, Miss Wallace? In private, if you please."

"I'm sorry but I'm busy right now. My lord," she added at the end.

"Go on," Ma said. She nodded towards the bench. "I sih an reh."

Ma *did* need to rest. Maybe it would be good to have it out with Morgan, once and for all.

"A few minutes," she said to him. He nodded and helped get Ma settled on the bench. "I'll be right back, Ma."

Molly walked away from the bench and the arbor, needing to separate herself from that place where she and Morgan had secretly met. She needed to be away from everything that happened a lifetime ago.

Morgan followed her and she knew it was against all protocol for him to do so. Hang the protocol. She would not walk beside him, nor behind. If they were to talk it would be on her terms.

When she reached a place that afforded a modicum of privacy she stopped and faced him. "I heard you tell your family you never loved me. Is that true?"

He seemed taken aback by her assertiveness. "Of course I loved you. The times we spent together on that bench . . . when I proposed, I meant every word of love I spoke to you."

She noticed he was talking about the past. "But the affection you showed me since I came back to the manor? The flirtation, the promises?"

He looked to the path. "I don't want to hurt you, Molly."

A wave of regret sped through her veins. "So that was all false?"

"I *was* glad to see you."

That was it? "You led me on. You made a fool of me—and yourself. And I was at fault for playing along."

To his credit, he met her eyes. "I am truly sorry."

She took in the sight of his gaze, knowing it would be the last time their eyes would meet, perhaps the last time they would speak. "I am sorry too," she said. It was odd to realize their connection was formally and completely broken.

He took a step away. "Very well then. I'm glad we can part on good terms."

She agreed, then thought of something. "Will you make me a promise?"

"If I can."

"Promise you will be a good—and faithful—husband to Miss Farrow."

"I will try."

"You must do more than that for she is a sweet, interesting, generous girl who is willing to accept your family and her position and responsibilities with an open heart and great enthusiasm. *If* you let her."

"I—"

"She does not deserve the pain, doubt, and uncertainty that you and I have given her. Do you understand?"

"I do. And I agree with everything you say."

Good. "One last thing. I am not yours anymore, Morgan. And you are not mine. Together, we enjoyed the sweetness of first love, and as such, those memories will remain special to both of us."

"Yes, they will," he said softly.

"But now? Now we move on. We move forward, better for our acquaintance, but on separate pathways, each with its own unique purpose."

His brow furrowed, but he nodded. "I hope you find happiness, Molly. For you deserve it."

"I will, and I do."

With that, she returned to her mother. She felt a spring in her step, as if the breeze swirling around her had the ability to lift her up and let her fly. She was soaring free at last!

Ma looked up when she approached. "Weh?"

Molly helped her to standing. "Let's continue our walk."

Ma held her ground. "Weh?"

"It's done with, Ma. I am free of him."

"Guh."

Yes indeed. Guh.

Genevieve let the lace curtain at her bedroom window fall into place. How she wished she could hear the words that were being exchanged between Morgan and Molly in the garden. Yet, she could tell by the way Morgan looked to the ground, and Molly gesticulated, that they were arguing. Molly appeared to have the upper hand, giving the last word and storming away.

As she did, Genevieve looked back at Morgan, seeking his reaction. *Please don't look sad. Please don't go after her.*

Morgan followed Molly with his eyes — for a brief moment. Then he looked to the roses, took a penknife from his pocket, and cut a single red bloom.

Genevieve's heart fell to her toes. *No! Don't go after Molly and bring her a rose!*

He turned in the opposite direction and walked towards the house, lifting the rose to his nose, taking in its fragrance.

Could he be bringing it to her?

Before she could fully comprehend the possibility, her mother entered her bedroom in a familiar flurry of complaints. "I am so weary of the people in this house treating me differently. I told them I was sorry. What do they want me to do? Kiss their toes?"

"It will take time to earn their trust again, Mamma. Be patient."

Her mother shook her head and checked her reflection in the dressing table mirror. "I sent a note to Lord Newley asking him to go riding and have received no reply. None at all. How rude of him."

Genevieve couldn't let her comment pass unchallenged. It was time to finish this discussion with her mother, once and for all. "How rude of you."

Mamma left her reflection and faced her. "I will not allow you to talk to me that way. What I did, I did for us. "

"That's not true."

Mamma fluttered a hand by her eyes, as if Genevieve's words were pesky gnats needing swatting. "I am the mother here. I did what I thought best."

"Best for you."

She came at Genevieve with a finger raised. "Best for us. I count in this too, you know."

Hearing the familiar argument made Genevieve weary. And brave.

"You tried but failed. Now it's time for me to run my own life, my way."

Mamma blinked. "But I am your mother."

"That, you are. But let's be honest. You made a mess of things by trying to get the earl as a husband, then flagrantly pursuing Lord Newley, *and* telling the family secrets."

"I—"

Genevieve moved towards the door, hoping her mother would follow. "You have no self-restraint, Mamma. Whatever you think, you say, without heed of the consequences."

"I am honest."

"You offend."

Mamma huffed. "As I've said, everything I did was for your benefit."

Genevieve leveled her with a look. "Whose benefit?"

For the first time in her life, Dorcas Farrow wilted under her daughter's gaze. Genevieve could almost see a mantle of shame fall across her shoulders. "Perhaps I did go a bit far."

Mamma still wasn't accepting the extent of her brazenness. "I know very well my own deficits. But you, Mamma, need to accept the deficits in your own character."

"Deficits? I do not appreciate talk of deficits."

Of course not. "I don't mean to be unkind . . ."

"Then don't be — don't be rude and don't offend."

Touché. "I merely hope you see what damage your impulsive behavior has caused and learn from it."

Mamma flipped a hand in the air. "So I didn't win the hand of the earl. He's much too boring for me anyway."

"You didn't win the hand of Lord Newley either. Was he boring?"

Her expression changed from arrogant to vulnerable. "He was the least boring man I've ever met. He was charming, extremely handsome, and . . ." She gave Genevieve a wistful look. "He made me feel young again."

Genevieve placed an arm around her shoulders. "You might have eventually gained a proposal from him if you had not gone too far. By showing an inability to be discerning and trustworthy, you gave Lord Newley no choice but to cut his ties with you."

Her face grew frantic. "Do you really think he's cut his ties completely? Is there no hope?"

Her mother's panic made Genevieve feel pity. "There is always hope. And second chances."

Mamma fell into her arms. "I'm so sorry, Genevieve. I will try to do better."

"I know you will." She also knew Mamma would try, and fail.

Yet no matter what, Genevieve would be there to pick up the pieces.

Genevieve was relieved when her mother left. She retrieved her copy of *Persuasion* when there was a soft rapping upon her door.

She remembered Morgan and the rose. Was it him? She set the book aside and smoothed her dress. "Come in."

It was him!

"Good afternoon, Genevieve."

"Good afternoon, Morgan."

He pulled the rose from behind his back. "For you."

Genevieve felt the pressure of happy tears, but willed them away. She took in the heady fragrance. "It's beautiful."

"As are you," he whispered.

She let herself believe that perhaps in his eyes — through the eyes of love — she *was* beautiful.

He offered her his arm. "Would you like to go to the music room? I'd love to hear you play."

"I'm not very good."

He pulled her hand through his arm and let his own linger upon it. "There, you are very, very wrong."

Sitting in the sunroom, Tilda looked up from her sketching of George. "I think this is my favorite room in the house."

He sighed and looked towards the stables. "It has its merits but I still prefer the out of doors." He pointed to a book. "Read to me some more about Robin of the Hood."

She set her drawing aside and picked up the book they'd been reading together. She found her place. ""Here is a little dagger," said Friar Tuck, pulling it out from under his gown. "Tis small, but to-morrow it may be of use. I can do no — ""

"I miss Friar Tuck and the other horses that were sold."

"Perhaps you can buy them back."

George shook his head and rubbed his sprained arm that was in a sling. "Not everything can be undone, Tilda."

She guessed he was talking about more than the horses. "I'll try to make it up to you."

He sighed deeply. "I didn't mean for you to turn my words upon yourself."

Oh, yes you did.

They looked towards the door as George's mother and father came into the room. "How are you feeling?" his mother asked.

"Better every hour. I really think I could go back to the stables." He tried to stand but grew dizzy and fell back into the chair, catching himself with his good hand.

"There will be none of that," Mr. Weston said. "Not until you're given a clean bill by Dr. Peter."

George nodded in disappointment. "Any word from Clarissa?"

Mrs. Weston stood at the bank of windows, looking across the estate. "Nothing."

Mr. Weston walked up behind her, and put a comforting hand upon her shoulder. "We are not going to worry. Her note said she'd be back tonight or tomorrow. She survived on her own for over a year. We must trust her to survive one more night."

"But where did she go?"

They exchanged ideas, but Tilda ceased listening. If she had her way, Clarissa would never come back.

"I'll help with that," Beth said. She unfastened the row of buttons down Clarissa's back.

"I wasn't planning on staying overnight at an inn or I would have brought a maid with me." She let Beth draw the bodice off. The cool night air refreshed.

"I could be your maid," Beth said as she began to undo the clasps of Clarissa's skirt.

Clarissa swung round to face her. "I am not bringing you back to the manor to be my maid or anyone else's maid."

"Then what will I do there?"

The girl didn't understand at all. "I found you in order to bring you home to live with me and my family, as family."

Beth's brow furrowed.

This is where it got complicated in Clarissa's mind. She was too young to have a daughter who was twelve—if that was indeed Beth's age, for even Beth wasn't sure—but there were also social repercussions to calling Beth her daughter. Some would believe it, hang the math. Some would shun them both because Beth was the product of her months in London living an improper life. And *if* a suitor forgave Clarissa's past, he would surely be put off by the responsibility of a child.

"Truly, I is fine being your maid. The people at the Village taught me all sorts a skills that would 'elp me earn a wage."

"You will not be my maid. You will be my daughter and that's that."

Beth's smile gave Clarissa the extra courage she needed, and assuaged her doubts. She drew the girl close and would forever remember the remarkable feeling of two small hands clasped around her waist. Her daughter's hands.

Chapter Twenty-Two

On the trip home to Summerfield Manor, Beth set a new record for the number of words a twelve-year-old could say per minute. It brought back memories of Clarissa's childhood, when she would rattle on and her parents would finally have to say, "Shush, girl. Let silence have a turn!"

But Clarissa didn't want silence. She loved Beth's innocent enthusiasm about everything she saw. For everything pleased her. From the ride in Timothy's wagon, to counting the colors of wildflowers in the meadow, to the way the horses flicked their tails, to the herd of sheep that captured the road ahead, filling in once the wagon was through like water flowing around an intrusive pebble.

Clarissa and Timothy had exchanged numerous smiles over the girl's head as she sat between them.

"Bethy-girl," Timothy said. "You make me see the world through fresh eyes."

"I agree," Clarissa said. "I'm noticing all the little things I usually ignore."

"But they're not little things." Beth suddenly pointed at the sky. "Look a' that cloud! It looks to be a rat, and that one looks like a pile of garbage at the end o' the street."

Clarissa lost her smile. Rats and garbage. *Those* were the reference points of a street ragamuffin. She wrapped an arm around Beth and vowed that those memories would be usurped by better ones. "I think those clouds look like a rabbit and a bale of hay. And over there is a big four-poster bed, and —"

"What's a four-poster?"

"You'll see soon enough. I have so much to show you. A whole other world."

"Your world?"

"Our world."

Clarissa's stomach knotted as they drove through the gates of Summerfield Manor. She was torn between wanting to jump off the wagon and run up the drive, or wanting to tell Timothy to turn the wagon around. The next few minutes could go well. Or badly.

"It will be fine," Timothy said.

"I hope so." Suddenly, all the should-have-saids assailed her. "Be polite, Beth, say please and thank you, and don't be offended if my family gives you odd looks, and —"

"Just be yourself, Bethy," Timothy said.

Clarissa took a fresh breath. "I'm so glad you'll be with us, Mr. Billings."

He pulled up on the reins. "I'm not going in with you."

"Why not? If it weren't for you, Beth wouldn't be here."

The girl nodded vigorously. "I wouldn't be 'ere."

He let the reins sag and looked down. "I've only been to the manor a few times on business. I've gone in the back door. I've not been amongst the family. I don't belong amongst the family."

Clarissa couldn't dispute anything he said, but found it odd she hadn't thought of it herself. "But you're a huge part of this."

He snickered. "That may or may not be considered a positive point. In fact, your family may be angry at me for helping you."

With that possibility, fear replaced excitement. Beyond their reaction to Beth, what would her family think about Clarissa going to London with Timothy — and staying overnight at an inn? At the very least there would be disappointment and condemnation for more rules of propriety ignored.

Timothy reached across Beth and touched Clarissa's knee for just a moment. "Remember that God puts people in the right place at the right time. He links them together so they can move forward and find out what might come next."

"You said that same thing up in Lila's nursery."

He shrugged. "Truth does not change."

Clarissa couldn't deny the truth that her path had crossed Beth's at just the right time. Back at her London flat, they'd had one evening and morning of personal time together—the time right before she was evicted. Without that perfect timing Clarissa would have returned to Summerfield with only the vague memory of the poor little girl on the stairs.

"It was meant to be, wasn't it?" she said.

"Appears so."

Beth took her hand. "You found me—twice."

The little girl's eyes were an incredible shade of cornflower blue. "We found each other."

Timothy tightened the reins. "With that settled it's time to share your discovery with the rest of the family." He nodded towards the manor. "They'll have seen the wagon. They're probably waiting for you."

Clarissa had an awful thought. "This is *not* the last time I'll see you or the last time we'll talk."

"We'll run into each other in the village."

"No!" she said, wishing she were standing so she could stomp her foot. "That's not enough."

They exchanged a long look over Beth's head and in that moment Clarissa knew Timothy was a man she would never forget. "You've done something no one else has ever been able to do."

"What's that?"

"You've made me believe in myself."

"I'm glad of that. Now you can help Beth believe in *her*self."

Am I up to such a task? Clarissa remembered something else Timothy had said to her back at Crompton Hall. "You told me that we each have a unique, God-given purpose. The trick is to find out what it is."

He smiled. "If I remember correctly, you responded by saying, 'Some trick.'"

"I've come a long way since then."

"Indeed you have. And now you're on the right road for that discovery. Coming home is always the—"

"Right road," Clarissa said. For he had said that too. "Thank you, Timothy. For all your wisdom, your kindness, and your friendship."

"You can never have too many friends," he said with a grin.

"I's your friend too," Beth said.

He flicked the tip of her nose. "Forever and always."

He clucked to the horses, and they rode the rest of the way up to the house.

With the family gathered in the drawing room, Genevieve opened the small trunk and gasped.

"Come now," the dowager said. "What is it?"

Genevieve removed an ornate silver centerpiece with curved branches holding smaller crystal bowls.

"What a beautiful epergne," Mrs. Weston said.

"What's it for?" Morgan asked.

"Decoration," the colonel said.

Mrs. Weston pooh-poohed them. "It's for the center of a table. You put flowers or fruit in the center and in all the surrounding bowls."

"We have one of those," the dowager said. "I got one for my wedding."

"Your first wedding," the colonel corrected.

There was the sound of a wagon and the earl moved to the window. "Probably another shipment of gifts. Not a practical thing in the bunch."

His brother laughed. "It's hardly appropriate to get a viscount and the heir to an earldom a new teapot or riding boots."

"Indeed not," Mrs. Farrow said.

Genevieve waited for her to say more, but she didn't. Ever since Mamma's humiliation and their talks, her mother had been more restrained. It was a good thing, yet it was unnatural enough to also be a worry.

Tilda ran a finger along the curve of the silver. "Can I put it with the display with the other gifts in the ball room?"

"If you're careful," Mrs. Weston said.

"Would you like my help?" George asked.

His mother pointed him back down in the chair. "You will do no such thing. Sit and rest."

He reluctantly did as he was told.

"It's Clarissa!" the earl said from the window.

They all rushed to the foyer as Dixon opened the door. Mrs. Weston ran to her daughter. "We're so glad you're back."

"We were worried," the dowager said. "Where have you been?"

"I left a note," she said. "Didn't you get my note?"

"Yes, we got your note," her father said. "But that doesn't negate worry. It was very generic."

"Plus, you were gone overnight," Mrs. Weston said. "Who brought you here?"

"Timothy Billings."

"The carpenter?" her father asked.

"My friend. Timothy had some business in London and was kind enough to provide the transportation. And support."

"Whyever did you go back to London?" the earl asked.

Clarissa turned away and motioned towards someone. The family watched in surprise as a little girl of about eleven or twelve stepped into the foyer. Clarissa drew her to a position in front and put her arms upon the girl's shoulders. "I would like to introduce you to Beth."

The girl scanned every face, looking like she was ready to run if the situation deemed it best. Genevieve offered her a smile—which was returned. The girl's face changed completely with that smile, as if a sunbeam had broken through the clouds.

"Hello," Beth said.

"Hello to you," the dowager said. "Clarissa. An explanation please."

Clarissa moved towards the drawing room, leading the girl inside. She sat her upon a settee before taking a place beside her. The rest of the family filed in. The earl and Clarissa's father stood. Tilda returned, assessed the room, then silently found a chair near George.

"Come now, daughter," Mrs. Weston said. "Explain yourself."

Clarissa—who had never broken physical contact with the girl—placed their clasped hands upon her own knee. "When I lived in London, Beth lived on the stairs of my building."

"What stairs?" the dowager asked.

"The main stairs leading up to my flat."

"I liked the third stair the best because it weren't broken and didn't 'ave splinters."

Mrs. Weston uttered an odd sound. "You mean she lived—actually lived—on the stairs?"

Clarissa lifted her chin. "She did. She was what you might call a street urchin."

"Might call?" Morgan asked.

"Would call." Clarissa pulled Beth under the protection of her arm. "She was homeless. She lived off the scraps of the street." She paused. "She has no family." Then Clarissa faced her family's gaze. "Until now. Until I rescued her and brought her here to live as my . . . as my daughter."

Although it was far from a comical moment, the way everyone gawked in unison, nearly made Genevieve smile.

The dowager was the first to speak. "Really, Clarissa. You go too far."

"Perhaps," she said, stilling the girl's swinging legs with a hand. "But didn't we just prove that as a family we have the strength to overcome all challenges?"

"Well, yes," her father said. "But—"

She pointed to Tilda. "Have we not taken Tilda into our home, treating her as a daughter?"

Tilda scooted back in her chair, as if she wished to merge with the upholstery.

"That's different," Mrs. Weston said.

"How? How is it different?" Clarissa asked. "Both girls are orphans and in need of care. I see no difference."

"Really, Clarissa," Mr. Weston said. "You can hardly compare the daughter of a soldier—the goddaughter of the colonel—with a girl whose background is completely unknown."

"My father was a tinker," Beth said. "And my mother a laundress. And—" She must have received the pressure of Clarissa's hand, for she stopped her explanation and looked in her direction. Clarissa shook her head. Beth finished by simply saying, "Da died and Ma ran off."

A different kind of silence filled the room. One that Genevieve felt compelled to fill. "How old were you when you were left alone?"

"Eight, I think."

"How old are you now?"

She shook her head. "I's not sure. I lost track."

Mr. Weston cleared his throat. "That's all very tragic, perhaps we should discuss it further in private . . . to say more, in front of the girl . . ."

Tilda stood. "I'll take her to the sunroom."

There was a palpable sigh of relief. "That would be good of you," Mrs. Weston said.

Tilda held out her hand and after a look to Clarissa, Beth went with her.

As soon as the girls were gone, Mr. Weston pounced. "Really, Clarissa. For you to go to London—"

"With a man," his wife added.

Clarissa stopped their objections with a hand. "Timothy has been a good friend and will remain a good friend. I owe him more than I can ever repay."

The women in the room exchanged glances and it was clear they again worried for Clarissa's reputation.

"Oh, please," Clarissa said "You worry about two days with Timothy when I lived for over a year on my own?"

It was a good point.

"You want an explanation for Beth's presence, I will give it to you."

Clarissa proceeded with a story of high hopes and dire desperation. Of an invisible girl turned real, of shared times with hats and laughter, and of a violent eviction where everything was lost in the escape. Including the girl.

"When I first returned to Summerfield and stayed with Joseph and Lila I was only concerned for myself. But as time passed . . ." She took a breath that seemed to start in her toes. "I could not forget her. Try as I might to think only of myself—and you all know how good I am at that—Beth remained in here," she pointed to her head. "And surprisingly, and more importantly, in here." She placed a hand above her heart. "For whatever reason, she and I are connected. Perhaps all that I endured was for the sole purpose of saving her. Perhaps none of this is about me at all, but about Beth."

Genevieve's first impulse was to applaud, but upon seeing the stunned looks on the faces of the others, she restrained herself.

"Well," the dowager finally said. "How extraordinary."

"Yes, it is," Clarissa said. She scanned the faces of her family. "I know it's unorthodox. I know it's out of character for me. Yet doesn't that make it more authentic? More . . . right?"

"I think it's commendable," the earl said.

With the gulf breached, Clarissa's mother rushed to her side. Clarissa stood and accepted her embrace. "I think so too," she said.

Genevieve wiped away a tear. It had been impossible not to sense the chasm that had stood between Clarissa and her mother, but now to witness that gorge bridged . . . She looked to her own mother, who had a handkerchief to her eyes. She moved to her side and took her hand.

Family. It always came down to family.

In the sunroom Tilda stood beside the girl and looked out over the rolling green hills of the Summerfield estate.

"All that's theirs?" she asked.

"Oh, more than that," Tilda said. "There's a village and fields and streams, and see those buildings over there? That's the stables. Dozens and dozens of horses and carriages for two people, or one, or four, covered and uncovered."

"I never imagined."

"Neither did I," Tilda said, mostly to herself.

"How long 'ave you been 'ere?"

"Not long." She thought of the mistakes she'd made. "When you lived on the streets you stole things, didn't you?"

Beth moved away from the view and sat on a wicker rocker, her spine curved to reach the back of the chair. "I had to. T'weren't no other way. But just food and stuff. I ne'er stole anythun worth real money."

Unlike me stealing jewelry for fun.

"They don want me 'ere, do they?"

Tilda considered lying, but knew the truth was fairly obvious. "You're a shock to them."

Beth nodded vigorously. "They's kinda a shock to me too."

Tilda laughed. Then she noticed her sketch pad nearby. "Can I draw you?"

"Draw?"

She showed Beth some of her drawings.

"That's the old lady."

"You can't call her that. She's the Dowager Countess of Summerfield."

"What's 'dowager' mean?"

Tilda thought a moment. "Old."

They giggled.

"What are you girls laughing about?"

They turned to see Clarissa in the doorway. Tilda hoped Beth wouldn't get them in trouble.

She needn't have worried, for Beth went to Clarissa and pulled her into the room. "Come see the drawings Tilda's made. They's really good."

Tilda watched nervously as Clarissa looked through the pages. "They are good." For the first time ever she looked at Tilda as if she *wasn't* mud on her shoe. "You're a good artist. Would you sketch Beth and me together?"

"Of course." Tilda wanted to ask how the discussion about Beth turned out, but by the look of joy on Clarissa's face, she could tell it went well.

Tilda set them together on a sofa and began to draw. *Please help me do a good job of it.*

Her hand shook as she began, but she was quickly lost in the task, glancing up, looking down, smudging the graphite for a shadow here, strengthening a line there.

Soon it was done. "There."

"Let us see."

Tilda brought the drawing to Clarissa and she and Beth studied it. Tilda held her breath, waiting for their opinion.

"I likes it," Beth proclaimed.

"So do I."

Tilda let herself breathe.

"May I keep it?" Clarissa asked.

Tilda's throat was too tight to speak, so she nodded.

Clarissa stood. "Come now, Beth. Let me show you around."

As they were leaving the room, Clarissa paused and turned back. "Thank you for this, Tilda."

"You're welcome."

"And accept my apologies for making you feel unwelcome in this house. I now see that Colonel Grady saved you just as I have saved my Beth."

Tilda's throat tightened, but she managed to say, "And accept my apologies for all I've done to hurt you and your family. I will do my best to make up for it."

"As will I," Clarissa said. She took Beth's hand and left the room.

The sunroom now seemed very sunny indeed.

"Shh!" Dottie said, as she and Molly stood before the door to the ballroom.

"We shouldn't be doing this," Molly said.

"It's not like we're going to take anything." Dottie opened the door and they went inside. The room was bathed in the light of dusk, causing a bluish glow to the growing shadows. They dared not light a lamp.

Dottie quickly moved to a specific table of wedding gifts. "With Miss Weston away I had some extra time, so I offered to dust in here. Look at these crystal goblets." She held one towards the window.

"Put it down!" Molly whispered. "What if you broke one?"

Dottie shrugged, but kept hold of it. "It doesn't sparkle much without sun coming in." She spread her arms wide. "But will you look at all this? Everything from silver candle-holders to fancy painted vases."

"Sterling silver candelabras and urns," Molly corrected. "Probably from China." Molly took it all in with a glance. She did not let her eyes linger.

Dottie noticed. "Don't you ever think that this could have been yours?"

Her stomach flipped once for good measure, but she said, "No, I don't. For if Morgan and I would have married, it would only be because he was *not* a titled gentleman. Therefore, any wedding gifts we received would be of a more normal, practical sort."

"You're no fun."

Perhaps not. "Come on then. You've shown me the spoils. Let's—"

They heard someone in the hall and turned to see Miss Farrow come in the room. "Oh. I'm sorry," she said.

Dottie immediately stepped behind Molly. "No, we're sorry, Miss Farrow," Molly said. "We were just looking at the beautiful gifts. Your beautiful gifts."

Miss Farrow nodded once, then strolled to a table of soup tureens and gravy boats. "It is rather ridiculous. I imagine the manor already has a bevy of such things."

There was nothing to say in response.

Then she sighed. "I can't believe I'm getting married soon." She turned towards Molly, and even in the dimming light Molly could see that her face was sincere. "I am sorry for . . ." she shrugged. "Happy too, of course, but sorry it has caused you pain."

In spite of herself, Molly was moved. "I'm not sorry, miss. For because of you I have found the true place where I belong."

Miss Farrow cocked her head.

Molly didn't want to say more. In fact, it gave her a wee bit of satisfaction to leave it at that.

"There now," Clarissa said as she pulled the bountiful covers over Beth. "Snug as a bug in a rug."

A furrow formed on Beth's forehead. "Bugs?" She shuddered. "I's had enough a bugs."

Clarissa touched the tip of her nose. "But now you're all clean from a bath and cozy in a warm bed."

Beth nodded, but her eyes strayed to the far corners of the room. "Tis a big room."

Yes, it was. Huge. And Beth looked even tinier than she was in the massive four-poster bed.

"Would you like to come stay with me in my room tonight?"

Beth bolted upright and immediately wiggled out of the covers.

Clarissa laughed. "I guess that's a yes. Come on then."

Once in her bedroom, Clarissa pulled back the covers and helped Beth get settled. "Better?"

"Much. Wills you be coming to bed soon?"

"Very soon."

Beth turned on her side, snuggling her face against a pillow. She took a long whiff of it. "I never smelled anythun so pretty."

Beth had already declared her bath 'heavenly', the dinner 'delicious', and the number of rooms in the manor to be a million and one.

Then Clarissa spotted something sitting in a chair across the room. She retrieved the china doll and held it before the girl. "This is Frances Marie," Clarissa said, fluffing the doll's skirt. "Frances Marie, this is Beth, your new mama."

Beth's eyes grew big. "She's mine?"

Clarissa suffered a stab of regret that she was giving up ownership of her favorite doll, but said, "She's yours now. Here. Let's tuck her in."

Beth shared her pillow with the doll and gently laid a hand on her. "She's beautiful."

Clarissa smoothed Beth's hair. "So are you."

Beth rewarded her with a smile. "God did good bringing us together again, didn't He?"

"He couldn't do it any better."

With that, Beth closed her eyes.

Clarissa turned away with tears of joy and gratitude.

Chapter Twenty-Three

Today I will be married.

This thought—nay, this fact—greeted Genevieve upon waking.

Even though the marriage arrangement had been in place for nearly a year, the reality of that day being *this* day shone bright, like the sun breaking through an overcast day, sending beams of God-light from heaven to earth.

She lingered in bed, stretching her arms until they found the massive headboard, letting them fall upon the pillows. *Tomorrow I will awaken with my husband beside me.*

Such a thought brought some fears. What would happen tonight, on the wedding night? Although she had enjoyed a few kisses, she had no other experience. Her female friends had offered little real information, only a lot of giggling and the rolling of eyes. She'd asked Mamma about such things, but had received the innocuous suggestion that she just "let it happen." Let *what* happen?

A breakfast tray was brought but her nerves prevented her from doing more than nibbling on a hard roll and sipping her tea.

There was a knock on the door. "Come in."

Genevieve had expected it to be her mother. Instead Mrs. Weston entered. "How are you this fine morning, my dear?"

She put a hand to her midsection. "Nervous."

"Morgan is nervous too."

"He is?"

She raised a calming hand. "It's totally normal and is to be expected. Life-changing occasions breed nerves like gardens breed weeds."

The analogy made her smile. "I'm sorry I didn't feel up to coming down for breakfast with all the guests. *And* that all week I've been leaving the card-playing, the riding, and the other activities early."

"You are forgiven," Mrs. Weston said. "If you remember I had my share of bowing out. Years of it." Her face looked pensive in the memories.

"Be assured that once this day is over, I am ready to fully participate."

"Good for you."

"That is *if* I can remember everyone's name and title."

Mrs. Weston laughed. "I remember my wedding day with all the barons, viscounts, marquises, dukes, and their female counterparts in attendance. I forgot their names as soon as they were introduced."

"Me too! And I'm so afraid I'll address them wrongly. A duke is "your grace", yes?"

Mrs. Weston put a hand upon Genevieve's cheek. "That's right, but don't worry too much about it. As the bride your main responsibility is to smile."

"They may forgive my ignorance today, but I want them to accept me. I know they call me 'the American' with a certain emphasis on the term, as one would emphasize the word *philanderer, gossip,* or heaven forbid, *commoner.*"

Mrs. Weston laughed again. "You will always be known as the American. Perhaps a few hundred years from now they will let it go. For now, bring the positive traits of that country to light."

"Those positive traits being . . .?"

Mrs. Weston ate a slice of apple from the breakfast tray. "Courage, tenacity, and being direct."

"I see those as Summerfield traits."

"There now. See how you already fit in?" She wiped her hands on a napkin and moved to the wedding dress. "You chose well."

Genevieve admired the duchesse satin. The dress stood as a symbol of the day, an exquisite costume for her role. "Though the dress is beautiful, I've worn beautiful gowns before. In many ways this dress is like gift-wrapping."

"It is the gift itself that has value."

Mrs. Weston's words touched her. "I am the gift to Morgan. Just as Morgan is the gift to me."

"Exactly." She moved to the dress, needing to touch it.

Mrs. Weston touched Genevieve's hand. "I do know this two-become-one, as long as we both shall live, is a little frightening."

Genevieve traced her finger along the tiny tucks on the bodice. "That's what worries me. To be alone and totally dependent on each other for companionship, amusement, and the travel logistics of the honeymoon is daunting. Other than sailing from New York to England, I have little experience with travel and all its languages and different customs."

Mrs. Weston took hold of both her hands and gave them a squeeze. "God will be with both of you from this day forward, helping you with every detail."

"You promise?"

"*He* promises."

There was a quick knock on her bedroom door, and her mother swept in, dressed in a gown of palest peach. She gave the two of them a questioning look, then set it aside to ask, "Why aren't you dressed? Where is Molly? We're to be at the church in an hour." She strode to the bell pull and tugged it sharply, three times.

Molly was not the next to arrive. Instead the dowager countess, Tilda, and Lila fluttered into the room, resplendent in their wedding garb, chattering to each other.

Clarissa came in next, with little Beth in tow. "What do you think of my Beth?" she asked the room. "I had Mrs. Camden and Albers hunt up my old dresses and boots. We added a bow in back and found some matching for her hair, so she doesn't look too out of fashion."

"You look very pretty, Beth," Mrs. Weston said.

The girl held the corners of the skirt and pulled them outward, offering a curtsy that was darling in its shakiness. The women's applause made her beam.

The dowager turned to Tilda. "You look very pretty too. Is that a new dress?"

"It's one of Clarissa's. She let me borrow it."

"I let you have it," Clarissa corrected. "Actually, I have many dresses that are too small for me."

"That's very generous of you, my dear," her mother said.

Molly entered, scanning the crowd. "Where have you been?" Mamma sniped. "Genevieve needs her hair done and needs to get dressed."

"If you please, Molly?" Genevieve asked.

The women parted, letting Molly go to work on her hair. Then it was time for the dress.

Genevieve felt like a doll whose arms were being manipulated into a new costume. Yet no doll had ever received the *oohs* and *aahs* that swept the room as Molly buttoned the row of satin covered buttons up the back.

"Oh, my darling daughter," Mamma said.

"You're stunning," Mrs. Weston said.

"My brother is a very lucky man," Lila said.

Genevieve glanced at Molly to see if she took offense, but she was busy smoothing the train-length veil.

"You's the prettiest girl in the world," Beth whispered.

"Woman, Bethy," Clarissa corrected. "For today she will become a married woman."

The phrase that had followed her all day returned.

Today is my wedding day.

Genevieve took a deep breath. "It's time to go. The groom awaits."

The bride was on her way to the church with the rest of the women. The bedroom was silent as Molly tidied the room for the last time.

She'd done her duty, she'd honored Mrs. Weston, her previous mistress, and had served the new viscountess well. She'd helped her own mother recover enough that even now, Ma was in the kitchen, offering another set of hands for the wedding feast. Her sister, Dottie, was doing well in her apprenticeship as a lady's maid to Miss Cavendish. And her little brother, Lon worked in the stables, happy to be out of doors.

Molly had given her time to all who had asked. She'd gone above and beyond to fulfill her responsibilities. Now, it was her turn.

She slipped upstairs and retrieved her carpet bag, packed and ready. She left two notes upon her pillow — one for Ma and one for Dottie. She hurried down the back stairs and out the side door. The front of the house was busy with a constant stream of carriages taking the guests and family to the church.

Suddenly, she remembered the last time she had exited the manor, bag in hand – hurt and angered by Morgan's newly discovered title, off to find a new job and home in London.

Yet this time was different. She felt no panic, no anger, or sadness. Replacing those feelings was a hint of wistfulness as she left a place where the majority of her life had been lived. Yet also present was the driving emotion of anticipation. Where one life was ending, another began.

She'd run away from a situation she could not control. But this time she was leaving for good, with everything settled. *She* was in control.

Or rather, God was. She was eager to see where He would take her.

Suddenly, Dottie burst through the side door, pointing at the carpet bag. "You're leaving?"

"I am."

"You're not going back to London, are you?"

"I'm not going far at all. I am finally home again and home is where I'm going to stay."

"But Summerfield Manor is your home."

"It's your home, and Ma's, and Lon's. And for many years, it was mine. But it's time to move on. There's a new kind of service for me now."

"Can't you do it from here?"

Molly shook her head once with determination. "I cannot. I'm going to the village. Mrs. Keening has a room to let over the bakery."

Dottie sighed with relief. "So you truly won't be far."

"Not at all. Now let me go, Dot. I need to be gone before the wedding party returns."

Dottie nodded, understanding. "You're a stronger woman than I can ever be."

"I accept the compliment, for I *am* far stronger than I ever thought I could be." She put a hand to Dottie's cheek. "I'll let you know when I'm settled."

She turned towards the back of the house and made her way to the village along familiar paths and meadows. As she went, she began to skip. And hum. And grin.

My, oh my, it felt good to be free!

The bride was resplendent and the groom dignified.

As it should be.

Clarissa sat in the church as the marriage ceremony commenced, hearing, but not listening to the words. It was the attendees that held her attention. For gathered in one place were the people of her life.

Standing near the bride was Lila, looking ever lovely in her gown of ribbed ivory satin, the skirt tiered with heavy Bedfordshire lace. Down the line Joseph stood near Morgan. Odd that Clarissa had been at their wedding — in secret — needing to see what could have been, but would never be, hers.

Would she ever have such a love? Would she ever stand in this church next to a man who would promise to love and cherish her until death did they part?

Tears stung, and Clarissa looked to her lap, glad that the occasion allowed tears. Beth looked up at her, her face showing concern. Clarissa smiled and patted her knee, allowing the girl to focus again on the ceremony.

Beth was one of the reasons her chance of marriage was slim. By proclaiming her a daughter, and considering her time spent in London on the stage . . . no gentleman would take her. They would assume her to be sullied by her experiences, and as such, not good and pure enough to be their wife.

So be it.

Clarissa was surprised by her own response. She'd been raised to be a married woman, with a grand house of her own, and many children. To discount all that so easily . . .

I made my own choices. But do I regret them?

She continued to scan the church. Her mother and father sat with their arms entwined, with George nearby, and Tilda a proper distance away.

Clarissa felt a twinge of guilt about that girl. Yes, she'd done wrong, and had been instrumental in bringing tension and havoc to the manor. Yet her motives were based on the desire to belong somewhere, to gain and keep a family. Wasn't Clarissa hoping to do the same for Beth?

Her uncle the earl sat with Grandmamma and the Colonel, pride evident upon their faces. For with the marriage of Morgan, the Weston line was secured for another generation. Above all else, above wealth and land and status, this was the ultimate goal of all who held titles. Although every family wished for the next to carry on, for those with a title, the pressure was intense as the ranks of history eternally stood guard over all that had been accomplished, a warning that it should not be carelessly undone.

On the other side of the aisle was Mrs. Farrow, sitting alone, for only a handful of the bride's friends had made the journey across the ocean to attend. She too dabbed at her eyes. Like Clarissa, were the happy tears tinged with regret? For ever since her humiliation, Mrs. Farrow had been more thoughtful in her actions and the words that came out of her mouth. A lesson learned perhaps?

There was always a lesson to be learned.

A few rows back sat Lord Newley, who kept his eyes on the bride and groom. Mrs. Farrow had set her sights on him—had made good progress. Yet through her brash actions she had caused him to withdraw. Clarissa almost felt sorry for the woman, because Clarissa, above all others, knew about brash actions and consequences.

Beth sought her hand, and Clarissa let their fingers intertwine. Was Beth a consequence?

When the little girl smiled up at her, Clarissa knew the answer to be otherwise.

Beth was a blessing. And if Clarissa received no others in her entire life, Beth would be enough.

Tilda looked at the grand people entering the manor, pausing to give well wishes to the bride and groom. The ceremony had been the most beautiful event she had ever witnessed. Yet she'd struggled to be happy for the couple because her daydreams of times past—the ones where *she* was a bride marrying the heir—would not completely fade no matter how often she tried to shove them away.

Tilda watched as Mrs. Farrow accept a greeting. The woman's eyes repeatedly strayed in the direction of Lord Newley, even though his eyes actively avoided her gaze. Tilda felt sorry for her, but took Mrs. Farrow's lesson as her own. Discretion was essential and family loyalty had to be placed at the top of any list of how to live one's life in Summerfield.

Tilda started when she felt a hand upon her shoulder.

"I startled you." Colonel Cummings said. "I'm sorry," He let his arm fully encompass her shoulders. "You seem deep in thought."

She nodded. "They're all so happy."

"That, they are."

"I almost ruined that."

"That, you did."

She looked up at him. "I've told them I'm sorry."

"And what did they say?"

"They've forgiven me."

"Then the slate is wiped clean."

"Really?" she asked.

"Have you told God you're sorry too?" he asked.
She nodded.

"Very good then. As I said."

"He forgives me too? The slate is truly wiped clean?"

"Jesus made certain of it."

"But I don't deserve it."

"And that, my very wise girl, is the point."

Tilda nodded, letting the immensity of this truth flood her entire being. She leaned her head against her godfather's chest, letting his arms lock the truth into her heart where it belonged.

Molly stopped at the crest of a hill that overlooked Summerfield Manor. The mansion teamed with guests, chatting and offering their congratulations.

There was Genevieve, accepting kisses to her cheek, her joy evident even from this distance.

Morgan stood beside her, shaking hands, beaming with his own happiness.

The ceremony was over. Morgan was married.

Peter stood beside her. "This must be difficult for you."

She let the statement land, then shoved it away and smiled at him. "How can being with you be difficult?"

"Good answer," he said.

"True answer," she said.

Their attention was diverted as a man ran up the hill towards them. "Doctor! Come quick! My son fell from an apple tree!"

Peter rushed after the man. After only a few steps he stopped and turned back to Molly. "Are you coming?"

Absolutely.

After the wedding ceremony, the reception, and the supper at Summerfield Manor, it was time for the bride and groom to leave on their honeymoon. A room for the night awaited them in London.

As Genevieve neared the carriage, her mother approached and took her into her arms. "Oh, my dear girl. I am so happy for you."

She pulled away, peering into her mother's eyes. "You be happy too, Mamma. Don't be too hard on yourself."

"Only as hard as I deserve." Then she ran her fingers along Genevieve's cheek. "You are the most beautiful bride I've ever seen. I mean that."

Genevieve believed her, believed it to be true. For if love could make a woman beautiful, it had accomplished that today.

Her mother offered one last kiss, then whispered in her ear, "I love you."

Genevieve felt warm inside. "I love you too. I wish Father were here."

Her mother looked heavenward. "He is. And I will be here too, for the Westons are letting me stay here until you return."

She relinquished Genevieve to Morgan's arm and together the couple entered the carriage that was adorned with garlands of flowers.

When they were nearly settled, Morgan paused. "Just a minute." He exited the carriage and plucked one of the red roses from the floral sprays and returned to his place beside her. "For you, dear wife."

She took in its fragrance, "I still have the other one you gave me."

"There will be many more," he said. "I promise."

She grinned at him. "I distinctly remember you saying that you were not a romantic."

He wove her fingers through his own and leaned close enough to kiss her. "I think you might change that in me, Mrs. Weston."

She'd do her best.

THE END

Discussion questions for
Bride of the Summerfields:

1. Chapter 5: Lady's maid, Agnes, insisted she be called by her surname. Clarissa points out that the hierarchy of the servants is almost more structured than that of the upper class. Here are nine servant positions. Put them in order, top to the bottom of the pecking order: Footman, Cook, Housekeeper, Kitchen maid, Housemaid, Butler, Lady's Maid, Scullery maid, Valet. (* answer below)

2. In Chapter 8, Molly and Dr. Peter talk about wisdom and life: "Wouldn't it be wonderful to say or do something that lingered on long after we die, like Socrates and King David?" What bit of wisdom would you like to leave future generations? (or at least the next one!)

3. In Chapter 10, Timothy and Clarissa talk about God's plan for their lives, and Timothy says, "I don't believe in destiny as if we don't have a choice. I believe in purpose. We each have a unique God-given purpose. The trick is to find out what it is." What do you think your purpose is? When/how did you discover it? If you've not discovered it, what do you think it might be?

4. Continuing the "purpose" talk between Clarissa and Timothy, he says, "Coming home is always the right road toward your purpose. You can't branch out until you return to your roots." Do you believe this is true? How was/could going "home" be the right road for you?

5. Chapter 10: Timothy (wise man that he is) says that going after a dream takes courage—even if it doesn't work out. What dream have you courageously pursued? Which dreams succeeded? Which did not? Was it a good thing some of them weren't successful?

6. Chapter 10: Timothy says "God puts people in the right place at the right time and links them together so they can move forward and find out what might come next." The people we meet, those who come in and out of our lives, have a purpose. Who are two of the most important person who came into your life?

7. Chapter 14: Peter tells Molly, "Love cannot be shut off like water in a spigot." Molly responds, "But neither can love overcome all boundaries." Who have you loved, perhaps longer than you should have? What boundaries have you overcome—or been unable to overcome?

8. Chapter 19: After things fall into place in Molly's life, she realizes God put roadblocks in her life to keep her and Morgan apart. When have you seen God use roadblocks to keep you safe or from an unhealthy relationship? Did you heed the roadblocks or go around them?

9. Chapter 19: Molly also realizes God had used her mother's stroke to bring her back to the manor—to meet Peter. What time in your life did God bring you to a place for a distinct reason?

10. Chapter 20: Timothy brings out the best in Clarissa. He notes her thoughtfulness, forgiveness, and determination. The first two are new traits to her, but it seems clear that Timothy does a lot to raise Clarissa's self-esteem. Thinking back on the Clarissa you came to know up to this point, how could her actions be the result of low self-esteem?

11. Little Beth came into Clarissa's life as a bit-player. Maturity and wisdom helped Clarissa see that Beth could be more to her, and that she could be more to Beth. What kind of mother do you think Clarissa will be?

* Answer to #1: Butler, Housekeeper, Valet, Lady's Maid, Cook, Footman, Housemaid, Kitchen maid, Scullery maid.

CLARISSA'S
Fashion

Victorian and Edwardian Fashion, p. 71

Chapter 12: "The bodice and pleated skirt were green mousseline de laine, broken up by a peach overskirt creating a lace-edged drapery to the knee, culminating in a soft bustle in back. The long-sleeved bodice was bisected from hip to neck with small ruffles, with matching cuffs. Two centered bows — at neck and hip — made Clarissa feel like a pretty package. Perhaps that's all she was"

TILDA'S Fashion

Victorian Fashions p. 24

Chapter 13: "Tilda felt a stitch of apprehension as she stepped toward the mirror. When she'd first seen this royal blue dress she'd thought it the most beautiful dress she'd ever seen. When she touched the ribbed texture of the faille fabric she marveled at its soft richness. And the lace . . . from the stand-up lace collar to the waist were white batiste tucks, outlined with ruffles made of wide cascading lace. It was the most elegant dress she'd ever seen—much less ever had on her body. She felt like she'd just been introduced to the dress of all dresses, that she had to wear."

Wedding Fashion:
LILA, GENEVIEVE, BETH, & TILDA

Wedding Fashions, p. 27

Chapter 15: "The long sleeves were adorned with ruffled lace cuffs, her bodice lined with flat lace, culminating in a V at her waist. The slim skirt was covered with yards of scalloped lace,, while a row of pleats edged the bottom of the dress and train. Over her hips were drapings of satin, and parading across the front of the skirt was a garland of white silk flowers, repeated in a corsage on her bodice, and as a crown for her scalloped veil."

About the Author

NANCY MOSER is the best-selling author of twenty-seven novels, including Christy Award winner, *Time Lottery;* Christy finalist *Washington's Lady;* and historical novels *Love of the Summerfields, Mozart's Sister, The Journey of Josephine Cain,* and *Masquerade.* Nancy has been married for forty years—to the same man. She and her husband have three grown children, six grandchildren, and live in the Midwest. She's been blessed with a varied life. She's earned a degree in architecture; run a business with her husband; traveled extensively in Europe; and has performed in various theatres, symphonies, and choirs. She knits voraciously, kills all her houseplants, and can wire an electrical fixture without getting shocked. She is a fan of anything antique—humans included.

Website: www.nancymoser.com
Blogs: Heroines, Heroes & History: www.hhhistory.com, and my author blog: www.authornancymoser.blogspot.com
Pinterest: www.pinterest.com/nancymoser1 (Check out my boards! I have a board for *Love of the Summerfields* that shows some of the real photographs and fashion pertaining to the story, as well as a board on 1880s fashion, History That Intrigues Me, and many others that involve history, fashion, and antiques.)
Facebook and Twitter:
www.facebook.com/nancymoser.author, and
www.twitter.com/MoserNancy
Goodreads:
www.goodreads.com/author/show/117288.Nancy_Moser

Look for Book Three
of the Manor House Series:

Rise of the Summerfields

Excerpt from Chapter One

Spring 1885

"It's a boy!"

Amid her exhaustion, Genevieve grabbed a fresh breath and forced herself to open her eyes. "Let me see him!'

Dr. Peter held him up for inspection. The baby screamed.

Genevieve's mother grasped her hand. "He has good lungs on him, that's for certain."

"Can I hold him?"

"Shortly," the doctor said. "Let us get him cleaned up."

Genevieve was vaguely aware of the doctor and his wife, Molly, taking care of her son.

Her son! She was a moth—

Her happy thoughts were interrupted by another contraction. "Ahhh!"

"What's going on, doctor?" asked her mother.

He was busy making an examination. "Oh my! We have another one!"

Another one?

"You're going to have to do it again, Lady Weston."

Genevieve knew that, without having to be told, as her body made its demands. *It* was in charge and all she could do was submit.

The here and now was consumed with pain. She heard voices, but they floated outside her consciousness. All that she was, was the baby, commanding release.

"Push!"

There was no alternative. Her mother and Molly supported her on either side, and with a scream she pushed the baby into its new life.

"It's a girl!"

Spent, Genevieve fell back on the pillows and laughed. "One of each?"

Her mother kissed her cheek. "One of each, my girl. How marvelous!"

She heard a door opening, and Morgan's voice. "I heard the scream. Is she all right?"

"Morgan . . ." Genevieve held out her hand and he rushed by her side, his eyes trying to take in everything around him.

"Two?" he said, pulling her hand to his lips. "Two?"

"A boy and a girl."

His eyes welled with tears as he kissed her. "Well done, my darling!"

Dr. Peter handed over their son, and Genevieve cradled him in her right arm. "He's beautiful."

"And here, Lord Weston, here is your daughter."

Morgan sat on the bed and took the little girl into his arms. He gently touched her chin and stroked her head. "Oh dear. Oh my. I am smitten."

"Let me see her," Genevieve asked.

He placed their daughter upon her left arm. The two babies snuggled and wriggled and cooed, making a myriad of expressions. "Our joy is complete," she said.

Morgan beamed down at them. "Our joy is just beginning."

Amen.

44012651R00229

Made in the USA
Middletown, DE
25 May 2017